THE COLLECTED WORKS OF WILLIAM FAULKNER

★

SOLDIERS' PAY

SOLDIERS' PAY

William Faulkner

1974

CHATTO & WINDUS

LONDON

PUBLISHED BY
Chatto & Windus Ltd
40 William IV Street
London WC2N 4DF

First published 1930
Published in The New Phoenix Library 1951
First published in a Uniform Edition 1957
This Edition first published 1974

ISBN 0 7011 0685 9

Printed and bound in Great Britain by
REDWOOD BURN LIMITED
Trowbridge & Esher

SOLDIERS' PAY

SOLDIER

"The hushèd plaint of wind in stricken trees
Shivers the grass in path and lane
And Grief and Time are tideless golden seas—
Hush, hush! He's home again."

SOLDIERS' PAY

CHAPTER I

I

Achilles—Did you shave this morning, Cadet?
Mercury—Yes, Sir.
Achilles—What with, Cadet?
Mercury—Issue, Sir.
Achilles—Carry on, Cadet.

—*Old Play.*
(*about 19—?*)

Lowe, Julian, number ——, late a Flying Cadet, Umptieth Squadron, Air Service, known as "One Wing" by the other embryonic aces of his flight, regarded the world with a yellow and disgruntled eye. He suffered the same jaundice that many a more booted one than he did, from Flight Commanders through Generals to the ambrosial single-barred (not to mention that inexplicable beast of the field which the French so beautifully call an aspiring aviator); they had stopped the war on him.

So he sat in a smoldering of disgusted sorrow, not even enjoying his Pullman prerogatives, spinning on his thumb his hat with its accursed white band.

"Had your nose in the wind, hey, buddy?" said Yaphank, going home and smelling to high heaven of bad whisky.

"Ah, go to hell," he returned sourly and Yaphank doffed his tortured hat.

"Why, sure, General—or should I of said Lootenant? Excuse me, madam. I got gassed doing k.p. and my sight ain't been the same since. On to Berlin! Yeh, sure, we're on to Berlin. I'm on to you, Berlin. I got your number. Number no thousand no hundred and naughty naught Private (very private) Joe Gilligan, late for parade, late for fatigue, late for breakfast when breakfast is late. The statue of liberty ain't never seen me, and if she do, she'll have to 'bout face."

Cadet Lowe raised a sophisticated eye. "Say, whatcher drinking, anyway?"

"Brother, I dunno. Fellow that makes it was gave a Congressional medal last Chuesday because he has got a plan to stop the war. Enlist all the Dutchmen in our army and make 'em drink so much of his stuff a day for forty days, see? Ruin any war. Get the idea?"

"I'll say. Won't know whether it's a war or a dance, huh?"

"Sure, they can tell. The women will all be dancing. Listen, I had a swell jane and she said, 'for Christ's sake, you can't dance.' And I said, 'like hell I can't.' And we was dancing and she said, 'what are you, anyways?' And I says, 'what do you wanta know for? I can dance as well as any general or major or even a sergeant, because I just win four hundred in a poker game,' and she said, 'oh, you did?' and I said, 'sure, stick with me, kid,' and she said, 'where is it?' Only I wouldn't show it to her and then this fellow come up to her and said, 'are you dancing this one?' And she said, 'sure, I am. This bird don't dance.' Well, he was a sergeant, the biggest one I ever seen. Say, he was like that fellow in Arkansaw that had some trouble with a nigger and a friend said to him, 'well, I hear you killed a nigger yesterday.' And he said, 'yes, weighed two hundred pounds.' Like a bear." He took the lurching of the train limberly and Cadet Lowe said, "For Christ's sake."

"Sure," agreed the other. "She won't hurt you, though.
I done tried it. My dog won't drink none of it of course,
but then he got bad ways hanging around Brigade H.Q. He's
the one trophy of the war I got: something that wasn't never
bawled out by a shave-tail for not saluting. Say, would you
kindly like to take a little something to keep off the sumnif-
erous dews of this goddam country? The honor is all mine
and you won't mind it much after the first two drinks. Makes
me homesick: like a garage. Ever work in a garage?"

Sitting on the floor between two seats was Yaphank's traveling companion, trying to ignite a splayed and sodden cigar.
Like devastated France, thought Cadet Lowe, swimming his
memory through the adenoidal reminiscences of Captain
Bleyth, an R.A.F. pilot delegated to temporarily re-inforce
their democracy.

"Why, poor soldier," said his friend, tearfully, "all alone
in no man's land and no matches. Ain't war hell? I ask you."
He tried to push the other over with his leg, then he fell to
kicking him, slowly. "Move over, you ancient mariner. Move
over, you goddam bastard. Alas, poor Jerks or something (I
seen that in a play, see? Good line) come on, come on; here's
General Pershing come to have a drink with the poor soldiers."
He addressed Cadet Lowe. "Look at him: ain't he sodden in
depravity?"

"Battle of Coonyak," the man on the floor muttered. "Ten
men killed. Maybe fifteen. Maybe hundred. Poor children
at home saying 'Alice, where art thou?' "

"Yeh, Alice. Where in hell are you? That other bottle.
What'n'ell have you done with it? Keeping it to swim in
when you get home?"

The man on the floor weeping said: "You wrong me as
ever man wronged. Accuse me of hiding mortgage on house?
Then take this soul and body; take all. Ravish me, big boy."

"Rayish a bottle of vinegar juice out of you, anyway," the other muttered, busy beneath the seat. He rose triumphant, clutching a fresh bottle. "Hark! the sound of battle and the laughing horses draws near. But shall they dull this poor unworthy head? No! But I would like to of seen one of them laughing horses. Must of been lady horses all together. Your extreme highness"—with ceremony, extending the bottle —"will you be kind enough to kindly condescend to honor these kind but unworthy strangers in a foreign land?"

Cadet Lowe accepted the bottle, drank briefly, gagged and spat his drink. The other supporting him massaged his back. "Come on, come on, they don't nothing taste that bad." Kindly cupping Lowe's opposite shoulder in his palm he forced the bottle mouthward again. Lowe released the bottle, defending himself. "Try again. I got you. Drink it, now."

"Jesus Christ," said Cadet Lowe, averting his head.

Passengers were interested and Yaphank soothed him. "Now, now. They won't nothing hurt you. You are among friends. Us soldiers got to stick together in a foreign country like this. Come on, drink her down. She ain't worth nothing to no one, spit on his legs like that."

"Hell, man, I can't drink it."

"Why, sure you can. Listen: think of flowers. Think of your poor gray-haired mother hanging on the front gate and sobbing her gray-haired heart out. Listen, think of having to go to work again when you get home. Ain't war hell? I would of been a corporal at least, if she had just hung on another year."

"Hell, I can't."

"Why, you got to," his new friend told him kindly, pushing the bottle suddenly in his mouth and tilting it. To be flooded or to swallow were his choices so he drank and retained it. His belly rose and hung, then sank reluctant.

"There now, wasn't so bad, was it? Remember, this hurts me to see my good licker going more than it does you. But she do kind of smack of gasoline, don't she?"

Cadet Lowe's outraged stomach heaved at its muscular moorings like a captive balloon. He gaped and his vitals coiled coldly in a passionate ecstasy. His friend again thrust the bottle in his mouth.

"Drink, quick! You got to protect your investment, you know."

His private parts, flooded, washed back to his gulping and a sweet fire ran through him, and the Pullman conductor came and regarded them in helpless disgust.

"Ten—shun," said Yaphank, springing to his feet. "Beware of officers! Rise, men, and salute the admiral here." He took the conductor's hand and held it. "Boys, this man commanded the navy," he said. "When the enemy tried to capture Coney Island he was there. Or somewhere between there and Chicago, anyway, wasn't you, Colonel?"

"Look out, men, don't do that." But Yaphank had already kissed his hand.

"Now, run along, Sergeant. And don't come back until dinner is ready."

"Listen, you must stop this. You will ruin my train."

"Bless your heart, Captain, your train couldn't be no safer with us if it was your own daughter." The man sitting on the floor moved and Yaphank cursed him. "Sit still, can't you? Say, this fellow thinks it's night. Suppose you have your hired man bed him down? He's just in the way here."

The conductor deciding Lowe was the sober one, addressed him.

"For God's sake, soldier, can't you do something with them?"

"Sure," said Cadet Lowe. "You run along; I'll look after them. They're all right."

"Well, do something with them. I can't bring a train into Chicago with the whole army drunk on it. My God, Sherman was sure right."

Yaphank stared at him quietly. Then he turned to his companions. "Men," he said solemnly, "he don't want us here. And this is the reward we get for giving our flesh and blood to our country's need. Yes, sir, he don't want us here; he begrudges us riding on his train, even. Say, suppose we hadn't sprang to the nation's call, do you know what kind of a train you'd have? A train full of Germans. A train full of folks eating sausage and drinking beer, all going to Milwaukee, that's what you'd have."

"Couldn't be worse than a train full of you fellows not knowing where you're going," the conductor replied.

"All right," Yaphank answered. "If that's the way you feel, we'll get off your goddam train. Do you think this is the only train in the world?"

"No, no," the conductor said hastily, "not at all. I don't want you to get off. I just want you to straighten up and not disturb the other passengers."

The sitting man lurched clumsily and Cadet Lowe met interested stares.

"No," said Yaphank, "no! You have refused the hospitality of your train to the saviors of your country. We could have expected better treatment than this in Germany, even in Texas." He turned to Lowe. "Men, we will get off his train at the next station. Hey, General?"

"My God," repeated the conductor. "If we ever have another peace I don't know what the railroads will do. I thought war was bad, but my God."

"Run along," Yaphank told him, "run along. You probably

won't stop for us, so I guess we'll have to jump off. Gratitude! Where is gratitude, when trains won't stop to let poor soldiers off? I know what it means. They'll fill trains with poor soldiers and run 'em off into the Pacific Ocean. Won't have to feed 'em any more. Poor soldiers! Woodrow, you wouldn't of treated me like this."

"Hey, what you doing?" But the man ignored him, tugging the window up and dragging a cheap paper suit-case across his companion's knees. Before either Lowe or the conductor could raise a hand he had pushed the suit-case out the window. "All out, men!"

His sodden companion heaved clawing from the floor. "Hey! That was mine you threw out!"

"Well, ain't you going to get off with us? We are going to throw 'em all off, and when she slows down we'll jump ourselves."

"But you threwed mine off first," the other said.

"Why, sure. I was saving you the trouble, see? Now don't you feel bad about it; you can throw mine off if you want, and then Pershing here, and the admiral can throw each other's off the same way. You got a bag, ain't you?" he asked the conductor. "Get yours, quick, so we won't have so damn far to walk."

"Listen, soldiers," said the conductor, and Cadet Lowe, thinking of Elba, thinking of his coiling guts and a slow alcoholic fire in him, remarked the splayed official gold breaking the man's cap. New York swam flatly past; Buffalo was imminent, and sunset.

"Listen, soldiers," repeated the conductor. "I got a son in France. Sixth Marines he is. His mother ain't heard from him since October. I'll do anything for you boys, see, but for God's sake act decent."

"No," replied the man, "you have refused us hospitality, so

we get off. When does the train stop? or have we got to jump?"

"No, no, you boys sit here. Sit here and behave and you'll be all right. No need to get off."

He moved swaying down the aisle and the sodden one removed his devastated cigar. "You throwed my suit-case out," he repeated.

Yaphank took Cadet Lowe's arm. "Listen. Wouldn't that discourage you? God knows, I'm trying to help the fellow get a start in life, and what do I get? One complaint after another." He addressed his friend again. "Why, sure, I throwed your suit-case off. Whatcher wanta do? wait till we get to Buffalo and pay a quarter to have it took off for you?"

"But you throwed my suit-case out," said the other again.

"All right. I did. Whatcher going to do about it?"

The other pawed himself erect, clinging to the window, and fell heavily over Lowe's feet. "For Christ's sake," his companion said, thrusting him into his seat, "watch whatcher doing."

"Get off," the man mumbled wetly.

"Huh?"

"Get off, too," he explained, trying to rise again. He got on to his legs and lurching, bumping and sliding about the open window he thrust his head through it. Cadet Lowe caught him by the brief skirt of his blouse.

"Here, here, come back, you damn fool. You can't do that."

"Why, sure he can," contradicted Yaphank, "let him jump off if he wants. He ain't only going to Buffalo, anyways."

"Hell, he'll kill himself."

"My God," repeated the conductor, returning at a heavy gallop. He leaned across Lowe's shoulder and caught the man's leg. The man, with his head and torso through the window, swayed lax and sodden as a meal sack. Yaphank pushed Lowe aside and tried to break the conductor's grip on the other's leg.

"Let him be. I don't believe he'll jump."

"But, good God, I can't take any chances. Look out, look out, soldier! Pull him back there!"

"Oh, for Christ's sake, let him go," said Lowe, giving up.

"Sure," the other amended, "let him jump. I'd kind of like to see him do it, since he suggested it himself. Besides, he ain't the kind for young fellows like us to associate with. Good riddance. Let's help him off," he added, shoving at the man's lumpy body. The would-be suicide's hat whipped from his head and the wind temporarily clearing his brain, he fought to draw himself in. He had changed his mind. His companion resisted, kindly.

"Come on, come on. Don't lose your nerve now. G'wan and jump."

"Help!" the man shrieked into the vain wind and "help!" the conductor chorused, clinging to him, and two alarmed passengers and the porter came to his assistance. They overcame Yaphank and drew the now thoroughly alarmed man into the car. The conductor slammed shut the window.

"Gentlemen," he addressed the two passengers, "will you sit here and keep them from putting him out that window? I am going to put them all off as soon as we reach Buffalo. I'd stop the train and do it now, only they'd kill him as soon as they get him alone. Henry," to the porter, "call the train conductor and tell him to wire ahead to Buffalo we got two crazy men on board."

"Yeh, Henry," Yaphank amended to the negro, "tell 'em to have a band there and three bottles of whisky. If they ain't got a band of their own, tell 'em to hire one. I will

pay for it." He dragged a blobby mass of bills from his
pocket and stripping off one, gave it to the porter. "Do you
want a band too?" he asked Lowe. "No," answering himself,
"no, you don't need none. You can use mine. Run now,"
he repeated.

"Yas suh, Cap'm." White teeth were like a suddenly
opened piano.

"Watch 'em, men," the conductor told his appointed guards.
"You, Henry!" he shouted, following the vanishing white
jacket.

Yaphank's companion, sweating and pale, was about to
become ill; Yaphank and Lowe sat easily respectively affable
and belligerent. The newcomers touched shoulders for mutual
support, alarmed but determined. Craned heads of other
passengers became again smugly unconcerned over books and
papers and the train rushed on along the sunset.

"Well, gentlemen," began Yaphank conversationally.

The two civilians sprang like plucked wires and one of
them said, "Now, now," soothingly, putting his hands on the
soldier. "Just be quiet, soldier, and we'll look after you.
Us Americans appreciates what you've done."

"Hank White," muttered the sodden one.

"Huh?" asked his companion.

"Hank White," he repeated.

The other turned to the civilian cordially. "Well, bless
my soul, if here ain't old Hank White in the flesh, that I
was raised with! Why, Hank! We heard you was dead,
or in the piano business or something. You ain't been fired,
have you? I notice you ain't got no piano with you."

"No, no," the man answered in alarm, "you are mistaken.
Schluss is my name. I got a swell line of ladies' under-
things." He produced a card.

"Well, well, ain't that nice. Say," he leaned confidentially toward the other, "you don't carry no women samples with you? No? I was afraid not. But never mind. I will get you one in Buffalo. Not buy you one, of course: just rent you one, you might say, for the time being. Horace," to Cadet Lowe, "where's that bottle?"

"Here she is, Major," responded Lowe, taking the bottle from beneath his blouse. Yaphank offered it to the two civilians.

"Think of something far, far away, and drink fast," he advised.

"Why, thanks," said the one called Schluss, tendering the bottle formally to his companion. They stooped cautiously and drank. Yaphank and Cadet Lowe drank, not stooping.

"Be careful, soldiers," warned Schluss.

"Sure," said Cadet Lowe. They drank again.

"Won't the other one take nothing?" asked the heretofore silent one, indicating Yaphank's traveling companion. He was hunched awkwardly in the corner. His friend shook him and he slipped limply to the floor.

"That's the horror of the demon rum, boys," said Yaphank solemnly and he took another drink. And Cadet Lowe took another drink. He tendered the bottle.

"No, no," Schluss said with passion, "not no more right now."

"He don't mean that," Yaphank said, "he just ain't thought." He and Lowe stared at the two civilians. "Give him time: he'll come to hisself."

After a while the one called Schluss took the bottle.

"That's right," Yaphank told Lowe confidentially. "For a while I thought he was going to insult the uniform. But you wasn't, was you?"

"No, no. They ain't no one respects the uniform like I do. Listen, I would of liked to fought by your side, see?

But someone got to look out for business while the boys are gone. Ain't that right?" he appealed to Lowe.

"I don't know," said Lowe with courteous belligerence, "I never had time to work any."

"Come on, come on," Yaphank reprimanded him, "all of us wasn't young enough to be lucky as you."

"How was I lucky?" Lowe rejoined fiercely.

"Well, shut up about it, if you wasn't lucky. We got something else to worry about."

"Sure," Schluss added quickly, "we all got something to worry about." He tasted the bottle briefly and the other said:

"Come on, now, drink it."

"No, no, thanks, I got a plenty."

Yaphank's eye was like a snake's. "Take a drink, now. Do you want me to call the conductor and tell him you are worrying us to give you whisky?"

The man gave him the bottle quickly. He turned to the other civilian. "What makes him act so funny?"

"No, no," said Schluss. "Listen, you soldiers drink if you want: we'll look after you."

The silent one added like a brother and Yaphank said:

"They think we are trying to poison them. They think we are German spies, I guess."

"No, no! When I see a uniform, I respect it like it was my mother."

"Then, come on and drink."

Schluss gulped and passed the bottle. His companion drank also and sweat beaded them.

"Won't he take nothing?" repeated the silent one and Yaphank regarded the other soldier with compassion.

"Alas, poor Hank," he said, "poor boy's done for, I fear. The end of a long friendship, men." Cadet Lowe said sure, seeing two distinct Hanks, and the other continued. "Look at that kind, manly face. Children together we was, picking flowers in the flowery meadows; him and me made the middle-weight mule-wiper's battalion what she was; him and me devastated France together. And now look at him.

"Hank! Don't you recognize this weeping voice, this soft hand on your brow? General," he turned to Lowe, "will you be kind enough to take charge of the remains? I will deputize these kind strangers to stop at the first harness factory we pass and have a collar suitable for mules made of dogwood with the initials H. W. in forget-me-nots."

Schluss in ready tears tried to put his arm about Yaphank's shoulders. "There, there, death ain't only a parting. Brace up: take a little drink, then you'll feel better."

"Why, I believe I will," he replied; "you got a kind heart, buddy. Fall in when fire call blows, boys."

Schluss mopped his face with a soiled, scented handkerchief and they drank again. New York in a rosy glow of alcohol and sunset streamed past breaking into Buffalo, and with fervent new fire in them they remarked the station. Poor Hank now slept peacefully in a spittoon.

Cadet Lowe and his friend being cold of stomach, rose and supported their companions. Schluss evinced a disinclination to get off. He said it couldn't possibly be Buffalo, that he had been to Buffalo too many times. Sure, they told him, holding him erect, and the conductor glared at them briefly and vanished. Lowe and Yaphank got their hats and helped the civilians into the aisle.

"I'm certainly glad my boy wasn't old enough to be a soldier," remarked a woman passing them with difficulty, and Lowe said to Yaphank:

"Say, what about him?"

"Him?" repeated the other, having attached Schluss to himself.

"That one back there," Lowe indicated the casual.

"Oh, him? You are welcome to him, if you want him."

"Why, aren't you together?"

Outside was the noise and smoke of the station. They saw through the windows hurrying people and porters, and Yaphank moving down the aisle answered:

"Hell, no. I never seen him before. Let the porter sweep him out or keep him, whichever he likes."

They half dragged, half carried the two civilians and with diabolical cunning Yaphank led the way through the train and dismounted from a day coach. On the platform Schluss put his arm around the soldier's neck.

"Listen, fellows," he said with passion, "y' know m' name, y' got addressh. Listen, I will show you 'Merica preshates what you done. Ol' Glory ever wave on land and sea. Listen, ain't nothing I got soldier can't have, nothing. N'if you wasn't soldiers I am still for you, one hundred pershent. I like you. I swear I like you."

"Why, sure," the other agreed, supporting him. After a while he spied a policeman and he directed his companion's gait toward the officer. Lowe with his silent one followed. "Stand up, can't you?" he hissed, but the man's eyes were filled with an inarticulate sadness, like a dog's. "Do the best you can, then," Cadet Lowe softened, added, and Yaphank, stopping before the policeman, was saying:

"Looking for two drunks, Sergeant? These men were annoying a whole trainload of people. Can't nothing be done to protect soldiers from annoyance? If it ain't top sergeants, it's drunks."

"I'd like to see the man can annoy a soldier," answered the officer. "Beat it, now."

"But say, these men are dangerous. What are you good for, if you can't preserve the peace?"

"Beat it, I said. Do you want me to run all of you in?"

"You are making a mistake, Sergeant. These are the ones you are looking for."

The policeman said, Looking for? regarding him with interest.

"Sure. Didn't you get our wire? We wired ahead to have the train met."

"Oh, these are the crazy ones, are they? Where's the one they were trying to murder?"

"Sure, they are crazy. Do you think a sane man would get hisself into this state?"

The policeman looked at the four of them with a blasé eye. "G'wan, now. You're all drunk. Beat it, or I'll run you in."

"All right. Take us in. If we got to go to the station to get rid of these crazy ones, we'll have to."

"Where's the conductor of this train?"

"He's with a doctor, working on the wounded one."

"Say, you men better be careful. Whatcher trying to do— kid me?"

Yaphank jerked his companion up. "Stand up," he said, shaking the man. "Love you like a brother," the other muttered. "Look at him," he said, "look at both of 'em. And there's a man hurt on that train. Are you going to stand here and do nothing?"

"I thought you was kidding me. These are the ones, are they?" he raised his whistle and another policeman ran up. "Here they are, Ed. You watch 'em and I'll get aboard and see about that dead man. You soldiers stay here, see?"

"Sure, Sergeant," Yaphank agreed. The officer ran heavily away and he turned to the civilians. "All right, boys. Here's

the bell-hops come to carry you out where the parade starts.
You go with them and me and this other officer will go back
and get the conductor and the porter. They want to come,
too."

Schluss again took him in his arms.

"Love you like a brother. Anything got's yours. Ask me."

"Sure," he rejoined. "Watch 'em, Cap, they're crazy as
hell. Now, you run along with this nice man."

"Here," the policeman said, "you two wait here."

There came a shout from the train and the conductor's
face was a bursting bellowing moon. "Like to wait and see
it explode on him," Yaphank murmured. The policeman
supporting the two men hurried toward the train. "Come
on here," he shouted to Yaphank and Lowe.

As he drew away Yaphank spoke swiftly to Lowe.

"Come on, General," he said, "let's get going. So long,
boys. Let's go, kid."

The policeman shouted, "Stop, there!" but they disre-
garded him, hurrying down the long shed, leaving the excitement to clot about itself, for all of them.

Outside the station in the twilight the city broke sharply
its skyline against the winter evening and lights were shim-
mering birds on motionless golden wings, bell notes in arrested
flight; ugly everywhere beneath a rumored retreating magic
of color.

Food for the belly, and winter, though spring was somewhere in the world, from the south blown up like forgotten
music. Caught both in the magic of change they stood feeling
the spring in the cold air, as if they had but recently come
into a new world, feeling their littleness and believing too that
lying in wait for them was something new and strange.
They were ashamed of this and silence was unbearable.

"Well, buddy," and Yaphank slapped Cadet Lowe smartly

on the back, "that's one parade we'll sure be A.W.O.L. from, huh?"

2

Who sprang to be his land's defense
And has been sorry ever since?
          Cadet!
Who can't date a single girl
Long as kee-wees run the world?
          Kay—det!

With food in their bellies and a quart of whisky snugly under Cadet Lowe's arm they boarded a train.

"Where are we going?" asked Lowe. "This train don't go to San Francisco, do she?"

"Listen," said Yaphank, "my name is Joe Gilligan. Gilligan, G-i-l-l-i-g-a-n, Gilligan, J-o-e, Joe; Joe Gilligan. My people captured Minneapolis from the Irish and taken a Dutch name, see? Did you ever know a man named Gilligan give you a bum steer? If you wanta go to San Francisco, all right. If you wanta go to St. Paul or Omyhaw, it's all right with me. And more than that, I'll see that you get there. I'll see that you go to all three of 'em if you want. But why'n hell do you wanta go so damn far as San Francisco?"

"I don't," replied Cadet Lowe. "I don't want to go anywhere especially. I like this train here—far as I am concerned. I say, let's fight this war out right here. But you see, my people live in San Francisco. That's why I am going there."

"Why, sure," Private Gilligan agreed readily. "Sometimes a man does wanta see his family—especially if he don't hafta live with 'em. I ain't criticizing you. I admire you for it, buddy. But say, you can go home any time. What I say is let's have a look at this glorious nation which we have fought for."

"Hell, I can't. My mother has wired me every day since the armistice to fly low and be careful and come home as soon as I am demobilized. I bet she wired the President to have me excused as soon as possible."

"Why, sure. Of course she did. What can equal a mother's love? Except a good drink of whisky. Where's that bottle? You ain't betrayed a virgin, have you?"

"Here she is." Cadet Lowe produced it and Gilligan pressed the bell.

"Claude," he told a superior porter, "bring us two glasses and a bottle of sassperiller or something. We are among gentlemen to-day and we aim to act like gentlemen."

"Whatcher want glasses for?" asked Lowe. "Bottle was all right yesterday."

"You got to remember we are getting among strangers now. We don't want to offend no savage customs. Wait until you get to be an experienced traveler and you'll remember these things. Two glasses, Othello."

The porter in his starched jacket became a symbol of self-sufficiency. "You can't drink in this car. Go to the buffet car."

"Ah, come on, Claude. Have a heart."

"We don't have no drinking in this car. Go to the buffet car if you want." He swung himself from seat to seat down the lurching car.

Private Gilligan turned to his companion. "Well! What do you know about that? Ain't that one hell of a way to treat soldiers? I tell you, General, this is the worst run war I ever seen."

"Hell, let's drink out of the bottle."

"No, no! This thing has got to be a point of honor,

now. Remember, we got to protect our uniform from insult. You wait here and I'll see the conductor. We bought tickets, hey, buddy?"

> With officers gone and officers' wives
> Having the grand old time of their lives——

an overcast sky, and earth dissolving monotonously into a gray mist, grayly. Occasional trees and houses marching through it; and towns like bubbles of ghostly sound beaded on a steel wire——

> Who's in the guard-room chewing the bars,
> Saying to hell with the government wars?
> Cadet!

And here was Gilligan returned, saying: "Charles, at ease." I might have known he would have gotten another one, thought Cadet Lowe, looking up. He saw a belt and wings, he rose and met a young face with a dreadful scar across his brow. My God he thought, turning sick. He saluted and the other peered at him with strained distraction. Gilligan, holding his arm, helped him into the seat. The man turned his puzzled gaze to Gilligan and murmured, "Thanks."

"Lootenant," said Gilligan, "you see here the pride of the nation. General, ring the bell for ice water. The lootenant here is sick."

Cadet Lowe pressed the bell, regarding with a rebirth of that old feud between American enlisted men and officers of all nations the man's insignia and wings and brass, not even wondering what a British officer in his condition could be doing traveling in America. Had I been old enough or lucky enough, this might have been me, he thought jealously.

The porter reappeared.

"No drinking in this car, I told you," he said. Gilligan

produced a bill. "No, sir. Not in this car." Then he saw the third man. He leaned down to him quickly, then glanced suspiciously from Gilligan to Lowe.

"What you all doing with him?" he asked.

"Oh, he's just a lost foreigner I found back yonder. Now, Ernest——"

"Lost? He ain't lost. He's from Gawgia. I'm looking after him. Cap'm"—to the officer—"is these folks all right?"

Gilligan and Lowe looked at each other. "Christ, I thought he was a foreigner," Gilligan whispered.

The man raised his eyes to the porter's anxious face. "Yes," he said slowly, "they're all right."

"Does you want to stay here with them, or don't you want me to fix you up in your place?"

"Let him stay here," Gilligan said. "He wants a drink."

"But he ain't got no business drinking. He's sick."

"Loot," Gilligan said, "do you want a drink?"

"Yes. I want a drink. Yes."

"But he oughtn't to have no whisky, sir."

"I won't let him have too much. I am going to look after him. Come on, now, let's have some glasses, can't we?"

The porter began again, "But he oughtn't——"

"Say, Loot," Gilligan interrupted, "can't you make your friend here get us some glasses to drink from?"

"Glasses?"

"Yeh! He don't want to bring us none."

"Does you want glasses, Cap'm?"

"Yes, bring us some glasses, will you?"

"All right, Cap'm." He stopped again. "You going to take care of him, ain't you?" he asked Gilligan.

"Sure, sure!"

The porter gone, Gilligan regarded his guest with envy. "You sure got to be from Georgia to get service on this train.

I showed him money but it never even shook him. Say,
General," to Lowe, "we better keep the lootenant with us,
huh? Might come in useful."

"Sure," agreed Lowe. "Say, sir, what kind of ships did
you use?"

"Oh, for Christ's sake," interrupted Gilligan, "let him be.
He's been devastating France, now he needs rest. Hey,
Loot?"

Beneath his scarred and tortured brow the man's gaze was
puzzled but kindly and the porter reappeared with glasses and
a bottle of ginger ale. He produced a pillow which he
placed carefully behind the officer's head, then he got two
more pillows for the others, forcing them with ruthless kindness to relax. He was deftly officious, including them impar-
tially in his activities, like Fate. Private Gilligan, unused
to this, became restive.

"Hey, ease up, George; lemme do my own pawing a while.
I aim to paw this bottle if you'll gimme room."

He desisted saying "Is this all right, Cap'm?"

"Yes, all right, thanks," the officer answered. Then:
"Bring your glass and get a drink."

Gilligan solved the bottle and filled the glasses. Ginger ale
hissed sweetly and pungently. "Up and at 'em, men."

The officer took his glass in his left hand and then Lowe
noticed his right hand was drawn and withered.

"Cheer-O," he said.

"Nose down," murmured Lowe. The man looked at him
with poised glass. He looked at the hat on Lowe's knee and
that groping puzzled thing behind his eyes became clear and
sharp as with a mental process, and Lowe thought that his
lips had asked a question.

"Yes, sir. Cadet," he replied, feeling warmly grateful, feeling again a youthful clean pride in his corps.

But the effort had been too much and again the officer's gaze was puzzled and distracted.

Gilligan raised his glass, squinting at it. "Here's to peace," he said. "The first hundred years is the hardest."

Here was the porter again, with his own glass. " 'Nother nose in the trough," Gilligan complained, helping him.

The negro patted and rearranged the pillow beneath the officer's head. "Excuse me, Cap'm, but can't I get you something for your head?"

"No, no, thanks. It's all right."

"But you're sick, sir. Don't you drink too much."

"I'll be careful."

"Sure," Gilligan amended, "we'll watch him."

"Lemme pull the shade down. Keep the light out of your eyes?"

"No, I don't mind the light. You run along. I'll call if I want anything."

With the instinct of his race the negro knew that his kindness was becoming untactful, yet he ventured again.

"I bet you haven't wired your folks to meet you. Whyn't you lemme wire 'em for you? I can look after you far as I go, but who's going to look after you, then?"

"No, I'm all right, I tell you. You look after me as far as you go. I'll get along."

"All right. But I am going to tell your paw how you are acting some day. You ought to know better than that, Cap'm." He said to Gilligan and Lowe: "You gentlemen call me if he gets sick."

"Yes, go on now, damn you. I'll call if I don't feel well."

Gilligan looked from his retreating back to the officer in admiration. "Loot, how do you do it?"

But the man only turned on them his puzzled gaze. He

finished his drink and while Gilligan renewed them Cadet Lowe, like a trailing hound, repeated:

"Say, sir, what kind of ships did you use?"

The man looked at Lowe kindly, not replying, and Gilligan said:

"Hush. Let him alone. Don't you see he don't remember himself? Do you reckon you would, with that scar? Let the war be. Hey, Lootenant?"

"I don't know. Another drink is better."

"Sure it is. Buck up, General. He don't mean no harm. He's just got to let her ride as she lays for a while. We all got horrible memories of the war. I lose eighty-nine dollars in a crap game once, besides losing, as that wop writer says, that an' which thou knowest at Chatter Teary. So how about a little whisky, men?"

"Cheer-O," said the officer again.

"What do you mean, Chateau Thierry?" said Lowe, boyish in disappointment, feeling that he had been deliberately ignored by one to whom Fate had been kinder than to himself.

"You talking about Chatter Teary?"

"I'm talking about a place you were not at, anyway."

"I was there in spirit, sweetheart. That's what counts."

"You couldn't have been there any other way. There ain't any such place."

"Hell there ain't! Ask the Loot here if I ain't right. How about it, Loot?"

But he was asleep. They looked at his face, young, yet old as the world, beneath the dreadful scar. Even Gilligan's levity left him. "My God, it makes you sick at the stomach, don't it? I wonder if he knows how he looks? What do you reckon his folks will say when they see him? or his girl—if he has got one. And I'll bet he has."

New York flew away: it became noon within, by clock, but the gray imminent horizon had not changed. Gilligan said: "If he has got a girl, know what she'll say?"

Cadet Lowe, knowing all the despair of abortive endeavor, asked, "What?"

New York passed on and Mahon beneath his martial harness slept. (Would I sleep? thought Lowe; had I wings, boots, would I sleep?) His wings indicated by a graceful sweep pointed sharply down above a ribbon. Purple, white, purple, over his pocket, over his heart (supposedly). Lowe descried between the pinions of a superimposed crown and three letters, then his gaze mounted to the sleeping scarred face. "What?" he repeated.

"She'll give him the air, buddy."

"Ah, come on. Of course she won't."

"Yes, she will. You don't know women. Once the new has wore off it'll be some bird that stayed at home and made money, or some lad that wore shiny leggings and never got nowheres so he could get hurt, like you and me."

The porter came to hover over the sleeping man.

"He ain't got sick, has he?" he whispered.

They told him no; and the negro eased the position of the sleeping man's head. "You gentlemen look after him and be sure to call me if he wants anything. He's a sick man."

Gilligan and Lowe, looking at the officer, agreed and the porter lowered the shade. "You want some more ginger ale?"

"Yes," said Gilligan, assuming the porter's hushed tone, and the negro withdrew. The two of them sat in silent comradeship, the comradeship of those whose lives had become pointless through the sheer equivocation of events, of the sorry jade, Circumstance. The porter brought ginger ale and they sat drinking while New York became Ohio.

Gilligan, that talkative unserious one, entered some dream within himself and Cadet Lowe, young and dreadfully disappointed, knew all the old sorrows of the Jasons of the world who see their vessels sink ere the harbor is left behind. . . . Beneath his scar the officer slept in all the travesty of his wings and leather and brass, and a terrible old woman paused, saying:

"Was he wounded?"

Gilligan waked from his dream. "Look at his face," he said fretfully; "he fell off of a chair on to an old woman he was talking to and done that."

"What insolence," said the woman, glaring at Gilligan. "But can't something be done for him? He looks sick to me."

"Yes, ma'am. Something can be done for him. What we are doing now—letting him alone."

She and Gilligan stared at each other, then she looked at Cadet Lowe, young and belligerent and disappointed. She looked back to Gilligan. She said from the ruthless humanity of money:

"I shall report you to the conductor. That man is sick and needs attention."

"All right, ma'am. But you tell the conductor that if he bothers him now, I'll knock his goddam head off."

The old woman glared at Gilligan from beneath a quiet, modish black hat and a girl's voice said:

"Let them alone, Mrs. Henderson. They'll take care of him all right."

She was dark. Had Gilligan and Lowe ever seen an Aubrey Beardsley, they would have known that Beardsley would have sickened for her: he had drawn her so often dressed in peacock hues, white and slim and depraved among meretricious trees and impossible marble fountains. Gilligan rose.

"That's right, miss. He is all right sleeping here with us. The porter is looking after him—" wondering why he should have to explain to her—"and we are taking him home. Just leave him be. And thank you for your interest."

"But something ought to be done about it," the old woman repeated futilely. The girl led her away and the train ran swaying in afternoon. (Sure, it was afternoon. Cadet Lowe's wrist watch said so. It might be any state under the sun, but it was afternoon. Afternoon or evening or morning or night, far as the officer was concerned. He slept.)

Damned old bitch, Gilligan muttered, careful not to wake him.

"Look how you've got his arm," the girl said, returning. She moved his withered hand from his thigh. (His hand, too, seeing the scrofulous indication of his bones beneath the blistered skin.) "Oh, his poor terrible face," she said, shifting the pillow under his head.

"Be quiet, ma'am," Gilligan said.

She ignored him. Gilligan, expecting to see him wake, admitted defeat and she continued:

"Is he going far?"

"Lives in Georgia," Gilligan said. He and Cadet Lowe seeing that she was not merely passing their section, rose. Lowe remarking her pallid distinction, her black hair, the red scar of her mouth, her slim dark dress, knew an adolescent envy of the sleeper. She ignored Lowe with a brief glance. How impersonal she was, how self-contained. Ignoring them.

"He can't get home alone," she stated with conviction. "Are you all going with him?"

"Sure," Gilligan assured her. Lowe wished to say something, something that would leave him fixed in her mind: something to reveal himself to her. But she glanced at the glasses, the bottle that Lowe feeling a fool yet clasped

"You seem to be getting along pretty well, yourselves," she said.

"Snake medicine, miss. But won't you have some?"

Lowe, envying Gilligan's boldness, his presence of mind, watched her mouth. She looked down the car.

"I believe I will, if you have another glass."

"Why, sure. General, ring the bell." She sat down beside Mahon and Gilligan and Lowe sat again. She seemed . . . she was young: she probably liked dancing, yet at the same time she seemed not young—as if she knew everything. (She is married, and about twenty-five, thought Gilligan.) (She is about nineteen, and she is not in love, Lowe decided.) She looked at Lowe.

"What's your outfit, soldier?"

"Flying Cadet," answered Lowe with slow patronage, "Air Service." She was a kid: she only looked old.

"Oh. Then of course you are looking after him. He's an aviator, too, isn't he?"

"Look at his wings," Lowe answered. "British. Royal Air Force. Pretty good boys."

"Hell," said Gilligan, "he ain't no foreigner."

"You don't have to be a foreigner to be with the British or French. Look at Lufbery. He was with the French until we come in."

The girl looked at him and Gilligan, who had never heard of Lufbery, said: "Whatever he is, he's all right. With us, anyway. Let him be whatever he wants."

The girl said: "I am sure he is."

The porter appeared. "Cap'm's all right?" he whispered, remarking her without surprise as is the custom of his race.

"Yes," she told him, "he's all right."

Cadet Lowe thought I bet she can dance and she added: "He couldn't be in better hands than these gentlemen." How

keen she is! thought Gilligan. She has known disappointment.
"I wonder if I could have a drink on your car?"

The porter examined her and then he said: "Yes, ma'am.
I'll get some fresh ginger ale. You going to look after
him?"

"Yes, for a while."

He leaned down to her. "I'm from Gawgia, too. Long
time ago."

"You are? I'm from Alabama."

"That's right. We got to look out for our own folks,
ain't we? I'll get you a glass right away."

The officer still slept and the porter returning hushed and
anxious, they sat drinking and talking with muted voices.
New York was Ohio, and Ohio became a series of identical
cheap houses with the same man entering gate after gate,
smoking and spitting. Here was Cincinnati and under the
blanched flash of her hand he waked easily.

"Are we in?" he asked. On her hand was a plain gold
band. No engagement ring. (Pawned it, maybe, thought
Gilligan. But she did not look poor.)

"General, get the Lootenant's hat."

Lowe climbed over Gilligan's knees and Gilligan said:

"Here's an old friend of ours, Loot. Meet Mrs. Powers."

She took his hand, helping him to his feet, and the porter
appeared.

"Donald Mahon," he said, like a parrot. Cadet Lowe
assisted by the porter returned with cap and stick and a
trench coat and two kit bags. The porter helped him into the
coat.

"I'll get yours, ma'am," said Gilligan, but the porter circumvented him. Her coat was rough and heavy and light
of color. She wore it carelessly and Gilligan and Cadet Lowe
gathered up their "issued" impedimenta. The porter handed

the officer his cap and stick, then he vanished with the lug-
gage belonging to them. She glanced again down the length
of the car.

"Where are my——"

"Yessum," the porter called from the door, across the
coated shoulders of passengers, "I got your things, ma'am."

He had gotten them and his dark gentle hand lowered the
officer carefully to the platform.

"Help the lootenant there," said the conductor officiously,
but he had already got the officer to the floor.

"You'll look after him, ma'am?"

"Yes. I'll look after him."

They moved down the shed and Cadet Lowe looked back.
But the negro was efficient and skillful, busy with other passengers. He seemed to have forgotten them. And Cadet
Lowe looked from the porter occupied with bags and the gar-
nering of quarters and half dollars, to the officer in his coat
and stick, remarking the set of his cap slanting backward
bonelessly from his scarred brow, and he marvelled briefly
upon his own kind.

But this was soon lost in the mellow death of evening in a
street between stone buildings, among lights, and Gilligan in
his awkward khaki and the girl in her rough coat, holding each
an arm of Donald Mahon, silhouetted against it in the doorway.

3

Mrs. Powers lay in her bed aware of her long body beneath
strange sheets, hearing the hushed night sounds of a hotel—
muffled footfalls along mute carpeted corridors, discreet opening and shutting of doors, somewhere a murmurous pulse of
machinery—all with that strange propensity which sounds,
anywhere else soothing, have, when heard in a hotel, for keep-

ing you awake. Her mind and body warming to the old
familiarity of sleep became empty, then as she settled her body
to the bed, shaping it for slumber, it filled with a remembered troubling sadness.

She thought of her husband youngly dead in France in a
recurrence of fretful exasperation with having been tricked by
a wanton Fate: a joke amusing to no one. Just when she had
calmly decided that they had taken advantage of a universal
hysteria for the purpose of getting of each other a brief
ecstasy, just when she had decided calmly that they were
better quit of each other with nothing to mar the memory of
their three days together and had written him so, wishing him
luck, she must be notified casually and impersonally that he
had been killed in action. So casually, so impersonally; as
if Richard Powers, with whom she had spent three days, were
one man and Richard Powers commanding a platoon in the
—Division were another.

And she being young must again know all the terror of
parting, of that passionate desire to cling to something concrete in a dark world, in spite of war departments. He had
not even got her letter! This in some way seemed the
infidelity: having him die still believing in her, bored though
they both probably were.

She turned feeling sheets like water, warmed by her bodily
heat, upon her legs.

Oh, damn, damn. What a rotten trick you played on
me. She recalled those nights during which they had tried
to eradicate to-morrows from the world. Two rotten tricks,
she thought. Anyway, I know what I'll do with the insurance, she added, wondering what Dick thought about it—if
he did know or care.

Her shoulder rounded upward, into her vision, the indication of her covered turning body swelled and died away toward

the foot of the bed: she lay staring down the tunnel of her room, watching the impalpable angles of furniture, feeling through plastered smug walls a rumor of spring outside. The airshaft was filled with a prophecy of April come again into the world. Like a heedless idiot into a world that had forgotten Spring. The white connecting door took the vague indication of a transom and held it in a mute and luminous plane, and obeying an impulse she rose and slipped on a dressing gown.

The door opened quietly under her hand. The room, like hers, was a suggestion of furniture, identically vague. She could hear Mahon's breathing and she found a light switch with her fingers. Under his scarred brow he slept, the light full and sudden on his closed eyes did not disturb him. And she knew in an instinctive flash what was wrong with him, why his motions were hesitating, ineffectual.

He's going blind, she said, bending over him. He slept and after a while there were sounds without the door. She straightened up swiftly and the noises ceased. Then the door opened to a blundering key and Gilligan entered supporting Cadet Lowe, glassy-eyed and quite drunk.

Gilligan standing his lax companion upright, said:

"Good afternoon, ma'am."

Lowe muttered wetly and Gilligan continued:

"Look at this lonely mariner I got here. Sail on, O proud and lonely," he told his attached and aimless burden. Cadet Lowe muttered again, not intelligible. His eyes were like two oysters.

"Huh?" asked Gilligan. "Come on, be a man: speak to the nice lady."

Cadet Lowe repeated himself liquidly and she whispered: "Shhh: be quiet."

"Oh," said Gilligan with surprise, "Loot's asleep, huh? What's he want to sleep for, this time of day?"

Lowe with quenchless optimism essayed speech again and Gilligan comprehending, said:

"That's what you want, is it? Why couldn't you come out like a man and say it? Wants to go to bed, for some reason," he explained to Mrs. Powers.

"That's where he belongs," she said; and Gilligan with alcoholic care led his companion to the other bed and with the exaggerated caution of the inebriate laid him upon it. Lowe drawing his knees up sighed and turned his back to them, but Gilligan dragging at his legs removed his puttees and shoes, taking each shoe in both hands and placing it on a table. She leaned against the foot of Mahon's bed, fitting her long thigh to the hard rail, until he had finished.

At last Lowe freed of his shoes turned sighing to the wall and she said:

"How drunk are you, Joe?"

"Not very, ma'am. What's wrong? Loot need something?"

Mahon slept and Cadet Lowe immediately slept.

"I want to talk to you, Joe. About him," she added quickly, feeling Gilligan's stare. "Can you listen or had you rather go to bed and talk it over in the morning?"

Gilligan, focusing his eyes, answered:

"Why, now suits me. Always oblige a lady."

Making her decision suddenly she said:

"Come in my room then."

"Sure: lemme get my bottle and I'm your man.'·

She returned to her room while he sought his bottle and when he joined her she was sitting on her bed clasping her knees, wrapped in a blanket. Gilligan drew up a chair.

"Joe, do you know he's going blind?" she said abruptly.

After a time her face became a human face and holding it in his vision he said:

"I know more than that. He's going to die."

"Die?"

"Yes, ma'am. If I ever seen death in a man's face, it's in his. Goddam this world," he burst out suddenly.

"Shhh!" she whispered.

"That's right, I forgot," he said swiftly.

She clasped her knees, huddled beneath the blanket, changing the position of her body as it became cramped, feeling the wooden head-board of the bed, wondering why there were not iron beds, wondering why everything was as it was— iron beds, why you deliberately took certain people to break your intimacy, why these people died, why you yet took others. . . . Will my death be like this: fretting and exasperating? Am I cold by nature, or have I spent all my emotional coppers, that I don't seem to feel things like others? Dick, Dick. Ugly and dead.

Gilligan sat brittly in his chair, focusing his eyes with an effort, having those instruments of vision evade him, slimy as broken eggs. Lights completing a circle, an orbit; she with two faces sitting on two beds, clasping four arms around her knees. . . . Why can't a man be very happy or very unhappy? It's only a sort of pale mixture of the two. Like beer when you want a shot—or a drink of water. Neither one nor the other.

She moved and drew the blanket closer about her. Spring in an airshaft, the rumor of spring; but in the room steam heat suggested winter, dying away.

"Let's have a drink, Joe."

He rose careful and brittle and walking with meticulous deliberation he fetched a carafe and glasses. She drew a small table near them and Gilligan prepared two drinks. She drank and set the glass down. He lit a cigarette for her.

"It's a rotten old world, Joe."

"You damn right. And dying ain't the half of it."

"Dying?"

"In his case, I mean. Trouble is, he probably won't die soon enough."

"Not die soon enough?"

Gilligan drained his glass. "I got the low down on him, see. He's got a girl at home: folks got 'em engaged when they was young, before he went off to war. And do you know what she's going to do when she sees his face?" he asked, staring at her. At last her two faces became one face and her hair was black. Her mouth was like a scar.

"Oh, no, Joe. She wouldn't do that." She sat up. The blanket slipped from her shoulders and she replaced it, watching him intently.

Gilligan breaking the orbit of visible things by an effort of will said:

"Don't you kid yourself. I've seen her picture. And the last letter he had from her."

"He didn't show them to you!" she said quickly.

"That's all right about that. I seen 'em."

"Joe. You didn't go through his things?"

"Hell, ma'am, ain't I and you trying to help him? Suppose I did do something that ain't exactly according to holy Hoyle: you know damn well that I can help him—if I don't let a whole lot of don'ts stop me. And if I know I'm right there ain't any don'ts or anything else going to stop me."

She looked at him and he hurried on:

"I mean, you and I know what to do for him, but if you are always letting a gentleman don't do this and a gentleman don't do that interfere, you can't help him. Do you see?"

"But what makes you so sure she will turn him down?"

"Why, I tell you I seen that letter: all the old bunk about knights of the air and the romance of battle, that even the fat crying ones outgrow soon as the excitement is over and uniforms and being wounded ain't only not stylish no more, but it is troublesome."

"But aren't you taking a lot for granted, not to have seen her, even?"

"I've seen that photograph: one of them flighty-looking pretty ones with lots of hair. Just the sort would have got herself engaged to him."

"How do you know it is still on? Perhaps she has forgotten him. And he probably doesn't remember her, you know."

"That ain't it. If he don't remember her he's all right. But if he will know his folks he will want to believe that something in his world ain't turned upside down."

They were silent a while, then Gilligan said: "I wish I could have knowed him before. He's the kind of a son I would have liked to have." He finished his drink.

"Joe, how old are you?"

"Thirty-two, ma'am."

"How did you ever learn so much about us?" she asked with interest, watching him.

He grinned briefly. "It ain't knowing, it's just saying things. I think I done it through practice. By talking so much," he replied with sardonic humor. "I talk so much I got to say the right thing sooner or later. You don't talk much, yourself."

"Not much," she agreed. She moved carelessly and the blanket slipped entirely, exposing her thin nightdress; raising her arms and twisting her body to replace it her long shank was revealed and her turning ankle and her bare foot.

Gilligan without moving said: "Ma'am, let's get married."

She huddled quickly in the blanket again, already knowing a faint disgust with herself.

"Bless your heart, Joe. Don't you know my name is Mrs.?"

"Sure. And I know, too, you ain't got any husband. I dunno where he is or what you done with him, but you ain't got a husband now."

"Goodness, I'm beginning to be afraid of you: you know too much. You are right: my husband was killed last year."

Gilligan looking at her said: "Rotten luck." And she tasting again a faint, warm sorrow, bowed her head to her arched clasped knees.

"Rotten luck. That's exactly what it was, what everything is. Even sorrow is a fake, now." She raised her face, her pallid face beneath her black hair, scarred with her mouth. "Joe, that was the only sincere word of condolence I ever had. Come here."

Gilligan went to her and she took his hand, holding it against her cheek. Then she removed it, shaking back her hair.

"You are a good fellow, Joe. If I felt like marrying anybody now, I'd take you. I'm sorry I played that trick, Joe."

"Trick?" repeated Gilligan, gazing upon her black hair. Then he said Oh, non-committally.

"But we haven't decided what to do with that poor boy in there," she said with brisk energy, clasping her blanket. "That's what I wanted to talk to you about. Are you sleepy?"

"Not me," he answered. "I don't think I ever want to sleep again."

"Neither do I." She moved across the bed, propping her back against the head board. "Lie down here and let's decide on something."

"Sure," agreed Gilligan. "I better take off my shoes, first. Ruin the hotel's bed."

"To hell with the hotel's bed," she told him. "Put your feet on it."

Gilligan lay down, shielding his eyes with his hand. After a time she said:

"Well, what's to be done?"

"We got to get him home first," Gilligan said. "I'll wire his folks to-morrow—his old man is a preacher, see. But it's that damn girl bothers me. He sure ought to be let die in peace. But what else to do I don't know. I know about some things," he explained, "but after all women can guess and be nearer right than whatever I could decide on."

"I don't think anyone could do much more than you. I'd put my money on you every time."

He moved, shading his eyes again. "I dunno: I am good so far, but then you got to have more'n just sense. Say, why don't you come with the general and me?"

"I intend to, Joe." Her voice came from beyond his shielding hand. "I think I intended to all the time."

(She is in love with him.) But he only said:

"Good for you. But I knowed you'd do the right thing. All right with your people, is it?"

"Yes. But what about money?"

"Money?"

"Well . . . for what he might need. You know. He might get sick anywhere."

"Lord, I cleaned up in a poker game and I ain't had time to spend it. Money's all right. That ain't any question." he said roughly.

"Yes, money's all right. You know I have my husband's insurance."

He lay silent, shielding his eyes. His khaki legs marring the bed ended in clumsy shoes. She nursed her knees, huddling in her blanket. After a space she said:

"Sleep, Joe?"

"It's a funny world, ain't it?" he asked irrelevantly, not moving.

"Funny?"

"Sure. Soldier dies and leaves you money, and you spend the money helping another soldier die comfortable. Ain't that funny?"

"I suppose so. . . . Everything is funny. Horribly funny."

"Anyway, it's nice to have it all fixed," he said after a while. "He'll be glad you are coming along."

(Dear dead Dick.) (Mahon under his scar, sleeping.) (Dick, my dearest one.)

She felt the head board against her head, through her hair, felt the bones of her long shanks against her arms clasping them, nursing them, saw the smug, impersonal room like an appointed tomb (in which how many, many discontents, desires, passions, had died?) high above a world of joy and sorrow and lust for living, high above impervious trees occupied solely with maternity and spring. (Dick, Dick. Dead, ugly Dick. Once you were alive and young and passionate and ugly, after a time you were dead, dear Dick: that flesh, that body, which I loved and did not love; your beautiful, young, ugly body, dear Dick, become now a seething of worms, like new milk. Dear Dick.)

Gilligan, Joseph, late a private, a democrat by enlistment and numbered like a convict, slept beside her, his boots (given him gratis by democrats of a higher rating among democrats) innocent and awkward upon a white spread of rented cloth, immaculate and impersonal.

She evaded her blanket and reaching her arm swept the room with darkness. She slipped beneath the covers, settling her cheek on her palm. Gilligan undisturbed snored, filling the room with a homely, comforting sound.

(Dick, dear, ugly dead. . . .)

4

In the next room Cadet Lowe waked from a chaotic dream, opening his eyes and staring with detachment, impersonal as God, at lights burning about him. After a time, he recalled his body, remembering where he was and by an effort he turned his head. In the other bed the man slept beneath his terrible face. (I am Julian Lowe I eat, I digest, evacuate: I have flown. This man . . . this man here, sleeping beneath his scar. . . . Where do we touch? Oh, God, oh, God: knowing his own body, his stomach.)

Raising his hand he felt his own undamaged brow. No scar there. Near him upon a chair was his hat severed by a white band, upon the table the other man's cap with its cloth crown sloping backward from a bronze initialed crest.

He tasted his sour mouth, knowing his troubled stomach. To have been him! he moaned. Just to be him. Let him take this sound body of mine! Let him take it. To have got wings on my breast, to have wings; and to have got his scar, too, I would take death to-morrow. Upon a chair Mahon's tunic evinced above the left breast pocket wings breaking from an initialed circle beneath a crown, tipping downward in an arrested embroidered sweep; a symbolized desire.

To be him, to have gotten wings, but to have got his scar

too!   Cadet Lowe turned to the wall with passionate disappointment like a gnawing fox at his vitals.   Slobbering
and moaning Cadet Lowe, too, dreamed again, sleeping.

5

Achilles—What preparation would you make for a cross-
    country flight, Cadet?
Mercury—Empty your bladder and fill your petrol tank, Sir.
Achilles—Carry on, Cadet.

> —*Old Play*
> (*About 19—?*)

Cadet Lowe, waking, remarked morning, and Gilligan entering the room, dressed.   Gilligan looking at him said:

"How you coming, ace?"

Mahon yet slept beneath his scar, upon a chair his tunic.
Above the left pocket, wings swept silkenly, breaking downward above a ribbon.   Purple, white, purple.

"Oh, God," Lowe groaned.

Gilligan with the assurance of physical well-being stood in
brisk arrested motion.

"As you were, fellow.   I'm going out and have some breakfast sent up.   You stay here until Loot wakes, huh?"

Cadet Lowe tasting his sour mouth groaned again.   Gilligan regarded him.   "Oh, you'll stay all right, won't you?
I'll be back soon."

The door closed after him and Lowe, thinking of water, rose
and took his wavering way across the room to a water pitcher.
Carafe.   Like giraffe or like café? he wondered.   The water
was good, but lowering the vessel he felt immediately sick.
After a while he recaptured the bed.

He dosed, forgetting his stomach, and remembering it he

dreamed and waked. He could feel his head like a dull infla-
tion, then he could distinguish the foot of his bed and thinking
again of water he turned on a pillow and saw another identical
bed and the suave indication of a dressing gown motionless
beside it. Leaning over Mahon's scarred supineness, she said:
"Don't get up."

Lowe said, I won't, closing his eyes, tasting his mouth,
seeing her long slim body against his red eyelids, opening
his eyes to light and her thigh shaped and falling away into
an impersonal fabric. With an effort he might have seen
her ankles. Her feet will be there, he thought, unable to
acomplish the effort and behind his closed eyes he thought
of saying something which would leave his mouth on hers.
Oh, God, he thought, feeling that no one had been so sick,
imagining that she would say I love you, too. If I had
wings, and a scar. . . . To hell with officers, he thought,
sleeping again:

To hell with kee-wees, anyway. I wouldn't be a goddam
kee-wee. Rather be a sergeant. Rather be a mechanic.
Crack up, Cadet. Hell, yes. Why not? War's over. Glad.
Glad. Oh, God. His scar: his wings. Last time.

He was briefly in a Jenny again, conscious of lubricating
oil and a slow gracious restraint of braced plane surfaces,
feeling an air blast and feeling the stick in his hand, watching
bobbing rocker arms on the horizon, laying her nose on the
horizon like a sighted rifle. Christ, what do I care? seeing
her nose rise until the horizon was hidden, seeing the arc
of a descending wing expose it again, seeing her become
abruptly stationary while a mad world spinning vortexed
about his seat. "Sure, what do you care?" asked a voice and
waking he saw Gilligan beside him with a glass of whisky.

"Drink her down, General," said Gilligan, holding the glass
under his nose.

"Oh, God, move it, move it."

"Come on, now; drink her down: you'll feel better. The Loot is up and at 'em, and Mrs. Powers. Whatcher get so drunk for, ace?"

"Oh, God, I don't know," answered Cadet Lowe, rolling his head in anguish. "Lemme alone."

Gilligan said: "Come on, drink her, now." Cadet Lowe said, Go away passionately.

"Lemme alone; I'll be all right."

"Sure you will. Soon as you drink this."

"I can't. Go away."

"You got to. You want I should break your neck?" asked Gilligan kindly, bringing his face up, kind and ruthless. Lowe eluded him and Gilligan reaching under his body, raised him.

"Lemme lie down," Lowe implored.

"And stay here forever? We got to go somewheres. We can't stay here."

"But I can't drink." Cadet Lowe's interior coiled passionately: an ecstasy. "For God's sake, let me alone."

"Ace," said Gilligan, holding his head up, "you got to. You might just as well drink this yourself. If you don't I'll put it down your throat, glass and all. Here, now."

The glass was between his lips, so he drank, gulping, expecting to gag. But gulping, the stuff became immediately pleasant. It was like new life in him. He felt a kind sweat and Gilligan removed the empty glass. Mahon, dressed except for his belt, sat beside a table. Gilligan vanished through a door and he rose, feeling shaky but quite fit. He took another drink. Water thundered in the bathroom and Gilligan returning said briskly: "Atta boy."

He pushed Lowe into the bathroom. "In you go, ace," he added.

Feeling the sweet bright needles of water burning his

shoulders, watching his body slipping an endless silver sheath of water, smelling soap: beyond that wall was her room, where she was, tall and red and white and black, beautiful. I'll tell her at once, he decided, sawing his hard young body with a rough towel. Glowing, he brushed his teeth and hair, then he had another drink under Mahon's quiet inverted stare and Gilligan's quizzical one. He dressed, hearing her moving in her room. Maybe she's thinking of me, he told himself, swiftly donning his khaki.

He caught the officer's kind, puzzled gaze and the man said:

"How are you?"

"Never felt better after my solo," he answered, wanting to sing. "Say, I left my hat in her room last night," he told Gilligan. "Guess I better get it."

"Here's your hat," Gilligan informed him unkindly, producing it.

"Well, then, I want to talk to her. Whatcher going to say about that?" asked Cadet Lowe, swept and garnished and belligerent.

"Why, sure, General," Gilligan agreed readily. "She can't refuse one of the saviors of her country." He knocked on her door. "Mrs. Powers?"

"Yes?" her voice was muffled.

"General Pershing here wants to talk to you. . . . Sure . . . All right." He turned about, opening the door. "In you go, ace."

Lowe, hating him, ignored his wink, entering. She sat in bed with a breakfast tray upon her knees. She was not dressed and Lowe looked delicately away. But she said blandly:

"Cherio, Cadet! How looks the air to-day?"

She indicated a chair and he drew it up to the bed, being so

careful not to seem to stare that his carriage became notice-
able. She looked at him quickly and kindly and offered him
coffee. Courageous with whisky on an empty stomach he
knew hunger suddenly. He took the cup.

"Good morning," he said with belated courtesy, trying to
be more than nineteen. (Why is nineteen ashamed of its
age?) She treats me like a child, he thought, fretted and
gaining courage, watching with increasing boldness her indicated shoulders and wondering with interest if she had
stockings on.

Why didn't I say something as I came in? Something
easy and intimate? Listen, when I first saw you my love for
you was like—my love was like—my love for you—God, if
I only hadn't drunk so much last night I could say it my love
for you my love is love is like . . . and found himself watching her arms as she moved and her loose sleeves fell away
from them, saying, yes, he was glad the war was over and
telling her that he had forty-seven hours flying time and
would have got wings in two weeks more and that his mother
in San Francisco was expecting him.

She treats me like a child, he thought with exasperation,
seeing the slope of her shoulders and the place where her
breast was.

"How black your hair is," he said, and she said:

"Lowe, when are you going home?"

"I don't know. Why should I go home? I think I'll have
to look at the country first."

"But your mother!" She glanced at him.

"Oh, well," he said largely, "you know what women are—
always worrying you."

"Lowe! How do you know so much about things? Women?
You—aren't married, are you?"

"Me married?" repeated Lowe with ungrammatical zest,

"me married? Not so's you know it. I have lots of girls, but married?" he brayed with brief unnecessary vigor. "What made you think so?" he asked with interest.

"Oh, I don't know. You look so—so mature, you see."

"Ah, that's flying does that. Look at him in there."

"Is that it? I had noticed something about you . . . You would have been an ace, too, if you'd seen any Germans, wouldn't you?"

He glanced at her quickly, like a struck dog. Here was his old dull despair again.

"I'm so sorry," she said with quick sincerity. "I didn't think: of course you would. Anyway, it wasn't your fault. You did your best, I know."

"Oh, for Christ's sake," he said, hurt, "what do you women want, anyway? I am as good a flyer as any ever was at the front—flying or any other way." He sat morose under her eyes. He rose suddenly. "Say, what's your name, anyway?"

"Margaret," she told him. He approached the bed where she sat and she said: "More coffee?" stopping him dead. "You've forgotton your cup. There it is, on the table."

Before he thought he had returned and fetched his cup, received coffee he did not want. He felt like a fool and being young he resented it. All right for you, he promised her and sat again in a dull rage. To hell with them all.

"I have offended you, haven't I?" she asked. "But, Lowe, I feel so bad, and you were about to make love to me."

"Why do you think that?" he asked, hurt and dull.

"Oh, I don't know. But women can tell. And I don't want to be made love to. Gilligan has already done that."

"Gilligan? Why, I'll kill him if he has annoyed you."

"No, no: he didn't offend me, any more than you did. It was flattering. But why were you going to make love to me? You thought of it before you came in, didn't you?"

Lowe told her youngly: "I thought of it on the train when I first saw you. When I saw you I knew you were the woman for me. Tell me, you don't like him better than me because he has wings and a scar, do you?"

"Why, of course not." She looked at him a moment, calculating. Then she said: "Mr. Gilligan says he is dying."

"Dying?" he repeated and "Dying?" How the man managed to circumvent him at every turn! As if it were not enough to have wings and a scar. But to die.

"Margaret," he said with such despair that she gazed at him in swift pity. (He was so young.) "Margaret, are you in love with him?" (Knowing that if he were a woman, he would be.)

"No, certainly not. I am not in love with anybody. My husband was killed on the Aisne, you see," she told him gently.

"Oh, Margaret," he said with bitter sincerity, "I would have been killed there if I could, or wounded like him, don't you know it?"

"Of course, darling." She put the tray aside. "Come here."

Cadet Lowe rose again and went to her. "I would have been, if I'd had a chance," he repeated.

She drew him down beside her, and he knew he was acting the child she supposed him to be, but he couldn't help it. His disappointment and despair were more than everything now. Here were her knees sweetly under his face, and he put his arms around her legs.

"I wanted to be," he confessed more than he had ever believed, "I would take his scar and all."

"And be dead, like he is going to be?"

But what was death to Cadet Lowe, except something true and grand and sad? He saw a tomb, open, and himself in boots and belt, and pilot's wings on his breast, a wound stripe. . . . What more could one ask of Fate?

"Yes, yes," he answered.

"Why, you have flown, too," she told him, holding his face against her knees, "you might have been him, but you were lucky. Perhaps you would have flown too well to have been shot down as he was. Had you thought of that?"

"I don't know. I guess I would let them catch me, if I could have been him. You are in love with him."

"I swear I am not." She raised his head to see his face. "I would tell you if I were. Don't you believe me?" her eyes were compelling: he believed her.

"Then, if you aren't, can't you promise to wait for me? I will be older soon and I'll work like hell and make money."

"What will your mother say?"

"Hell, I don't have to mind her like a kid forever. I am nineteen, as old as you are, and if she don't like it, she can go to hell."

"Lowe!" she reproved him, not telling him she was twenty-four, "the idea! You go home and tell your mother—I will give you a note to her—and you can write what she says."

"But I had rather go with you."

"But, dear heart, what good will that do? We are going to take him home, and he is sick. Don't you see, darling, we can't do anything until we get him settled, and that you would only be in the way?"

"In the way?" he repeated with sharp pain.

"You know what I mean. We can't have anything to think about until we get him home, don't you see?"

"But you aren't in love with him?"

"I swear I'm not. Does that satisfy you?"

"Then, are you in love with me?"

She drew his face against her knees again. "You sweet child," she said; "of course I won't tell you—yet."

And he had to be satisfied with this. They held each other

in silence for a time. "How good you smell," remarked Cadet Lowe at last.

She moved. "Come up here by me," she commanded, and when he was beside her she took his face in her hands and kissed him. He put his arms around her, and she drew his head between her breasts. After a while she stroked his hair and spoke.

"Now, are you going home at once?"

"Must I?" he asked vacuously.

"You must," she answered. "To-day. Wire her at once. And I will give you a note to her."

"Oh, hell, you know what she'll say."

"Of course I do. You haven't any sisters and brothers, have you?"

"No," he said in surprise. She moved and he sensed the fact that she desired to be released. He sat up. "How did you know?" he asked in surprise.

"I just guessed. But you will go, won't you? Promise."

"Well, I will, then. But I will come back to you."

"Of course you will. I will expect you. Kiss me."

She offered her face coolly and he kissed her as she wished: coldly, remotely. She put her hands on his cheeks. "Dear boy," she said, kissing him again, as his mother kissed him.

"Say, that's no way for engaged people to kiss," he objected.

"How do engaged people kiss?" she asked. He put his arms around her, feeling her shoulder blades, and drew her mouth against his with the technique he had learned. She suffered his kiss a moment, then thrust him away.

"Is that how engaged people kiss?" she asked, laughing. 'I like this better." She took his face in her palms and touched his mouth briefly and coolly. "Now swear you'll wire your mother at once."

"But will you write to me?"

"Surely. But swear you will go to-day, in spite of what Gilligan may tell you."

"I swear," he answered, looking at her mouth. "Can't I kiss you again?"

"When we are married," she said, and he knew he was being dismissed. Thinking, knowing that she was watching him, he crossed the room with an air, not looking back.

Here were yet Gilligan and the officer. Mahon said:

"Morning, old chap."

Gilligan looked at Lowe's belligerent front from a quizzical reserve of sardonic amusement.

"Made a conquest, hey, ace?"

"Go to hell," replied Lowe. "Where's that bottle? I'm going home to-day."

"Here she is, General. Drink deep. Going home?" he repeated. "So are we, hey, Loot?"

CHAPTER II

I

Jones, Januarius Jones, born of whom he knew and cared not, becoming Jones alphabetically, January through a conjunction of calendar and biology, Januarius through the perverse conjunction of his own star and the compulsion of food and clothing—Januarius Jones baggy in gray tweed, being lately a fellow of Latin in a small college, leaned upon a gate of iron grill-work breaking a levee of green and embryonically starred honeysuckle, watching April busy in a hyacinth bed. Dew was on the grass and bees broke apple bloom in the morning sun while swallows were like plucked strings against a pale windy sky. A face regarded him across a suspended trowel and the metal clasps of crossed suspenders made a cheerful glittering.

The rector said: "Good morning, young man." His shining dome was friendly against an ivy-covered wall above which the consummate grace of a spire and a gilded cross seemed to arc across motionless young clouds.

Januarius Jones, caught in the spire's illusion of slow ruin, murmured: "Watch it fall, sir." The sun was full on his young round face.

The horticulturist regarded him with benevolent curiosity. "Fall? Ah, you see an aeroplane," he stated. "My son was in that service during the war." He became gigantic in black trousers and broken shoes. "A beautiful day for flying," he said from beneath his cupped hand. "Where do you see it?"

"No, sir," replied Jones, "no aeroplane, sir. I referred in a fit of unpardonable detachment to your spire. It was ever my childish delight to stand beneath a spire while clouds are moving overhead. The illusion of slow falling is perfect. Have you ever experienced this, sir?"

"To be sure I have, though it has been—let me see—more years than I care to remember. But one of my cloth is prone to allow his own soul to atrophy in his zeal for the welfare of other souls that——"

"—that not only do not deserve salvation, but that do not particularly desire it," finished Jones.

The rector promptly rebuked him. Sparrows were delirious in ivy and the rambling façade of the rectory was a dream in jonquils and clipped sward. There should be children here, thought Jones. He said:

"I most humbly beg your pardon for my flippancy, Doctor. I assure you that I—ah—took advantage of the situation without any ulterior motive whatever."

"I understand that, dear boy. My rebuke was tendered in the same spirit. There are certain conventions which we must observe in this world: one of them being an outward deference to that cloth which I unworthily, perhaps, wear. And I have found this particularly incumbent upon us of the—what shall I say——?"

> "Integer vitae scelerisque purus
>   non eget Mauris iaculis neque arcu
>   nec venenatis sagittas,
>   Fusce, pharetra—" began Jones.

The rector chimed in:

> "—sive per Syrtis iter aestuosas
>   sive facturus per inhospitalem
>   Causasum vel quae loac fabulosas
>   lambit Hydaspes,"

they concluded in galloping duet and stood in the ensuing silence regarding each other with genial enthusiasm.

"But come, come," cried the rector. His eyes were pleasant. "Shall I let the stranger languish without my gates?" The grilled iron swung open and his earthy hand was heavy on Jones' shoulder. "Come, let us try the spire."

The grass was good. A myriad bees vacillated between clover and apple bloom, apple bloom and clover, and from the Gothic mass of the church the spire rose, a prayer imperishable in bronze, immaculate in its illusion of slow ruin across motionless young clouds.

"My one sincere parishioner," murmured the divine. Sunlight was a windy golden plume about his bald head, and Januarius Jones' face was a round mirror before which fauns and nymphs might have wantoned when the world was young.

"Parishioner, did I say? It is more than that: it is by such as this that man may approach nearest to God. And how few will believe this! How few, how few!" He stared unblinking into the sun-filled sky: drowned in his eyes was a despair long since grown cool and quiet.

"That is very true, sir. But we of this age believe that he who may be approached informally, without the intercession of an office-boy of some sort, is not worth the approaching. We purchase our salvation as we do our real estate. Our God," continued Jones, "need not be compassionate, he need not be very intelligent. But he must have dignity."

The rector raised his great dirty hand. "No, no. You do them injustice. But who has ever found justice in youth, or any of those tiresome virtues with which we coddle and cradle our hardening arteries and souls? Only the ageing need conventions and laws to aggregate to themselves some of the beauty of this world. Without laws the young would rieve us of it as corsairs of old combed the blue seas."

The rector was silent a while. The intermittent shadows of young leaves were bird cries made visible and sparrows in ivy were flecks of sunlight become vocal. The rector continued:

"Had I the arranging of this world I should establish a certain point, say at about the age of thirty, upon reaching which a man would be automatically relegated to a plane where his mind would no longer be troubled with the futile recollection of temptations he had resisted and of beauty he had failed to garner to himself. It is jealousy, I think, which makes us wish to prevent young people doing the things we had not the courage or the opportunity ourselves to accomplish once, and have not the power to do now."

Jones, wondering what temptations he had ever resisted and then recalling the women he might have seduced and hadn't, said: "And then what? What would the people who have been unlucky enough to reach thirty do?"

"On this plane there would be no troubling physical things such as sunlight and space and birds in the trees—but only unimportant things such as physical comfort: eating and sleeping and procreation."

What more could you want? thought Jones. Here was a swell place. A man could very well spend all his time eating and sleeping and procreating, Jones believed. He rather wished the rector (or anyone who could imagine a world consisting solely of food and sleep and women) had had the creating of things and that he, Jones, could be forever thirty-one years of age. The rector, though, seemed to hold different opinions.

"What would they do to pass the time?" asked Jones for the sake of argument, wondering what the others would do to pass the time, what with eating and sleeping and fornication taken from them.

"Half of them would manufacture objects and another portion would coin gold and silver with which to purchase these objects. Of course, there would be storage places for the coins and objects, thus providing employment for some of the people. Others naturally would have to till the soil."

"But how would you finally dispose of the coins and objects? After a while you would have a single vast museum and a bank, both filled with useless and unnecessary things. And that is already the curse of our civilization—Things, Possessions, to which we are slaves, which require us to either labor honestly at least eight hours a day or do something illegal so as to keep them painted or dressed in the latest mode or filled with whisky or gasoline."

"Quite true. And this would remind us too sorely of the world as it is. Needless to say, I have provided for both of these contingencies. The coins might be reduced again to bullion and coined over, and—" the reverend man looked at Jones in ecstasy—"the housewives could use the objects for fuel with which to cook food."

Old fool, thought Jones, saying: "Marvelous, magnificent! You are a man after my own heart, Doctor."

The rector regarded Jones kindly. "Ah, boy, there is nothing after youth's own heart: youth has no heart."

"But, Doctor. This borders on borders upon lese majesty. I thought we had declared a truce regarding each other's cloth."

Shadows moved as the sun moved, a branch dappled the rector's brow: a laureled Jove.

"What is your cloth?"

"Why—" began Jones.

"It is the diaper still, dear boy. But forgive me," he added quickly on seeing Jones' face. His arm was heavy and solid as an oak branch across Jones' shoulder. "Tell me, what do you consider the most admirable of virtues?"

Jones was placated. "Sincere arrogance," he returned

promptly. The rector's great laugh boomed like bells in the sunlight, sent the sparrows like gusty leaves whirling.

"Shall we be friends once more, then? Come, I will make a concession: I will show you my flowers. You are young enough to appreciate them without feeling called upon to comment."

The garden was worth seeing. An avenue of roses bordered a graveled path which passed from sunlight beneath two overarching oaks. Beyond the oaks, against a wall of poplars in a restless formal row were columns of a Greek temple, yet the poplars themselves in slim, vague green were poised and vain as girls in a frieze. Against a privet hedge would soon be lilies like nuns in a cloister and blue hyacinths swung soundless bells, dreaming of Lesbos. Upon a lattice wall wistaria would soon burn in slow inverted lilac flame, and following it they came lastly upon a single rose bush. The branches were huge and knotted with age, heavy and dark as a bronze pedestal, crowned with pale impermanent gold. The divine's hands lingered upon it with soft passion.

"Now, this," he said, "is my son and my daughter, the wife of my bosom and the bread of my belly: it is my right hand and my left hand. Many is the night I have stood beside it here after having moved the wrappings too soon, burning newspapers to keep the frost out. Once I recall I was in a neighboring town attending a conference. The weather—it was March—had been most auspicious and I had removed the covering.

"The tips were already swelling. Ah, my boy, no young man ever awaited the coming of his mistress with more impatience than do I await the first bloom on this bush. (Who was the old pagan who kept his Byzantine goblet at his bedside and slowly wore away the rim kissing it? there is an analogy.) . . . But what was I saying?—ah, yes. So

I left the bush uncovered against my better judgment and repaired to the conference. The weather continued perfect until the last day, then the weather reports predicted a change. The bishop was to be present; I ascertained that I could not reach home by rail and return in time. At last I engaged a livery man to drive me home.

"The sky was becoming overcast, it was already turning colder. And then, three miles from home, we came upon a stream and found the bridge gone. After some shouting we attracted the attention of a man plowing across the stream and he came over to us in a skiff. I engaged my driver to await me, was ferried across, walked home and covered my rose, walked back to the stream and returned in time. And that night—" the rector beamed upon Januarius Jones "—snow fell!"

Jones fatly supine on gracious grass, his eyes closed against the sun, stuffing his pipe: "This rose has almost made history. You have had the bush for some time, have you not? One does become attached to things one has long known." Januarius Jones was not particularly interested in flowers.

"I have a better reason than that. In this bush is imprisoned a part of my youth, as wine is imprisoned in a wine jar. But with this difference: my wine jar always renews itself."

"Oh," remarked Jones, despairing, "there is a story here, then."

"Yes, dear boy. Rather a long story. But you are not comfortable lying there."

"Who ever is completely comfortable," Jones rushed into the breach, "unless he be asleep? It is the fatigue caused by man's inevitable contact with the earth which bears him, be he sitting, standing or lying, which keeps his mind in a continual fret over futilities. If a man, if a single man, could be freed for a moment from the forces of gravity, concentrating his weight upon that point of his body which touches the earth, what would he not do? He would be a god, the lord of life, causing the high gods to tremble on their thrones: he would thunder at the very gates of infinity like a mailed knight. As it is, he must ever have behind his mind a dull wonder how anything composed of fire and air and water and omnipotence in equal parts can be so damn hard."

"That is true. Man cannot remain in one position long enough to really think. But about the rose bush——"

"Regard the buzzard," interrupted Jones with enthusiasm, fighting for time, "supported by air alone: what dignity, what singlenes of purpose! What cares he whether or not Smith is governor? What cares he that the sovereign people annually commission comparative strangers about whom nothing is known save that they have no inclination toward perspiration, to meddle with impunity in the affairs of the sovereign people?"

"But, my dear boy, this borders on anarchism."

"Anarchism? Surely. The hand of Providence with money-changing blisters. That is anarchism."

"At least you admit the hand of Providence."

"I don't know. Do I?" Jones, his hat over his eyes and his pipe projecting beneath, heaved a box of matches from his jacket. He extracted one and scraped it on the box. It failed and he threw it weakly into a clump of violets. He tried another. He tried another. "Turn it around," murmured the rector. He did so and the match flared.

"How do you find the hand of Providence here?" he puffed around his pipe stem.

The rector gathered the dead matches from the clump of violets. "In this way: it enables man to rise and till the soil, so that he might eat. Would he, do you think, rise and labor if he could remain comfortably supine over long? Even that part of the body which the Creator designed for sitting on serves him only a short time, then it rebels, then it, too, gets his sullen bones up and hales them along. And there is no help for him save in sleep."

"But he cannot sleep for more than a possible third of his time," Jones pointed out. "And soon it will not even be a third of his time. The race is weakening, degenerating: we cannot stand nearly as much sleep as our comparatively recent (geologically speaking of course) forefathers could, not even as much as our more primitive contemporaries can. For we, the self-styled civilized peoples, are now exercised over our minds and our arteries instead of our stomachs and sex, as were our progenitors and some of our uncompelled contemporaries."

"Uncompelled?"

"Socially, of course. Doe believes that Doe and Smith should and must do this or that because Smith believes that Smith and Doe should and must do this or that."

"Ah, yes." The divine again lifted his kind, unblinking eyes straight into the sun. Dew was off the grass and jonquils and narcissi were beginning to look drowsy, like girls after a ball. "It is drawing toward noon. Let us go in: I can offer you refreshment and lunch, if you are not engaged."

Jones rose. "No, no. Thank you a thousand times. But I sha'n't trouble you."

The rector was hearty. "No trouble, no trouble at all. I am alone at present."

Jones demurred. He had a passion for food, and an instinct. He had only to pass a house for his instinct to inform him whether or not the food would be good. Jones did not, gastronomically speaking, react favorably to the rector.

The divine, however, overrode him with hearty affability: the rector would not take No. He attached Jones to himself and they trod their shadows across the lawn, herding them beneath the subdued grace of a fanlight of dim-colored glass lovely with lack of washing. After the immaculate naked morning, the interior of the hall vortexed with red fire. Jones, temporarily blind, stumbled violently over an object and the handle of a pail clasped his ankle passionately. The rector, bawling Emmy! dragged him, pail and all, erect: he thanked his lucky stars that he had not been attached to the floor as he rose a sodden Venus, disengaging the pail. His dangling feet touched the floor and he felt his trouser leg with despair, fretfully. He's like a derrick, he thought with exasperation.

The rector bawled Emmy again. There was an alarmed response from the depths of the house and one in gingham brushed them. The divine's great voice boomed like surf in the narrow confines, and opening a door upon a flood of light, he ushered the trickling Jones into his study.

"I shall not apologize," the rector began, "for the meagerness of the accommodation which I offer you. I am alone at present, you see. But, then, we philosophers want bread for the belly and not for the palate, eh? Come in, come in."

Jones despaired. A drenched trouser leg, and bread for the belly alone. And God only knew what this great lump of a divine meant by bread for the belly and no bread for the palate. Husks, probably. Regarding food, Jones was sybaritically rather than æsthetically inclined. Or even philosophically. He stood disconsolate, swinging his dripping leg.

"My dear boy, you are soaking!" exclaimed his host. "Come, off with your trousers."

Jones protested weakly. "Emmy!" roared the rector again.

"All right, Uncle Joe. Soon's I get this water up."

"Never mind the water right now. Run to my room and fetch me a pair of trousers."

"But the rug will be ruined!"

"Not irreparably, I hope. We'll take the risk. Fetch me the trousers. Now, dear boy, off with them. Emmy will dry them in the kitchen and then you will be right as rain."

Jones surrendered in dull despair. He had truly fallen among moral thieves. The rector assailed him with ruthless kindness and the gingham-clad one reappeared at the door with a twin of the rector's casual black nether coverings over her arm.

"Emmy, this is Mr. —— I do not recall having heard your name?—he will be with us at lunch. And, Emmy, see if Cecily wishes to come also."

This virgin shrieked at the spectacle of Jones, ludicrous in his shirt and his fat pink legs and the trousers jerked solemn and lethargic into the room. "Jones," supplied Januarius Jones, faintly. Emmy, however, was gone.

"Ah, yes, Mr. Jones." The rector fell upon him anew, doing clumsy and intricate things with the waist and bottoms of the trousers, and Jones, decently if voluminously clad, stood like a sheep in a gale while the divine pawed him heavily.

"Now," cried his host, "make yourself comfortable (even Jones found irony in this) while I find something that will quench thirst."

The guest regained his composure in a tidy, shabby room. Upon a rag rug a desk bore a single white hyacinth in a handleless teacup, above a mantel cluttered with pipes and twists of paper hung a single photograph. There were books everywhere—on shelves, on window ledges, on the floor: Jones saw the Old Testament in Greek in several volumes, a depressing huge book on international law, Jane Austen and "Les Contes Drolatiques" in dog-eared amity: a mutual supporting caress. The rector reëntered with milk in a pitcher of blue glass and two mugs. From a drawer he extracted a bottle of Scotch whisky.

"A sop to the powers," he said, leering at Jones with innocent depravity. "Old dog and new tricks, my boy. But your pardon: perhaps you do not like this combination?"

Jones' morale rose balloon-like. "I will try any drink once," he said, like Jurgen.

"Try it, anyway. If you do not like it you are at perfect liberty to employ your own formula."

The beverage was more palatable than he would have thought. He sipped with relish. "Didn't you mention a son, sir?"

"That was Donald. He was shot down in Flanders last spring." The rector rose and took the photograph down from above the mantel. He handed it to his guest. The boy was about eighteen and coatless: beneath unruly hair, Jones saw a thin face with a delicate pointed chin and wild, soft eyes. Jones' eyes were clear and yellow, obscene and old in sin as a goat's.

"There is death in his face," said Jones.

His host took the photograph and gazed at it. "There is always death in the faces of the young in spirit, the eternally young. Death for themselves or for others. And dishonor. But death, surely. And why not? why should death desire only those things which life no longer has use for? Who gathers the withered rose?" The rector dreamed darkly in space for a while. After a time he added: "A companion sent back a few of his things." He propped the photograph upright on the desk and from a drawer he took a tin box. His great hand fumbled at the catch.

"Let me, sir," offered Jones, knowing that it was useless to

volunteer, that the rector probably did this every day. But
the lid yielded as he spoke and the divine spread on the desk
the sorry contents: a woman's chemise, a cheap paper-covered
"Shropshire Lad," a mummied hyacinth bulb. The rector
picked up the bulb and it crumbled to dust in his hand.

"Tut, tut! How careless of me!" he ejaculated, sweeping
the dust carefully into an envelope. "I have often deplored
the size of my hands. They should have been given to someone who could use them for something other than thumbing
books or grubbing in flower beds. Donald's hands, on the
contrary, were quite small, like his mother's: he was quite
deft with his hands. What a surgeon he would have made."

He placed the things upon the desk, before the propped
photograph like a ritual, and propping his face in his earthy
hands he took his ruined dream of his son into himself as one
inhales tobacco smoke.

"Truly, there is life and death and dishonor in his face.
Had you noticed Emmy? Years ago, about the time this
picture was made. . . . But that is an old story. Even Emmy has probably forgotten it. . . . You will notice that he
has neither coat nor cravat. How often has he appeared after
his mother had seen him decently arrayed, on the street, in
church, at formal gatherings, carrying hat, coat and collar in
his hands. How often have I heard him say 'Because it is
too hot.' Education in the bookish sense he had not: the
schooling he got was because he wanted to go, the reading he
did was because he wanted to read. Least of all did I teach
him fortitude. What is fortitude? Emotional atrophy, gan-
grene. . . ." He raised his face and looked at Jones. "What
do you think? was I right? Or should I have made my son
conform to a type?"

"Conform that face to a type? (So Emmy has already
been dishonored, once, anyway.) How could you? (I owe

that dishonored one a grudge, too.)   Could you put a faun into
formal clothes?"

The rector sighed.   "Ah, Mr. Jones, who can say?"   He
slowly replaced the things in the tin box and sat clasping the
box between his hands.   "As I grow older, Mr. Jones, I
become more firmly convinced that we learn scarcely anything
as we go through this world, and that we learn nothing whatever which can ever help us or be of any particular benefit
to us, even.   However! . . ."   He sighed again, heavily.

2

Emmy, the dishonored virgin, appeared, saying: "What
do you want for dinner, Uncle Joe?   Ice cream or strawberry
shortcake?"   Blushing, she avoided Jones' eye.

The rector looked at his guest, yearning.   "What would
you like, Mr. Jones?   But I know how young people are about
ice cream.   Would you prefer ice cream?"

But Jones was a tactful man in his generation and knowing about food himself he had an uncanny skill in anticipating
other peoples' reactions to food.   "If it is the same to you,
Doctor, let it be shortcake."

"Shortcake, Emmy," the rector instructed with passion.
Emmy withdrew.   "Do you know," he continued with apolo-
getic gratitude, "do you know, when a man becomes old,
when instead of using his stomach, his stomach uses him, as
his other physical compulsions become weaker and decline, his
predilections toward the food he likes obtrude themselves."

"Not at all, sir."   Jones assured him.   "I personally prefer
a warm dessert to an ice."

"Then you must return when there are peaches.   I will
give you a peach cobbler, with butter and cream. . . .   But
ah, my stomach has attained a sad ascendency over me."

"Why shouldn't it, sir? Years rieve us of sexual compulsions: why shouldn't they fill the interval with compulsions of food?"

The rector regarded him kindly and piercingly. "You are becoming specious. Man's life need not be always filled with compulsions of either sex or food, need it?"

But here came quick tapping feet down the uncarpeted hall and she entered, saying: "Good morning, Uncle Joe," in her throaty voice, crossing the room with graceful effusion, not seeing Jones at once. Then she remarked him and paused like a bird in midflight, briefly. Jones rose and under his eyes she walked mincing and graceful, theatrical with body-consciousness to the desk. She bent sweetly as a young tree and the divine kissed her cheek. Jones' goat's eyes immersed her in yellow contemplation.

"Good morning, Cecily." The rector rose. "I had expected you earlier, on such a day as this. But young girls must have their beauty sleep regardless of weather," he ended with elephantine joviality. "This is Mr. Jones, Cecily. Miss Saunders, Mr. Jones."

Jones bowed with obese incipient grace as she faced him, but at her expression of hushed delicate amazement he knew panic. Then he remembered the rector's cursed trousers and he felt his neck and ears slowly burn, knowing that not only was he ridiculous looking but that she supposed he wore such things habitually. She was speechless and Jones damned the hearty oblivious rector slowly and completely. Curse the man: one moment it was Emmy and no trousers at all, next moment an attractive stranger and nether coverings like a tired balloon. The rector was saying bland as Fate:

"I had expected you earlier. I had decided to let you take some hyacinths."

"Uncle Joe! How won—derful!" Her voice was rough,

like a tangle of golden wires. She dragged her fascinated gaze from Jones and hating them both Jones felt perspiration under his hair. "Why didn't I come sooner? But I am always doing the wrong thing, as Mr.—Mr. Jones will know from my not coming in time to get hyacinths."

She looked at him again, as she might at a strange beast. Jones' confusion became anger and he found his tongue.

"Yes, it is too bad you didn't come earlier. You would have seen me more interestingly gotten up than this even. Emmy seemed to think so, at least."

"I beg your pardon?" she said.

The rector regarded him with puzzled affability. Then he understood. "Ah, yes, Mr. Jones suffered a slight accident and was forced to don a garment of mine."

"Thanks for saying 'was forced,' " Jones said viciously. "Yes, I stumbled over that pail of water the doctor keeps just inside the front door, doubtless for the purpose of making his parishioners be sure they really require help from heaven, on their second visit," he explained, Greek-like, giving his dignity its death-stroke with his own hand. "You, I suppose, are accustomed to it and can avoid it."

She looked from Jones' suffused angry face to the rector's kind, puzzled one and screamed with laughter.

"Forgive me," she pleaded, sobering as quickly. "I simply couldn't help it, Mr. Jones. You'll forgive me, won't you?"

"Certainly. Even Emmy enjoyed it. Doctor, Emmy cannot have been so badly outraged after all, to suffer such shock from seeing a man's bare——"

She covered up this gaucherie, losing most of the speech in her own words. "So you showed Mr. Jones your flowers? Mr. Jones should be quite flattered: that is quite a concession for Uncle Joe to make," she said smoothly, turning to the divine, graceful and insincere as a French sonnet. "Is Mr.

Jones famous, then? You haven't told me you knew famous men."

The rector boomed his laugh. "Well, Mr. Jones, you seem to have concealed something from me." (Not as much as I would have liked to, Jones thought.) "I didn't know I was entertaining a celebrity."

Jones' essential laziness of temper regained its ascendency and he answered civilly: "Neither did I, sir."

"Ah, don't try to hide your light, Mr. Jones. Women know these things. They see through us at once."

"Uncle Joe," she cautioned swiftly at this unfortunate remark, watching Jones. But Jones was safe now.

"No, I don't agree with you. If they saw through us they would never marry us."

She was grateful and her glance showed a faint interest. (what color are her eyes?)

"Oh, that's what Mr. Jones is! an authority on women."

Jones' vanity swelled and the rector saying, "Pardon me," fetched a chair from the hall. She leaned her thigh against the desk and her eyes (are they gray or blue or green?) met his yellow unabashed stare. She lowered her gaze and he remarked her pretty self-conscious mouth. This is going to be easy, he thought. The rector placed the chair for her and she sat and when the rector had taken his desk chair again, Jones resumed his own seat. How long her legs are, he thought, seeing her frail white dress shape to her short torso. She felt his bold examination and looked up.

"So Mr. Jones is married," she remarked. She did something to her eyes and it seemed to Jones that she had touched him with her hands. I've got your number, he thought vulgarly. He replied:

"No, what makes you think so?" The rector filling his pipe regarded them kindly.

"Oh, I misunderstood, then."

"That isn't why you thought so."

"No?"

"It's because you like married men," he told her boldly.

"Do I?" without interest. It seemed to Jones that he could see her interest ebb away from him, could feel it cool.

"Don't you?"

"You ought to know."

"I?" asked Jones. "How should I know?"

"Aren't you an authority on women?" she replied with sweet ingenuousness. Speechless he could have strangled her. The divine applauded:

"Checkmate, Mr. Jones!"

Just let me catch her eye again, he vowed, but she would not look at him. He sat silent and under his seething gaze she took the photograph from the desk and held it quietly for a time. Then she replaced it and reaching across the desk-top she laid her hand on the rector's.

"Miss Saunders was engaged to my son," the divine explained to Jones.

"Yes?" said Jones, watching her profile, waiting for her to look at him again. Emmy, that unfortunate virgin, appeared at the door.

"All right, Uncle Joe," she said, vanishing immediately.

"Ah, lunch," the rector announced, starting up. They rose.

"I can't stay," she demurred, yielding to the divine's hand upon her back. Jones fell in behind. "I really shouldn't stay," she amended.

They moved down the dark hall and Jones watching her white dress flow indistinctly to her stride, imagining her kiss, cursed her. At a door she paused and stood aside courteously, as a man would. The rector stopped also as perforce did Jones and here was a French comedy regarding precedence. Jones with counterfeit awkwardness felt her soft uncorseted thigh against the back of his hand and her sharp stare was like ice water. They entered the room. "Made you look at me then," he muttered.

The rector remarking nothing said:

"Sit here, Mr. Jones," and the virgin Emmy gave him a haughty antagonistic stare. He returned her a remote yellow one. I'll see about you later, he promised her mentally, sitting to immaculate linen. The rector drew the other guest's chair and sat himself at the head of the table.

"Cecily doesn't eat very much," he said, carving a fowl, "so the burden will fall upon you and me. But I think we can be relied upon, eh, Mr. Jones?"

She propped her elbows opposite him. And I'll attend to you, too, Jones promised her darkly. She still ignored his yellow gaze and he said: "Certainly, sir," employing upon her the old thought process which he had used in school when he was prepared upon a certain passage, but she ignored him with such thorough perfection that he knew a sudden qualm of unease, a faint doubt. I wonder if I am wrong? he pondered. I'll find out, he decided suddenly.

"You were saying, sir"—still watching her oblivious shallow face—"as Miss Saunders so charmingly came in, that I am too specious. But one must always generalize about fornication. Only after——"

"Mr. Jones!" the rector exclaimed heavily.

"—the fornication is committed should one talk about it at all, and then only to generalize, to become—in your words—specious. He who kisses and tells is not very much of a fellow, is he?"

"Mr. Jones," the rector remonstrated.

"Mr. Jones!" she echoed. "What a terrible man you are! Really, Uncle Joe——"

Jones interrupted viciously. "As far as the kiss itself goes, women do not particularly care who does the kissing. All they are interested in is the kiss itself."

"Mr. Jones!" she repeated, staring at him, then looking quickly away. She shuddered.

"Come, come, sir. There are ladies present." The rector achieved his aphorism.

Jones pushed his plate from him, Emmy's raw and formless hand removed it and here was a warm golden brow crowned with strawberries. Dam'f I look at her, he swore, and so he did. Her gaze was remote and impersonal, green and cool as sea water and Jones turned his eyes first. She turned to the rector, talking smoothly about flowers. He was politely ignored and he moodily engaged his spoon as Emmy appeared again.

Emmy emanated a thin hostility and staring from Jones to the girl she said:

"Lady to see you, Uncle Joe."

The rector poised his spoon. "Who is it, Emmy?"

"I dunno. I never saw her before. She's waiting in the study."

"Has she had lunch? Ask her in here."

(She knows I am watching her. Jones knew exasperation and a puerile lust.)

"She don't want anything to eat. She said not to disturb you until you had finished dinner. You better go in and see what she wants." Emmy retreated.

The rector wiped his mouth and rose. "I suppose I must. You young people sit here until I return. Call Emmy if you want anything."

Jones sat in sullen silence, turning a glass in his fingers. At last she looked at his bent ugly face.

"So you are unmarried, as well as famous," she remarked

"Famous because I'm unmarried," he replied darkly.

"And courteous because of which?"

"Either one you like."

"Well, frankly, I prefer courtesy."

"Do you often get it?"

"Always . . . eventually." He made no reply and she continued: "Don't you believe in marriage?"

"Yes, as long as there are no women in it." She shrugged indifferently. Jones could not bear seeming a fool to any one as shallow as he considered her and he blurted, wanting to kick himself: "You don't like me, do you?"

"Oh, I like anyone who believes there may be something he doesn't know," she replied without interest.

"What do you mean by that?" (are they green or gray?) Jones was a disciple of the cult of boldness with women. He rose and the table wheeled smoothly as he circled it: he wished faintly that he were more graceful. Those thrice unhappy trousers! You can't blame her, he thought with fairness. What would I think had she appeared in one of her grandma's mother hubbards? He remarked her reddish dark hair and the delicate slope of her shoulder. (I'll put my hand there and let it slip down her arm as she turns.)

Without looking up, she said suddenly: "Did Uncle Joe tell you about Donald?" (Oh hell, thought Jones.) "Isn't it funny," her chair scraped to her straightening knees, "we both thought of moving at the same time?" She rose, her chair intervened woodenly and Jones stood ludicrous and foiled. "You take mine and I'll take yours," she added, moving around the table.

"You bitch," said Jones evenly and her green-blue eyes took him sweetly as water.

"What made you say that?" she asked quietly. Jones, having to an extent eased his feelings, thought he saw a recurring interest in her expression. (I was right, he gloated.)

"You know why I said that."

"It's funny how few men know that women like to be talked to that way," she remarked irrelevantly.

I wonder if she loves someone? I guess not—like a tiger loves meat. "I am not like other men," he told her.

He thought he saw derision in her brief glance, but she merely yawned delicately. At last he had her classified in the animal kingdom. Hamadryad, a slim jeweled one.

"Why doesn't George come for me!" she said as if in answer to his unspoken speculation, patting her mouth with the tips of petulant, delicate fingers. "Isn't it boring, waiting for some one?"

"Yes. Who is George, may I ask?"

"Certainly, you may ask."

"Well, who is he?" (I don't like her type, anyway.) "I had gathered that you were pining for the late lamented."

"The late lamented?"

"That fox-faced Henry or Oswald or something."

"Oh, Donald. Do you mean Donald?"

"Surely. Let him be Donald, then."

She regarded him impersonally. (I can't even make her angry, he thought fretfully.) "Do you know, you are impossible."

"All right. So I am," he answered with anger. "But then I wasn't engaged to Donald. And George is not calling for me."

"What makes you so angry? Because I won't let you put your hands on me?"

"My dear woman, if I had wanted to put my hands on you I would have done it."

"Yes?" Her rising inflection was a polite maddening derision.

"Certainly. Don't you believe it?" his own voice gave him courage.

"I don't know . . . but what good would it do to you?"

"No good at all. That's the reason I don't want to."

Her green eyes took him again. Sparse old silver on a buffet shadowed heavily under a high fanlight of colored glass identical with the one above the entrance, her fragile white dress across the table from him: he could imagine her long subtle legs, like Atalanta's reft of running.

"Why do you tell yourself lies?" she asked with interest.

"Same reason you do."

"I?"

"Surely. You intend to kiss me and yet you are going to all this damn trouble about it."

"Do you know," she remarked with speculation, "I believe I hate you."

"I don't doubt it. I know damn well I hate you."

She moved in her chair, sloping the light now across her shoulders, releasing him and becoming completely another person. "Let's go to the study. Shall we?"

"All right. Uncle Joe should be done with his caller by now." He rose and they faced each other across the broken meal. She did not rise.

"Well?" she said.

"After you, ma'am," he replied with mock deference.

"I have changed my mind. I think I'll wait here and talk to Emmy, if you don't object."

"Why Emmy?"

"Why not Emmy?"

"Ah, I see. You can feel fairly safe with Emmy: she probably won't want to put her hands on you. That's it, isn't it?" She glanced briefly at him. "What you really mean is, that you will stay if I am going out of the room, don't you?"

"Suit yourself." She became oblivious of him, breaking a biscuit upon a plate and dripping water upon it from a glass. Jones moved fatly in his borrowed trousers, circling the table again. As he approached she turned slightly in her chair, extending her hand. He felt its slim bones in his fat moist palm, its nervous ineffectual flesh. Not good for anything. Useless. But beautiful with lack of character. Beautiful hands. Its very fragility stopped him like a stone barrier.

"Oh, Emmy," she called sweetly, "come here, darling. I have something to show you."

Emmy regarded them balefully from the door and Jones said quickly: "Will you fetch me my trousers, Miss Emmy?"

Emmy glanced from one to the other ignoring the girl's mute plea. (Oho, Emmy has fish of her own to fry, thought Jones.) Emmy vanished and he put his hands on the girl's shoulders.

"Now what will you do? Call the reverend?"

She looked at him across her shoulder from beyond an inaccessible barrier. His anger grew and his hands wantonly crushed her dress.

"Don't ruin my clothes, please," she said icily. "Here, if you must." She raised her face and Jones felt shame, but his boyish vanity would not let him stop now. Her face a prettiness of shallow characterless planes blurred into his, her mouth was motionless and impersonal, unresisting and cool. Her face from a blur became again a prettiness of characterless shallowness icy and remote, and Jones, ashamed of himself and angry with her therefore, said with heavy irony: "Thanks."

"Not at all. If you got any pleasure from it you are quite welcome." She rose. "Let me pass, please."

He stood awkwardly aside. Her frigid polite indifference was unbearable. What a fool he had been! He had ruined everything.

"Miss Saunders," he blurted, "I—forgive me: I don't usually act that way, I swear I don't."

She spoke over her shoulder. "You don't have to, I suppose? I imagine you are usually quite successful with us?"

"I am very sorry. But I don't blame you. . . . One hates to convict oneself of stupidity."

After a while hearing no further sound of movement he looked up. She was like a flower stalk or a young tree relaxed against the table: there was something so fragile, so impermanent since robustness and strength were unnecessary, yet strong withal as a poplar is strong through very absence of strength, about her; you knew that she lived, that her clear delicate being was nourished by sunlight and honey until even digestion was a beautiful function . . . as he watched something like a shadow came over her, somewhere between her eyes and her petulant pretty mouth, in the very clear relaxation of her body, that caused him to go quickly to her. She stared into his unblinking goat's eyes as his hands sliding across her arms met at the small of her back, and Jones did not know the door had opened until she jerked her mouth from his and twisted slimly from his clasp.

The rector loomed in the door, staring into the room as if he did not recognize it. He has never seen us at all, Jones knew, then seeing the divine's face he said: "He's ill."

The rector spoke. "Cecily——"

"What is it, Uncle Joe?" she replied in sharp terror, going to him. "Aren't you well?"

The divine balanced his huge body with a hand on either side of the doorway.

"Cecily, Donald's coming home," he said.

3

There was that subtle effluvia of antagonism found inevitably in a room where two young "pretty" women are, and they sat examining each other with narrow care. Mrs. Powers temporarily engaged in an unself-conscious accomplishment and being among strangers as well, was rather oblivious of it; but Cecily never having been engaged in an unself-conscious action of any kind and being among people whom she knew, examined the other closely with that attribute women have for gaining correct instinctive impressions of another's character, clothes, morals, etc. Jones' yellow stare took the newcomer at intervals, returning, however, always to Cecily, who ignored him.

The rector tramped heavily back and forth. "Sick?" he boomed. "Sick? But we'll cure him. Get him home here with good food and rest and attention and we'll have him well in a week. Eh, Cecily?"

"Oh, Uncle Joe! I can't believe it yet. That he is really safe." She rose as the rector passed her chair and sort of undulated into his arms, like a slim wave. It was beautiful.

"Here's the medicine for him, Mrs. Powers," he said with heavy gallantry, embracing Cecily, speaking over her head toward the contemplative pallor of the other woman's quiet watching face. "There, there, don't cry," he added, kissing her. The audience watched this, Mrs. Powers with speculative detached interest and Jones with morose speculation.

"It's because I am so happy—for you, dear Uncle Joe,"
she answered. She turned graceful as a flower stalk against
the rector's black bulk. "And we owe it all to Mrs.—Mrs.
Powers," she continued in her slightly rough voice, like a
tangle of golden wires, "she was so kind to bring him back
to us." Her glance swept past Jones and flickered like a
knife toward the other woman. (Damn little fool thinks I
have tried to vamp him, Mrs. Powers thought.) Cecily moved
toward her with studied impulse. "May I kiss you? do you
mind?"

It was like kissing a silken smooth steel blade and Mrs.
Powers said brutally: "Not at all. I'd have done the same
for anyone sick as he is, nigger or white. And you would,
too," she added with satisfying malice.

"Yes, it was so sweet of you," Cecily repeated, coolly non-
committal, exposing a slim leg from the arm of the caller's
chair. Jones, statically remote, watched the comedy.

"Nonsense," the rector interposed. "Mrs. Powers merely
saw him fatigued with traveling. I am sure he will be a different man to-morrow."

"I hope so," Mrs. Powers answered with sudden weariness,
recalling his devastated face and that dreadful brow, his
whole relaxed inertia of constant dull pain and ebbing morale.
It's too late, she thought with instinctive perspicuity. Shall
I tell them about the scar? she pondered. Prevent a scene
when this—this creature (feeling the girl's body against her
shoulder) sees it. But no, I won't, she decided, watching
the tramping rector leonine in his temporary happiness. What
a coward I am. Joe should have come: he might have
known I'd bungle it some way.

The rector fetched his photograph. She took it: thin faced,
with the serenity of a wild thing, the passionate serene alert-

ness of a faun; and that girl leaning against the oaken branch
of the rector's arm, believing that she is in love with the
boy, or his illusion—pretending she is, anyway. No, no, I
won't be catty. Perhaps she is—as much as she is capable
of being in love with anyone. It's quite romantic, being
reft of your love and then having him returned unexpectedly
to your arms. And an aviator, too. What luck that girl
has playing her parts. Even God helps her. . . . You cat!
she's pretty and you are jealous. That's what's the matter
with you, she thought in her bitter weariness. What makes
me furious is her thinking that I am after him, am in love
with him! Oh, yes, I'm in love with him! I'd like to hold
his poor ruined head against my breast and not let him
wake again ever. . . . Oh, hell, what a mess it all is! And
that dull fat one yonder in somebody else's trousers, watching
her with his yellow unwinking eyes—like a goat's. I suppose
she's been passing the time with him.

"—he was eighteen then," the rector was saying. "He
would never wear hat nor tie: his mother could never make
him. She saw him correctly dressed, but it mattered not
how formal the occasion, he invariably appeared without
them."

Cecily rubbing herself like a cat on the rector's arm: "Oh,
Uncle Joe, I love him so!"

And Jones like another round and arrogant cat, blinking
his yellow eyes, muttered a shocking phrase. The rector
was oblivious in speech and Cecily in her own graceful im-
mersion but Mrs. Powers half heard, half saw, and Jones
looking up met her black stare. He tried to look her down
but her gaze was impersonal as a dissection so he averted
his and fumbled for his pipe.

There came a prolonged honking of a motor horn from
without and Cecily sprang to her feet.

"Oh, there's—there's a friend of ours. I'll send him away and come straight back. Will you excuse me a moment, Uncle Joe?"

"Eh?" The rector broke his speech. "Oh, yes."

"And you Mrs. Powers?" She moved toward the door and her glance swept Jones again. "And you, Mr. Jones?"

"George got a car, has he?" Jones asked as she passed him. "Bet you don't come back."

She gave him her cool stare and from beyond the study door she heard the rector's voice resume the story again— of Donald, of course. And now I'm engaged again, she thought complacently, enjoying George's face in anticipation when she would tell him. And that long black woman has been making love to him—or he to her. I guess it's that, from what I know of Donald. Oh, well, that's how men are, I guess. Perhaps he'll want to take us both. . . . She tripped down the steps into the sunlight: the sunlight caressed her with joy, as though she were a daughter of sunlight. How would I like to have a husband and a wife, too, I wonder? Or two husbands? I wonder if I want one even, want to get married at all. . . . I guess it's worth trying, once. I'd like to see that horrible fat one's face if he could hear me say that, she thought. Wonder why I let him kiss me? Ugh!

George leaned from his car watching her restricted swaying stride with faint lust. "Come on, come on," he called.

She did not increase her gait at all. He swung the door open, not bothering to dismount himself. "My God, what took you so long?" he asked plaintively. "Dam'f I thought you were coming at all."

"I'm not," she told him, laying her hand on the door. Her white dress in the nooning sun was unbearable to the eye, sloped to her pliant fragility. Beyond her, across the lawn, was another pliant gesture though this was only a tree, a poplar.

"Huh?"

"Not coming. My fiancé is arriving to-day."

"Aw hell, get in."

"Donald's coming to-day," she repeated, watching him. His face was ludicrous: blank as a plate, then shocked to slow amazement.

"Why, he's dead," he said vacuously.

"But he isn't dead," she told him sweetly. "A lady friend he's traveling with came on ahead and told us. Uncle Joe's like a balloon."

"Ah, come on, Cecily. You're kidding me."

"I swear I'm not. I'm telling you the God's truth."

His smooth empty face hung before her like a handsome moon, empty as a promise. Then it filled with an expression of a sort.

"Hell, you got a date with me to-night. Whatcher going to do about that?"

"What can I do? Donald will be here by then."

"Then it's all off with us?"

She gazed at him, then looked quickly away. Funny how only an outsider had been able to bring home to her the significance of Donald's imminence, his return. She nodded dumbly, beginning to feel miserable and lost.

He leaned from the car and caught her hand. "Get in here," he commanded.

"No, no, I can't," she protested, trying to draw back. He held her wrist. "No, no, let me go. You are hurting me."

"I know it," he answered grimly. "Get in."

"Don't, George, don't! I must go back."

"Well, when can I see you?"

Her mouth trembled. "Oh, I don't know. Please, George.

Don't you see how miserable I am?" Her eyes became blue, dark; the sunlight made bold the wrenched thrust of her body, her thin taut arm. "Please, George."

"Are you going to get in or do you want me to pick you up and put you in?"

"I'm going to cry in a minute. You'd better let me go."

"Oh, damn. Why, sugar, I didn't mean it that way. I just wanted to see you. We've got to see each other if it's going to be all off with us. Come on, I've been good to you."

She relaxed. "Well, but just around the block then. I've got to get back to them." She raised a foot to the running board. "Promise?" she insisted.

"Sure. Round the block it is. I won't run off with you if you say not."

She got in and as they drove off she looked quickly to the house. There was a face in the window, a round face.

4

George turned from the street and drove down a quiet lane bordered by trees, between walls covered with honey-suckle. He stopped the car and she said swiftly:

"No, no, George! Drive on."

But he cut the switch. "Please," she repeated. He turned in his seat.

"Cecily, you are kidding me, aren't you?"

She turned the switch and tried to reach the starter with her foot. He caught her hands, holding her. "Look at me."

Her eyes grew blue again with foreboding.

"You are kidding me, aren't you?"

"I don't know. Oh, George, it all happened so suddenly! I don't know what to think. When we were in there talking about him it all seemed so grand for Donald to be coming back, in spite of that woman with him; and to be engaged to a man who will be famous when he gets here—oh, it seemed then that I did love him: it was exactly the thing to do. But now . . . I'm just not ready to be married yet. And he's been gone so long, and to take up with another woman on his way to me—I don't know what to do. I—I'm going to cry," she ended suddenly, putting her crooked arm on the seat-back and burying her face in her elbow. He put his arm around her shoulders and tried to draw her to him. She raised her hands between them straightening her arms.

"No, no, take me back."

"But, Cecily——"

"You mustn't! Don't you know I'm engaged to be married? He'll probably want to be married to-morrow, and I'll have to do it."

"But you can't do that. You aren't in love with him."

"But I've got to, I tell you!"

"Are you in love with him?"

"Take me back to Uncle Joe's. Please."

He was the stronger and at last he held her close, feeling her small bones, her frail taut body beneath her dress. "Are you in love with him?" he repeated.

She burrowed her face into his coat.

"Look at me." She refused to lift her face and he slipped his hand under her chin, raising it. "Are you?"

"Yes, yes," she said wildly, staring at him. "Take me back!"

"You are lying. You aren't going to marry him."

She was weeping. "Yes, I am. I've got to. He expects it and Uncle Joe expects it. I must, I tell you."

"Darling, you can't. Don't you love me? You know you do. You can't marry him." She stopped struggling and lay against him, crying. "Come on, say you won't marry him."

"George, I can't," she said hopelessly. "Don't you see I have got to marry him?"

Young and miserable they clung to each other. The slumbrous afternoon lay about them in the empty lane. Even the sparrows seemed drowsy and from the spire of the church pigeons were remote and monotonous, unemphatic as sleep. She raised her face.

"Kiss me, George."

He tasted tears: their faces were coolly touching. She drew her head back, searching his face. "That was the last time, George."

"No, no," he objected, tightening his arms. She resisted a moment, then kissed him passionately.

"Darling!"

"Darling!"

She straightened up, dabbing at her eyes with his handkerchief. "There! I feel better now. Take me home, kind sir."

"But, Cecily," he protested, trying to embrace her again. She put him aside coolly.

"Not any more, ever. Take me home, like a nice boy."

"But, Cecily——"

"Do you want me to get out and walk? I can, you know: it isn't far."

He started the engine and drove on in a dull youthful sorrow. She patted at her hair, her fingers bloomed slimly in it, and they turned onto the street again. As she descended at the gate he made a last despairing attempt.

"Cecily, for God's sake!"

She looked over her shoulder at his stricken face. "Don't be silly, George. Of course I'll see you again. I'm not married—yet."

Her white dress in the sun was an unbearable shimmer sloping to her body's motion and she passed from sunlight to shadow, mounting the steps. At the door she turned, flashed him a smile and waved her hand. Then her white dress faded beyond a fanlight of muted color dim with age and lovely with lack of washing, leaving George to stare at the empty maw of the house in hope and despair and baffled youthful lust.

5

Jones at the window saw them drive away. His round face was enigmatic as a god's, his clear obscene eyes showed no emotion. You are good, you are, he thought in grudging, unillusioned admiration. I hand it to you. He was still musing upon her when the mean-looking black-haired woman, interrupting the rector's endless reminiscences of his son's boyhood and youth, suggested that it was time to go to the station.

The divine became aware of the absence of Cecily, who was at that moment sitting in a stationary motor car in an obscure lane, crying on the shoulder of a man whose name was not Donald. Jones, the only one who had remarked the manner of her going, was for some reason he could not have named safely non-committal. The rector stated fretfully that Cecily, who was at that moment kissing a man whose name was not Donald, should not have gone away at that time. But the other woman (I bet she's mean as hell, thought Jones) interrupted again, saying that it was better so.

"But she should have gone to the station to meet him," the rector stated with displeasure.

"No, no. Remember, he is sick. The less excitement the better for him. Besides it is better for them to meet privately."

"Ah, yes, quite right, quite right. Trust a woman in these things, Mr. Jones. And for that reason perhaps you had better wait also, don't you think?"

"By all means, sir. I will wait and tell Miss Saunders why you went without her. She will doubtless be anxious to know."

After the cab had called for them and gone Jones, still standing, stuffed his pipe with moody viciousness. He wandered aimlessly about the room, staring out the windows in turn, puffing his pipe; then pausing to push a dead match beneath a rug with his toe he crossed deliberately to the rector's desk. He drew and closed two drawers before finding the right one.

The bottle was squat and black and tilted took the light pleasantly. He replaced it, wiping his mouth on the back of his hand. And just in time, too, for her rapid brittle steps crossed the veranda and he heard a motor car retreating.

The door framed her fragile surprise. She remarked, "Oh! Where are the others?"

"What's the matter? Have a puncture?" Jones countered nastily. Her eyes flew like birds and he continued: "The others? They went to the station, the railroad station. You know: where the trains come in. The parson's son or something is coming home this afternoon. Fine news, isn't it? But won't you come in?"

She entered hesitant, watching him.

"Oh, come on in, sister. I won't hurt you."

"But why didn't they wait for me?"

"They thought you didn't want to go, I suppose. Hadn't you left that impression?"

In the silence of the house was a clock like a measured respiration, and Emmy was faintly audible somewhere. These sounds reassured her and she entered a few steps. "You saw me go. Didn't you tell them where I was?"

"Told them you went to the bathroom."

She looked at him curiously, knowing in some way that he was not lying. "Why did you do that?"

"It was your business where you were going, not mine. If you wanted them to know you should have told them yourself."

She sat alertly. "You're a funny sort of a man, aren't you?"

Jones moved casually, in no particular direction. "How funny?"

She rose. "Oh, I don't know exactly . . . you don't like me and yet you told a lie for me."

"Hell, you don't think I mind telling a lie, do you?"

She said with speculation:

"I wouldn't put anything past you—if you thought you could get any fun out of it." Watching his eyes she moved toward the door.

The trousers hampered him but despite them his agility was amazing. But she was alert and her studied grace lent her muscular control and swiftness, and so it was a bland rubbed panel of wood that he touched. Her dress whipped from sight, he heard a key and her muffled laugh, derisive.

"Damn your soul," he spoke in a quiet toneless emotion, "open the door."

The wood was bland and inscrutable: baffling, holding up to him in its polished depths the fat white blur of his own face. Holding his breath he heard nothing beyond it save a clock somewhere.

"Open the door," he repeated, but there was no sound. Has she gone away, or not? He wondered, straining his ears, bending to the bulky tweeded Narcissus of himself in the polished wood. He thought of the windows and walking quietly he crossed the room, finding immovable gauze wire. He returned to the center of the room without trying to muffle his steps and stood in a mounting anger, cursing her slowly. Then he saw the door handle move.

He sprang to it. "Open the door, you little slut, or I'll kick your screens out."

The lock clicked and he jerked the door open upon Emmy, his trousers over her arm, meeting him with her frightened antagonistic eyes.

"Where—" began Jones, and Cecily stepped from the shadows, curtsying like a derisive flower.

"Checkmate, Mr. Jones." Jones paraphrased the rector in a reedy falsetto. "Do you know——"

"Yes," said Cecily quickly, taking Emmy's arm. "But tell us on the veranda." She led the way and Jones followed in reluctant admiration. She and the baleful speechless Emmy preceding him sat arm in arm in a porch swing while afternoon sought interstices in soon-to-be lilac wistaria: afternoon flowed and ebbed upon them as they swung and their respective silk and cotton shins took and released sunlight in running planes.

"Sit down, Mr. Jones," she continued, gushing. "Do tell us about yourself. We are so interested, aren't we, Emmy dear?" Emmy was watchful and inarticulate, like an animal. "Emmy, dear Mr. Jones, has missed all of your conversation and admiring you as we all do—we simply cannot help it, Mr. Jones—she is naturally anxious to make up for it."

Jones cupped a match in his palms and there were two little flames in his eyes, leaping and sinking to pin points.

"You are silent, Mr. Jones? Emmy and I both would like to hear some more of what you have learned about us

from your extensive amatory career. Don't we, Emmy darling?"

"No, I won't spoil it for you," Jones replied heavily. "You
are on the verge of getting some first-hand information of
your own. As for Miss Emmy, I'll teach her sometime later,
in private."

Emmy continued to watch him with fierce dumb distrust.
Cecily said: "At first hand?"

"Aren't you being married to-morrow? You can learn from
Oswald. He should certainly be able to tell you, traveling
as he seems to with a sparring partner. Got caught, at last,
didn't you?"

She shivered. She looked so delicate, so needing to be
cared for that Jones, becoming masculine and sentimental,
felt again like a cloddish brute. He lit his pipe again and
Emmy, convicting herself of the power of speech, said:

"Yonder they come."

A cab had drawn up to the gate and Cecily sprang to her
feet and ran along the porch to the steps. Jones and Emmy
rose and Emmy vanished somewhere as four people descended
from the cab. So that's him, thought Jones ungrammatically,
following Cecily, watching her as she stood poised on the
top step like a bird, her hand to her breast. Trust her!

He looked again at the party coming through the gate, the
rector looming above them all. There was something changed
about the divine: age seemed to have suddenly overtaken
him, unresisted, coming upon him like a highwayman. He's
sure sick, Jones told himself. The woman, that Mrs. Some-
thing-or-other, left the party and hastened ahead. She
mounted the steps to Cecily.

"Come darling," she said taking the girl's arm, "come
inside. He is not well and the light hurts his eyes. Come
in and meet him there, hadn't you rather?"

"No, no: here. I have waited so long for him."

The other woman was kind but obdurate. And she led the girl into the house. Cecily reluctant, with reverted head cried: "Uncle Joe! his face! is he sick?"

The divine's face was gray and slack as dirty snow. At the steps he stumbled slightly and Jones sprang forward, taking his arm. "Thanks, buddy," said the third man, in a private's uniform, whose hand was beneath Mahon's elbow. They mounted the steps and crossing the porch passed under the fanlight, into the dark hall.

"Take your cap, Loot," murmured the enlisted man. The other removed it and handed it to him. They heard swift tapping feet crossing a room and the study door opened letting a flood of light fall upon them and Cecily cried:

"Donald! Donald! She says your face is hur—oooooh!" she ended, screaming as she saw him.

The light passing through her fine hair gave her a halo and lent her frail dress a fainting nimbus about her crumpling body like a stricken poplar. Mrs. Powers moving quickly caught her, but not before her head had struck the door jamb.

CHAPTER III

I

Mrs. Saunders said: "You come away now, let your sister alone."

Young Robert Saunders fretted but optimistic, joining again that old battle between parent and child, hopeful in the face of invariable past defeat:

"But can't I ask her a civil question? I just want to know what his scar l——"

"Come now, come with mamma."

"But I just want to know what his sc——"

"Robert."

"But mamma," he essayed again, despairing. His mother pushed him firmly doorward.

"Run down to the garden and tell your father to come here. Run, now."

He left the room in exasperation. His mamma would have been shocked could she have read his thoughts. It wasn't her especially. They're all alike, he guessed largely, as has many a man before him and as many will after him. He wasn't going to hurt the old 'fraid cat.

Cecily freed of her clothing lay crushed and pathetic between cool linen, surrounded by a mingled scent of cologne and ammonia, her fragile face coiffed in a towel. Her mother drew a chair to the side of the bed and examined her daughter's pretty shallow face, the sweep of her lashes upon her white cheek, her arms paralleling the shape of her body beneath the covers, her delicate blue-veined wrists and her long slender hands relaxed and palm-upward beside her. Then young Robert Saunders, without knowing it, had his revenge.

"Darling, what did his face look like?"

Cecily shuddered, turning her head on the pillow. "Ooooh, don't, don't, mamma! I c-can't bear to think of it."

(But I just want to ask you a civil question.) "There, there. We won't talk about it until you feel better."

"Not ever, not ever. If I have to see him again I'll—I'll just die. I can't bear it, I can't bear it."

She was crying again frankly like a child, not even concealing her face. Her mother rose and leaned over her. "There, there. Don't cry any more. You'll be ill." She gently brushed the girl's hair from her temples, rearranging the towel. She bent down and kissed her daughter's pale cheek. "Mamma's sorry, baby. Suppose you try to sleep. Shall I bring you a tray at supper time?"

"No, I couldn't eat. Just let me lie here alone and I'll feel better."

The older woman lingered, still curious. (I just want to ask her a civil question.) The telephone rang and with a last ineffectual pat at the pillow she withdrew.

Lifting the receiver she remarked her husband closing the garden gate behind him.

"Yes? . . . Mrs. Saunders. . . . Oh, George? . . . Quite well, thank you. How are you . . . no, I am afraid not. . . . What? . . . yes, but she is not feeling well . . . later, perhaps. . . . Not to-night. Call her to-morrow . . . yes, yes, quite well, thank you. Good-by."

She passed through the cool darkened hall and onto the veranda letting her tightly corseted figure sink creaking into a rocking chair as her husband carrying a sprig of mint and his hat mounted the steps. Here was Cecily in the masculine and gone to flesh: the same slightly shallow good looks and somewhere an indicated laxness of moral fiber. He had once been precise and dapper but now he was clad slovenly in careless uncreased gray and earthy shoes. His hair still curled youthfully upon his head and he had Cecily's eyes. He was a Catholic, which was almost as sinful as being a republican; his fellow townsmen, while envying his social and financial position in the community, yet looked askance at him because he and his family made periodical trips to Atlanta to attend church.

"Tobe!" he bellowed, taking a chair near his wife.

"Well, Robert," she began with zest, "Donald Mahon came home to-day."

"Government sent his body back, did they?"

"No, he came back himself. He got off the train this afternoon."

"Eh? Why, he's dead."

"But he isn't dead. Cecily was there and saw him. A strange fat young man brought her home in a cab—completely collapsed. She said something about a scar on him. She fainted, poor child. I made her go to bed at once. I never did find who that strange young man was," she ended fretfully.

Tobe in a white jacket appeared with a bowl of ice, sugar, water and a decanter. Mr. Saunders sat staring at his wife. "Well, I'll be damned," he said at last. And again, "I'll be damned."

His wife rocked complacent over her news. After a while Mr. Saunders breaking his trance, stirred. He crushed his mint sprig between his fingers and taking a cube of ice he rubbed the mint over it, then dropped both into a tall glass. Then he spooned sugar into the glass and dribbled whisky from the decanter slowly, and slowly stirring it he stared at his wife. "I'll be damned," he said for the third time.

Tobe filled the glass from a water bottle and withdrew.

"So he come home. Well, well. I'm glad on the parson's account. Pretty decent feller."

"You must have forgotten what it means."

"Eh?"

"To us."

"To us?"

"Cecily was engaged to him, you know."

Mr. Saunders sipped and setting his glass on the floor beside him he lit a cigar. "Well, we've given our consent, haven't we? I ain't going to back out now." A thought occurred to him. "Does Sis still want to?"

"I don't know. It was such a shock to her, poor child, his coming home and the scar and all. But do you think it is a good thing?"

"I never did think it was a good thing. I never wanted it."

"Are you putting it off on me? Do you think I insisted on it?"

Mr. Saunders from long experience said mildly: "She ain't old enough to marry yet."

"Nonsense. How old was I when we married?"

He raised his glass again. "Seems to me you are the one insisting on it." Mrs. Saunders rocking, stared at him: he was made aware of his stupidity. "Why do you think it ain't a good thing, then?"

"I declare, Robert. Sometimes . . ." she sighed and then as one explains to a child in fond exasperation at its stupidity: "Well, an engagement in war time and an engagement in peace time are two different things. Really, I don't see how he can expect to hold her to it."

"Now look here, Minnie. If he went to war expecting her to wait for him and come back expecting her to take him, there's nothing else for them to do. And if she still wants to don't you go persuading her out of it, you hear?"

"Are you going to force your daughter into marriage? You just said yourself she is too young."

"Remember, I said if she still wants to. By the way, he ain't lame or badly hurt, is he?" he asked quickly.

"I don't know. Cecily cried when I tried to find out."

"Sis is a fool, sometimes. But don't you go monkeying with them, now." He raised his glass and took a long draught, then he puffed his cigar furiously, righteously.

"I declare, Robert, I don't understand you sometimes. The idea of driving your own daughter into marriage with a man who has nothing and who may be half dead, and who probably won't work anyway. You know yourself how these ex-soldiers are."

"You are the one wants her to get married. I ain't. Who do you want her to take, then?"

"Well, there's Dr. Gary. He likes her, and Harrison Maurier from Atlanta. Cecily likes him, I think."

Mr. Saunders inelegantly snorted. "Who? That Maurier feller? I wouldn't have that damn feller around here at all. Slick hair and cigarettes all over the place. You better pick out another one."

"I'm not picking out anybody. I just don't want you to drive her into marrying that Mahon boy."

"I ain't driving her, I tell you. You have already taught me better than to try to drive a woman to do anything. But I don't intend to interfere if she does want to marry Mahon."

She sat rocking and he finished his julep. The oaks on the lawn became still with dusk, and the branches of trees were as motionless as coral fathoms deep under seas. A tree frog took up his monotonous trilling and the west was a vast green lake, still as eternity. Tobe appeared silently.

"Supper served, Miss Minnie."

The cigar arced redly into a canna bed and they rose.

"Where is Bob, Tobe?"

"I don't know'm. I seed him gwine to'ds de garden a while back, but I ain't seed him since."

"See if you can find him. And tell him to wash his face and hands."

"Yessum." He held the door for them and they passed into the house, leaving the twilight behind them filled with Tobe's mellow voice calling across the dusk.

2

But young Robert Saunders could not hear him. He was at that moment climbing a high board fence which severed the dusk above his head. He conquered it at last and sliding downward his trousers evinced reluctance, then accepting the gambit accompanied him with a ripping sound. He sprawled in damp grass feeling a thin shallow fire across his young behind, and said Damn, regaining his feet and disjointing his hip trying to see down his back.

Ain't that hell, he remarked to the twilight. I have rotten luck. It's all your fault, too, for not telling me, he thought, gaining a vicarious revenge on all sisters. He picked up the object he had dropped in falling and crossed the rectory lawn through dew, toward the house. There was a light in a heretofore unused upper room and his heart sank. Had he gone to bed this early? Then he saw silhouetted feet on the balustrade of the porch and the red eye of a cigarette. He sighed with relief. That must be him.

He mounted the steps, saying: "Hi, Donald."

"Hi, Colonel," answered the one sitting there. Approaching, he discerned soldier clothes. That's him. Now I'll see, he thought exultantly, snapping on a flash light and throwing its beam full on the man's face. Aw, shucks. He was becoming thoroughly discouraged. Did anyone ever have such luck? There must be a cabal against him.

"You ain't got no scar," he stated with dejection. "You ain't even Donald, are you?"

"You guessed it, bub. I ain't even Donald. But say, how about turning that searchlight some other way?"

He snapped off the light in weary disillusion. He burst out: "They won't tell me nothing. I just want to know what his scar looks like but they won't tell me nothing about it. Say, has he gone to bed?"

"Yes, he's gone to bed. This ain't a good time to see his scar."

"How about to-morrow morning?" hopefully. "Could I see it then?"

"I dunno. Better wait till then."

"Listen," he suggested with inspiration, "I tell you what: to-morrow about eight when I am going to school you kind of get him to look out of the window and I'll be passing and I'll see it. I asked Sis, but she wouldn't tell me nothing."

"Who is Sis, bub?"

"She's just my sister. Gosh, she's mean. If I'd seen his scar I'd a told her now, wouldn't I?"

"You bet. What's your sister's name?"

"Name's Cecily Saunders, like mine only mine's Robert Saunders. You'll do that, won't you?"

"Oh . . . Cecily. . . . Sure, you leave it to me, Colonel."

He sighed with relief, yet still lingered. "Say, how many soldiers has he got here?"

"About one and a half, bub."

"One and a half? Are they live ones?"

"Well, practically."

"How can you have one and a half soldiers if they are live ones?"

"Ask the war department. They know how to do it."

He pondered briefly. "Gee, I wish we could get some soldiers at our house. Do you reckon we could?"

"Why, I expect you could."

"Could? How?" he asked eagerly.

"Ask your sister. She can tell you."

"Aw, she won't tell me."

"Sure she will. You ask her."

"Well, I'll try," he agreed without hope, yet still optimistic. "Well, I guess I better be going. They might be kind of anxious about me," he explained, descending the steps. "Good-by, mister," he added politely.

"So long, Colonel."

I'll see his scar to-morrow, he thought with elation. I wonder if Sis does know how to get us a soldier? She don't know much but maybe she does know that. But girls don't never know nothing, so I ain't going to count on it. Anyway I'll see his scar to-morrow.

Tobe's white jacket looming around the corner of the house gleamed dully in the young night and as young Robert mounted the steps toward the yellow rectangle of the front door Tobe's voice said:

"Whyn't you come on to yo' supper? Yo' mommer gwine tear yo' hair and my hair bofe out if you late like this. She say fer you to clean up befo' you goes to de dinin' room: I done drawed you some nice water in de baff room. Run 'long now. I tell 'em you here."

He paused only to call through his sister's door: "I'm going to see it to-morrow. Yaaaah!" Then soaped and hungry he clattered into the dining room, accomplishing an intricate field maneuver lest his damaged rear be exposed. He ignored his mother's cold stare.

"Robert Saunders, where have you been?"

"Mamma, there's a soldier there says we can get one too."

"One what?" asked his father through his cigar smoke.

"A soldier."

"Soldier?"

"Yes, sir. That one says so."

"That one what?"

"That soldier where Donald is. He says we can get a soldier, too."

"How get one?"

"He wouldn't tell me. But he says that Sis knows how to get us one."

Mr. and Mrs. Saunders looked at each other above young Robert's oblivious head as he bent over his plate spooning food into himself.

3

On board the Frisco Limited,

Missouri, April 2, 1919.

Dear Margaret—

I wonder if you miss me like I miss you. Well I never had much fun in St. Louis. I was there only a half a day. This is just a short note to remind you of waiting for me. It's too bad I had to leave you so soon after. I will see my mother and attend to a few business matters and I will come back pretty soon. I will work like hell for you Margaret. This is just a short note to remind you of waiting for me. This dam train rocks so I cannot write any way. Well, give my reguards to Giligan tell him not to break his arm crooking it until I get back. I will love you all ways.

With love

JULIAN.

"What is that child's name, Joe?"

Mrs. Powers in one of her straight dark dresses stood on

the porch in the sun. The morning breeze was in her hair, beneath her clothing like water, carrying sun with it: pigeons about the church spire leaned upon it like silver and slanting splashes of soft paint. The lawn sloping fenceward was gray with dew, and a negro informal in undershirt and overalls passed a lawn mower over the grass, leaving behind his machine a darker green stripe like an unrolling carpet. Grass sprang from the whirling blades and clung wetly to his legs.

"What child?" Gilligan, uncomfortable in new hard serge and a linen collar, sat on the balustrade moodily smoking. For reply she handed him the letter and with his cigarette tilted in the corner of his mouth he squinted through the smoke, reading.

"Oh, the ace. Name's Lowe."

"Of course: Lowe. I tried several times after he left us but I never could recall it."

Gilligan returned the letter to her. "Funny kid, ain't he? So you scorned my affections and taken his, huh?"

Her windy dress molded her longly. "Let's go to the garden so I can have a cigarette."

"You could have it here. The padre wouldn't mind, I bet."

"I'm sure he wouldn't. I am considering his parishioners. What would they think to see a dark strange woman smoking a cigarette on the rectory porch at eight o'clock in the morning?"

"They'll think you are one of them French what-do-you-call-'ems the Loot brought back with him. Your good name won't be worth nothing after these folks get through with it."

"My good name is your trouble, not mine, Joe."

"My trouble? How you mean?"

"Men are the ones who worry about our good names,

because they gave them to us. But we have other things to
bother about, ourselves. What you mean by a good name
is like a dress that's too flimsy to wear comfortably. Come
on, let's go to the garden."

"You know you don't mean that," Gilligan told her. She
smiled faintly, not turning her face to him.

"Come on," she repeated, descending the steps.

They left a delirium of sparrows and the sweet smell of
fresh grass behind them and were in a graveled path between
rose bushes. The path ran on beneath two formal arching
oaks; lesser roses rambling upon a wall paralleled them and
Gilligan following her long stride trod brittle and careful.
Whenever he was among flowers he always felt as if he had
entered a room full of women: he was always conscious of
his body, of his walk, feeling as though he trod in sand. So
he believed that he really did not like flowers.

Mrs. Powers paused at intervals, sniffing, tasting dew upon
buds and blooms, then the path passed between violet beds
to where against a privet hedge there would soon be lilies.
Beside a green iron bench beneath a magnolia she paused
again, staring up into the tree. A mocking bird flew out and
she said:

"There's one, Joe. See?"

"One what? Bird nest?"

"No, a bloom. Not quite, but in a week or so. Do you
know magnolia blooms?"

"Sure: not good for anything if you pick 'em. Touch it,
and it turns brown on you. Fades."

"That's true of almost everything, isn't it?"

"Yeh, but how many folks believe it? Reckon the Loot
does?"

"I don't know. . . . I wonder if he'll have a chance to
touch that one?"

"Why should he want to? He's already got one that's turning brown on him."

She looked at him, not comprehending at once. Her black eyes, her red mouth like a pomegranate blossom. She said then: "Oh! Magnolia. . . . I'd thought of her as a—something like an orchid. So you think she's a magnolia?"

"Not an orchid, anyways. Find orchids anywhere but you wouldn't find her in Illinoy or Denver, hardly."

"I guess you are right. I wonder if there are any more like her anywhere?"

"I dunno. But if there ain't there's already one too many."

"Let's sit down a while. Where's my cigarette?" She sat on the bench and he offered her his paper pack and struck a match for her. "So you think she won't marry him, Joe?"

"I ain't so sure any more. I think I am changing my mind about it. She won't miss a chance to marry what she calls a hero—if only to keep somebody else from getting him." (Meaning you, he thought.)

(Meaning me, she thought.) She said: "Not if she knows he's going to die?"

"What does she know about dying? She can't even imagine herself getting old, let alone imagining anybody she is interested in dying. I bet she believes they can even patch him up so it won't show."

"Joe, you are an incurable sentimentalist. You mean you think she'll marry him because she is letting him think she will and because she is a 'good' woman. You are quite a gentle person, Joe."

"I ain't!" he retorted with warmth. "I am as hard as they make 'em: I got to be." He saw she was laughing at him and he grinned ruefully. "Well, you got me that time, didn't you?" He became suddenly serious. "But it ain't her I'm worrying about. It's his old man. Why didn't you tell him how bad off he was?"

She quite feminine and Napoleonic:

"Why did you send me on ahead instead of coming yourself? I told you I'd spoil it." She flipped her cigarette away and put her hand on his arm. "I didn't have the heart to, Joe. If you could have seen his face! and heard him! He was like a child, Joe. He showed me all of Donald's things. You know: pictures, and a slingshot, and a girl's undie and a hyacinth bulb he carried with him in France. And there was that girl and everything. I just couldn't. Do you blame me?"

"Well, it's all right now. It was a kind of rotten trick, though, to let him find it all out before them people at the station. We done the best we could, didn't we?"

"Yes, we did the best we could. I wish we could do more." Her gaze brooded across the garden where in the sun beyond the trees, bees were already at work. Across the garden, beyond a street and another wall you could see the top of a pear tree like a branching candelabra, closely bloomed, white, white. . . . She stirred, crossing her knees. "That girl fainting, though. What do you——"

"Oh, I expected that. But here comes Othello, like he was looking for us."

They watched the late conductor of the lawn mower as he shuffled his shapeless shoes along the gravel. He saw them and halted.

"Mr. Gillmum, Rev'un say fer you to come to de house."

"Me?"

"You Mist' Gillmum, ain't you?"

"Oh, sure." He rose. "Excuse me, ma'am. You coming, too?"

"You go and see what he wants. I'll come along after a while."

The negro had turned shuffling on ahead of him and the lawn mower had resumed its chattering song as Gilligan mounted the steps. The rector stood on the veranda. His face was calm but it was evident he had not slept.

"Sorry to trouble you, Mr. Gilligan, but Donald is awake, and I am not familiar with his clothing as you are. I gave away his civilian things when he—when he——"

"Sure, sir," Gilligan answered in sharp pity for the gray-faced man. He don't know him yet! "I'll help him."

The divine, ineffectual, would have followed, but Gilligan leaped away from him up the stairs. He saw Mrs. Powers coming from the garden and he descended to the lawn, meeting her.

"Good morning, Doctor," she responded to his greeting. "I have been looking at your flowers. I hope you don't mind?"

"Not at all, not at all, my dear madam. An old man is always flattered when his flowers are admired. The young are so beautifully convinced that their emotions are admirable: young girls wear the clothes of their older sisters who require clothes, principally because they do not need them themselves, just for fun, or perhaps to pander to an illusion of the male; but as we grow older what we are loses importance, giving place to what we do. And I have never been able to do anything well save to raise flowers. And that is, I think, an obscure emotional house-wifery in me: I had thought to grow old with my books among my roses: until my eyes became too poor to read longer I would read, after that I would sit in the sun. Now, of course, with my son at home again, I must put that by. I am anxious for you to see

Donald this morning. You will notice a marked improvement."

"Oh, I'm sure I shall," she answered, wanting to put her arms around him. But he was so big and so confident. At the corner of the house was a tree covered with tiny white-bellied leaves like a mist, like a swirl of arrested silver water. The rector offered his arm with heavy gallantry.

"Shall we go in to breakfast?"

Emmy had been before them with narcissi, and red roses in a vase repeated the red of strawberries in flat blue bowls. The rector drew her chair. "When we are alone Emmy sits here, but she has a strange reluctance to dining with strangers, or when guests are present."

Mrs. Powers sat and Emmy appeared briefly and disappeared, for no apparent reason. At last there came slow feet on the staircase slanting across the open door. She saw their legs, then their bodies crossed her vision and the rector rose as they appeared in the door. "Good morning, Donald," he said.

(That my father? Sure, Loot. That's him.) "Good morning, sir."

The divine stood huge and tense and powerless as Gilligan helped Mahon into his seat.

"Here's Mrs. Powers, too, Loot."

He turned his faltering puzzled gaze upon her. "Good morning," he said, but her eyes were on his father's face. She lowered her gaze to her plate feeling hot moisture against her lids. What have I done? she thought, what have I done?

She tried to eat but could not, watching Mahon, awkward with his left hand, peering into his plate, eating scarcely anything, and Gilligan's healthy employment of knife and fork, and the rector tasting nothing, watching his son's every move with gray despair.

Emmy appeared again with fresh dishes. Averting her face she set the dishes down awkwardly and was about to flee precipitately when the rector looking up stopped her. She turned in stiff self-conscious fright, hanging her head.

"Here's Emmy, Donald," his father said.

Mahon raised his head and looked at his father. Then his puzzled gaze touched Gilligan's face and returned to his plate, and his hand rose slowly to his mouth. Emmy stood for a space and her black eyes became wide and the blood drained from her face slowly. Then she put the back of one red hand against her mouth and fled, blundering into the door.

I can't stand this. Mrs. Powers rose unnoticed save by Gilligan and followed Emmy. Upon a table in the kitchen Emmy leaned bent almost double, her head cradled in her red arms. What a terrible position to cry in, Mrs. Powers thought, putting her arms around Emmy. The girl jerked herself erect, staring at the other. Her face was wrung with weeping, ugly.

"He didn't speak to me!" she gasped.

"He didn't know his father, Emmy. Don't be silly." She held Emmy's elbows, smelling harsh soap. Emmy clung to her.

"But me, me! He didn't even look at me!" she repeated.

It was on her tongue to say Why should he? but Emmy's blurred sobbing and her awkward wrung body; the very kinship of tears to tears, something to cling to after having been for so long a prop to others. . . .

Outside the window was a trellised morning-glory vine with a sparrow in it, and clinging to Emmy, holding each other in a recurrent mutual sorrow she tasted warm salt in her throat.

Damn, damn, damn, she said amid her own racking infrequent tears.

4

In front of the post office the rector was the center of an interested circle when Mr. Saunders saw him. The gathering was representative, embracing the professions with a liberal leavening of those inevitable casuals, cravatless, overalled or unoveralled, who seem to suffer no compulsions whatever, which anything from a captured still to a negro with an epileptic fit or a mouth organ attracts to itself like atoms to a magnet, in any small southern town—or northern town or western town, probably.

"Yes, yes, quite a surprise," the rector was saying. "I had no intimation of it, none whatever, until a friend with whom he was traveling—he is not yet fully recovered, you see—preceded him in order to inform me."

(One of them airy-plane fellers.)

(S'what I say: if the Lord had intended folks to fly around in the air He'd 'a' give 'em wings.)

(Well, he's been closter to the Lord'n you'll ever git.)

This outer kindly curious fringe made way for Mr. Saunders.

(Closter'n that feller'll ever git, anyway. Guffaws.) This speaker was probably a Baptist.

Mr. Saunders extended his hand.

"Well, Doctor, we are mighty glad to hear the good news."

"Ah, good morning, good morning." The rector took the proffered hand in his huge paw. "Yes, quite a surprise. I was hoping to see you. How is Cecily this morning?" he asked in a lower tone. But there was no need, no lack of privacy. There was a general movement into the post office. The mail was in and the window had opened and even those who expected no mail, who had received no mail in months must needs answer one of the most enduring compulsions of the American nation. The rector's news had become stale in the face of the possibility of a stamped personal communication of some kind, of any kind.

Charlestown, like numberless other towns throughout the south, had been built around a circle of tethered horses and mules. In the middle of the square was the courthouse— a simple utilitarian edifice of brick and sixteen beautiful Ionic columns stained with generations of casual tobacco. Elms surrounded the courthouse and beneath these trees, on scarred and carved wood benches and chairs the city fathers, progenitors of solid laws and solid citizens who believed in Tom Watson and feared only God and drouth, in black string ties or the faded brushed gray and bronze meaningless medals of the Confederate States of America, no longer having to make any pretense toward labor, slept or whittled away the long drowsy days while their juniors of all ages, not yet old enough to frankly slumber in public, played checkers or chewed tobacco and talked. A lawyer, a drug clerk and two nonedescripts tossed iron discs back and forth between two holes in the ground. And above all brooded early April sweetly pregnant with noon.

Yet all of them had a pleasant word for the rector as he and Mr. Saunders passed. Even the slumberers waked from the light sleep of the aged to ask about Donald. The divine's progress was almost triumphal.

Mr. Saunders walked beside him, returning greetings, preoccupied. Damn these women-folks, he fretted. They passed beneath a stone shaft bearing a Confederate soldier shading his marble eyes forever in eternal rigid vigilance and the rector repeated his question.

"She is feeling better this morning. It is too bad she fainted yesterday, but she isn't strong, you know."

"That was to be expected; his unannounced arrival rather

startled us all. Even Donald acknowledges that, I am sure. Their attachment also, you see."

Trees arching greenly over the street made a green tunnel of quiet, the sidewalk was checkered with shade. Mr. Saunders felt the need of mopping his neck. He took two cigars from his pocket, but the rector waved them away. Damn these women! Minnie should have done this.

The rector said: "We have a beautiful town, Mr. Saunders. These streets, these trees. . . . This quiet is just the thing for Donald."

"Yes, yes, just the thing for him, Doctor——"

"You and Mrs. Saunders must come in to see him this afternoon. I had expected you last night, but remembering that Cecily had been quite overcome— It is as well you did not, though. Donald was fatigued and Mrs. P—— I thought it better to have a doctor (just as a precaution, you see), and he advised Donald to go to bed."

"Yes, yes. We had intended to come, but, as you say, his condition, first night at home; and Cecily's condition, too—" He could feel his moral fiber disintegrating. Yet his course had seemed so logical last night after his wife had taken him to task, taking him, as a clinching argument, in to see his daughter weeping in bed. Damn these women! he repeated for the third time. He puffed his cigar and flung it away, mentally girding himself.

"About this engagement, Doctor——"

"Ah, yes, I was thinking of it myself. Do you know, I believe Cecily is the best medicine he can have? Wait," as the other would have interrupted, "it will naturally take her some time to become accustomed to his—to him—" he faced his companion confidentially, "he has a scar, you see. But I am confident this can be removed, even though Cecily does

become accustomed to it. In fact, I am depending on her
to make a new man of him in a short time."

Mr. Saunders gave it up. To-morrow, he promised himself. To-morrow I will do it.

"He is naturally a bit confused now," the divine continued,
"but care and attention, and above all, Cecily, will remedy
that. Do you know," he turned his kind gaze on Mr. Saunders again, "do you know, he didn't even know me at first
when I went into his room this morning? Merely a temporary condition, though, I assure you. Quite to be expected,"
he added quickly. "Don't you think it was to be expected?"

"I should think so, yes. But what happened to him? How
did he manage to turn up like this?"

"He won't talk about it. A friend who came home with
him assures me that he doesn't know, cannot remember. But
this happens quite often, the young man—a soldier himself—tells me, and that it will all come back to him some day.
Donald seems to have lost all his papers save only a certificate
of discharge from a British hospital. But pardon me: you
were saying something about the engagement."

"No, no. It was nothing." The sun was overhead: it was
almost noon. Around the horizon were a few thick clouds
fat as whipped cream. Rain this afternoon. Suddenly he
spoke: "By the way, Doctor, I wonder if I might stop in and
speak to Donald?"

"By all means. Certainly. He will be glad to see an old
friend. Stop in, by all means."

The clouds were steadily piling higher. They passed beneath the church spire and crossed the lawn. Mounting the
steps of the rectory, they saw Mrs. Powers sitting with a
book. She raised her eyes, seeing the resemblance immediately; the rector's "Mr. Saunders is an old friend of Donald's"

was unnecessary. She rose, shutting her book on her fore-finger.

"Donald is lying down. Mr. Gilligan is with him, I think. Let me call."

"No, no," Mr. Saunders objected quickly, "don't disturb him. I will call later."

"After you have come out of your way to speak to him? He will be disappointed if you don't go up. You are an old friend, you know. You said Mr. Saunders is an old friend of Donald's, didn't you, Doctor?"

"Yes, indeed. He is Cecily's father."

"Then you must come up by all means." She put her hand on his elbow.

"No, no, ma'am. Don't you think it would be better not to disturb him now, Doctor?" he appealed to the rector.

"Well, perhaps so. You and Mrs. Saunders are coming this afternoon, then?"

But she was obdurate. "Hush, Doctor. Surely Donald can see Miss Saunders' father at any time." She firmly com-pelled him through the door, and he and the divine followed her up the stairs. To her knock, Gilligan's voice replied and she opened the door.

"Here is Cecily's father to see Donald, Joe," she said, standing aside. The door opened and flooded the narrow passage with light, closing, it reft the passage of light again, and moving through a walled twilight, she descended the stairs again slowly. The lawn mower was long since stilled and beneath a tree she could see the recumbent form and one propped knee of its languid conductor lapped in slumber. Along the street passed slowly the hourly quota of negro children who, seeming to have no arbitrary hours, seemingly free of all compulsions of time or higher learning, went to and from school at any hour of a possible lighted eight, car-

rying lunch pails of ex-molasses and -lard tins. Some of them
also carried books. The lunch was usually eaten on the way
to school, which was conducted by a fattish negro in a lawn
tie and an alpaca coat who could take a given line from any
book from the telephone directory down and soon have the
entire present personnel chanting it after him, like Vachel
Lindsay. Then they were off for the day.

The clouds had piled higher and thicker, taking a lavender
tinge, making bits of sky laked among them more blue. The
air was becoming sultry, oppressive; and the church spire had
lost perspective until now it seemed but two dimensions of
metal and cardboard.

The leaves hung lifeless and sad, as if life were being recalled from them before it was fully given, leaving only the
ghosts of young leaves. As she lingered near the door, she
could hear Emmy clashing dishes in the dining-room and at
last she heard that for which she waited.

"—expect you and Mrs. Saunders this afternoon, then,"
the rector was saying as they appeared.

"Yes, yes," the caller answered with detachment. His eyes
met Mrs. Powers'. How like her he is! she thought, and her
heart sank. Have I blundered again? She examined his face
fleetingly and sighed with relief.

"How do you think he looks, Mr. Saunders?" she asked.

"Fine, considering his long trip, fine."

The rector said happily: "I had noticed it myself this
morning. Didn't you also, Mrs. Powers?" His eyes implored
her and she said yes. "You should have seen him yesterday,
to discern the amazing improvement in him. Eh, Mrs.
Powers?"

"Yes, indeed, sir. We all commented on it this morning."

Mr. Saunders, carrying his limp panama hat, moved toward
the steps. "Well, Doctor, it's fine having the boy home again.

We are all glad for our own sakes as well as yours. If there is anything we can do—" he added with neighborly sincerity.

"Thank you, thank you. I will not hesitate. But Donald is in a position to help himself now, provided he gets his medicine often enough. We depend on you for this, you know," the rector answered with jovial innuendo.

Mr. Saunders added a complement of expected laughter. "As soon as she is herself again we, her mother and I, expect it to be the other way: we expect to be asking you to lend us Cecily occasionally."

"Well, that might be arranged, I imagine—especially with a friend." The rector laughed in turn and Mrs. Powers, listening, exulted. Then she knew a brief misgiving. They are so much alike! Will they change his mind for him, those women? She said:

"I think I'll walk as far as the gate with Mr. Saunders, if he doesn't mind."

"Not at all, ma'am. I'll be delighted."

The rector stood in the door and beamed upon them as they descended the steps. "Sorry you cannot remain to dinner," he said.

"Some other time, Doctor. My missus is waiting for me to-day."

"Yes, some other time," the rector agreed. He entered the house again, and they crossed grass beneath the imminent heavens. Mr. Saunders looked at her sharply. "I don't like this," he stated. "Why doesn't someone tell him the truth about that boy?"

"Neither do I," she answered. "But if they did, would he believe it? Did anyone have to tell you about him?"

"My God, no! Anybody could look at him. It made me sick. But, then, I'm chicken-livered, anyway," he added with mirthless apology. "What did the doctor say about him?"

"Nothing definite, except that he remembers nothing that happened before he was hurt. The man that was wounded is dead and this is another person, a grown child. It's his apathy, his detachment, that's so terrible. He doesn't seem to care where he is nor what he does. He must have been passed from hand to hand, like a child."

"I mean, about his recovery."

She shrugged. "Who can tell? There is nothing physically wrong with him that surgeons can remedy, if that's what you mean."

He walked on in silence. "His father should be told, though," he said at last.

"I know, but who is to do it? Besides, he is bound to know some day, so why not let him believe as he wishes as long as he can? The shock will be no greater at one time than at another. And he is old, and so big and happy now. And Donald may recover, you know," she lied.

"Yes, that's right. But do you think he will?"

"Why not? He can't remain forever as he is now." They had reached the gate. The iron was rough and hot with sun under her hand, but there was no blue anywhere in the sky.

Mr. Saunders, fumbling with his hat, said: "But suppose he—he does not recover?"

She gave him a direct look. "Dies, you mean?" she asked brutally.

"Well, yes. Since you put it that way."

"Now that's what I want to discuss with you. It is a question of strengthening his morale, of giving him some reason to—well, buck up. And who could do that better than Miss Saunders?"

"But, ma'am, ain't you asking a lot, asking me to risk my daughter's happiness on such a poor bet as that?"

"You don't understand. I am not asking that the engagement be insisted upon. I mean, why not let Cecily—Miss Saunders—see him as often as she will, let her be sweethearts with him if necessary until he gets to know her again and will make an effort for himself. Time enough then to talk of engagements. Think, Mr. Saunders: suppose he were your son. That wouldn't be very much to ask of a friend, would it?"

He looked at her again in admiration, keenly. "You've got a level head on your shoulders, young lady. So what I'm to do is to prevail on her to come and see him, is it?"

"You must do more than that: you must see that she does come, that she acts just as she acted toward him before." She gripped his arm. "You must not let her mother dissuade her. You must not. Remember, he might have been your son."

"What makes you think her mother might object?" he asked in amazement.

She smiled faintly. "You forget I'm a woman, too," she said. Then her face became serious, imminent. "But you mustn't let that happen, do you hear?" Her eyes compelled him. "Is that a promise?"

"Yes," he agreed, meeting her level glance. He took her firm, proffered hand and felt her clean, muscular clasp.

"A promise, then," she said as warm great drops of rain dissolving from the fat, dull sky splashed heavily. She said good-by and fled, running across the lawn toward the house before assaulting gray battalions of rain. Her long legs swept her up and onto the veranda as the pursuing rain, foiled, whirled like cavalry with silver lances across the lawn.

5

Mr. Saunders, casting an uneasy look at the dissolving sky, let himself out the gate and here, returning from school, was his son, saying: "Did you see his scar, daddy? Did you see his scar?"

The man stared at this troublesome small miniature of himself, and then he knelt suddenly, taking his son into his arms, holding him close.

"You seen his scar," young Robert Saunders accused, trying to release himself as the rain galloped over them, through the trees.

6

Emmy's eyes were black and shallow as a toy animal's and her hair was a sun-burned shock of no particular color. There was something wild in Emmy's face: you knew that she outran, out-fought, out-climbed her brothers: you could imagine her developing like a small but sturdy greenness on a dunghill. Not a flower. But not dung, either.

Her father was a house painter, with the house painter's inevitable penchant for alcohol, and he used to beat his wife. She, fortunately, failed to survive the birth of Emmy's fourth brother, whereupon her father desisted from the bottle long enough to woo and wed an angular shrew who, serving as an instrument of retribution, beat him soundly with stove wood in her lighter moments.

"Don't never marry a woman, Emmy," her father, maudlin and affectionate, advised her. "If I had it to do all over again I'd take a man every time."

"I won't never marry nobody," Emmy had promised herself passionately, especially after Donald had gone to war and her laboriously worded letters to him had gone unanswered. (And now he don't even know me, she thought dully.)

"I won't never marry nobody," she repeated, putting dinner on the table. "I think I'll just die," she said, staring through a streaming window into the rain, watching the gusty rain surge by like a gray yet silver ship crossing her vision, nursing a final plate between her hands. She broke her revery, and putting the plate on the table she went and stood without the study door where they were sitting watching the streaming window panes, hearing the gray rain like a million little feet across the roof and in the trees.

"All right, Uncle Joe," she said, fleeing kitchenward.

Before they were halfway through lunch the downpour had ceased, the ships of rain had surged onward, drawing before the wind, leaving only a whisper in the wet green waves of leaves, with an occasional gust running in long white lines like elves holding hands across the grass. But Emmy did not appear with dessert.

"Emmy!" called the rector again.

Mrs. Powers rose. "I'll go see," she said.

The kitchen was empty. "Emmy?" she called quietly. There was no reply, and she was on the point of leaving when an impulse bade her look behind the open door. She swung it away from the wall and Emmy stared at her dumbly.

"Emmy, what is it?" she asked.

But Emmy marched wordless from her hiding place, and taking a tray she placed the prepared dessert on it and handed it to Mrs. Powers.

"This is silly, Emmy, acting this way. You must give him time to get used to us again."

But Emmy only looked at her from beyond the frontiers of her inarticulate despair, and the other woman carried the tray in to the table. "Emmy's not feeling well," she explained.

"I am afraid Emmy works too hard," the rector said. "She was always a hard worker, don't you remember, Donald?"

Mahon raised his puzzled gaze to his father's face. "Emmy?" he repeated.

"Don't you remember Emmy?"

"Yes, sir," he repeated tonelessly.

7

The window panes had cleared, though it yet rained. She sat after the men had left the table and at last Emmy peered through the door, then entered. She rose and together the two of them cleared the table, over Emmy's mild protest, and carried the broken meal to the kitchen. Mrs. Powers turned back her sleeves briskly.

"No, no, lemme do it," Emmy objected. "You'll spoil your dress."

"It's an old one: no matter if I do."

"It don't look old to me. I think it's right pretty. But this is my work. You go on and lemme do it."

"I know, but I've got to do something or I'll go wild. Don't you worry about this dress: I don't."

"You are rich, you don't have to, I guess," Emmy answered coldly, examining the dress.

"Do you like it?" Emmy made no reply. "I think clothes of this sort suit people of your and my type, don't you?"

"I dunno. I never thought about it," splashing water in the sink.

"I tell you what," said Mrs. Powers, watching Emmy's firm, sturdy back, "I have a new dress up in my trunk that doesn't suit me, for some reason. When we get through, suppose you come up with me and we'll try it on you. I can sew a little, and we can make it fit you exactly. What about it?"

Emmy thawed imperceptibly. "What use would I have for it? I don't go anywhere, and I got clothes good enough to wash and sweep and cook in."

"I know, but it's always well to have some dress-up things.

I will lend you stockings and things to go with it, and a hat, too."

Emmy slid dishes into hot water and steam rose about her reddened arms. "Where's your husband?" she asked irrelevantly.

"He was killed in the war, Emmy."

"Oh," she said. Then, after a while: "And you so young, too." She gave Mrs. Powers a quick, kind glance: sisters in sorrow. (My Donald was killed, too.)

Mrs. Powers rose quickly. "Where's a cup towel? Let's get done so we can try that dress."

Emmy drew her hands from the water and dried them on her apron. "Wait, lemme get an apron for you, too."

A bedraggled sparrow eyed her from the limp, glistening morning-glory vine, and Emmy dropped the apron over her head and knotted the cords at the back. Steam rose again about Emmy's forearms, wreathing her head, and the china was warm and smooth and sensuous to the touch; glass gleamed under Mrs. Powers' toweling and a dull parade of silver took the light mutely, hushing it as like two priestesses they repeated the orisons of Clothes.

As they passed the study door they saw the rector and his son gazing quietly into a rain-perplexed tree, and Gilligan sprawled on his back upon a battered divan, smoking and reading.

8

Emmy, outfitted from head to heel, thanked her awkwardly.

"How good the rain smells!" Mrs. Powers interrupted her. "Sit down a while, won't you?"

Emmy, admiring her finery, came suddenly from out her Cinderella dream. "I can't. I got some mending to do. I nearly clean forgot it."

"Bring your mending in here, then, so we can talk. I haven't had a woman to talk to in months, it seems like. Bring it in here and let me help you."

Emmy said, flattered: "Why do you want to do my work?"

"I told you if I don't have something to do I'll be a crazy woman in two days. Please, Emmy, as a favor. Won't you?"

"All right. Lemme get it." She gathered up her garments and leaving the room she returned with a heaped basket. They sat on either side of it.

"His poor huge socks," Mrs. Powers raised her encased hand. "Like chair covers, aren't they?"

Emmy laughed happily above her needle, and beneath swooning gusts of rain across the roof the pile of neatly folded and mended garments grew steadily.

"Emmy," Mrs. Powers said after a time, "what was Donald like before? You knew him a long time, didn't you?"

Emmy's needle continued its mute, tiny flashing, and after a while Mrs. Powers leaned across the basket and putting her hand under Emmy's chin, raised her bent face. Emmy twisted her head aside and bent again over her needle. Mrs. Powers rose and drew the shades, darkening the room against the rain-combed afternoon. Emmy continued to peer blindly at her darning until the other woman took it from her hand, then she raised her head and stared at her new friend with beast-like, unresisting hopelessness.

Mrs. Powers took Emmy's arms and drew her erect. "Come, Emmy," she said, feeling the bones in Emmy's hard, muscular arms. Mrs. Powers knew that lacking a bed any reclining intimacy was conducive to confidence, so she drew Emmy down beside her in an ancient obese armchair. And with heedless rain filling the room with hushed monotonous sound, Emmy told her brief story.

"We was in school together—when he was there at all. He

never came, mostly. They couldn't make him. He'd just go off into the country by himself, and not come back for two or three days. And nights, too. It was one night when he—when he——"

Her voice died away and Mrs. Powers said: "When he what, Emmy? Aren't you going too fast?"

"Sometimes he used to walk home from school with me. He wouldn't never have a hat or a coat, and his face was like—it was like he ought to live in the woods. You know: not like he ought to went to school or had to dress up. And so you never did know when you'd see him. He'd come in school at almost any time and folks would see him way out in the country at night. Sometimes he'd sleep in folks' houses in the country and sometimes niggers would find him asleep in sand ditches. Everybody knew him. And then one night——"

"How old were you then?"

"I was sixteen and he was nineteen. And then one night——"

"But you are going too fast. Tell me about you and him before that. Did you like him?"

"I liked him better than anybody. When we was both younger we dammed up a place in a creek and built a swimming hole and we used to go in every day. And then we'd lie in a old blanket we had and sleep until time to get up and go home. And in summer we was together nearly all the time. Then one day he'd just disappear and nobody wouldn't know where he was. And then he'd be outside our house some morning, calling me.

"The trouble was that I always lied to pappy where I had been and I hated that. Donald always told his father: he never lied about nothing he ever did. But he was braver than me, I reckon.

"And then when I was fourteen pappy found out about how I like Donald, and so he took me out of school and kept me at home all the time. So I didn't hardly ever get to see Donald. Pappy made me promise I wouldn't go around with him any more. He had come for me once or twice and I told him I couldn't go, and then one day he came and pappy was at home.

"Pappy ran out to the gate and told him not to come fooling around there no more, but Donald stood right up to him. Not acting bad, but just like pappy was a fly or something. And so pappy come in the house mad and said he wasn't going to have any such goings-on with his girls, and he hit me and then he was sorry and cried (he was drunk, you see), and made me swear I wouldn't never see Donald again. And I had to. But I thought of how much fun we used to have, and I wanted to die.

"And so I didn't see Donald for a long time. Then folks said he was going to marry that—that—her. I knew Donald didn't care much about me: he never cared about anybody. But when I heard that he was going to marry her——

"Anyway, I didn't sleep much at night, and so I'd sit on the porch after I'd undressed lots of times, thinking about him and watching the moon getting bigger every night. And then one night, when the moon was almost full and you could see like day almost, I saw somebody walk up to our gate and stop there. And I knew it was Donald, and he knew I was there because he said:

" 'Come here, Emmy.'

"And I went to him. And it was like old times because I forgot all about him marrying her, because he still liked me, to come for me after so long. And he took my hand and we walked down the road, not talking at all. After a while we came to the place where you turn off the road to go to our

swimming hole, and when we crawled through the fence my
nightie got hung and he said, 'Take it off.' And I did and we
put it in a plum bush and went on.

"The water looked so soft in the moonlight you couldn't
tell where the water was hardly, and we swam a while and
then Donald hid his clothes, too, and we went on up on top
of a hill. Everything was so kind of pretty and the grass felt so
good to your feet, and all of a sudden Donald ran on ahead of
me. I can keep up with Donald when I want to, but for some
reason I didn't want to to-night, and so I sat down. I could
see him running along the top of the hill, all shiny in the
moonlight, then he ran back down the hill toward the creek.

"And so I laid down. I couldn't see anything except the
sky, and I don't know how long it was when all of a sudden
there was his head against the sky, over me, and he was wet
again and I could see the moonlight kind of running on his
wet shoulders and arms, and he looked at me. I couldn't see
his eyes, but I could feel them somehow like things touching
me. When he looks at you—you feel like a bird, kind of:
like you was going swooping right away from the ground or
something. But now there was something different, too. I
could hear him panting from running, and I could feel something inside me panting, too. I was afraid and I wasn't afraid.
It was like everything was dead except us. And then he said:

" 'Emmy, Emmy.'

"Kind of like that. And then—and then——"

"Yes. And then he made love to you."

Emmy turned suddenly, and the other held her close. "And
now he don't even know me, he don't even know me!" she
wailed.

Mrs. Powers held her and at last Emmy raised her hand
and pushed her hair from her face. "And then?" Mrs. Powers
prompted.

"And afterwards we laid there and held each other, and I felt so quiet, so good, and some cows came up and looked at us and went away. And I could feel his hand going right slow from my shoulder along my side as far as he could reach and then back again, slow, slow. We didn't talk at all, just his hand going up and down my side, so smooth and quiet. And after a while I was asleep.

"Then I waked up. It was getting dawn and I was cramped and wet and cold, and he was gone. But I knew he would come back. And so he did, with some blackberries. We ate 'em and watched it getting light in the east. Then when the blackberries were gone I could feel the cold, wet grass under me again and see the sky all yellow and chilly behind his head.

"After a while we went back by the swimming hole and he put on his clothes and we got my nightie and I put it on. It was getting light fast and he wanted to go all the way home with me, only I wouldn't let him: I didn't care what happened to me now. And when I went through the gate there was pappy standing on the porch."

She was silent. Her story seemed to be finished. She breathed regularly as a child against the other's shoulder.

"And what then, Emmy?" Mrs. Powers prompted again.

"Well, when I came to the porch I stopped and he said, 'Where have you been?' and I said, 'None of your business,' and he said, 'You whore, I'll beat you to death,' and I said, 'Touch me.' But he didn't. I think I would have killed him if he had. He went into the house and I went in and dressed and bundled up my clothes and left. And I haven't been back since, either."

"What did you do then?"

"I got a job sewing for a dressmaker named Mrs. Miller,

and she let me sleep in her shop until I could earn some money. I hadn't been there but three days when one day Mr. Mahon walked in. He said that Donald had told him about us and that Donald had gone to the war, and that he had come for me. So I have been here ever since. So I didn't see Donald any more, and now he don't know me at all."

"You poor child," Mrs. Powers said. She raised Emmy's face: it was calm, purged. She no longer felt superior to the girl. Suddenly Emmy sprang to her feet and gathered up the mended clothes. "Wait, Emmy," she called. But Emmy was gone.

She lit a cigarette and sat smoking slowly in her great, dim room with its heterogeneous collection of furniture. After a while she rose to draw the curtains; the rain had ceased and long lances of sunlight piercing the washed immaculate air struck sparks amid the dripping trees.

She crushed out her cigarette, and descending the stairs she saw a strange retreating back, and the rector, turning from the door, said hopelessly, staring at her:

"He doesn't give us much hope for Donald's sight."

"But he's only a general practitioner. We'll get a specialist from Atlanta," she encouraged him, touching his sleeve.

And here was Miss Cecily Saunders tapping her delicate way up the fast-drying path, between the fresh-sparkled grass.

9

Cecily sat in her room in pale satin knickers and a thin orange-colored sweater, with her slim legs elevated to the arm of another chair, reading a book. Her father, opening the door without knocking, stared at her in silent disapproval. She met his gaze for a time, then lowered her legs.

"Do nice girls sit around half-naked like this?" he asked coldly. She laid her book aside and rose.

"Maybe I'm not a nice girl," she answered flippantly. He watched her as she enveloped her narrow body in a flimsy diaphanous robe.

"I suppose you consider that an improvement, do you?"

"You shouldn't come in my room without knocking, daddy," she told him fretfully.

"No more I will, if that's the way you sit in it." He knew he was creating an unfortunate atmosphere in which to say what he wished, but he felt compelled to continue. "Can you imagine your mother sitting in her room half undressed like this?"

"I hadn't thought about it." She leaned against the mantel combatively respectful. "But I can if she wanted to."

He sat down. "I want to talk to you, Sis." His tone was changed and she sank onto the foot of the bed, curling her legs under her, regarding him hostilely. How clumsy I am, he thought, clearing his throat. "It's about young Mahon."

She looked at him.

"I saw him this noon, you know."

She was forcing him to do all the talking. Dammit, what an amazing ability children have for making parental admonition hard to achieve. Even Bob was developing it.

Cecily's eyes were green and fathomless. She extended her arm, taking a nail file from her dressing-table. The downpour had ceased and the rain was only a whisper in the wet leaves. Cecily bent her face above the graceful slender gesturing of her hands.

"I say, I saw young Mahon to-day," her father repeated with rising choler.

"You did? How did he look, daddy?" Her tone was so soft, so innocent that he sighed with relief. He glanced at her sharply, but her face was lowered sweetly and demurely: he could see only her hair filled with warm reddish lights and the shallow plane of her cheek and her soft, unemphatic chin.

"That boy's in bad shape, Sis."

"His poor father," she commiserated above her busy hands. "It is so hard on him, isn't it?"

"His father doesn't know."

She looked quickly up and her eyes became gray and dark, darker still. He saw that she didn't know, either.

"Doesn't know?" she repeated. "How can he help seeing that scar?" Her face blanched and her hand touched her breast delicately. "Do you mean——"

"No, no," he said hastily. "I mean his father thinks—that he—his father doesn't think—I mean his father forgets that his journey has tired him, you see," he finished awkwardly. He continued swiftly: "That's what I wanted to talk to you about."

"About being engaged to him? How can I, with that scar? How can I?"

"No, no, not engaged to him, if you don't want to be. We won't think about the engagement at all now. But just keep on seeing him until he gets well, you see."

"But, daddy, I can't. I just can't."

"Why, Sis?"

"Oh, his face. I can't bear it any more." Her own face was wrung with the recollection of a passed anguish. "Don't you see I can't? I would if I could."

"But you'll get used to it. And I expect a good doctor can patch him up and hide it. Doctors can do anything these days. Why, Sis, you are the one who can do more for him right now than any doctor."

She lowered her head to her arms folded upon the foot-rail

of the bed and her father stood beside her, putting his arm about her slim, nervous body.

"Can't you do that much, Sis? Just drop in and see him occasionally?"

"I just can't," she moaned, "I just can't."

"Well, then, I guess you can't see that Farr boy any more, either."

She raised her head quickly and her body became taut beneath his arm. "Who says I can't?"

"I say so, Sis," he replied gently and firmly.

Her eyes became blue with anger, almost black.

"You can't prevent it. You know you can't." She thrust herself back against his arm, trying to evade it. He held her and she twisted her head aside, straining from him.

"Look at me," he said quietly, putting his other hand under her cheek. She resisted, he felt her warm breath on his hand, but he forced her face around. Her eyes blazed at him. "If you can't occasionally see the man you are engaged to, and a sick man to boot, I'm damned if I'll have you running around with anybody else."

There were red prints of his fingers on her cheek, and her eyes slowly filled. "You are hurting me," she said, and feeling her soft, vague chin in his palm and her fragile body against his arm, he knew a sudden access of contrition. He picked her up bodily and sat again in a chair, holding her on his lap.

"Now, then," he whispered, rocking, holding her face against his shoulder, "I didn't mean to be so rough about it."

She lay against him limply, weeping, and the rain filled the interval, whispering across the roof, among the leaves of trees. After a long space in which they could hear dripping eaves and the happy sound of gutters and a small ivory clock in the room, she moved and still holding her face against his coat, she clasped her father about the neck.

"We won't think about it any more," he told her, kissing her cheek. She clasped him again tightly, then slipping from his lap, she stood at the dressing-table, dabbing powder upon her face. He rose, and in the mirror across her shoulder he saw her blurred face and the deft nervousness of her hands. "We won't think of it any more," he repeated, opening the door. The orange sweater was a hushed incandescence under the formal illusion of her robe, molding her narrow back, as he closed the door after him.

As he passed his wife's room she called to him.

"What were you scolding Cecily for, Robert?" she asked.

But he stumped on down the stairs, ignoring her and soon she heard him cursing Tobe from the back porch.

Mrs. Saunders entered her daughter's room and found her swiftly dressing. The sun broke suddenly through the rain and long lances of sunlight piercing the washed immaculate air struck sparks amid the dripping trees.

"Where are you going, Cecily?" she asked.

"To see Donald," she replied, drawing on her stockings, twisting them skillfully and deftly at the knees.

10

Januarius Jones, lounging through the wet grass, circled the house and peering through the kitchen window saw Emmy's back and one angled arm sawing across her body. He mounted the steps quietly and entered. Emmy's stare above her poised iron was impersonally combative. Jones' yellow eyes, unabashed, took her and the ironing board and the otherwise empty kitchen boldly. Jones said:

"Well, Cinderella."

"My name is Emmy," she told him icily.

"That's right," he agreed equably, "so it is. Emmy, Emmeline, Emmylune, Lune—'*La lune en grade aucune rancune.*' But does it? Or perhaps you prefer '*Noir sur la lune?*' Or do you make finer or less fine distinctions than this? It might be jazzed a bit, you know. Aelia thought so, quite successfully, but then she had a casement in which to lean at dusk and harp her sorrow on her golden hair. You don't seem to have any golden hair, but, then, you might jazz your hair up a little, too. Ah, this restless young generation! Wanting to jazz up everything, not only their complexes, but the shapes of their behinds as well."

She turned her back on him indifferently, and again her arm sawed the iron steadily along a stretched fabric. He became so still that after a while she turned to see what had become of him. He was so close behind her that her hair brushed his face. Clutching her iron, she shrieked.

"Hah, my proud beauty!" hissed Jones in accepted style, putting his arms around her.

"Let me go!" she said, glaring at him.

"Your speech is wrong," Jones informed her helpfully. " 'Release me, villain, or it will be the worse for you,' is what you should say."

"Let me go," she repeated.

"Not till you divulge them papers," he answered, fat and solemn, his yellow eyes expressionless as a dead man's.

"Lemme go, or I'll burn you," she cried hotly, brandishing the iron. They stared at one another. Emmy's eyes were fiercely implacable and Jones said at last:

"Dam'f I don't believe you would."

"See if I don't," she said with anger. But releasing her, he sprang away in time. Her red hand brushed her hair from

her hot face and her eyes blazed at him. "Get out, now," she
ordered, and Jones, sauntering easily toward the door, remarked plaintively:

"What's the matter with you women here, anyway? Wildcats. Wildcats. By the way, how is the dying hero to-day?"

"Go on now," she repeated, gesturing with the iron. He
passed through the door and closed it behind him. Then he
opened it again and making her a deep fattish bow from the
threshold he withdrew.

In the dark hallway he halted, listening. Light from the
front door fell directly in his face: he could see only the edged
indication of sparse furniture. He paused, listening. No,
she isn't here, he decided. Not enough talk going on for
her to be here. That femme hates silence like a cat does
water. Cecily and silence: oil and water. And she'll be
on top of it, too. Little bitch, wonder what she meant by
that yesterday. And Georgie, too. She's such a fast worker
I guess it takes a whole string to keep her busy. Oh, well,
there's always to-morrow. Especially when to-day ain't over
yet. Go in and pull the Great Dane's leg a while.

At the study door he met Gilligan. He didn't recognize
him at first.

"Bless my soul," he said at last. "Has the army disbanded
already? What will Pershing do now, without any soldiers
to salute him? We had scarcely enough men to fight a war
with, but with a long peace ahead of us—man, we are helpless."

Gilligan said coldly: "Whatcher want?"

"Why, nothing, thank you. Thank you so much. I merely
came to call upon our young friend in the kitchen and to
incidentally inquire after Mercury's brother."

"Whose brother?"

"Young Mr. Mahon, in a manner of speaking, then."

"Doctor's with him," Gilligan replied curtly. "You can't go in now." He turned on his heel.

"Not at all," murmured Jones, after the other's departing back. "Not at all, my dear fellow." Yawning, he strolled up the hall. He stood in the entrance, speculative, filling his pipe. He yawned again openly. At his right was an open door and he entered a stuffily formal room. Here was a convenient window ledge on which to put spent matches, and sitting beside it he elevated his feet to another chair.

The room was depressingly hung wth glum portraits of someone's forebears, between which the principal strain of kinship appeared to be some sort of stomach trouble. Or perhaps they were portraits of the Ancient Mariner at different ages before he wore out his albatross. (Not even a dead fish could make a man look like that, thought Jones, refusing the dyspeptic gambit of their fretful painted eyes. No wonder the parson believes in hell.) A piano had not been opened in years, and opened would probably sound like the faces looked. Jones rose and from a bookcase he got a copy of "Paradise Lost" (cheerful thing to face a sinner with, he thought), and returned to his chair. The chair was hard, but Jones was not. He elevated his feet again.

The rector and a stranger came into his vision, pausing at the front door in conversation. The stranger departed and that black woman appeared. She and the rector exchanged a few words. Jones remarked with slow, lustful approval her firm, free carriage, and——

And here came Miss Cecily Saunders in pale lilac with a green ribbon at her waist, tapping her delicate way up the fast-drying gravel path between the fresh-sparkled grass.

"Uncle Joe!" she called, but the rector had already withdrawn to his study. Mrs. Powers met her and she said: "Oh. How do you do? May I see Donald?"

She entered the hall beneath the dim lovely fanlight, and her roving glance remarked one sitting with his back to a window. She said Donald! and sailed into the room like a bird. One hand covered her eyes and the other was outstretched as she ran with quick tapping steps and sank before him at his feet, burying her face in his lap.

"Donald, Donald! I will try to get used to it, I will try! Oh, Donald, Donald! Your poor face! But I will, I will," she repeated hysterically. Her fumbling hand touched his sleeve and slipping down his arm she drew his hand under her cheek, clasping it. "I didn't mean to, yesterday. I wouldn't hurt you for anything, Donald. I couldn't help it, but I love you, Donald, my precious, my own." She burrowed deeper into his lap.

"Put your arms around me, Donald," she said, "until I get used to you again."

He complied, drawing her upward. Suddenly, struck with something familiar about the coat, she raised her head. It was Januarius Jones.

She sprang to her feet. "You beast, why didn't you tell me?"

"My dear ma'am, who am I to refuse what the gods send?"

But she did not wait to hear him. At the door Mrs. Powers stood watching with interest. Now she's laughing at me! Cecily thought furiously. Her glance was a blue dagger and her voice was like dripped honey.

"How silly of me, not to have looked," she said sweetly. "Seeing you, I thought at once that Donald would be near by. I am sure if I were a man I'd always be as near you as possible. But I didn't know you and Mr.—Mr. Smith were such good friends. Though they say that fat men are awfully attractive. May I see Donald—do you mind?"

Her anger lent her fortitude. When she entered the study she looked at Mahon without a qualm, scar and all. She greeted the rector, kissing him, then she turned swift and graceful to Mahon, averting her eyes from his brow. He watched her quietly, without emotion.

You have caused me to look foolish, she told him with whispered smooth fury, sweetly kissing his mouth.

Jones, ignored, followed down the hall and stood without the closed door to the study, listening, hearing her throaty, rapid speech beyond the bland panel. Then, stooping, he peered through the keyhole. But he could see nothing and feeling his creased waistline constricting his breathing, feeling his braces cutting into his stooped fleshy shoulders, he rose under Gilligan's detached, contemplative stare. Jones' own yellow eyes became quietly empty and he walked around Gilligan's immovable belligerence and on toward the front door, whistling casually.

II

Cecily Saunders returned home nursing the yet uncooled embers of her anger. From beyond the turning angle of the veranda her mother called her name and she found her parents sitting together.

"How is Donald?" her mother asked, and not waiting for a reply, she said: "George Farr 'phoned again after you left. I wish you'd leave a message for him. It keeps Tobe forever stopping whatever he is doing to answer the 'phone."

Cecily, making no reply, would have passed on to a French window opening upon the porch, but her father caught her hand, stopping her.

"How is Donald looking to-day?" he asked, repeating his wife.

Her unrelaxed hand tried to withdraw from his. "I don't know and I don't care," she said harshly.

"Why, didn't you go there?" Her mother's voice was faintly laced with surprise. "I thought you were going there."

"Let me go, daddy." She wrenched her hand nervously. "I want to change my dress." He could feel her rigid, delicate bones. "Please," she implored and he said:

"Come here, Sis."

"Now, Robert," his wife interposed. "You promised to let her alone."

"Come here, Sis," he repeated, and her hand becoming lax, she allowed herself to be drawn to the arm of his chair. She sat nervously, impatiently, and he put his arm around her. "Why didn't you go there?"

"Now, Robert, you promised," his wife parroted futilely.

"Let me go, daddy." She was rigid beneath her thin, pale dress. He held her and she said: "I did go there."

"Did you see Donald?"

"Oh, yes. That black, ugly woman finally condescended to let me see him a few minutes. In her presence, of course."

"What black, ugly woman, darling?" asked Mrs. Saunders, with interest.

"Black woman? Oh, you mean Mrs. What's-her-name. Why, Sis, I thought you and she would like each other. She has a good, level head, I thought."

"I don't doubt it. Only——"

"What black woman, Cecily?"

"——only you'd better not let Donald see that you are smitten with her."

"Now, now, Sis. What are you talking about?"

"Oh, it's well enough to talk that way," she said, taut and passionate, "but haven't I eyes of my own? Haven't I seen? Why did she come all the way from Chicago or wherever it was with him? And yet you expect me——"

"Who came from where? What woman, Cecily? What woman, Robert?" They ignored her.

"Now, Sis, you ain't just to her. You're just excited."

His arm held her fragile rigidity.

"I tell you, it isn't that—just her. I had forgiven that, because he is sick and because of how he used to be about—about girls. You know, before the war. But he has humiliated me in public: this afternoon he—he— Let me go, daddy," she repeated, imploring, trying to thrust herself away from him.

"But what woman, Cecily? What is all this about a woman?" Her mother's voice was fretted.

"Sis, honey, remember he is sick. And I know more about Mrs.—er—Mrs. Powers than you do." He removed his arm, yet held her by the wrist. "Now, you——"

"Robert, who is this woman?"

"—think about it to-night and we'll talk it over in the morning."

"No, I am through with him, I tell you. He has humiliated me before her." Her hand came free and she sprang toward the window.

"Cecily!" her mother called after the slim whirl of her vanishing dress, "are you going to call George Farr?"

"No! Not if he was the last man in the world. I hate men." The swift staccato of her feet died away upon the stairs, and then a door slammed. Mrs. Saunders sank creaking into her chair.

"Now, Robert."

So he told her.

12

Cecily did not appear at breakfast. Her father mounted to her room, and knocked this time.

"Yes?" her voice penetrated the wood, muffled thinly.

"It's me, Sis. Can I come in?"

There was no reply, so he entered. She had not even bathed her face, and upon the pillow she was flushed and childish with sleep. The room was permeated with her body's intimate repose; it was in his nostrils like an odor and he felt ill at ease, cumbersome and awkward. He sat on the edge of the bed and took her surrendered hand diffidently. It was unresponsive.

"How do you feel this morning?"

She made no reply, lazily feeling her ascendency and he continued with assumed lightness: "Do you feel better about poor young Mahon this morning?"

"I've put him out of my mind. He doesn't need me any more."

"Course he does," heartily, "we expect you to be his best medicine."

"How can I?"

"How? What do you mean?"

"He brought his own medicine with him."

Her calmness, her exasperating calmness. He must flog himself into yesterday's rage. That was the only way to do anything with 'em, damn 'em.

"Did it ever occur to you that I, in my limited way, may know more about this than you?"

She withdrew her hand and slid it beneath the covers, making no reply, not even looking at him.

He continued: "You are acting like a fool, Cecily. What did the man do to you yesterday?"

"He simply insulted me before another woman. But I don't care to discuss it."

"But listen, Sis. Are you refusing to even see him when seeing him meant whether or not he will get well again?"

"He's got that black woman. If she can't cure him with all her experience, I certainly can't."

Her father's face slowly suffused. She glanced at him impersonally then turned her head on the pillow, staring out the window.

"So you refuse to see him any more?"

"What else can I do? He very evidently does not want me to bother him any longer. Do you want me to go where I am not wanted?"

He swallowed his anger, trying to speak calmly, trying to match her calm. "Don't you see that I'm not trying to make you do anything? that I am only trying to help that boy get on his feet again? Suppose he was Bob, suppose Bob was lying there like he is."

"Then you'd better get engaged to him yourself. I'm not."

"Look at me," he said with such quiet, such repression that she lay motionless, holding her breath. He put a rough hand on her shoulder.

"You don't have to man-handle me," she told him calmly, turning her head.

"Listen to me. You are not to see that Farr boy, any more. Understand?"

Her eyes were unfathomable as sea water.

"Do you understand me?" he repeated.

"Yes, I hear you."

He rose. They were amazingly alike. He turned at the door meeting her stubborn, impersonal gaze. "I meant it, Sis."

Her eyes clouded suddenly. "I am sick and tired of men. Do you think I care?"

The door closed behind him and she lay staring at its inscrutable, painted surface, running her fingers lightly over her breasts, across her belly, drawing concentric circles upon her body beneath the covers, wondering how it would feel to have a baby, hating that inevitable time when she'd have to have one, blurring her slim epicenity, blurring her body with pain. . . .

13

Miss Cecily Saunders, in pale blue linen, entered a neighbor's house, gushing, paying a morning call. Women did not like her, and she knew it. Yet she had a way with them, a way of charming them temporarily with her conventional perfection, insincere though she might be. Her tact and her graceful deference were such that they discussed her disparagingly only behind her back. None of them could long resist her. She always seemed to enjoy other people's gossip. It was not until later you found that she had gossiped none herself. And this, indeed, requires tact.

She chatted briefly while her hostess pottered among tubbed flowers, then asking and receiving permission, she entered the house to use the telephone.

14

Mr. George Farr, lurking casually within the courthouse portals, saw her unmistakable approaching figure far down the shady street, remarking her quick, nervous stride. He gloated, fondling her in his eyes with a slow sensuality. That's the way to treat 'em: make 'em come to you. Forgetting that he had 'phoned her vainly five times in thirty hours. But her surprise was so perfect, her greeting so impersonal, that he began to doubt his own ears.

"My God," he said, "I thought I'd never get you on the 'phone."

"Yes?" She paused, creating an unpleasant illusion of arrested haste.

"Been sick?"

"Yes, sort of. Well," moving on, "I'm awfully glad to have seen you. Call me again sometime, when I'm in, won't you?"

"But say, Cecily——"

She paused again and looked at him over her shoulder with courteous patience. "Yes?"

"Where are you going?"

"Oh, I'm running errands to-day. Buying some things for mamma. Good-bye." She moved again, her blue linen shaping delicate and crisp to her stride. A negro driving a wagon passed between them, interminable as Time: he thought the wagon would never pass, so he darted around it to overtake her.

"Be careful," she said quickly, "Daddy's downtown to-day. I am not supposed to see you any more. My folks are down on you."

"Why?" he asked in startled vacuity.

"I don't know. Perhaps they have heard of your running around with women, and they think you will ruin me. That's it, probably."

Flattered, he said: "Aw, come on."

They walked beneath awnings. Wagons tethered to slumbering mules and horses were motionless in the square. They were lapped, surrounded, submerged by the frank odor of unwashed negroes, most of whom wore at least one ex-garment of the army O.D.; and their slow, unemphatic voices and careless, ready laughter which has also somehow beneath it something elemental and sorrowful and unresisting, lay drowsily upon the noon.

At the corner was a drug store in each window of which

was an identical globe, containing liquids, once red and green, respectively, but faded now to a weak similar brown by the suns of many summers. She stayed him with her hand.

"You mustn't come any further, George, please."

"Oh, come on, Cecily."

"No, no. Good-by." Her slim hand stopped him dead in his tracks.

"Come in and have a coca-cola."

"No, I can't. I have so many things to do. I'm sorry."

"Well, after you get through, then," he suggested as a last resort.

"I can't tell. But if you want to, you can wait here for me and I'll come back if I have time. If you want to, you know."

"All right. I'll wait here for you. Please come, Cecily."

"I can't promise. Good-by."

He was forced to watch her retreating from him, mincing and graceful, diminishing. Hell, she won't come, he told himself. But he daren't leave for fear she might. He watched her as long as he could see her, watching her head among other heads, sometimes seeing her whole body, delicate and unmistakable. He lit a cigarette and lounged into the drug store.

After a while the clock on the courthouse struck twelve and he threw away his fifth cigarette. God damn her, she won't have another chance to stand me up, he swore. Cursing her he felt better and pushed open the screen door.

He sprang suddenly back into the store and stepped swiftly out of sight and the soda clerk, glassy-haired and white-jacketed, said: "Whatcher dodging?" with interest. She passed, walking and talking gayly with a young married man who clerked in a department store. She looked in as they passed, without seeing him.

He waited, wrung and bitter with anger and jealousy, until he knew she had turned the corner. Then he swung the door outward furiously. He cursed her again, blindly, and someone behind him saying, "Mist' George, Mist' George," monotonously drew up beside him. He whirled upon a negro boy.

"What in hell you want?" he snapped.

"Letter fer you," replied the negro equably, shaming him with better breeding. He took it and gave the boy a coin. It was written on a scrap of wrapping paper and it read: "Come to-night after they have gone to bed. I may not get out. But come—if you want to."

He read and reread it, he stared at her spidery, nervous script until the words themselves ceased to mean anything to his mind. He was sick with relief. Everything, the ancient, slumbering courthouse, the elms, the hitched somnolent horses and mules, the stolid coagulation of negroes and the slow unemphasis of their talk and laughter, all seemed some way different, lovely and beautiful under the indolent noon.

He drew a long breath.

CHAPTER IV

I

MR. GEORGE FARR considered himself quite a man. I wonder if it shows in my face? he thought, keenly examining the faces of men whom he passed, trying to fancy that he did see something in some faces that other faces had not. But he had to admit that he could see nothing, and he knew a slight depression, a disappointment. Strange. If that didn't show in your face what could you do for things to show in your face? It would be fine if (George Farr was a gentleman), if without talking men who had women could somehow know each other on sight—some sort of involuntary sign: an automatic masonry. Of course women were no new thing to him. But not like this. Then the pleasing thought occurred to him that he was unique in the world, that nothing like this had happened to any other man, that no one else had ever thought of such a thing. Anyway I know it. He gloated over a secret thought like a pleasant taste in the mouth.

When he remembered (remember? had he thought of anything else?) how she had run into the dark house in her nightgown, weeping, he felt quite masculine and superior and gentle. She's all right now though, I guess they all do that.

His Jove-like calm was slightly shaken, however, after he had tried twice unsuccessfully to get her over the 'phone and it was completely shattered when late in the afternoon she drove serenely by him in a car with a girl friend, utterly ignoring him. She didn't see me. (You know she did.) She didn't see me! (You know damn well she did.)

By nightfall he was on the verge of his possible, mild unemphatic insanity. Then this cooled away as the sun cooled from the sky. He felt nothing, yet like an unattached ghost he felt compelled to linger around the corner which she would pass if she did come downtown. Suddenly he knew terror. What if I were to see her with another man? It would be worse than death he knew, trying to make himself leave, to hide somewhere like a wounded beast. But his body would not go.

He saw her time after time and when it turned out to be someone else he did not know what he felt. And so when she did turn the corner he did not believe his eyes at first. It was her brother that he first recognized, then he saw her and all his life went into his eyes leaving his body but an awkward, ugly gesture in unquicked clay. He could not have said how long it was that he was unconscious of the stone base of the monument on which he sat while she and her brother moved slowly and implacably across his vision, then his life flowed completely, emptying his eyes and filling his body again, giving him dominion over his arms and legs, and temporarily sightless he sprang after her.

"Hi, George," young Robert greeted him casually, as an equal. "Goin' to the show?"

She looked at him swiftly, delicately, with terror and something like loathing.

"Cecily—" he said.

Her eyes were dark, black, and she averted her head and hurried on.

"Cecily," he implored, touching her arm.

At his touch she shuddered, shrinking from him. "Don't, don't touch me," she said piteously. Her face was blanched, colorless, and he stood watching her frail dress flowing to the fragile articulation of her body as she and her brother passed on, leaving him.   And he, too, partook of her pain and terror, not knowing what it was.

2

Donald Mahon's homecoming, poor fellow, was hardly a nine days' wonder even.   Curious, kindly neighbors came in —men who stood or sat jovially respectable, cheerful: solid business men interested in the war only as a by-product of the rise and fall of Mr. Wilson, and interested in that only as a matter of dollars and cents, while their wives chatted about clothes to each other across Mahon's scarred, oblivious brow; a few of the rector's more casual acquaintances democratically uncravated, hushing their tobacco into a bulged cheek, diffidently but firmly refusing to surrender their hats; girls that he had known, had danced with or courted of summer nights, come now to look once upon his face, and then quickly aside in hushed nausea, not coming any more unless his face happened to be hidden on the first visit (upon which they finally found opportunity to see it); boys come to go away fretted because he wouldn't tell any war stories—all this going on about him while Gilligan, his glum major-domo, handled them all with impartial discouraging efficiency.

"Beat it, now," he repeated to young Robert Saunders, who with sundry contemporaries to whom he had promised something good in the way of damaged soldiers, had called.

"He's going to marry my sister. I'd like to know why I can't see him," young Robert protested. He was in the uncomfortable position of one who has inveigled his friends into a gold mine and then cannot produce the mine. They jeered at him and he justified his position hotly, appealing to Gilligan.

"G'wan now, beat it. Show's over. G'wan now." Gilligan

shut the door on him. Mrs. Powers, descending the stairs, said:

"What is it, Joe?"

"That damn Saunders hellion brought his whole gang around to see his scar. We got to stop this," he stated with exasperation, "can't have these damn folks in and out of here all day long, staring at him."

"Well, it is about over," she told him, "they have all called by now. Even their funny little paper has appeared. 'War Hero Returns,' you know—that sort of thing."

"I hope so," he answered without hope. "God knows they've all been here once. Do you know, while I was living and eating and sleeping with men all the time I never thought much of them, but since I got civilized again and seen all these women around here saying, Ain't his face terrible, poor boy, and Will she marry him? and Did you see her down-town yesterday almost nekkid? why, I think a little better of men after all. You'll notice them soldiers don't bother him, specially the ones that was over-seas. They just kind of call the whole thing off. He just had hard luck and whatcher going to do about it? is the way they figure. Some didn't and some did, the way they think of it."

They stood together looking out of the window upon the sleepy street. Women, quite palpably "dressed," went steadily beneath parasols in one direction. "Ladies' Aid," murmured Gilligan. "W. C. T. U. maybe."

"I think you are becoming misanthropic, Joe."

Gilligan glanced at her smooth contemplative profile almost on a level with his own.

"About women? When I say soldiers I don't mean me. I wasn't no soldier any more than a man that fixes watches is a watchmaker. And when I say women I don't mean you."

She put her arm over his shoulder. It was firm, latent in

strength, comforting. He knew that he could embrace her
in the same way, that if he wished she would kiss him, frankly
and firmly, that her eyelids would never veil her eyes at the
touch of his mouth. What man is for her? he wondered,
knowing that after all no man was for her, knowing that she
would go through with all physical intimacies, that she would
undress to a lover (?) with this same impersonal efficiency.
(He should be a—a—he should be a gladiator or a statesman or a victorious general: someone hard and ruthless who
would expect nothing from her, of whom she would expect
nothing. Like two gods exchanging golden baubles. And I,
I am no gladiator nor statesman nor general: I am nothing.
Perhaps that's why I want so much from her.) He put his
arm over her shoulders.

Niggers and mules. Afternoon lay in a coma in the street,
like a woman recently loved. Quiet and warm:
nothing now that the lover has gone away. Leaves were
like a green liquid arrested in mid-flow, flattened and spread;
leaves were as though cut with scissors from green paper and
pasted flat on the afternoon: someone dreamed them and then
forgot his dream. Niggers and mules.

Monotonous wagons drawn by long-eared beasts crawled
past. Negroes humped with sleep, portentous upon each
wagon and in the wagon bed itself sat other negroes upon
chairs: a pagan catafalque under the afternoon. Rigid, as
though carved in Egypt ten thousand years ago. Slow dust
rising veiled their passing, like Time; the necks of mules
limber as rubber hose swayed their heads from side to side,
looking behind them always. But the mules were asleep also.
"Ketch me sleep, he kill me. But I got mule blood in me:
when he sleep, I sleep; when he wake, I wake."

In the study where Donald sat, his father wrote steadily
on to-morrow's sermon. The afternoon slept without.

The Town:

War Hero Returns. . . .

His face . . . the way that girl goes on with that Farr boy. . . .

Young Robert Saunders:

I just want to see his scar. . . .

Cecily:

And now I'm not a good woman any more.   Oh, well, it had to be sometime, I guess. . . .

George Farr:

Yes! Yes! She was a virgin!   But if she won't see me, it means somebody else.   Her body in another's arms. . . . Why must you? Why must you? What do you want? Tell me: I will do anything, anything. . . .

Margaret Powers:

Can nothing at all move me again? Nothing to desire? Nothing to stir me, to move me, save pity? . . .

Gilligan:

Margaret, tell me what you want. I will do it. Tell me, Margaret. . . .

The rector wrote "The Lord is my shepherd: I shall not want."

Donald Mahon knowing Time as only something which was taking from him a world he did not particularly mind losing, stared out a window into green and motionless leaves: a motionless blur.

The afternoon dreamed on toward sunset. Niggers and mules. . . . At last Gilligan broke the silence.

"That old fat one is going to send her car to take him riding."

Mrs. Powers made no reply.

3

San Francisco, Cal.
April 5, 1919.

Dear Margaret—

Well I am at home again I got here this afternoon. As
soon as I got away from mother I am sitting down to write
to you. Home seems pretty good after you have been doing
a pretty risky thing like lots of them cracked up at. Its
boreing all these girls how they go on over a flying man
if you ever experienced it isn't it. There was a couple of
janes on the train I met. Well anyway they saw my hat
band and they gave me the eye they were society girls they
said but I am not so dumb any way they were nice kids and
they might of been society girls. Anyway I got there phone
numbers and I am going to give them a call. Just kidding
them see there is only one woman for me Margaret you
know it. Well we rode on into San Francisco talking and
laughing in there stateroom so I am going to take the best
looking of them out this week I made a date with her except
she wants me to bring a fellow for her friend so I guess I
will poor kids they probably havent had much fun dureing the
war like a man can have dureing the war. But I am just
kidding them Margaret you mustnt be jealous like I am not
jealous over Lieut Mahon. Well mother is dragging me out
to tea I had rather I had be shot than go except she
insists. Give my reguards to Joe.

With love

Julian.

Mrs. Powers and Gilligan met the specialist from Atlanta
at the station. In the cab he listened to her attentively.

"But, my dear madam," he objected when she had finished,
"you are asking me to commit an ethical violation."

"But, surely, Doctor, it isn't a violation of professional ethics to let his father believe as he wishes to believe, is it?"

"No, it is a violation of my personal ethics."

"Then, you tell me and let me tell his father."

"Yes, I will do that. But pardon me, may I ask what exactly is your relation to him?"

"We are to be married," she answered, looking at him steadily.

"Oho. Then that is quite all right. I will promise not to say anything before his father that can disturb him."

He kept his promise. After lunch he joined her where she sat on the shaded quiet veranda. She put aside her embroidery frame and he took a chair, puffing furiously at his cigar until it burned evenly.

"What is he waiting for?" he asked suddenly.

"Waiting for?" she repeated.

He flashed her a keen gray glance. "There is no ultimate hope for him, you know."

"For his sight, you mean?"

"That's practically gone now. I mean for him."

"I know. That's what Mr. Gilligan said two weeks ago."

"H'm. Is Mr. Gilligan a doctor?"

"No. But it doesn't take a doctor to see that, does it?"

"Not necessarily. But I think Mr. Gilligan rather overshot himself, making a public statement like that."

She rocked gently. He veiled his head in smoke, watching the evenly burning ash at the cigar tip. She said:

"You think that there is no hope for him, then?"

"Frankly, I do not." He tilted the ash carefully over the balustrade. "He is practically a dead man now. More than that, he should have been dead these three months were it not for the fact that he seems to be waiting for something. Something he has begun, but has not completed, something he has carried from his former life that he does not remember consciously. That is his only hold on life that I can see." He gave her another keen glance. "How does he regard you now? He remembers nothing of his life before he was injured."

She met his sharp, kind gaze a moment, then she suddenly decided to tell him the truth. He watched her intently until she had finished.

"So you are meddling with Providence, are you?"

"Wouldn't you have done the same?" she defended herself.

"I never speculate on what I would have done," he answered shortly. "There can be no If in my profession. I work in tissue and bone, not in circumstance."

"Well, it's done now. I am in it too far to withdraw. So you think he may go at any time?"

"You are asking me to speculate again. What I said was that he will go whenever that final spark somewhere in him is no longer fed. His body is already dead. Further than that I cannot say."

"An operation?" she suggested.

"He would not survive it. And in the second place, the human machine can only be patched and parts replaced up to a certain point. And all that has been done for him, or he would have never been released from any hospital."

Afternoon drew on. They sat quietly talking while sunlight, becoming lateral, broke through the screening leaves and sprinkled the porch with flecks of yellow, like mica in a stream. The same negro in the same undershirt droned up and down the lawn with his mower, an occasional vehicle passed slumbrous and creaking behind twitching mules, or moving more swiftly, leaving a fretful odor of gasoline to die beneath the afternoon.

The rector joined them after a while.

"Then there's nothing to do except let him build himself up, eh, Doctor?" he asked.

"Yes, that is my advice.   Attention, rest and quiet, let him resume old habits. About his sight, though——"

The rector looked up slowly. "Yes, I realize his sight must go.   But there are compensations.   He is engaged to be married to a very charming lady.   Don't you think that will give him incentive to help himself?"

"Yes, that should, if anything can."

"What do you think?   Shall we hurry the marriage along?"

"We—ll—" the doctor hesitated: he was not exactly accustomed to giving advice on this subject.

Mrs. Powers came to his rescue. "I think we had better not hurry him at all," she said quickly. "Let him accustom himself leisurely, you see. Don't you think so, Doctor Baird?"

"Yes, Reverend, you let Mrs. Powers here advise you about that. I have every confidence in her judgment. You let her take charge of this thing. Women are always more capable than we are, you know."

"That's quite true. We are already under measureless obligations to Mrs. Powers."

"Nonsense. I have almost adopted Donald myself."

The cab came at last and Gilligan appeared with the doctor's things. They rose and Mrs. Powers slipped her arm through the rector's. She squeezed his arm and released him. As she and Gilligan, flanking the doctor, descended the steps the rector said again, timidly:

"You are sure, Doctor, that there is nothing to be done immediately? We are naturally anxious, you know," he ended apologetically.

"No, no," the doctor replied testily, "he can help himself more than we can help him."

The rector stood watching until the cab turned the corner. Looking back, she could see him in the door staring after them. Then they turned a corner.

As the train drew into the station the doctor said, taking her hand:

"You've let yourself in for something that is going to be unpleasant, young lady."

She gave him a straight glance in return.

"I'll take the risk," she said, shaking his hand firmly.

"Well, good-bye, then, and good luck."

"Good-bye, sir," she answered, "and thank you."

He turned to Gilligan, offering his hand.

"And the same to you, Doctor Gilligan," he said with faint sarcasm. They saw his neat gray back disappear and Gilligan, turning to her, asked:

"What'd he call me Doctor for?"

"Come on, Joe," she said, not replying to his questions, "let's walk back. I want to walk through the woods again."

4

The air was sweet with fresh-sawed lumber and they walked through a pale yellow city of symmetrical stacked planks. A continuous line of negroes carried boards up a cleated incline like a chicken run into a freight car and flung them clashing to the floor, under the eye of an informally clad white man who reclined easily upon a lumber pile, chewing indolent tobacco. He watched them with interest as they passed, following the faint wagon road.

They crossed grass-grown steel rails, and trees obscured the lumber yard, but until they reached the bottom of the hill the voices of the negroes raised in bursts of meaningless laughter or snatches of song in a sorrowful minor came to them, and the slow reverberations of the cast boards smote at measured intervals. Quietly under the spell of the still late afternoon woods they descended a loamy hill, following the faint downward winding of the road. At the foot of the hill a dogwood tree spread flat palm-like branches in invocation among dense green, like a white nun.

"Niggers cut them for firewood because they are easy to chop," she said, breaking the silence. "Shame, isn't it?"

"Do they?" he murmured without interest. With the soft, sandy soil giving easily under their feet they came upon water. It ran somberly from out massed honeysuckle vines and crossed the dim road into another impenetrable thicket, murmuring. She stopped, and bending slightly, they could see their heads and their two fore-shortened bodies repeating themselves.

"Do we look that funny to people, I wonder?" she said. Then she stepped quickly across. "Come on, Joe."

The road passed from the dim greenness into sunlight again. It was still sandy and the going was harder, exasperating.

"You'll have to pull me, Joe." She took his arm, feeling her heels sink and slip treacherously at each step. Her unevenly distributed weight made his own progress more difficult, and he disengaged his arm and put his hand against her back.

"That's better," she said, leaning against his firm hand. The road circled the foot of a hill and trees descending the hill were halted by the curving road's green canyon as though waiting to step across when they had passed. Sun was in the trees like an arrested lateral rain and ahead where circling, the green track of the stream approached the road again, they heard young voices and a sound of water.

They walked slowly through the shifting sand, and the voices beyond a screen of thick leaves became louder. She squeezed his arm for silence and they left the road and parted leaves cautiously upon glinted disturbed water, taking and giving the sun in a flashing barter of gold for gold, dazzling the eyes. Two wet matted heads spread opening fans of water like muskrats and on a limb, balanced precariously to dive, stood a third swimmer. His body was the color of old paper, beautiful as a young animal's.

They stepped into view and Gilligan said:

"Hi, Colonel."

The diver took one quick, terrified look and releasing his hold he fell like a stone into the water. The other two, shocked and motionless, stared at the intruders, then when the diver reappeared above the surface they whooped at him in merciless derision. He swam like an eel across the pool and took refuge beneath the overhanging bank, out of sight. His companions still squalled at him in inarticulate mirth. She raised her voice above the din.

"Come on, Joe. We've spoiled their fun."

They left the noise behind and again in the road, she remarked:

"We shouldn't have done that. Poor boy, they'll tease him to death now. What makes men so silly, Joe?"

"Dam'f I know. But they sure are. Do you know who that was?"

"No. Who was it?"

"Her brother."

"Her——"

"Young Saunders."

"Oh, was it? Poor boy, I'm sorry I shocked him."

And well she might have been, could she have seen his malevolent face watching her retreating figure as he swiftly donned his clothes. I'll fix you! he swore, almost crying.

The road wound through a depression between two small

ridges. The sun was yet in the tops of trees and here were cedars unsunned and solemn, a green quiet nave. A thrush sang and they stopped as one, listening to its four notes, watching the fading patches of sun on the top of the ridge.

"Let's sit down and have a cigarette," she suggested.

She lowered herself easily and he sat beside her as young Robert Saunders, panting up the hill behind them, saw them and fell flat, creeping as near as he dared. Gilligan, reclining on his elbow, watched her pallid face. Her head was lowered and she dug in the earth with a stick. Her unconscious profile was in relief against a dark cedar and she said, feeling his eyes on her:

"Joe, we have got to do something about that girl. We can't expect Dr. Mahon to take sickness as an excuse much longer. I hoped her father would make her come, but they are so much alike. . . ."

"Whatcher want to do? Want me to go and drag her up by the hair?"

"I expect that would be the best way, after all." Her twig broke and casting it aside she searched for another one.

"Sure it would—if you got to fool with her kind at all."

"Unluckily, though, this is a civilized age and you can't do that."

"So called," muttered Gilligan. He sucked at his cigarette, then watched the spun white arc of its flight. The thrush sang again, filling the interval liquidly and young Robert, thinking, is it Sis they're talking about? felt fire on his leg and brushed from it an ant almost half an inch long. Drag her by the hair, huh? he muttered. I'd like to see 'em. Ow, but he stings! rubbing his leg, which did not help it any.

"What are we going to do, Joe? Tell me. You know about people."

Gilligan shifted his weight and his corrugated elbow tingled under his other hand.

"We've been thinking of them ever since we met. Let's think about you and me for a while," he said roughly.

She looked at him quickly. Her black hair and her mouth like a pomegranate blossom. Her eyes were black and they became quite gentle as she said:

"Please, Joe."

"Oh, I ain't going to propose. I just want you to talk to me about yourself for a while."

"What do you want me to tell you?"

"Nothing you don't want to. Just quit thinking about the loot for a while. Just talk to me."

"So you are surprised to find a woman doing something without some obvious material end in view. Aren't you?" He was silent, nursing his knees, staring between them at the ground. "Joe, you think I'm in love with him, don't you?" (Uhuh! Stealing Sis' feller. Young Robert Saunders squirming nearer, taking sand into his bosom.) "Don't you, Joe?"

"I don't know," he replied sullenly and she asked:

"What kind of women have you known, Joe?"

"The wrong kind, I guess. Leastways none of 'em ever made me lose a night's sleep until I saw you."

"It isn't me that made you lose a night's sleep. I just happened to be the first woman you ever knew doing something you thought only a man would do. You had nice fixed ideas about women and I upset them. Wasn't that it?"

She looked at his averted face, at his reliable homely face. (Are they going to talk all night? thought young Robert Saunders. Hunger was in his belly and he was gritty and uncomfortable with sand.)

The sun was almost down. Only the tips of trees were yet

dipped in fading light and where they sat the shadow became a violet substance in which the thrush sang and then fell still.

"Margaret," said Gilligan at last, "were you in love with your husband?"

Her face in the dusk was a smooth pallor, and after a while:

"I don't know, Joe. I don't think I was. You see, I lived in a small town and I had got kind of sick lazing around home all morning and dressing up just to walk downtown in the afternoon and spending the evenings messing around with men, so after we got in the war I persuaded some friends of my mother's to get me a position in New York. Then I got into the Red Cross—you know, helping in canteens, dancing with those poor country boys on leave, lost as sheep, trying to have a good time. And nothing in the world is harder to do in New York.

"And one night Dick (my husband) came in. I didn't notice him at first, but after we had danced together and I saw he was—well—impressed, I asked him about himself. He was in an officers' training camp.

"Then I started getting letters from him and at last he wrote that he would be in New York until he sailed. I had got in the habit of Dick by that time and when I saw him again, all spic and span, and soldiers saluting him, I thought he was grand. You remember how it was then—everybody excited and hysterical, like a big circus.

"So every night we went out to dinner and to dance, and after we would sit in my room and smoke and talk until all hours, till daylight. You know how it was: all soldiers talking of dying gloriously in battle without really believing it or knowing very much about it, and how women kind of got the same idea, like the flu—that what you did to-day would not matter to-morrow, that there really wasn't a to-morrow at all.

"You see, I think we both had agreed that we were not in love with each other for always, but we were both young, and so we might as well get all the fun we could. And then, three days before he sailed, he suggested that we get married. I had had proposals from nearly every soldier I had been at all kind to, just as all the other girls did, and so I wasn't surprised much. I told him I had other men friends and I knew that he knew other women, but neither of us bothered about that. He told me he expected to know women in France and that he didn't expect me to be a hermit while he was gone. And so we met the next morning and got married and I went to work.

"He called for me at the canteen while I was dancing with some boys on leave, and the other girls all congratulated us (lots of them had done the same thing), only some of them teased me about being a highbrow and marrying an officer. You see, we all got so many proposals we hardly listened to them. And I don't think they listened to us, either.

"He called for me and we went to his hotel. You see, Joe, it was like when you are a child in the dark and you keep on saying, It isn't dark, it isn't dark. We were together for three days and then his boat sailed. I missed him like the devil at first. I moped around without anybody to feel sorry for me: so many of my friends were in the same fix, with no sympathy to waste. Then I got dreadfully afraid I might be going to have a baby and I almost hated Dick. But when I was sure I wasn't I went back to the canteen, and after a while I hardly thought of Dick at all.

"I got more proposals, of course, and I didn't have such a bad time. Sometimes at night I'd wake up, wanting Dick, but after a time he got to be a shadowy sort of person, like

George Washington. And at last I didn't even miss him any more.

"Then I began to get letters from him, addressed to his dear little wife, and telling me how he missed me and so forth. Well, that brought it all back again and I'd write him every day for a time. And then I found that writing bored me, that I no longer looked forward to getting one of those dreadful flimsy envelopes, that had already been opened by a censor.

"I didn't write any more. And one day I got a letter saying that he didn't know when he'd be able to write again, but it would be as soon as he could. That was when he was going up to the front, I guess. I thought about it for a day or two and then I made up my mind that the best thing for both of us was just to call the whole thing off. So I sat down and wrote him, wishing him luck and asking him to wish me the same.

"And then, before my letter reached him, I received an official notice that he had been killed in action. He never got my letter at all. He died believing that everything was the same between us."

She brooded in the imminent twilight. "You see, I feel some way that I wasn't square with him. And so I guess I am trying to make it up to him in some way."

Gilligan felt impersonal, weary. He took her hand and rubbed his cheek against it. Her hand turned in his and patted his cheek, withdrawing. (Holding hands! gloated young Robert Saunders.) She leaned down, peering into Gilligan's face. He sat motionless, taut. Take her in my arms, he debated, overcome her with my own passion. Feeling this, she withdrew from him, though her body had not moved.

"That wouldn't do any good, Joe. Don't you know it wouldn't?" she asked.

"Yes, I know it," he said. Let's go."

"I'm sorry, Joe," she told him in a low voice, rising. He rose and helped her to her feet. She brushed her skirt and walked on beside him. The sun was completely gone and they walked through a violet silence soft as milk. "I wish I could, Joe," she added.

He made no reply and she said: "Don't you believe me?"

He strode on and she grasped his arm, stopping. He faced her and in her firm sexless embrace he stood staring at the blur of her face almost on a level with his own, in longing and despair. (Uhuh, kissing! crowed young Robert Saunders, releasing his cramped limbs, trailing them like an Indian.)

They then turned and walked on, out of his sight. Night was almost come: only the footprint of day, only the odor of day, only a rumor, a ghost of light among the trees.

5

He burst into his sister's room. She was fixing her hair and she saw him in the mirror, panting and regrettably soiled.

"Get out, you little beast," she said.

Undaunted, he gave his news: "Say, she's in love with Donald, that other one says, and I seen them kissing."

Her arrested hands bloomed delicately in her hair.

"Who is?"

"That other lady at Donald's house."

"Saw her kissing Donald?"

"Naw, kissing that soldier feller that ain't got no scar."

"Did she say she was in love with Donald?" she turned, trying to grasp her brother's arm.

"Naw, but that soldier said she is and she never said nothing. So I guess she is, don't you?"

"The cat! I'll fix her."

"That's right," he commended. "That's what I told her

when she sneaked up on me nekkid. I knowed you wouldn't
let no woman beat you out of Donald."

6

Emmy put supper on the table. The house was quiet and
dark. No lights yet. She went to the study door. Mahon
and his father sat in the dusk, quietly watching the darkness
come slow and soundless as a measured respiration. Donald's
head was in silhouette against a fading window and Emmy
saw it and felt her heart contract as she remembered that
head above her against the sky, on a night long, long ago.

But now the back of it was toward her and he no longer
remembered her. She entered that room silently as the twilight itself and standing beside his chair, looking down upon
his thin worn hair that had once been so wild, so soft, she
drew his unresisting head against her hard little hip. His
face was quiet under her slow hand, and as she gazed out
into the twilight upon which they two gazed she tasted the
bitter ashes of an old sorrow and she bent suddenly over his
devastated head, moaning against it, making no sound.

The rector stirred heavily in the dusk. "That you, Emmy?"

"Supper's ready," she said quietly. Mrs. Powers and Gilligan mounted the steps onto the veranda.

7

Doctor Gary could waltz with a level glass of water on his
head, without spilling a drop. He did not care for the more
modern dances, the nervous ones. "All jumping around—
like monkeys. Why try to do something a beast can do
so much better?" he was wont to say. "But a waltz, now.
Can a dog waltz, or a cow?" He was a smallish man, bald

and dapper, and women liked him. Such a nice bedside manner. Doctor Gary was much in demand, both professionally and socially. He had also served in a French hospital in '14, '15, and '16. "Like hell," he described it. "Long alleys of excrement and red paint."

Doctor Gary, followed by Gilligan, descended nattily from Donald's room, smoothing the set of his coat, dusting his hands with a silk handkerchief. The rector appeared hugely from his study, saying: "Well, Doctor?"

Doctor Gary rolled a slender cigarette from a cloth sack returning the sack to its lair in his cuff. When carried in his pocket it made a bulge in the cloth. He struck a match.

"Who feeds him at table?"

The rector, surprised, answered: "Emmy has been giving him his meals—helping him, that is," he qualified.

"Put it in his mouth for him?"

"No, no. She merely guides his hand. Why do you ask?"

"Who dresses and undresses him?"

"Mr. Gilligan here assists him. But why——"

"Have to dress and undress him like a baby, don't you?" he turned sharply to Gilligan.

"Kind of," Gilligan admitted. Mrs. Powers came out of the study and Doctor Gary nodded briefly to her. The rector said:

"But why do you ask, Doctor?"

The doctor looked at him sharply. "Why? Why?" he turned to Gilligan. "Tell him," he snapped.

The rector gazed at Gilligan. Don't say it, his eyes seemed to plead. Gilligan's glance fell. He stood dumbly gazing at his feet and the doctor said abruptly: "Boy's blind. Been blind three or four days. How you didn't know it I can't see." He settled his coat and took his derby hat. "Why didn't you tell?" he asked Gilligan. "You knew, didn't you?

Well, no matter, I'll look in again to-morrow. Good-day, madam. Good-day."

Mrs. Powers took the rector's arm. "I hate that man," she said. "Damn little snob. But don't you mind, Uncle Joe. Remember, that Atlanta doctor told us he would lose his sight. But doctors don't know everything: who knows, perhaps when he gets strong and well he can have his sight restored."

"Yes, yes," the rector agreed, clinging to straws. "Let's get him well and then we can see."

He turned heavily and reëntered his study. She and Gilligan looked at one another a long moment.

"I could weep for him, Joe."

"So could I—if it would do any good," he answered somberly. "But for God's sake, keep people out to-day."

"I intend to. But it's hard to refuse them: they mean so well, so kind and neighborly."

"Kind, hell. They are just like that Saunders brat: come to see his scar. Come in and mill around and ask him how he got it and if it hurt. As if he knowed or cared."

"Yes. But they sha'n't come in and stare at his poor head any more. We won't let them in, Joe. Tell them he is not well, tell them anything."

She entered the study. The rector sat at his desk, a pen poised above an immaculate sheet, but he was not writing. His face was propped on one great fist and his gaze brooded darkly upon the opposite wall.

She stood beside him, then she touched him. He started like a goaded beast before he recognized her.

"This had to come, you know," she told him quietly.

"Yes, yes. I have expected it. We all have, have we not?"

"Yes, we all have," she agreed.

"Poor Cecily. I was just thinking of her. It will be a blow

to her, I am afraid. But she really cares for Donald, thank God. Her affection for him is quite pretty. You have noticed it, haven't you?"

"Yes, yes."

"It's too bad she is not strong enough to come every day. But she is quite delicate, as you know, don't you?"

"Yes, yes. I'm sure she will come when she can."

"So am I. Thank God, there is one thing which has not failed him."

His hands were clasped loosely upon the paper before him.

"Oh, you are writing a sermon and I have interrupted you. I didn't know." she apologized, withdrawing.

"Not at all. Don't go, I can do this later."

"No, you do it now. I will go and sit with Donald. Mr. Gilligan is going to fix a chair for him on the lawn to-day, it is so nice out."

"Yes, yes. I will finish my sermon and join you."

From the door she looked back. But he was not writing. His face was propped on one great fist and his gaze brooded darkly upon the opposite wall.

Mahon sat in a deck chair. He wore blue glasses and a soft, limp hat concealed his brow. He liked to be read to, though no one could tell whether or not the words meant anything to him. Perhaps it was the sound of the voice that he liked. This time it was Gibbons' "History of Rome," and Gilligan wallowed atrociously among polysyllabic words when Mrs. Powers joined them. He had brought a chair for her, and she sat, neither hearing nor not hearing, letting Gilligan's droning voice sooth her as it did Mahon. The leaves above her head stirred faintly, agitated upon the ineffable sky, dappling her dress with shadow. Clover was again thrusting above the recently mown grass and bees broke it; bees were humming

golden arrows tipped or untipped with honey and from the
church spire pigeons were remote and unemphatic as sleep.

A noise aroused her and Gilligan ceased reading. Mahon
sat motionless, hopeless as Time, as across the grass came an
old negro woman, followed by a strapping young negro in a
private's uniform. They came straight toward the sitting
group and the woman's voice rose upon the slumbrous afternoon.

"Hush yo' mouf, Loosh," she was saying, "it'll be a po'
day in de mawnin' when my baby don't wanter see his ole
Cal'line. Donald, Mist' Donald honey, here Callie come
ter you, honey; here yo' mammy come ter you." She completed the last steps in a shuffling lope. Gilligan rose, inter-
cepting her.

"Hold up, Aunty. He's asleep. Don't bother him."

"Naw, suh! He don't wanter sleep when his own folks
comes ter see him." Her voice rose again and Donald moved
in his chair. "Whut I tell you? he wake: look at 'im. Mist'
Donald, honey!"

Gilligan held her withered arm while she strained like a
leashed hound.

"Bless de Lawd, done sont you back ter yo' mammy. Yes,
Jesus! Ev'y day I prayed, and de Lawd heard me." She
turned to Gilligan. "Lemme go, please, suh."

"Let her go, Joe," Mrs. Powers seconded, and Gilligan released her. She knelt beside Donald's chair, putting her hands
on his face. Loosh stood diffidently in the background.

"Donald, baby, look at me. Don't you know who dis is?
Dis yo' Callie whut use ter put you ter bed, honey. Look
here at me. Lawd, de white folks done ruint you, but num-
mine, yo' mammy gwine look after her baby. You, Loosh!"
still kneeling, she turned and called to her grandson. "Come
up here and speak ter Mist' Donald. Here whar he kin see

you. Donald, honey, here dis triflin' nigger talking ter you. Look at him, in dem soldier clothes."

Loosh took two paces and came smartly to attention, saluting. "If de lootenant please, Co'pul Nelson glad to see— Co'pul Nelson glad to see de lootenant looking so well."

"Don't you stand dar wavin' yo' arm at yo' Mist' Donald, nigger boy. Come up here and speak ter him like you been raised to."

Loosh lost his military bearing and he became again that same boy who had known Mahon long ago, before the world went crazy. He came up diffidently and took Mahon's hand in his kind, rough black one. "Mist' Donald?" he said.

"Dat's it," his grandmother commended. "Mist' Donald, dat Loosh talkin' ter you. Mist' Donald?"

Mahon stirred in his chair and Gilligan forcibly lifted the old woman to her feet. "Now, Aunty. That's enough for one time. You come back to-morrow."

"Lawd! ter hear de day when white man tell me Mist' Donald don't wanter see me!"

"He's sick, Aunty," Mrs. Powers explained. "Of course, he wants to see you. When he is better you and Loosh must come every day."

"Yes, ma'am! Dey ain't enough water in de sevum seas to keep me from my baby. I'm coming back, honey. I gwine to look after you."

"Get her away, Loosh," Mrs. Powers whispered to the negro. "He's sick, you know."

"Yessum. He one sick man in dis world. Ef you wants me fer anything, any black man kin tell you whar I'm at, ma'am." He took his grandmother's arm. "Come on here, mammy. Us got to be goin'."

"I'm a-comin' back, Donald, honey. I ain't gwine to leave you." They retreated and her voice died away. Mahon said:

"Joe."

"Whatcher say, Loot?"

"When am I going to get out?"

"Out of what, Loot?"

But he was silent, and Gilligan and Mrs. Powers stared at each other tensely. At last he spoke again:

"I've got to go home, Joe." He raised his hand, fumbling, striking his glasses and they fell from his face. Gilligan replaced them.

"Whatcher wanta go home for, Loot?"

But he had lost his thought. Then:

"Who was that talking, Joe?"

Gilligan told him and he sat slowly plaiting the corner of his jacket (the suit Gilligan had got for him) in his fingers. Then he said: "Carry on, Joe."

Gilligan picked up the book again and soon his voice resumed its soporific drone. Mahon became still in his chair. After a while Gilligan ceased, Mahon did not move, and he rose and peered over the blue glasses.

"You never can tell when he's asleep and when he ain't," he said fretfully.

CHAPTER V

I

CAPTAIN GREEN, who raised the company, had got a captain's commission from the governor of the state thereby. But Captain Green was dead. He might have been a good officer, he might have been anything: certainly he remembered his friends. Two subaltern's commissions were given away politically in spite of him, so the best he could do was to make his friend Madden, First Sergeant. Which he did.

And so here was Green in bars and shiny putties, here was Madden trying to acquire the habit of saying Sir to him, here was Tom and Dick and Harry with whom both Green and Madden had gambled and drunk whisky trying to learn to remember that there was a difference not only between them and Green and Madden, but that there was also a difference between Madden and Green.

"Oh, well," they said in American camps, "he's working hard: let him get used to it. It's only on parade, hey, Sergeant?"

"Sure," Sergeant Madden replied. "The Colonel is giving us hell about our appearance. Can't we do better than this?"

But at Brest:

"What in hell does he think he is? Pershing?" they asked Sergeant Madden.

"Come on, come on, snap into it. If I hear another word from a man he goes before the Captain." Sergeant Madden had also changed.

In wartime one lives in to-day. Yesterday is gone and to-morrow may never come. Wait till we get into action, they told each other, we'll kill the son-of-a-bitch. "Not Madden?" asked one horrified. They only looked at him. "For Christ's sake," remarked one at last.

But Fate, using the War Department as an instrument, circumvented them. When Sergeant Madden reported to his present captain and his old friend he found Green alone.

"Sit down, dammit," Green told him, "nobody's coming in. I know what you're going to say. I am moving, anyhow. should get my papers tonight. Wait," as Madden would have interrupted. "If I want to hold my commission I have got to work. These goddam training camps turn out officers trained. But I wasn't. And so I am going to school for a while. Christ. At my age. I wish to God somebody else had gotten up this damn outfit. Do you know where I would like to be now? Out yonder with them, calling somebody else a son-of-a-bitch, as they are calling me now. Do you think I get any fun out of this?"

"Ah, hell, let 'em talk. What do you expect?"

"Nothing. Only I had to promise the mother of every goddam one of them that I'd look out for him and not let him get hurt. And now there's not a bastard one wouldn't shoot me in the back if he got a chance."

"But what do you expect from them? What do you want? This is no picnic, you know."

They sat silent across a table from each other. Their faces were ridged and sharp, cavernous in the unshadowed glare of light while they sat thinking of home, of quiet elm-shaded streets along which wagons creaked and crawled through the dusty day and along which girls and boys walked in the evening to and from the picture show or to sip sweet chilled liquids in drug stores; of peace and quiet and all homely things, of a time when there was no war.

They thought of young days not so far behind them, of the

faint unease of complete physical satisfaction, of youth and lust like icing on a cake, making the cake sweeter. . . . Outside was Brittany and mud, an equivocal city, temporary and twice foreign, lust in a foreign tongue. To-morrow we die.

At last Captain Green said diffidently:

"You are all right?"

"Hell, yes. They wanted to reduce me at one time, but I am all right now."

Green opened his mouth twice, like a fish, and Madden said quickly: "I'll look after them. Don't you worry."

"Ah, I'm not. Not about those bastards."

An orderly entered, saluting. Green acknowledged him and the man delivered his message stiffly and withdrew.

"There it is," said the captain.

"You'll go to-morrow, then?"

"Yes. Yes. I hope so," he answered, vaguely staring at the sergeant. Madden rose.

"Well, I think I'll run along. I feel tired to-night."

Green rose also and they stared at each other like strangers across the table.

"You'll come in to see me in the morning?"

"I guess so. Sure, I'll come in."

Madden wished to withdraw and Green wanted him to, but they stood awkwardly, silent. At last Green said: "I am obliged to you." Madden's light-caverned eyes held a question. Their shadows were monstrous. "For helping me get by with that dose. Court-martial, you know. . . ."

"What did you expect of me?" No less, Green acknowledged and Madden continued: "Why don't you let those women alone? They are all rotten with it."

"Easy to say." Green laughed mirthlessly. "For you, I mean."

Madden's hand strayed to the pocket of his blouse, then

fell to his side again. After a while he repeated: "Well, I'll be going."

The captain moved around the table, extending his hand. "Well, good-bye."

Madden did not take it. "Good-bye?"

"I may not see you again," the other explained lamely.

"Hell. You talk like you were going home. Don't be a fool. Those birds don't mean anything by panning you. It will be the same with anybody."

Green watched his knuckles whitening on the table. "I didn't mean that. I meant—" He could not say I may be killed. A man simply didn't say a thing like that. "You will get to the front before I do, I expect."

"Perhaps so. But there is enough for all of us, I reckon."

The rain had ceased for some reason and there came up faintly on the damp air that sound made by battalions and regiments being quiet, an orderly silence louder than a riot. Outside, Madden felt mud, knew darkness and damp, he smelled food and excrement and slumber beneath a sky too remote to distinguish between peace and war.

2

He thought at times of Captain Green as he crossed France, seeing the intermittent silver smugness of rain spaced forever with poplars like an eternal frieze giving way upon vistas fallow and fecund, roads and canals and villages shining their roofs violently; spires and trees; roads, villages; villages, towns, a city; villages, villages, then cars and troops and cars and troops at junction points. He saw people going about warfare in a businesslike way, he saw French soldiers playing croquet in stained horizon-blue, he saw American soldiers watching them, giving them American cigarettes; he saw American and British troops fighting, saw nobody minding them particularly. Save the M. P's. A man must be in a funny frame of mind to be an M.P. Or a nigger general. The war zone. Business as usual. The golden age of non-combatants.

He thought at times of Green, wondering where the other was, even after he got to know his new company commander. A man quite different from Green. He had been a college instructor and he could explain to you where Alexander and Napoleon and Grant made their mistakes. He was mild: his voice could scarcely be heard on a parade ground and his men all said, Wait till we get into the lines. We'll fix the son-of-a-bitch.

Sergeant Madden, however, got along quite well with his officers, particularly with a lieutenant named Powers. And with the men, too. Even after a training period with dummies and a miniature sector he got along with them. They had become accustomed to the sound of far guns (shooting at other people, however) and the flickering horizon at night; they had been bombed by aeroplanes while lined up for mess at a field kitchen, while the personnel of a concealed French battery watched them without interest from a dug-out; they had received much advice from troops that had been in the lines.

At last they were going in themselves after a measureless space of aimless wandering here and there, and the sound of guns though seemingly no nearer was no longer impersonal. They tramped by night, feeling their feet sink, then hearing them suck in mud. Then they felt sloping ground and were in a ditch. It was as if they were burying themselves, descending into their own graves in the bowels of the wet black earth, into a darkness so dense as to constrict breathing, constrict the heart. They stumbled on in the darkness.

Out of the gratis advice they had received, they recalled

strongest to drop when a gun went off or when they heard a shell coming; so when a machine gun, far to the right, stuttered, breaking the slow hysteria of decay which buried them, some-one dropped, someone stumbled over him, then they all went down as one man. The officer cursed them, non-coms kicked them erect again. Then while they stood huddled in the dark, smelling death, the lieutenant ran back along the line making them a brief bitter speech.

"Who in hell told you to lie down? The only guns within two miles of you are those things in your hands there. Feel this? this thing here"—slapping the rifles—"this is a gun. Sergeants, if another man drops, tramp him right into the mud and leave him."

They plowed on, panting and cursing in whispers. Sud-denly they were among men, and a veteran of four days, sens-ing that effluvia of men new to battle, said:

"Why, look at the soldiers come to fight in the war."

"Silence there!" a non-com's voice, and a sergeant came jumping along saying, Where is your officer? Men going out brushed them, passing on in the pitch wet darkness and a voice whispered wickedly, Look out for gas. The word Gas passed from mouth to mouth and Authority raged them into silence again. But the mischief had been done.

Gas. Bullets and death and damnation. But Gas. It looked like mist, they had been told. First thing you know you are in it. And then—Good-night.

Silence broken by muddy movements of unrest and breath-ing. Eastward the sky paled impalpably, more like a death than a birth of anything; and they peered out in front of them, seeing nothing. There seemed to be no war here at all, though to the right of them a rumorous guttural of guns rose and fell thickly and heavily on the weary dawn. Powers, the officer, had passed from man to man. No one must fire:

there was a patrol out there somewhere in the darkness. Dawn grew gray and slow; after a while the earth took a vague form and someone seeing a lesser darkness screamed, "Gas!"

Powers and Madden sprang among them as they fought blindly, fumbling and tearing at their gas masks, trampling each other, but they were powerless. The lieutenant laid about him with his fists, trying to make himself heard, and the man who had given the alarm whirled suddenly on the fire-step, his head and shoulders sharp against the sorrowful dawn.

"You got us killed," he shrieked, shooting the officer in the face at point-blank range.

3

Sergeant Madden thought of Green again on a later day as he ran over broken ground at Cantigny saying, Come on, you bastards, do you want to live forever? He forgot Green temporarily as he lay beside a boy who had sold him shoes back home, in a shell-hole too small for them, feeling his exposed leg whipped by a gale as a tufted branch is whipped by a storm. After a while night came and the gale passed away and the man beside him died.

While in hospital he saw Captain Green's name in a published casualty list. He also discovered in hospital that he had lost his photograph. He asked hospital orderlies and nurses about it, but no one recalled having seen it among his effects. It was just as well, though. She had in the meantime married a lieutenant on the staff of a college R.O.T.C. unit.

4

Mrs. Burney's black was neat and completely air-proof: she did not believe in air save as a necessary adjunct to

breathing. Mr. Burney, a morose, silent man, whose occu-
pation was that of languidly sawing boards and then mildly
nailing them together again, took all his ideas from his wife,
so he believed this, too.

She toiled, neat as a pin, along the street, both fretted with
and grateful to the heat because of her rheumatism, making
a call. When she thought of her destination, of her changed
status in the town, above her dull and quenchless sorrow she
knew a faint pride: the stroke of Fate which robbed her
likewise made of her an aristocrat. The Mrs. Worthingtons,
the Mrs. Saunderses, all spoke to her now as one of them,
as if she, too, rode in a car and bought a half dozen new
dresses a year. Her boy had done this for her, his absence
accomplishing that which his presence had never done, could
never do.

Her black gown drank heat and held it in solution about
her, her cotton umbrella became only a delusion. How hot
for April, she thought, seeing cars containing pliant women's
bodies in cool, thin cloth passing her. Other women walking
in delicate, gay shades nodded to her bent small rotundity,
greeting her pleasantly. Her flat "common sense" shoes
carried her steadily and proudly on.

She turned a corner and the sun through maples was directly
in her face. She lowered her umbrella to it, and remarking
after a while a broken drain, and feeling an arching thrust
of poorly laid concrete, she slanted her umbrella back. Pigeons
in the spire were coolly remote from the heat, unemphatic
as sleep, and she passed through an iron gate, following a
graveled path. The rambling façade of the rectory dreamed
in the afternoon above a lawn broken by geranium beds and
a group of chairs beneath a tree. She crossed grass and the
rector rose, huge as a rock, black and shapeless, greeting her.

(Oh, the poor man, how bad he looks. And so old, so old

we are for this to happen to us. He was not any good, but he was my son. And now Mrs. Worthington and Mrs. Saunders and Mrs. Wardle speak to me, stop in to chat about this and that while there is my Dewey dead. They hadn't no sons and now his son come back and mine didn't, and how gray his face, poor man.)

She panted with heat, like a dog, feeling pain in her bones, and she hobbled horribly across to the grouped figures. It was because the sun was in her eyes that she couldn't see, sun going down beyond a lattice wall covered with wistaria. Pigeons crooned liquid gutturals from the spire, slanting like smears of paint, and the rector was saying:

"This is Mrs. Powers, Mrs. Burney, a friend of Donald's. Donald, here is Mrs. Burney. You remember Mrs. Burney: she is Dewey's mother, you remember."

Mrs. Burney took a proffered chair blindly. Her dress held heat, her umbrella tripped her bonelessly, then bonelessly avoided her. The rector closed it and Mrs. Powers settled her in the chair. She rubbed at her eyes with a black-bordered cotton handkerchief.

Donald Mahon waked to voices. Mrs. Powers was saying: "How good of you to come. All Donald's old friends have been so nice to him. Especially the ones who had sons in the war. They know, don't they?"

(Oh, the poor man, the poor man. And your scarred face! Madden didn't tell me your face was scarred, Donald.)

Pigeons like slow sleep, afternoon passing away, dying. Mrs. Burney, in her tight, hot black, the rector, huge and black and shapeless, Mrs. Burney with an unhealed sorrow, Mrs. Powers—(Dick, Dick. How young, how terribly young: to-morrow must never come. Kiss me, kiss me through my hair. Dick, Dick. My body flowing away from me, dividing. How ugly men are, naked. Don't leave me, don't leave me! No, no! we don't love each other! we don't! we don't! Hold me close, close: my body's intimacy is broken, unseeing: thank God my body cannot see. Your body is so ugly, Dick! Dear Dick. Your bones, your mouth hard and shaped as bone: rigid. My body flows away: you cannot hold it. Why do you sleep, Dick? My body flows on and on. You cannot hold it, for yours is so ugly, dear Dick. . . . "You may not hear from me for some time. I will write when I can. . . .")

Donald Mahon, hearing voices, moved in his chair. He felt substance he could not see, heard what did not move him at all. "Carry on, Joe."

The afternoon dreamed on, unbroken. A negro, informal in an undershirt, restrained his lawn mower, and stood beneath a tree, talking to a woman across the fence. Mrs. Burney in her rigid unbearable black: Mrs. Worthington speaks to me, but Dewey is dead. Oh, the poor man, his gray face. My boy is dead, but his boy has come home, come home . . . with a woman. What is she doing here? Mrs. Mitchell says. . . . Mrs. Mitchell says . . . that Saunders girl is engaged to him. She was downtown yesterday almost nekkid. With the sun on her. . . . She wiped her eyes again under inevitable spring.

Donald Mahon, hearing voices: "Carry on, Joe."

"I come to see how your boy is getting along, what with everything." (Dewey, my boy.)

(I miss you like the devil, Dick. Someone to sleep with? I don't know. Oh, Dick, Dick. You left no mark on me, nothing. Kiss me through my hair, Dick, with all your ugly body, and let's don't ever see each other again, ever. . . . No, we won't, dear, ugly Dick.)

(Yes, that was Donald. He is dead.) "He is much better,

thank you.   Give him a few weeks' rest and he will be well
again."

"I am so glad, so glad," she answered, pitying him, envying
him. (My son died, a hero: Mrs. Worthington, Mrs. Saunders, chat with me about nothing at all.) "Poor boy, don't
he remember his friends at all?"

"Yes, yes." (This was Donald, my son.) "Donald, don't
you remember Mrs. Burney? She is Dewey's mother, you
know."

(. . . but not forever. I wish you all the luck and love
in the world. Wish me luck, dear Dick. . . .)

Donald Mahon, hearing voices: "Carry on, Joe."

The way that girl goes on with men! she thought exultantly.
Dewey may be dead, but thank God he ain't engaged to her.
"Your boy is home, he'll be married soon and everything.
So nice for you, so nice. . . ."

"There, there," the rector said, touching her shoulder
kindly, "you must come often to see him."

"Yes, I will come often," she replied through her black-
bordered cotton handkerchief. "It's so nice he come home
safe and well. Some didn't." (Dewey, Dewey.)

The sun flamed slowly across the wistaria, seeking interstices. She would see Mrs. Worthington downtown now,
probably. Mrs. Worthington would ask her how she was, how
her husband was. (My rheumatism, but I am old. Yes,
yes. When we get old. . . . You are old, too, she would
think with comfortable malice, older than me. Old, old,
too old for things like this to happen to us. He was so good
to me, so big and strong: brave. . . .) She rose and someone
handed her the cotton umbrella.

"Yes, yes. I will come again to see him." (Poor boy.
Poor man, his face: so gray.)

The lawn mower chattered slowly, reluctantly breaking the

evening. Mrs. Burney, disturbing bees, crossed grass blindly. Someone passed her at the gate and remarking an arching thrust of poorly laid concrete and a broken drain, she slanted her umbrella backward, shielding her neat, black-clad, airproof back.

Sucking silver sound of pigeons slanting to and from the spire like smears of soft paint on a cloudless sky. The sun lengthened the shadow of the wistaria-covered wall, immersing the grouped chairs in cool shadow. Waiting for sunset.

(Dick, my love, that I did not love, Dick, your ugly body breaking into mine like a burglar, my body flowing away, washing away all trace of yours. . . . Kiss and forget me: remember me only to wish me luck, dear, ugly, dead Dick. . . .)

(This was my son, Donald. He is dead.)

Gilligan, crossing the lawn, said: "Who was that?"

"Mrs. Burney," the rector told him. "Her son was killed. You've probably heard of him downtown."

"Yeh, I've heard of him. He was the one under indictment for stealing fifty pounds of sugar and they let him go to enlist, wasn't he?"

"There were stories. . . ." The rector's voice died away.

Donald Mahon, hearing silence: "You stopped, Joe."

Gilligan stood near him settling the colored glasses over his eyes. "Sure, Loot. More Rome?"

The shadow of the wall took them completely and at last he said:

"Carry on, Joe."

5

She missed Mrs. Worthington. She saw the old woman drive smoothly away from Price's in her car, alone in the back seat. The negro driver's head was round as a cannon ball

and Mrs. Burney watched it draw away, smelling gasoline.
The shadow of the courthouse was like thinned tobacco smoke
filling one side of the square, and standing in the door of
a store she saw an acquaintance, a friend of her son's. He
had been in Dewey's company, an officer or something, but
he hadn't got killed, not him! Trust them generals and
things.

(No, no! I won't feel like this! He done the best he
could. It ain't his fault if he wasn't brave enough to get
killed, like Dewey was. They are all jealous of Dewey anyway: won't talk about him except that he done what was
right. Done what was right! Didn't I know he would?
Dewey, Dewey. So young he was, so big and brave. Until
that Green man took him off and got him killed.)

She felt sorry for the man, felt kindly toward him, pitying
him. She stopped beside him. Yes, ma'am, he was all right.
Yes, the other boys were all right.

"But then you wasn't killed," she explained. "All soldiers
wasn't like Dewey: so brave—foolhardy, almost. . . . I always told him not to let that Green get him—get him——"

"Yes, yes," he agreed, looking at her meticulous, bent
neatness.

"He was all right? He didn't want for nothing?"

"No, no, he was all right," he assured her. Sunset was
almost come. Sparrows in a final delirium in the dusty elms,
the last wagons going slowly country-ward.

"Men don't know," she said bitterly. "You probably never
done for him what you could. That Mr. Green. . . . I
always misdoubted him."

"He is dead, too, you know," he reminded her.

(I won't be unjust to him!) "You was a officer or something: seems like you'd have took better care of a boy you
knowed."

"We did all we could for him," he told her patiently. The square, empty of wagons, was quiet. Women went slowly in the last of the sun, meeting husbands, going home to supper. She felt her rheumatism more, now that the air was getting cooler, and she became restive in her fretful black.

"Well. You seen his grave, you say. . . . You are sure he was all right?" So big and strong he was, so good to her.

"Yes, yes. He was all right."

Madden watched her bent, neat rotundity going down the street among shadows, beneath metallic awnings. The shadow of the courthouse had taken half the town like a silent victorious army, not firing a shot. The sparrows completed a final dusty delirium and went away, went away across evening into morning, retracing months: a year:

Someone on a fire-step had shouted Gas and the officer leaped among them striking, imploring. Then he saw the officer's face in red and bitter relief as the man on the fire-step, sharp against the sorrowful dawn, turned screaming, You have got us killed, and shot him in the face at point-blank range.

6

San Francisco, Cal.
April 14, 1919.

Dear Margaret—

I got your letter and I intended to answering it sooner but I have been busy running around. Yes she was not a bad kid she has shown me a good time no she is not so good looking but she takes a good photo she wants to go in the movies. And a director told her she photographs better than any girl he has seen. She has a car and she

is a swell dancer but of coarse I just like to play around
with her she is to young for me. To really care for. No
I have not gone to work yet. This girl goes to the U and
she is talking about me going there next year. So I may
go there next year. Well there is no news I have done a
little flying but mostly dancing and running around. I have
got to go out on a party now or I would write more. Next
time more next time give my reguards to everybody I know.

Your sincere friend

JULIAN LOWE

7

Mahon liked music; so Mrs. Worthington sent her car
for them. Mrs. Worthington lived in a large, beautiful old
house which her husband, conveniently dead, had bequeathed,
with a colorless male cousin who had false teeth and no occu-
pation that anyone knew of, to her. The male cousin's articulation was bad (he had been struck in the mouth with an ax
in a dice game in Cuba during the Spanish-American War):
perhaps this was why he did nothing.

Mrs. Worthington ate too much and suffered from gout and
a flouted will. So her church connection was rather trying
to the minister and his flock. But she had money—that
panacea for all ills of the flesh and spirit. She believed in
rights for women, as long as women would let her dictate what
was right for them.

One usually ignored the male relation. But sometimes
one pitied him.

But she sent her car for them and with Mrs. Powers and
Mahon in the rear, and Gilligan beside the negro driver, they
rolled smoothly beneath elms, seeing stars in a clear sky,
smelling growing things, hearing a rhythmic thumping soon
to become music.

8

This, the spring of 1919, was the day of the Boy, of him who had been too young for soldiering. For two years he had had a dry time of it. Of course, girls had used him during the scarcity of men, but always in such a detached impersonal manner. Like committing fornication with a beautiful woman who chews gum steadily all the while. O Uniform, O Vanity. They had used him but when a uniform showed up he got the air.

Up to that time uniforms could all walk: they were not only fashionable and romantic, but they were also quite keen on spending what money they had and they were also going too far away and too immediately to tell on you. Of course it was silly that some uniforms had to salute others, but it was nice, too. Especially, if the uniform you had caught happened to be a salutee. And heaven only knows how much damage among feminine hearts a set of pilot's wings was capable of.

And the shows:

Beautiful, pure girls (American) in afternoon or evening gowns (doubtless under Brigade Orders) caught in deserted fire trenches by Prussian Hussars (on passes signed by Belasco) in parade uniform; courtesans in Paris frocks demoralizing Brigade staffs, having subalterns with arrow collar profiles and creased breech, whom the generals all think may be German spies, and handsome old generals, whom the subalterns all think may be German spies, glaring at each other across her languid body while corporal comedians entertain the beautiful-limbed and otherwise idle Red Cross nurses (American). The French women present are either marquises or whores or German spies, sometimes both, sometimes all three. The marquises may be told immediately because they all wear sabots, having given their shoes with the rest of their cloth-ing to the French army, retaining only a pair of forty carat diamond earrings. Their sons are all aviators who have been out on a patrol since the previous Tuesday, causing the mar-quises to be a trifle distrait. The regular whores patronize them, while the German spies make love to the generals.

A courtesan (doubtless also under Brigade Orders) later saves the sector by sex appeal after gun-powder had failed, and the whole thing is wound up with a sort of garden party near a papier-mâché dugout in which the army sits in sixty-pound packs, all three smoking cigarettes, while the Prussian Guard gnashes its teeth at them from an adjacent card-board trench.

A chaplain appears who, to indicate that the soldiers love him because he is one of them, achieves innuendoes about home and mother and fornication. A large new flag is flown and the enemy fires at it vainly with .22 rifles. The men on our side cheer, led by the padre.

"What," said a beautiful, painted girl, not listening, to James Dough who had been for two years a corporal-pilot in a French chasse escadrille, "is the difference between an American Ace and a French or British aviator?"

"About six reels," answered James Dough glumly (such a dull man! Where did Mrs. Wardle get him?) who had shot down thirteen enemy craft and had himself been crashed twice, giving him eleven points without allowing for evapora-tion.

"How nice. Is that so, really? You had movies in France, too, then?"

"Yes. Gave us something to do in our spare time."

"Yes," she agreed, offering him her oblivious profile. "You must have had an awfully good time while we poor women were slaving here rolling bandages and knitting things. I hope women can fight in the next war: I had much rather march and shoot guns than knit. Do you think they will let women fight in the next war?" she asked, watching a young man dancing, limber as a worm.

"I expect they'll have to." James Dough shifted his artificial leg, nursing his festering arm between the bones of which a tracer bullet had passed. "If they want to have another one."

"Yes." She yearned toward the agile, prancing youth. His body was young in years, his hair was glued smoothly to his skull. His face, under a layer of powder, was shaved and pallid, sophisticated, and he and his blonde and briefly-skirted partner slid and poised and drifted like a dream. The negro cornetist stayed his sweating crew and the assault arrested withdrew, leaving the walls of silence peopled by the unconquered defenders of talk. Boys of both sexes swayed arm in arm, taking sliding tripping steps, waiting for the music and the agile youth, lounging immaculately, said: "Have this dance?"

She said "Hel—lo," sweetly drawling. "Have you met Mr. Dough? Mr. Rivers, Mr. Dough. Mr. Dough is a visitor in town."

Mr. Rivers patronized Mr. Dough easily and repeated: "Dance the next?" Mr. Rivers had had a year at Princeton.

"I'm sorry. Mr. Dough doesn't dance," answered Miss Cecily Saunders faultlessly. Mr. Rivers, well bred, with all the benefits of a year at a cultural center, mooned his blank face at her.

"Aw, come on. You aren't going to sit out all evening, are you? What did you come here for?"

"No, no: later, perhaps. I want to talk to Mr. Dough. You hadn't thought of that, had you?"

He stared at her quietly and emptily. At last he mumbled "Sorry," and lounged away.

"Really," began Mr. Dough, "not on my account, you know. If you want to dance——"

"Oh, I have to see those—those infants all the time. Really, it is quite a relief to meet someone who knows more than dancing and—and—dancing. But tell me about yourself. Do you like Charlestown? I can see that you are accustomed to larger cities, but don't you find something charming about these small towns?"

Mr. Rivers roved his eye, seeing two girls watching him in poised invitation, but he moved on toward a group of men standing and sitting near the steps, managing in some way to create the illusion of being both participants and spectators at the same time. They were all of a kind: there was a kinship like an odor among them, a belligerent self-effacement. Wallflowers. Wallflowers. Good to talk to the hostess and dance with the duds. But even the talkative hostess had given them up now. One or two of them, bolder than the rest, but disseminating that same faint identical odor stood beside girls, waiting for the music to start again, but the majority of them herded near the steps, touch, ing each other as if for mutual protection. Mr. Rivers heard phrases in bad French and he joined them, aware of his own fitted dinner jacket revealing his matchless linen.

"May I see you a minute, Madden?"

The man quietly smoking detached himself from the group. He was not big, yet there was something big and calm about him: a sense of competent inertia after activity.

"Yes?" he said.

"Do me a favor, will you?"

"Yes?" the man repeated courteously non-committal.

"There's a man here who can't dance, that nephew of Mrs. Wardle's, that was hurt in the war. Cecily—I mean Miss Saunders—has been with him all evening. She wants to dance."

The other watched him with calm intentness and Mr. Rivers suddenly lost his superior air.

"To tell the truth, I want to dance with her. Would you mind sitting with him a while? I'd be awfully obliged to you if you would."

"Does Miss Saunders want to dance?"

"Sure she does. She said so." The other's gaze was so penetrating that he felt moisture and drew his handkerchief, wiping his powdered brow lightly, not to disarrange his hair. "God damn it," he burst out, "you soldiers think you own things, don't you?"

Columns, imitation Doric, supported a remote small balcony, high and obscure, couples strolled in, awaiting the music, talk and laughter and movement distorted by a lax transparency of curtains inside the house. Along the balustrade of the veranda red eyes of cigarettes glowed; a girl stooping ostrich-like drew up her stocking and light from a window found her young shapeless leg. The negro cornetist, having learned in his thirty years a century of the white man's lust, blinked his dispassionate eye, leading his crew in a fresh assault. Couples erupted in, clasped and danced; vague blurs locked together on the lawn beyond the light.

". . . Uncle Joe, Sister Kate, all shimmy like jelly on a plate. . . ."

Mr. Rivers felt like a chip in a current: he knew a sharp puerile anger. Then as they turned the angle of the porch he saw Cecily clothed delicately in a silver frock, fragile as spun glass. She carried a green feather fan and her slim, animated turned body, her nervous prettiness, filled him with speculation. The light falling diffidently on her, felt her arm, her short body, suavely indicated her long, virginal legs.

". . . Uncle Bud, ninety-two, shook his cane and shimmied too. . . ."

Dr. Gary danced by without his glass of water: they avoided him and Cecily looked up, breaking her speech.

"Oh, Mr. Madden! How do you do?" She gave him her hand and presented him to Mr. Dough. "I'm awfully flattered that you decided to speak to me—or did Lee have to drag you over? Ah, that's how it was. You were going to ignore me, I know you were. Of course we can't hope to compete with French women——"

Madden protested conventionally and she made room for him beside her.

"Sit down. Mr. Dough was a soldier, too, you know."

Mr. Rivers said heavily: "Mr. Dough will excuse you. How about a dance? Time to go home soon."

She civilly ignored him and James Dough shifted his leg. "Really, Miss Saunders, please dance, I wouldn't spoil your evening for anything."

"Do you hear that, Mr. Madden? The man is driving me away. Would you do that?" she tilted her eyes at him effectively. Then she turned to Dough with restrained graceful impulsiveness. "I still call him Mr. Madden, though we have known each other all our lives. But then he was in the war, and I wasn't. He is so—so experienced, you see. And I am only a girl. If I had been a boy like Lee I'd have gone and been a lieutenant in shiny boots or a general or something by now. Wouldn't I?" Her turning body was graceful, impulsive: a fragile spontaneity. "I cannot call you mister any more. Do you mind?"

"Let's dance." Mr. Rivers, tapping his foot to the music,

watched this with sophisticated boredom. He yawned openly.
"Let's dance."

"Rufus, ma'am," said Madden.

"Rufus. And you mustn't say ma'am to me any longer.
You won't, will you?"

"No ma—I mean, no."

"Oh, you nearly forgot then——"

"Let's dance," repeated Mr. Rivers.

"—but you won't forget any more. You won't, will you?"

"No, no."

"Don't let him forget, Mr. Dough. I am depending on
you."

"Good, good. But you go and dance with Mr. Smith
here."

She rose. "He is sending me away," she stated with mock
humility. Then she shrugged narrowly, nervously. "I know
we aren't as attractive as French women, but you must make
the best of us. Poor Lee, here, doesn't know any French
women so we can please him. But you soldiers don't like us
any more, I'm afraid."

"Not at all: we give you up to Mr. Lee only on condition that you come back to us."

"Now that's better. But you are saying that just to be
polite," she accused.

"No, no, if you don't dance with Mr. Lee, here, you will be
impolite. He has asked you several times."

She shrugged again nervously. "So I guess I must dance,
Lee. Unless you have changed your mind, too, and don't
want me?"

He took her hand. "Hell, come on."

Restraining him, she turned to the other two, who had
risen also. "You will wait for me?"

They assured her, and she released them. Dough's creaking, artificial knee was drowned by the music and she gave herself to Mr. Rivers' embrace. They took the syncopation, he felt her shallow breast and her knees briefly, and said: "What you doing to him?" slipping his arm further around her, feeling the swell of her hip under his hand.

"Doing to him?"

"Ah, let's dance."

Locked together they poised and slid and poised, feeling the beat of the music, toying with it, eluding it, seeking it again, drifting like a broken dream.

9

George Farr, from the outer darkness, glowered at her, watching her slim body cut by a masculine arm, watching her head beside another head, seeing her limbs beneath her silver dress anticipating her partner's limbs, seeing the luminous plane of her arm across his black shoulders and her fan drooping from her arched wrist like a willow at evening. He heard the rhythmic troubling obscenities of saxophones, he saw vague shapes in the darkness and he smelled the earth and things growing in it. A couple passed them and a girl said, "Hello, George. Coming in?" "No," he told her, wallowing in all the passionate despair of spring and youth and jealousy, getting of them an exquisite bliss.

His friend beside him, a soda-clerk, spat his cigarette. "Let's have another drink."

The bottle was a combination of alcohol and sweet syrup purloined from the drug store. It was temporarily hot to the throat, but this passed away leaving in its place a sweet, inner fire, a courage.

"To hell with them," he said.

"You ain't going in, are you?" his friend asked. They had

another drink. The music beat on among youthful leaves, into the darkness, beneath the gold and mute cacophony of stars. The light from the veranda mounting was lost, the house loomed huge against the sky: a rock against which waves of trees broke, and breaking were forever arrested; and stars were golden unicorns neighing unheard through blue meadows, spurning them with hooves sharp and scintillant as ice. The sky, so remote, so sad, spurned by the unicorns of gold, that, neighing soundlessly from dusk to dawn, had seen them, had seen her—her taut body prone and naked as a narrow pool sweetly dividing: two silver streams from a single source. . . .

"I'm not going in," he answered, moving away. They crossed the lawn and in the shadow of a crepe-myrtle one with a sound of breath became two. They walked quickly on, averting their eyes.

"Hell, no," he repeated, "I'm not going in."

10

This was the day of the Boy, male and female.

"Look at them, Joe," Mrs. Powers said, "sitting there like lost souls waiting to get into hell."

The car had stopped broad-side on, where they could get a good view.

"They don't look like they're sitting to me," Gilligan answered with enthusiasm. "Look at them two: look where he's got his hand. This is what they call polite dancing, is it? I never learned it: I would have got throwed out of any place I ever danced doing that. But I had a unfortunate youth: I never danced with nice people."

Through two heavy identical magnolias the lighted porch

was like a stage. The dancers moved, locked two and two, taking the changing light, eluding it.

". . . shake it and break it, don't let it fall. . . ."

Along the balustrade they sat like birds, effacingly belligerent. Wallflowers.

"No, no, I mean those ex-soldiers there. Look at them. Sitting there, talking their army French, kidding themselves. Why did they come, Joe?"

"Same reason we come. Like a show, ain't it? But how do you know they're soldiers? . . . Look at them two there," he crowed suddenly, with childish intentness. The couple slid and poised, losing the syncopation deliberately, seeking and finding it, losing it again. . . . Her limbs eluded his, anticipated his: the breath of a touch and an escape, which he, too, was quick to assist. Touch and retreat: no satiety. "Wow, if that tune ever stops!"

"Don't be silly, Joe. I know them. I have seen their sort at the canteen too often, acting just that way: poor kind dull boys going to war, and because they were going girls were nice to them. But now there is no war for them to go to. And look how the girls treat them."

"What was you saying?" asked Gilligan with detachment. He tore his eyes from the couple. "Wow, if the loot could see this it'd sure wake him up, wouldn't it?"

Mahon sat quietly beside Mrs. Powers. Gilligan turning in his seat beside the negro driver looked at his quiet shape. The syncopation pulsed about them, a reiteration of wind and strings warm and troubling as water. She leaned toward him.

"Like it, Donald?"

He stirred, raising his hand to his glasses.

"Come on, Loot," said Gilligan quickly; "don't knock 'em

off. We might lose 'em here." Mahon lowered his hand obediently. "Music's pretty good, ain't it?"

"Pretty good, Joe," he agreed.

Gilligan looked at the dancers again. "Pretty good ain't the half of it. Look at 'em."

". . . oh, oh, I wonder where my easy rider's gone. . . ."

He turned suddenly to Mrs. Powers. "You know who that is there?"

Mrs. Powers saw Dr. Gary, without his glass of water, she saw a feather fan like a willow at evening and the luminous plane of a bare arm upon conventional black. She saw two heads as one head, cheek to cheek, expressionless and fixed as a ritual above a slow synchronization of limbs. "That Saunders lady," Gilligan explained.

She watched the girl's graceful motion, a restrained delicate abandon, and Gilligan continued: "I think I'll go closer, with them birds sitting there. I got to see this."

They greeted him with the effusiveness of people who are brought together by invitation yet are not quite certain of themselves and of the spirit of the invitation; in this case the eternal country boys of one national mental state, lost in the comparative metropolitan atmosphere of one diametrically opposed to it. To feel provincial: finding that a certain conventional state of behavior has become inexplicably obsolete over night.

Most of them Gilligan knew by name and he sat also upon the balustrade. He was offered and accepted a cigarette and he perched among them while they talked loudly, drowning the intimation of dancers they could not emulate, of girls who once waited upon their favors and who now ignored them—the hang-over of warfare in a society tired of warfare. Puzzled and lost, poor devils. Once Society drank war, brought them into manhood with a cultivated taste for war;

but now Society seemed to have found something else for a beverage, while they were not yet accustomed to two and seventy-five per cent.

"Look at those kids that grew up while we were away," one advised him with passion. "The girls don't like it. But what can they do? We can't do them dances. It ain't just going through the motions. You could learn that, I guess. It's—it's—" he sought vainly for words. He gave it up and continued: "Funny, too. I learned things from French women. . . . Say, the girls don't like it, do they? They haven't changed that much, you know."

"Naw, they don't like it," Gilligan. answered. "Look at them two."

"Sure, they don't like it. These are nice girls: they will be the mothers of the next generation. Of course they don't like it."

"Somebody sure does, though," Gilligan replied. Dr. Gary passed, dancing smoothly, efficiently, quite decorous, yet enjoying himself. His partner was young and briefly skirted: you could see that she danced with him because it was the thing to dance with Dr. Gary—no one knew exactly why. She was conscious of physical freedom, of her young, uncorseted body, flat as a boy's and, like a boy's, pleasuring in freedom and motion, as though freedom and motion were water, pleasuring her flesh to the intermittent teasing of silk. Her glance followed over Dr. Gary's shoulder (it was masculine because it was drably conventional in black) an arrested seeking for a lost rhythm, lost deliberately. Dr. Gary's partner, skillfully following him, watched the other couple, ignoring the girl. (If there's justice in heaven, I'll get him next time.)

"Dancing with you," said Dr. Gary, "is like a poem by a

minor poet named Swinburne." Dr. Gary preferred Milton:
he had the passages all designated, like a play.

"Swinburne?" She smiled vaguely, watching the other
couple, not losing the rhythm, not cracking her paint. Her
face was smooth, as skillfully done and as artificial as an
orchid. "Did he write poems, too?" (Is he thinking of
Ella Wilcox or Irene Castle? He is a grand dancer: takes a
good dancer to get along with Cecily.) "I think Kipling is
awfully cute, don't you?" (What a funny dress Cecily has
on.)

Gilligan, watching the dancers, said: "What?"

The other repeated defensively: "He was in a French base.
Sure he was. Two or three years. Good fellow." He added:
"Even if he can dance like they do."

Light, motion, sound: no solidity. A turgid compulsion,
passionate and evanescent. And outside spring, like a young
girl reft of happiness and incapable of sorrow.

". . . throw it on the wall. Oh, oh, oh, oh . . ." ". . .
wont never forget his expression when he said, 'Jack, mine's
got syph. Had her . . . '" "shake it and break it, shake it.
. . ." "First night in Paris . . . then the other one. . . ."
". . . don't let it fall. . . ." ". . . with a gun . . . twenty
dollars in gold pinned to my. . . ." "I wonder where my
easy, easy rider's. . . ."

"Sure," Gilligan agreed. He wondered where Madden,
whom he liked, was, and not expecting an answer he was informed. (There she is again. Her feather fan like a willow at
evening, her arm crossing conventional black a slim warm
plane. Jove would have said, How virginal her legs are, but
Gilligan, not being Jove, said, For Christ's sake, wishing Donald Mahon were her partner or failing this, being glad he
couldn't see her.

The music stopped. The dancers stood waiting its re-newal. The hostess talking interminably appeared and as before a plague people scattered before her passage. Gilligan caught, submerged beneath waves of talk, suffered her, watching couples pass from the veranda onto the vague lawn. How soft their bodies look, their little backs and hips, he thought, saying, yes ma'am or no ma'am. At last he walked away and left her talking, and in a swing he saw Madden and a stranger.

"This is Mr. Dough," Madden said, greeting him. "How's Mahon?"

Gilligan shook hands. "He's outside there, now, with Mrs. Powers."

"He is? Mahon was with the British," he explained to his companion. "Aviation."

He betrayed a faint interest. "R.A.F.?"

"I guess so," Gilligan replied. "We brought him over to hear the music a while."

"Brought him?"

"Got his in the head. Don't remember much," Madden informed the other. "Did you say Mrs. Powers is with him?" he asked Gilligan.

"Yeh, she came. Why not come out and speak to her?"

Madden looked at his companion. Dough shifted his cork leg. "I think not," he said. "I'll wait for you."

Madden rose. "Come on," Gilligan said, "she'll be glad to see you. She ain't a bad sort, as Madden can tell you."

"No, I'll wait here, thanks. But come back, will you?"

Madden read his unexpressed thought. "She's dancing now. I'll be back before then."

They left him lighting a cigarette. The negro cornetist had restrained his men and removed them temporarily and the porch was deserted save for the group sitting on the balustrade. These, the hostess, with a renascence of optimism, had run to earth and captured.

Gilligan and Madden crossed grass, leaving lights behind. "Mrs. Powers, you remember Mr. Madden," Gilligan informed her formally. He was not big, yet there was something big and calm about him, a sense of competent inertia after activity. Madden saw her colorless face against the canopied darkness of the car, her black eyes and her mouth like a scar. Beside her Mahon sat motionless and remote, waiting for music which you could not tell whether or not he heard.

"Good evening, ma'am," Madden said enveloping her firm, slow hand, remembering a figure sharp against the sky screaming, You got us killed and firing point-blank into another man's face red and bitter in a relief of transient flame against a sorrowful dawn.

II

Jones, challenging the competition, danced with her twice, once for six feet and then for nine feet. She could not dance with the muscular facility of some of the other girls. Perhaps this was the reason she was in such demand. Dancing with the more skilled ones was too much like dancing with agile boys. Anyway, men all seemed to want to dance with her, to touch her.

Jones, foiled the second time, became yellowly speculative: tactical; then, watching his chance, he cut in upon glued hair and a dinner coat. The man raised his empty ironed face fretfully, but Jones skillfully cut her out of the prancing herd and into the angle made by the corner of the balustrade. Here only his back could be assailed.

He knew his advantage was but temporary, so he spoke quickly.

"Friend of yours here to-night."

Her feather fan drew softly across his neck. He sought her knee with his and she eluded him with efficiency, trying vainly to maneuver from the corner. One desiring to cut in importuned him from behind and she said with exasperation: "Do you dance, Mr. Jones? They have a good floor here. Suppose we try it."

"Your friend Donald dances. Ask him for one," he told her, feeling her shallow breast and her nervous efforts to evade him. One importuned him from behind and she raised her pretty unpretty face. Her hair was soft and fine, carelessly caught about her head and her painted mouth was purple in this light.

"Here? Dancing?"

"With his two Niobes. I saw the female one and I imagine the male one is here also."

"Niobes?"

"That Mrs. Powers, or whatever her name is."

She held her head back so as to see his face. "You are lying."

"No, I'm not. They are here."

She stared at him. He could feel her fan drooping from her arched wrist on his cheek softly and one importuned him from behind. "Sitting out now, in a car," he added.

"With Mrs. Powers?"

"Watch your step, sister, or she'll have him."

She slipped from him suddenly. "If you aren't going to dance——"

One importuning him from behind repeated tirelessly, "May I cut in," and she evaded Jones' arm.

"Oh, Lee. Mr. Jones doesn't dance."

"M'I've this dance," mumbled the conventional one conventionally, already encircling her. Jones stood baggy and yellow, yellowly watching her fan upon her partner's coat, like a hushed splash of water, her arching neck and her arm crossing a black shoulder with luminous warmth, the indicated silver evasion of her limbs anticipating her partner's like a broken dream.

"Got a match?" Jones, pausing, asked abruptly of a man sitting alone in a swing. He lit his pipe and lounged in slow and fat belligerence among a group sitting upon the balustrade near the steps, like birds. The negro cornetist spurred his men to fiercer endeavor, the brass died and a plaintive minor of hushed voices carried the rhythm until the brass, suspiring again, took it. Jones sucked his pipe, thrusting his hands in his jacket and a slim arm slid suddenly beneath his tweed sleeve.

"Wait for me, Lee." Jones, looking around, remarked her fan and the glass-like fragility of her dress. "I must see some people in a car."

The boy's ironed face was a fretted fatuity above his immaculate linen. "Let me go with you."

"No, no. You wait for me. Mr. Jones will take me: you don't even know them. You dance until I come back. Promise?"

"But say——"

Her hand flashed slimly staying him. "No, no. Please. Promise?"

He promised and stood to stare at them as they descended the steps passing beneath the two magnolias and so on into darkness, where her dress became a substanceless articulation beside the man's shapeless tweed. . . . After a while he turned and walked down the emptying veranda. Where'd that slob come from? he wondered, seeing two girls watching him in poised invitation. Do they let anybody in here?

As he hesitated, the hostess appeared talking interminably, but he circumvented her with skill of long practice. Beyond a shadowed corner in the half-darkness of a swing a man sat alone. He approached and before he could make his request the man extended a box of matches.

"Thanks," he murmured, without surprise, lighting a cigarette. He strolled away, and the owner of the matches fingered the small, crisp wood box, wondering mildly who the third one would be.

12

"No, no, let's go to them first."

She arrested their progress and after a time succeeded in releasing her arm. As they stood, a couple passed them, and the girl, leaning to her, whispered: "See right through you. Stay out of the light."

They passed on and she looked after them, watching the other girl. Cat! What a queer dress she is wearing. Funny ankles. Funny. Poor girl.

But she had little time for impersonal speculation, being attached temporarily to Jones. "No, no," she repeated, twisting the hand he held, drawing him in the direction of the car. Mrs. Powers, looking over Madden's head, saw them.

Jones released the fragile writhing of her fingers, and she sped delicately over the damp grass. He followed fatly and she put her hands on the door of the car, her narrow nervous hands, between which the green fan splashed graciously.

"Oh, how do you do? I didn't have any idea you were coming! If I had I would have arranged partners for you. I'm sure you dance awfully well. But then, as soon as the men see you here you won't lack for partners, I know."

(What does she want with him now? Watching me: doesn't trust me with him.)

"Awfully nice dance. And Mr. Gilligan!" (What's she wanta come worrying him now for? She bothers damn little

while he's sitting at home there.) "Of course, one simply
does not see Donald without Mr. Gilligan. It must be nice to
have Mr. Gilligan fond of you like that. Don't you think so,
Mrs. Powers?" Her braced straightening arms supportèd a
pliant slow backward curve from her hips. "And Rufus.
(Yes, she is pretty. And silly. But—but pretty.) You deserted me for another woman! Don't say you didn't. I
tried to make him dance with me, Mrs. Powers, but he
wouldn't do it. Perhaps you had better luck?" A dropped
knee molded the glass-like fragility of her silver dress. "Ah,
you needn't say anything: we know how attractive Mrs.
Powers is, don't we, Mr. Jones?" (See your behind, the shape
of it. And your whole leg, when you stand like that. Knows
it, too.)

Her eyes became hard, black. "You told me they were
dancing," she accused.

"He can't dance, you know," Mrs. Powers said. "We
brought him so he could hear the music."

"Mr. Jones told me you and he were dancing. And I
believed him: I seem to know so much less than other people
about him. But, of course, he is sick, he does not—remember
his old friends, now that he has made new ones."

(Is she going to cry? It would be just like her. The fool,
the little fool.) "I think you are not fair to him. But won't
you get in and sit down? Mr. Madden, will you——?"

Madden had already opened the door.

"No, no: if he likes the music I'd only disturb him. He
had much rather sit with Mrs. Powers, I know."

(Yes, she's going to make a scene.) "Please. Just a
moment. He hasn't seen you to-day, you know."

She hesitated, then Jones regarded the dividing soft curves
of her thighs and the fleeting exposure of a stocking, and borrowed a match from Gilligan. The music had ceased and

through the two identical magnolias the porch was like an empty stage. The negro driver's head was round as a capped cannon-ball: perhaps he slept. She mounted and sank into the dark seat beside Mahon, sitting still and resigned. Mrs. Powers suddenly spoke:

"Do you dance, Mr. Madden?"

"Yes, a little," he admitted. She descended from the car and turning, met Cecily's startled shallow face.

"I'll leave you to visit with Donald while I have a dance or two with Mr. Madden, shall I?" She took Madden's arm. "Don't you want to come in, too, Joe?"

"I guess not," Gilligan answered. "Competition'll be too strong for me. I'll get you to learn me private, some time, so I can be a credit to you."

Cecily, in exasperation, saw the other woman stealing part of her audience. But here were still Jones and Gilligan. Jones climbed heavily into the vacated seat, uninvited. Cecily gave him a fierce glance and turned her back upon him, feeling his arm against her side.

"Donald, sweetheart," she said, putting her arm about Mahon. From here she could not see the scar so she drew his face to hers with her hand, laying her cheek against his. Feeling her touch, hearing voices, he stirred. "It's Cecily, Donald," she said sweetly.

"Cecily," he parroted.

"Yes. Put your arm around me like you used to, Donald, dear heart." She moved nervously, but the length of Jones' arm remained against her closely as though it were attached by suction, like an octopus' tentacle. Trying to avoid him, her clasp about Mahon tightened convulsively, and he raised his hand, touching her face, fumbling at his glasses. "Easy there, Loot," Gilligan warned quickly, and he lowered his hand.

Cecily kissed his cheek swiftly and sat up, releasing him. "Oh, there goes the music again, and I have this dance." She stood up in the car, looking about. One lounging immaculately, smoking, strolled past. "Oh, Lee," she called, in happy relief, "here I am."

She opened the door and sprang out as the conventional one approached. Jones descended fatly, baggily, and stood dragging his jacket across his thick, heavy hips, staring yellowly at Mr. Rivers. Her body poised again, turning, and she said to Gilligan: "You aren't dancing to-night?"

"Not like that," he replied, "no, ma'am. Where I come from you'd have to have a license to dance that way."

Her laugh was in three notes and she was like a swept tree. Her eyes, beneath lowered lids, her teeth, between her purple lips, glittered briefly.

"I think that's awfully clever. And Mr. Jones doesn't dance either, so all I have left is Lee."

Lee—Mr. Rivers—stood waiting, and Jones said heavily: "This is my dance."

"I'm sorry. I promised Lee," she answered swiftly. "But you cut in, won't you?" Her hand was briefly on his sleeve and Jones, contemplating Mr. Rivers, yellowly repeated:

"This is my dance."

Mr. Rivers looked at him and then looked quickly away.

"Oh, beg pardon. Your dance?"

"Lee!" she said sharply, reaching her hand again. Mr. Rivers met Jones' stare once more.

"Beg pardon," he muttered, "I'll cut in." He lounged onward. Cecily let her glance follow him, then she shrugged and turned to Jones. Her neck, her arm, took faint light warmly, smoothly. She took Jones' tweed sleeve.

"Say," Gilligan murmured, watching their retreat, "you can see right through her."

"Dat's de war," explained the negro driver, sleeping again immediately.

13

Jones dragged her resisting among shadows. A crepe-myrtle bush obscured them.

"Let me go!" she said, struggling.

"What's the matter with you? You kissed me once, didn't you?"

"Let me go," she repeated.

"What for? For that goddam dead man? What does he care about you?" He held her until her nervous energy, deserting her, left her fragile as a captured bird. He stared at the white blur which was her face and she was aware of the shapeless looming bulk of his body in the darkness, smelling wool and tobacco.

"Let me go," she repeated piteously, and finding herself suddenly free, she fled across grass, knowing dew on her shoes, seeing gratefully a row of men sitting like birds on the balustrade. Mr. Rivers' ironed face, above his immaculate linen, met her and she grasped his arm.

"Let's dance, Lee," she said thinly, striking her body sharply against him, taking the broken suggestion of saxophones.

14

Mrs. Powers had a small triumph: the railbirds had given her a "rush."

"Say," they had nudged each other, "look who Rufe's got."

And while the hostess stood in effusive volubility beside her straight, dark dress, two of them, whispering together, beckoned Madden aside.

"Powers?" they asked, when he joined them. But he hushed them.

"Yes, that was him. But that's not for talk, you know. Don't tell them, see." His glance swept the group along the rail. "Won't do any good, you know."

"Hell, no," they assured him. Powers!

And so they danced with her, one or two at first, then having watched her firm, capable performance, all of them that danced at all were soon involved in a jolly competition, following her while she danced with another of their number, importuning her between dances: some of them even went so far as to seek out other partners whom they knew.

Madden after a time merely looked on, but his two friends were assiduous, tireless; seeing that she did not dance too long with the poor dancers, fetching her cups of insipid punch; kind and a little tactless.

Her popularity brought the expected harvest of feminine speculation. Her clothes were criticized, her "nerve" in coming to a dance in a street dress, in coming at all. Living in a house with two young men, one of them a stranger. No other woman there . . . except a servant. And there had been something funny about that girl, years ago. Mrs. Wardle spoke to her, however. But she speaks to everyone who can't avoid her. And Cecily Saunders stopped between dances, holding her arm, chatting in her coarse, nervous, rushing speech, rolling her eyes about at all the inevitable men, talking all the time. . . . The negro cornetist unleashed his indefatigable pack anew and the veranda broke again into clasped couples.

Mrs. Powers, catching Madden's eye, signaled him. "I must go," she said. "If I have to drink another cup of that punch——"

They threaded their way among dancers, followed by her

protesting train. But she was firm and they told her good-night with regret and gratitude, shaking her hand.

"It was like old times," one of them diffidently phrased it, and her slow, friendly, unsmiling glance took them all.

"Wasn't it? Again soon, I hope. Good-bye, good-bye." They watched her until her dark dress merged with shadow beyond the zone of light. The music swept on, the brass swooned away and the rhythm was carried by a hushed plain-tive minor of voices until the brass recovered.

"Say, you could see right through her," Gilligan remarked with interest as they came up. Madden opened the door and helped her in, needlessly.

"I'm tired, Joe. Let's go."

The negro driver's head was round as a capped cannon-ball and he was not asleep. Madden stood aside, hearing the spitting engine merge into a meshed whine of gears, watching them roll smoothly down the drive.

Powers . . . a man jumping along a trench of demoralized troops caught in a pointless hysteria. Powers. A face briefly spitted on the flame of a rifle: a white moth beneath a reluctant and sorrowful dawn.

15

George Farr and his friend the soda-clerk walked beneath trees that in reverse motion seemed to swim backward above them, and houses were huge and dark or else faintly luminous shapes of flattened lesser dark where no trees were. People were asleep in them, people lapped in slumber, temporarily freed of the flesh. Other people elsewhere dancing under the spring sky: girls dancing with boys while other boys whose bodies had known all intimacies with the bodies of girls, walked dark streets alone, alone. . . .

"Well," his friend remarked, "we got two more good drinks left."

He drank fiercely, feeling the fire in his throat become an inner grateful fire, pleasuring in it like a passionate muscular ecstasy. (Her body prone and naked as a narrow pool, flowing away like two silver streams from a single source.) Dr. Gary would dance with her, would put his arm around her, anyone could touch her. (Except you: she doesn't even speak to you who have seen her prone and silver . . . moonlight on her like sweetly dividing water, marbled and slender and unblemished by any shadow, the sweet passion of her constricting arms that constricting hid her body beyond the obscuring prehensileness of her mouth—) Oh God, oh God!

"Say, whatcher say we go back to the store and mix another bottle?"

He did not answer and his friend repeated the suggestion.

"Let me alone," he said suddenly, savagely.

"Goddam you, I'm not hurting you!" the other answered with justifiable heat.

They stopped at a corner, where another street stretched away beneath trees into obscurity, in uncomfortable intimacy. (I'm sorry: I'm a fool. I'm sorry I flew out at you, who are not at all to blame.) He turned heavily.

"Well, I guess I'll go in. Don't feel so good to-night. See you in the morning."

His friend accepted the unspoken apology. "Sure. See you to-morrow."

The other's coatless figure faded and after a while his footsteps died away. And George Farr had the town, the earth, the world to himself and his sorrow. Music came faint as a troubling rumor beneath the spring night, sweetened by distance: a longing knowing no ease. (Oh God, oh God!)

CHAPTER VI

At last George Farr gave up trying to see her. He had 'phoned vainly and time after time, at last the telephone became the end in place of the means: he had forgotten why he wanted to reach her. Finally he told himself that he hated her, that he would go away; finally he was going to as much pains to avoid her as he had been to see her. So he slunk about the streets like a criminal, avoiding her, feeling his very heart stop when he did occasionally see her unmistakable body from a distance. And at night he lay sleepless and writhing to think of her, then to rise and don a few garments and walk past her darkened house, gazing in slow misery at the room in which he knew she lay, soft and warm, in intimate slumber, then to return to home and bed, to dream of her brokenly.

When her note came at last, he knew relief, sharp and bitter as the pain had been. When he took the square white paper from the post office, when he saw her nervous spidery script sprawled thinly across it, he felt something like a shocking silent concussion at the base of his brain. I won't go, he told himself, knowing that he would, and he re-read it, wondering if he could bear to see her, if he could speak to her, touch her again.

He was ahead of the appointed time, sitting hidden from view at a turn of the stairs ascending to the balcony. The stairs were enclosed by a solid wood balustrade and from the foot of the steps the long tunnel of the drug store swept toward light and the entrance, a tunnel filled with the mingled scents of carbolic and sweet syrups: a medicated, a synthetic purity.

He saw her as she entered the door and, rising, he saw her pause on seeing him, then, as in a dream, silhouetted against the door, with light toying with her white dress, giving it a shallow nimbus, she came tap-tapping on her high heels toward him. He sat back trembling and heard her mount the steps. He saw her dress, and feeling his breath catch, he raised his eyes to her face as without pausing she sank into his arms like a settling bird.

"Cecily, oh, Cecily," he said brokenly, taking her kiss. He withdrew his mouth. "You damn near killed me."

She drew his face quickly back to hers, murmuring against his cheek. He held her close and they sat so for a long time. At last he whispered: "You'll ruin your dress sitting here." But she only shook her head, clinging to him. Finally she sat up.

"Is this my drink?" she asked, picking up one of the glassed, sweetish liquids beside him. She put the other glass in his hand, and he closed his fingers about it, still looking at her.

"Now, we'll have to get married," he said, fatuously.

"Yes?" sipping her drink.

"Well, won't we?" he asked, in surprise.

"You've got it backward. Now we don't have to get married." She gave him a quick glance, and seeing his face, she laughed. Her occasional coarseness so out of keeping with her innate and utter delicacy always shocked him. But then George Farr, like most men, was by nature a prude. He eyed her with disapproval, silent. She set her glass down and leaned her breast against him. "George?"

He thawed, putting his arm about her, but she refused her

mouth. She thrust herself away from him and he, feeling that he had conquered, released her.

"But aren't you going to marry me?"

"Darling, aren't we already married, now? Do you doubt me, or is it only a marriage license will keep you true to me?"

"You know it isn't." He couldn't tell her that it was jealousy, that he didn't trust her. "It's only that——"

"Only what?"

"Only that if you won't marry me, you don't love me."

She moved from him. Her eyes became dark blue. "Can you say that?" She looked away, and her movement was half shiver, half shrug. "I might have known it, though. Well, I've been a fool, I guess. You were just—just passing the time with me, then?"

"Cecily—" trying to take her in his arms again. She evaded him and rose.

"I don't blame you. I suppose that's what any man would have done in your place. That's all men ever want of me, anyway. So it might as well have been you, as anyone. . . . Only I'm sorry you didn't tell me before—sooner, George. I thought you were different." She gave him her narrow back. How little, how—how helpless she is! And I have hurt her, he thought, in sharp pain, rising and putting his arm about her, careless of who might see.

"Don't, don't!" she whispered quickly turning. Her eyes were quite green again. "Someone will see! Sit down!"

"Not till you take that back."

"Sit down, sit down! Please, George! Please, please!"

"Take that back, then."

Her eyes were dark again, and he read terror in her face, and he released her, sitting down again.

"Promise me not ever, ever, ever to do that again."

He promised dully and she sat beside him. She slid her hand into his and he looked up.

"Why do you treat me like this?"

"Like what?" he asked.

"Saying I don't love you. What other proof do you want? What other proof can I give? What do you consider proof? Tell me: I'll try to do it." She looked at him in delicate humility.

"I'm sorry: forgive me," he said abjectly.

"I've already forgiven you. It's forgetting it I can't promise. I don't doubt you, George. Or I couldn't have. . . ." Her voice died away and she clutched his hand convulsively, releasing it. She rose. "I must go."

He caught her hand. It was unresponsive. "May I see you this afternoon?"

"Oh, no. I can't come back this afternoon. I have some sewing to do."

"Oh, come on, put it off. Don't treat me again like you did. I nearly went crazy. I swear I did."

"Sweetheart, I can't, I simply can't. Don't you know I want to see you as badly as you want to see me; that I would come if I could?"

"Let me come down there, then."

"I believe you are crazy," she told him, with contemplation. "Don't you know I'm not supposed to see you at all?"

"Then I'm coming to-night."

"Hush!" she whispered, quickly, descending the steps.

"But I am," he repeated stubbornly. She looked hurriedly about the store, and her heart turned to water. Here, sitting at a table in the alcove made by the ascending stairs, was that fat man, with a half-empty glass before him.

She knew dreadful terror, and as she stared at his round, bent head, all her blood drained from her icy heart. She

put her hand on the railing, lest she fall. Then this gave
way to anger. The man was a nemesis: every time she had
seen him since that first day at luncheon with Uncle Joe,
he had flouted her, had injured her with diabolic ingenuity.
And now, if he had heard——

George had risen, following her, but at her frantic gesture,
her terror-stricken face, he retreated again. Then she changed
her expression as readily as you would a hat. She descended
the steps.

"Good morning, Mr. Jones."

Jones looked up with his customary phlegmatic calm, then
he rose, lazily courteous. She watched him narrowly with
the terror-sharpened cunning of an animal, but his face and
manner told nothing.

"Good morning, Miss Saunders."

"You have the morning coca-cola habit, too, I see. Why
didn't you come up and join me?"

"I am still cursing myself for missing that pleasure. You
see, I didn't know you were alone." His yellow bodiless
stare was as impersonal as the jars of yellowish liquid in the
windows and her heart sank.

"I didn't see nor hear you come in, or I would have called
to you."

He was non-committal. "Thank you. The misfortune is
mine, however."

She said suddenly: "I wonder if you will do me a favor?
I have a thousand million things to do this morning. Will
you go with me and help me remember them—do you mind?"
Her eyes held a desperate coquetry.

Jones' eyes were fathomless, slowly yellow. "I'll be delighted."

"Finish your drink, then."

George Farr's good-looking face, wrung and jealous, peered

down at them. She made no sign, yet there was such pitiful
terror in her whole attitude that even George's dull and
jealous intelligence took her meaning. His face sank again
from view. Jones said:

"Let the drink go. I don't know why I keep on trying
the things. Make myself think I have a highball, perhaps."

She laughed in three notes. "You can't expect to satisfy
tastes like that in this town. In Atlanta now——"

"Yes, you can do lots of things in Atlanta you can't do
here."

She laughed again, flatteringly, and they moved up the anti-
septic tunnel of the drug store, toward the entrance. She
could laugh in such a way as to lend the most innocent
remark a double entendre: you immediately accepted the fact
that you had said something clever, without recalling what
it was at all. Jones' yellow idol's stare remarked her body's
articulation, her pretty, nervous face, while George Farr, in
a sick, dull rage, watched them in silhouette, flatly. Then
they reassumed depth and she, fragile as a Tanagra, and
he, slouching and shapeless and tweeded, disappeared.

2

"Say," said young Robert Saunders, "are you a soldier,
too?"

Jones, lunching to a slow completion, heavily courteous,
deferentially conversational, had already won Mrs. Saunders.
Of Mr. Saunders he was not so sure, nor did he care. Finding that the guest knew practically nothing about money
or crops or politics, Mr. Saunders soon let him be to gossip
trivially with Mrs. Saunders. Cecily was perfect: pleasantly
tactful, letting him talk. Young Robert though was bent on
a seduction of his own.

"Say," he repeated, for the third time, watching Jones' every move with admiration—"was you a soldier, too?"

"Were, Robert," corrected his mother.

"Yessum. Was you a soldier in the war?"

"Robert. Let Mr. Jones alone, now."

"Sure, old fellow," Jones answered. "I fought some."

"Oh, did you?" asked Mrs. Saunders. "How interesting," she commented without interest. Then: "I suppose you never happened to run across Donald Mahon in France, did you?"

"No. I had very little time in which to meet people, you see," replied Jones with gravity, who had never seen the Statute of Liberty—even from behind.

"What did you do?" asked young Robert indefatigable.

"I suppose so." Mrs. Saunders sighed with repletion and rang a bell. "The war was so big. Shall we go?"

Jones drew her chair and young Robert repeated tirelessly: "What did you do in the war? Did you kill folks?"

The older people passed on to the veranda. Cecily, with a gesture of her head, indicated a door and Jones entered, followed by young Robert, still importunate. The scent of Mr. Saunders' cigar wafted down the hall and into the room where they sat and young Robert, refraining his litany, caught Jones' yellow, fathomless eye, like a snake's, and young Robert's spine knew an abrupt, faint chill. Watching Jones cautiously he moved nearer his sister.

"Run along, Bobby. Don't you see that real soldiers never like to talk about themselves?"

He was nothing loath. He suddenly desired to be in the warm sun. This room had got cold. Still watching Jones he sidled past him to the door. "Well," he remarked, "I guess I'll be going."

"What did you do to him?" she asked, when he had gone.

"I? Nothing. Why?"

"You scared him, some way. Didn't you see how he watched you?"

"No, I didn't notice it." He filled his pipe, slowly.

"I suppose not. But then you frighten lots of people, don't you?"

"Not as many as you'd think. Lots of them I'd like to frighten can take care of themselves too well."

"Yes? But why frighten them?"

"Sometimes that's the only way to get what you want from people."

"Oh. . . . They have a name for that, haven't they? Blackmail, isn't it?"

"I don't know. Is it?"

She shrugged with assumed indifference. "Why do you ask me about it?"

His yellow stare became unbearable and she looked away. How quiet it is outside, under the spell of noon. Trees shaded the house, the room was dark and cool. Furniture was slow unemphatic gleams of lesser dark and young Robert Saunders, at the age of sixty-five, was framed and indistinct above the mantel: her grandfather.

She wished for George. He should be here to help her. But what could he do? she reconsidered with that vast tolerance of their men which women must gain by giving their bodies (else how do they continue to live with them?) that the conquering male is after all no better than a clumsy, tactless child. She examined Jones with desperate speculation. If he were not so fat! Like a worm.

She repeated: "Why do you ask me?"

"I don't know. You have never been frightened by anyone, have you?"

She watched him, not replying.

"Perhaps that's because you have never done anything to be afraid of?"

She sat on a divan, her hands palm up on either side, watching him. He rose suddenly and she as suddenly shed her careless laxness, becoming defensive, watchful. But he only scratched a match on the iron grate screen. He sucked it into his pipe bowl while she watched the fleshy concavity of his cheeks and the golden pulsations of the flame in his eyes. He pushed the match through the screen and resumed his seat. But she did not relax.

"When are you to be married?" he asked suddenly.

"Married?"

"Yes. Isn't it all arranged?"

She felt slow, slow blood in her throat and wrists, in her palms: her blood seemed to mark away an interval that would never pass. Jones, watching the light in her fine hair, lazy and yellow as an idol, Jones released her at last. "He expects it, you know."

Her blood liquefied again and became cold. She could feel the skin all over her body. She said: "What makes you think he does? He is too sick to expect anything, now."

"He?"

"You said Donald expects it."

"My dear girl, I said. . . ." He could see a nimbus of light in her hair and the shape of her, but her face he could not see. He rose. She did not move as he sat beside her. The divan sank luxuriously beneath his weight, sensuously enfolding him. She did not move, her hand lay palm up between them, but he ignored it. "Why don't you ask me how much I heard?"

"Heard? When?" Her whole attitude expressed ingenuous interest.

He knew that in her examination of his face there was

calm speculation and probably contempt. He considered moving beyond her so that she must face the light and leave his own face in shadow. . . . The light in her hair, caressing the shape of her cheek. Her hand between them, naked and palm upward, grew to be a monstrous size: it was the symbol of her body. His hand a masculine body for hers to curl inside. Browning, is it? seeing noon become afternoon, becoming gold and slightly wearied among leaves like the limp hands of women. Her hand was a frail, impersonal barrier, restraining him.

"You attach a lot of importance to a kiss, don't you?" she asked at length. He shaped her unresponsive hand to his and she continued lightly: "That's funny, in you."

"Why, in me?"

"You've had lots of girls crazy about you, haven't you?"

"What makes you think that?"

"I don't know. The way you—everything about you." She could never decide exactly about him. The feminine predominated so in him, and the rest of him was feline: a woman with a man's body and a cat's nature.

"I expect you are right. You are an authority regarding your own species yourself." He released her hand saying, "Excuse me," and lit his pipe again. Her hand remained lax, impersonal between them: it might have been a handkerchief. He pushed the dead match through the screen and said:

"What makes you think I attach so much importance to a kiss?"

Light in her hair was the thumbed rim of a silver coin, the divan embraced her quietly and light quietly followed the long slope of her limbs. A wind came among leaves without the window, stroking them together. Noon was past.

"I mean, you think that whenever a woman kisses a man or tells him something, that she means something by it."

"She does mean something by it. Of course it never is what the poor devil thinks she means, but she means something."

"Then you certainly don't blame the woman if the man chooses to think she meant something she didn't at all mean, do you?"

"Why not? It would be the devil of a chaotic world if you never could count on whether or not people mean what they say. You knew damn well what I meant when you let me kiss you that day."

"But I don't know that you meant anything, any more than I did. You are the one who——"

"Like hell you didn't," Jones interrupted roughly. "You knew what I meant by it."

"I think we are getting personal," she told him, with faint distaste.

Jones sucked his pipe. "Certainly, we are. What else are we interested in except you and me?"

She crossed her knees. "Never in my life——"

"In God's name, don't say it. I have heard that from so many women. I had expected better of someone as vain as I am."

He would be fairly decent looking, she thought, if he were not so fat—and could dye his eyes another color. After a while, she spoke.

"What do you think I mean when I do either of them?"

"I couldn't begin to say. You are a fast worker, too fast for me. I doubt if I could keep up with the men you kiss and lie to, let alone with what you mean in each case. I don't think you can yourself."

"So you cannot imagine letting people make love to you and saying things to them without meaning anything by it?"

"I cannot. I always mean something by what I say or do."

"For instance?" her voice was faintly interested, ironical.

Again he considered moving, so that her face would be in light and his in shadow. But then he would no longer be beside her. He said roughly: "I meant by that kiss that some day I intend to have your body."

"Oh," she said sweetly, "it's all arranged, then? How nice. I can now understand your success with us. Just a question of will power, isn't it? Look the beast in the eye and he—I mean she—is yours. That must save you a lot of your valuable time and trouble, I imagine?"

Jones' stare was calm, bold and contemplative, obscene as a goat's. "You don't believe I can?" he asked.

She shrugged delicately, nervously, and her lax hand between them grew again like a flower: it was as if her whole body became her hand. The symbol of a delicate, bodyless lust. Her hand seemed to melt into his yet remain without volition, her hand unawaked in his and her body also yet sleeping, crushed softly about with her fragile clothing. Her long legs, not for locomotion, but for the studied completion of a rhythm carried to its *nth*: compulsion of progress, movement; her body created for all men to dream after. A poplar, vain and pliant, trying attitude after attitude, gesture after gesture—"a girl trying gown after gown, perplexed but in pleasure." Her unseen face nimbused with light and her body, which was no body, crumpling a dress that had been dreamed. Not for maternity, not even for love: a thing for the eye and the mind. Epicene, he thought, feeling her slim bones, the bitter nervousness latent in her flesh.

"If I really held you close you'd pass right through me like a ghost, I am afraid," he said and his clasp was loosely about her.

"Quite a job," she said coarsely. "Why are you so fat?"

"Hush," he told her, "you'll spoil it."

His embrace but touched her and she, with amazing tact, suffered him. Her skin was neither warm nor cool, her body in the divan's embrace was nothing, her limbs only an indication of crushed texture. He refused to hear her breath as he refused to feel a bodily substance in his arms. Not an ivory carving: this would have body, rigidity; not an animal that eats and digests—this is the heart's desire purged of flesh. "Be quiet," he told himself as much as her, "don't spoil it."

The trumpets in his blood, the symphony of living, died away. The golden sand of hours bowled by day ran through the narrow neck of time into the corresponding globe of night, to be inverted and so flow back again. Jones felt the slow, black sand of time marking his life away. "Hush," he said, "don't spoil it."

The sentries in her blood lay down, but they lay down near the ramparts with their arms in their hands, waiting the alarm, the inevitable stand-to, and they sat clasped in the vaguely gleamed twilight of the room, Jones a fat Mirandola in a chaste Platonic nympholepsy, a religio-sentimental orgy in gray tweed, shaping an insincere, fleeting articulation of damp clay to an old imperishable desire, building himself a papier mâché Virgin: and Cecily Saunders wondering what, how much, he had heard, frightened and determined. What manner of man was this? she thought alertly, wanting George to be there and put an end to this situation, how she did not know; wondering if the fact of his absence were significant.

Outside the window leaves stirred and cried soundlessly. Noon was past. And under the bowled pale sky, trees and grass, hills and valleys, somewhere the sea, regretted him, with relief.

No, no, he thought, with awakened despair, don't spoil it. But she had moved and her hair brushed his face. Hair. Everyone, anyone, has hair. (To hold it, to hold it.) But it was hair and here was a body in his arms, fragile and delicate it might be, but still a body, a woman: something to answer the call of his flesh, to retreat pausing, touching him tentatively, teasing and retreating, yet still answering the call of his flesh. Impalpable and dominating. He removed his arm.

"You little fool, don't you know you had me?"

Her position had not changed. The divan embraced her in its impersonal clasp. Light like the thumbed rim of a coin about her indistinct face, her long legs crushed to her dress. Her hand, relaxed, lay slim and lax between them. But he ignored it.

"Tell me what you heard," she said.

He rose. "Good-bye," he said. "Thanks for lunch, or dinner, or whatever you call it."

"Dinner," she told him. "We are common people." She rose also and studiedly leaned her hip against the arm of a chair. His yellow eyes washed over her warm and clear us urine, and he said, "God damn you." She sat down again leaning back into the corner of the divan and as he sat beside her, seemingly without moving, she came to him.

"Tell me what you heard."

He embraced her, silent and morose. She moved slightly and he knew that she was offering her mouth.

"How do you prefer a proposal?" he asked.

"How?"

"Yes. What form do you like it in? You have had **two or** three in the last few days, haven't you?"

"Are you proposing?"

"That was my humble intention. Sorry I'm dull. That was why I asked for information."

"So when you can't get your women any other way, you marry them, then?"

"Dammit, do you think all a man wants of you is your body?" She was silent and he continued: "I am not going to tell on you, you know." Her tense body, her silence, was a question. "What I heard, I mean."

"Do you think I care? You have told me yourself that women say one thing and mean another. So I don't have to worry about what you heard. You said so yourself." Her body became a direct challenge, yet she had not moved. "Didn't you?"

"Don't do that," he said sharply. "What makes you so beautiful and disturbing and so goddammed dull?"

"What do you mean? I am not used——"

"Oh, I give up. I can't explain to you. And you wouldn't understand, anyway. I know I am temporarily a fool, so if you tell me I am, I'll kill you."

"Who knows? I may like that." Her soft, coarse voice was quiet.

Light in her hair, her mouth speaking and the vague, crushed shape of her body. "Atthis," he said.

"What did you call me?"

He told her. " 'For a moment, an æon, I pause plunging above the narrow precipice of thy breast' and on and on and on. Do you know how falcons make love? They embrace at an enormous height and fall locked, beak to beak, plunging: an unbearable ecstasy. While we have got to assume all sorts of ludicrous postures, knowing our own sweat. The falcon breaks his clasp and swoops away swift and proud and lonely, while a man must rise and take his hat and walk out."

She was not listening, hadn't heard him. "Tell me what you heard," she repeated. Where she touched him was a cool fire; he moved but she followed like water. "Tell me what you heard."

"What difference does it make, what I heard? I don't care anything about your jelly-beans. You can have all the Georges and Donalds you want. Take them all for lovers if you like. I don't want your body. If you can just get that through your beautiful thick head, if you will just let me alone, I will never want it again."

"But you have proposed to me. What do you want of me?"

"You wouldn't understand, if I tried to tell you."

"Then if I did marry you, how would I know how to act toward you? I think you are crazy."

"That's what I have been trying to tell you," Jones answered in a calm fury. "You won't have to act anyway toward me. I will do that. Act with your Donalds and Georges, I tell you."

She was like a light globe from which the current has been shut. "I think you're crazy," she repeated.

"I know I am." He rose abruptly. "Good-bye. Shall I see your mother, or will you thank her for lunch for me?"

Without moving she said: "Come here."

In the hall, he could hear Mrs. Saunders' chair as it creaked to her rocking, through the front door he saw trees, the lawn and the street. She said Come here again. Her body was a vague white shape as he entered the room again and light was the thumbed rim of a coin about her head. He said:

"If I come back, you know what it means."

"But I can't marry you. I am engaged."

"I wasn't talking about that."

"Then what do you mean?"

"Good-bye," he repeated. At the front door he could hear Mr. and Mrs. Saunders talking but from the room he had left came a soft movement, louder than any other sound. He thought she was following him, but the door remained empty and when he looked into the room again she sat as he had left her. He could not even tell if she were looking at him.

"I thought you had gone," she remarked.

After a time he said: "Men have lied to you a lot, haven't they?"

"What makes you say that?"

He looked at her a long moment. Then he turned to the door again. "Come here," she repeated quickly.

She made no movement, save to slightly avert her face as he embraced her. "I'm not going to kiss you," he told her.

"I'm not so sure of that." Yet his clasp was impersonal.

"Listen. You are a shallow fool, but at least you can do as you are told. And that is, let me alone about what I heard. Do you understand? You've got that much sense, haven't you? I'm not going to hurt you: I don't even want to see you again. So just let me alone about it. If I heard anything I have already forgotten it—and it's damn seldom I do anything this decent. Do you hear?"

She was cool and pliant as a young tree in his arms and against his jaw she said: "Tell me what you heard."

"All right then," he said savagely. His hand cupped her shoulder, holding her powerless and his other hand ruthlessly brought her face around. She resisted, twisting her face against his fat palm.

"No, no; tell me first."

He dragged her face up brutally and she said in a smoth-
ered whisper: "You are hurting me!"

"I don't give a damn.   That might go with George, but
not with me."

He saw her eyes go dark, saw the red print of his fingers
on her cheek and chin.   He held her face where the light
could fall on it, examining it with sybaritish anticipation.
She exclaimed quickly, staring at him: "Here comes daddy!
Stop!"

But it was Mrs. Saunders in the door, and Jones was
calm, circumspect, lazy and remote as an idol.

"Why, it's quite cool in here, isn't it?   But so dark.
How do you keep awake?" said Mrs. Saunders, entering.   "I
nearly went to sleep several times on the porch.   But the
glare is so bad on the porch.   Robert went off to school
without his hat: I don't know what he will do."

"Perhaps they haven't a porch at the school house," murmured Jones.

"Why, I don't recall.   But our school is quite modern.   It
was built in—when was it built, Cecily?"

"I don't know, mamma."

"Yes.   But it is quite new.   Was it last year or the year
before, darling?"

"I don't know, mamma."

"I told him to wear his hat because of the glare, but of
course, he didn't.   Boys are so hard to manage.   Were you
hard to manage when you were a child, Mr. Jones?"

"No, ma'am," answered Jones, who had no mother that he
could name and who might have claimed any number of
possible fathers, "I never gave my parents much trouble.   I
am of a quiet nature, you see.   In fact, until I reached my
eleventh year, the only time I ever knew passion was one
day when I discovered beneath the imminent shadow of our

annual picnic that my Sunday school card was missing. At our church they gave prizes for attendance and knowing the lesson, and my card bore forty-one stars, when it disappeared." Jones grew up in a Catholic orphanage, but like Henry James, he attained verisimilitude by means of tediousness.

"How dreadful. And did you find it again?"

"Oh, yes. I found it in time for the picnic. My father had used it to enter a one dollar bet on a race horse. When I went to my father's place of business to prevail on him to return home, as was my custom, just as I passed through the swinging doors, one of his business associates there was saying. 'Whose card is this?' I recognized my forty-one stars immediately, and claimed it, collecting twenty-two dollars, by the way. Since then I have been a firm believer in Christianity."

"How interesting," Mrs. Saunders commented, without having heard him. "I wish Robert liked Sunday school as much as that."

"Perhaps he would, at twenty-two to one."

"Pardon me?" she said. Cecily rose, and Mrs. Saunders said: "Darling, if Mr. Jones is going, perhaps you had better lie down. You look tired. Don't you think she looks tired, Mr. Jones?"

"Yes, indeed. I had just commented on it."

"Now, mamma," said Cecily.

"Thank you for lunch." Jones moved doorward and Mrs. Saunders replied conventionally, wondering why he did not try to reduce. (But perhaps he is trying, she added, with belated tolerance.) Cecily followed him.

"Do come again," she told him, staring at his face. "How much did you hear?" she whispered, with fierce desperation. "You MUST tell me."

Jones bowed fatly to Mrs. Saunders, and again bathed the

girl in his fathomless, yellow stare. She stood beside him in the door and the afternoon fell full upon her slender fragility. Jones said:

"I am coming to-night."

She whispered, "What?" and he repeated.

"You heard that?" Her mouth shaped the words against her blanched face. "You heard that?"

"I say that."

Blood came beneath her skin again and her eyes became opaque, cloudy. "No, you aren't," she told him. He looked at her calmly, and her knuckles whitened on his sleeve. "Please," she said, with utter sincerity. He made no answer, and she added: "Suppose I tell daddy?"

"Come in again, Mr. Jones," Mrs. Saunders said. Jones' mouth shaped You don't dare. Cecily stared at him in hatred and bitter desperation, in helpless terror and despair. "So glad to have you," Mrs. Saunders was saying. "Cecily, you had better lie down: you don't look at all well. Cecily is not very strong, Mr. Jones."

"Yes, indeed. One can easily see she isn't strong," Jones agreed, politely. The screen door severed them and Cecily's mouth, elastic and mobile as red rubber, shaped Don't.

But Jones made no reply. He descended wooden steps and walked beneath locust trees in which bees were busy. Roses were slashed upon green bushes, roses red as the mouths of courtesans, red as Cecily's mouth, shaping Don't.

She watched his fat, lazy, tweed back until he reached the gate and the street, then she turned to where her mother stood in impatient anticipation of her freed stout body. The light was behind her and the older woman could not see her face, but there was something in her attitude, in the relaxed hopeless tension of her body that caused the other to look at her in quick alarm.

"Cecily?"

The girl touched her and Mrs. Saunders put her arm around her daughter. The older woman had eaten too much, as usual, and she breathed heavily, knowing her corsets, counting the minutes until she would be free of them.

"Cecily?"

"Where is daddy, mamma?"

"Why, he's gone to town. What is it, baby?" She asked, quickly, "what's the matter?"

Cecily clung to her mother. The other was like a rock, a panting rock: something imperishable, impervious to passion and fear. And heartless.

"I must see him," she answered. "I have just got to see him."

The other said: "There, there. Go to your room and lie down a while." She sighed heavily. "No wonder you don't feel well. Those new potatoes at dinner! When will I learn when to stop eating? But if it isn't one thing, it's another, isn't it? Darling, would you mind coming in and unlacing me? I think I'll lie down a while before I dress to go to Mrs. Coleman's."

"Yes, mamma. Of course," she answered, wanting her father, George, anyone, to help her.

3

George Farr, lurking along a street, climbed a fence swiftly when the exodus from the picture show came along. Despite himself, he simply could not act as though he were out for a casual stroll, but must drift aimlessly and noticeably back and forth along the street with a sort of skulking frankness. He was too nervous to go somewhere else and time his return; he was too nervous to conceal himself and stay there. So he gave up and became frankly skulking, climbing a fence smartly when the exodus from the picture show began.

Nine-thirty

People sat on porches rocking and talking in low tones, enjoying the warmth of April, people passing beneath dark trees along the street, old and young, men and women, making comfortable, unintelligible sounds, like cattle going to barn and bed. Tiny red eyes passed along at mouth-height and burning tobacco lingered behind sweet and pungent. Spitting arc lights, at street corners, revealed the passers-by, temporarily dogging them with elastic shadows. Cars passed under the lights and he recognized friends: young men and the inevitable girls with whom they were "going"—coiffed or bobbed hair and slim young hands fluttering forever about it, keeping it in place. . . . The cars passed on into darkness, into another light, into darkness again.

Ten o'clock

Dew on the grass, dew on small unpickable roses, making them sweeter, giving them an odor. Otherwise, they had no odor, except that of youth and growth, as young girls have no particular attributes, save the kinship of youth and growth. Dew on the grass, the grass assumed a faint luminousness as if it had stolen light from day and the moisture of night were releasing it, giving it back to the world again. Tree-frogs shrilled in the trees, insects droned in the grass. Tree frogs are poison, negroes had told him. If they spit on you, you'll die. When he moved they fell silent (getting ready to spit, perhaps), when he became still again, they released the liquid flute-like monotony swelling in their throats, filling the night with the imminence of summer. Spring, like a girl

loosing her girdle. . . . People passed in belated ones and
twos. Words reached him in meaningless snatches. Fireflies had not yet come.

Ten-thirty

Rocking blurs on the verandas of houses rose and went
indoors, entering rooms, and lights went off here and there,
beyond smoothly descending shades. George Farr stole across
a deserted lawn to a magnolia tree. Beneath it, fumbling
in a darkness so inky that the rest of the world seemed
quite visible in comparison, he found a water tap. Water
gushed, filling his incautious shoe, and a mocking bird flew
darkly and suddenly out. He drank, wetting his dry hot
mouth, and returned to his post. When he was still again, the
frogs and insects teased at silence gently, not to break it
completely. As the small odorless roses unfolded under the
dew their scent grew as though they, too, were growing, doub-
ling in size.

Eleven o'clock

Solemnly the clock on the courthouse, staring its four bland
faces across the town, like a kind and sleepless god, dropped
eleven measured golden bells of sound. Silence carried them
away, silence and dark that passing along the street like a
watchman, snatched scraps of light from windows, palming
them as a pickpocket palms snatched handkerchiefs. A belated car passed swiftly. Nice girls must be home by eleven.
The street, the town, the world, was empty for him.

He lay on his back in a slow consciousness of relaxing
muscles, feeling his back and thighs and legs luxuriously.
It became so quiet that he dared to smoke, though being careful not to expose the match unduly. Then he lay down
again, stretching, feeling the gracious earth through his cloth-

ing. After a while his cigarette burned down and he spun
it from two fingers and sickled his knee until he could reach
his ankle, scratching. Life of some sort was also down his
back, or it felt like it, which was the same thing. He
writhed his back against the earth and the irritation
ceased. . . . It must be eleven-thirty by now. He waited
for what he judged to be five minutes, then he held his
watch this way and that, trying to read it. But it only
tantalized him: he could have sworn to almost any hour or
minute you could name. So he cupped another cautious
match. It was eleven-fourteen. Hell.

He lay back again cradling his head in his clasped arms.
From this position the sky became a flat plane, flat as the
brass-studded lid of a dark blue box. Then, as he watched, it
assumed depth again, it was as if he lay on the bottom of
the sea while sea-weed, clotting blackly, lifted surfaceward
unshaken by any current, motionless; it was as if he lay on
his stomach, staring downward into water into which his
gorgon's hair, clotting blackly, hung motionless. Eleven-
thirty.

He had lost his body. He could not feel it at all. It was
as though vision were a bodiless Eye suspended in dark-blue
space, an Eye without Thought, regarding without surprise
an antic world where wanton stars galloped neighing like
unicorns in blue meadows- . . . After a while, the Eye, having
nothing in or by which to close itself, ceased to see, and he
waked, thinking that he was being tortured, that his arms
were being crushed and wrung from his body. He dreamed
that he had screamed, and finding that to move his arms
was an agony equaled only by that of letting them stay where
they were, he rolled writhing, chewing his lip. His whole
blood took fire: the pain became a swooning ecstasy that
swooned away. Yet they still felt like somebody else's arms,

even after the pain had gone. He could not even take out his watch, he was afraid he would not be able to climb the fence.

But he achieved this, knowing it was midnight, because the street lamps had been turned off, and in the personal imminent desertion of the street he slunk, feeling, though there was none to see him, more like a criminal than ever, now that his enterprise was really under way. He walked on trying to bolster his moral courage, trying not to look like a sneaking nigger, but, in spite of him, it seemed that every dark quiet house stared at him, watching him with blank and lightless eyes, making his back itch after he had passed. But what if they do see me? What am I doing, that anyone should not do? Walking along a deserted street after midnight. That's all. But this did not stop the prickling of hair on the back of his neck.

His gait faltered, not quite stopping altogether: near the trunk of a tree, he discerned movement, a thicker darkness. His first impulse was to turn back, then he cursed himself for an excitable fool. Suppose it were someone. He had as much right to the street as the other had—more, if the other were concealing himself. He strode on no longer skulking, feeling on the contrary quite righteous. As he passed the tree, the thicker darkness shifted slowly. Whoever it was did not wish to be seen. The other evidently feared him more than he did the other, so he passed on boldly. He looked back once or twice, but saw nothing.

Her house was dark, but remembering the shadow behind the tree, and for the sake of general precaution, he passed steadily on. After a block or so he halted, straining his ears. Nothing save the peaceful, unemphatic sounds of night. He crossed the street and stopped again, listening. Nothing. Frogs and crickets, and that was all. He walked in the grass beside the pavement, stealing quiet as a shadow to the corner of her lawn.   He climbed the fence and, crouching, stole along beside a hedge until he was opposite the house, where he stopped again.   The house was still, unlighted, bulking huge and square in slumber and he sped swiftly from the shadow of the hedge to the shadow of the veranda at the place where a french window gave upon it.   He sat down in a flower bed, leaning his back against the wall.

The turned flower bed filled the darkness with the smell of fresh earth, something friendly and personal in a world of enormous vague formless shapes of greater and lesser darkness.   The night, the silence, was complete and profound: a formless region filled with the smell of fresh earth and the measured ticking of the watch in his pocket.   After a time, he felt soft damp earth through his trousers upon his thighs and he sat in a slow physical content, a oneness with the earth, waiting a sound from the dark house at his back.   He heard a sound after a while but it was from the street.   He sat still and calm.   With the inconsistency of his kind, he felt safer here, where he had no business being, than on the street to which he had every right.   The sound, approaching, became two vague figures, and Tobe and the cook passed along the drive toward their quarters, murmuring softly to each other. . . .   Soon the night was again vague and vast and empty.

Again he became one with the earth, with dark and silence, with his own body . . . with her body, like a little silver water sweetly dividing . . . turned earth and hyacinths along a veranda, swinging soundless bells. . . .   How can breasts be as small as yours, and yet be breasts . . . the dull gleam of her eyes beneath lowered lids, of her teeth beneath her lip, her arms rising like two sweet wings of a dream. . . .   Her body like.

He took breath into himself, holding it. Something came slow and shapeless across the lawn toward him, pausing opposite. He breathed again, held his breath again. The thing moved and came directly toward him and he sat motionless until it had almost reached the flower bed in which he sat. Then he sprang to his feet and before the other could raise a hand he fell upon the intruder, raging silently. The man accepted battle and they fell clawing and panting, making no outcry. They were at such close quarters, it was so dark, that they could not damage each other, and intent on battle, they were oblivious of their surroundings until Jones hissed suddenly beneath George Farr's armpit:

"Look out! Somebody's coming!"

They paused mutually and sat clasping each other like the first position of a sedentary dance. A light had appeared suddenly in a lower window and with one accord they rose and hurled themselves into the shadow of the porch, plunging into the flower bed as Mr. Saunders stepped through the window. Crushing themselves against the brick wall, they lay in a mutual passion for concealment, hearing Mr. Saunders' feet on the floor above their heads. They held their breath, closing their eyes like ostriches and the man came to the edge of the veranda, and standing directly over them, he shook cigar ashes upon them and spat across their prone bodies . . . after years had passed, he turned and went away.

After a while Jones heaved and George Farr released his cramped body. The light was off again and the house bulked huge and square, sleeping among the trees. They rose and stole across the lawn and after they had passed the frogs and crickets resumed their mild monotonies.

"What—" began George Farr, once they were on the street again.

"Shut up," Jones interrupted. "Wait until we are further away."

They walked side by side, and George Farr, seething, decided upon what he considered a safe distance. Stopping he faced the other.

"What in hell were you doing there?" he burst out.

Jones had dirt on his face and his collar had burst. George Farr's tie was like a hangman's noose under his ear and he wiped his face with his handkerchief.

"What were you doing there?" Jones countered.

"None of your damn business," he answered hotly. "What I ask is, what in hell do you mean, hanging around that house?"

"Maybe she asked me to. What do you think of that?"

"You lie," said George Farr, springing upon him. They fought again in the darkness, beneath the arching silence of elms. Jones was like a bear and George Farr, feeling his soft enveloping hug, kicked Jones' legs from under him. They fell, Jones uppermost, and George lay gasping, with breath driven from his lungs, while Jones held him upon his back.

"How about it?" Jones asked, thinking of his shin. "Got enough?"

For reply, George Farr heaved and struggled, but the other held him down, thumping his head rhythmically upon the hard earth. "Come on, come on. Don't act like a child. What do we want to fight for?"

"Take back what you said about her, then," he panted. Then he lay still and cursed Jones. Jones, unmoved, repeated:

"Got enough? Promise?"

George Farr arched his back, writhing, trying vainly to cast off Jones' fat enveloping bulk. At last he promised in weak

rage, almost weeping, and Jones removed his soft weight.
George sat up.

"You better go home," Jones advised him, rising to his feet.
"Come on, get up." He took George's arm and tugged at it.

"Let go, you bastard!"

"Funny how things get around," remarked Jones mildly,
releasing him. George got slowly to his feet and Jones continued: "Run along, now. You have been out late enough
Had a fight and everything."

George Farr, panting, rearranged his clothes. Jones bulked
vaguely beside him. "Good-night," said Jones, at last.

"Good-night."

They faced each other and after a time Jones repeated:
"Good-night, I said."

"I heard you."

"What's the matter? Not going in now?"

"Hell, no."

"Well, I am." He turned away. "See you again." George
Farr followed him, doggedly. Jones, slow and fat, shapeless,
in the darkness, remarked: "Do you live down this way now?
You've moved recently, haven't you?"

"I live wherever you do to-night," George told him, stubbornly.

"Thanks, awfully. But I have only one bed and I don't
like to sleep double. So I can't ask you in. Some other
time."

They walked slowly beneath dark trees, in dogged intimacy.
The clock on the courthouse struck one and the stroke died
away into silence. After a while Jones stopped again. "Look
here, what are you following me for?"

"She didn't ask you to come there to-night."

"How do you know? If she asked you, she would ask
someone else."

"Listen," said George Farr, "if you don't let her alone, I'll kill you. I swear I will."

"*Salut,*" murmured Jones. "*Ave, Cæsar.* . . . Why don't you tell her father that? Perhaps he'll let you set up a tent on the lawn to protect her. Now, you go on and let me alone, do you hear?" George held his ground stubbornly. "You want me to beat hell out of you again?" Jones suggested.

"Try it," George whispered with dry passion. Jones said: "Well, we've both wasted this night, anyway. It's too late, now——"

"I'll kill you! She never told you to come at all. You just followed me. I saw you behind that tree. You let her alone, do you hear?"

"In God's name, man! Don't you see that all I want now is sleep? Let's go home, for heaven's sake."

"You swear you are going home?"

"Yes, yes. I swear. Good-night."

George Farr watched the other's shapeless fading figure, soon it became but a thicker shadow among shadows. Then he turned homeward himself in cooled anger and bitter disappointment and desire. That blundering idiot had interfered this time, perhaps he would interfere every time. Or perhaps she would change her mind, perhaps, since he had failed her to-night. . . . Even Fate envied him this happiness, this unbearable happiness, he thought bitterly. Beneath trees arching the quiet sky, spring loosing her girdle languorous . . . her body, like a narrow pool, sweetly. . . . I thought I had lost you, I found you again, and now he. . . . He paused, sharply struck by a thought, an intuition. He turned and sped swiftly back.

He stood near a tree at the corner of the lawn and after a short time he saw something moving shapeless and slow across

the faint grass, along a hedge. He strode out boldly and the
other saw him and paused, then that one, too, stood erect
and came boldly to meet him. Jones joined him, murmuring,
"Oh, hell," and they stood in static dejection, side by side.

"Well?" challenged George Farr, at last.

Jones sat down heavily on the sidewalk. "Let's smoke a
while," he suggested, in that impersonal tone which people
sitting up with corpses use.

George Farr sat beside him and Jones held a match to his
cigarette, then lit his own pipe. He sighed, clouding his
head with an unseen pungency of tobacco. George Farr
sighed also, resting his back against a tree. The stars swam
on like the mast-head lights of squadrons and squadrons on
a dark river, going on and on. Darkness and silence and a
world turning through darkness toward another day. . . .
The bark of the tree was rough, the ground was hard. He
wished vaguely that he were fat like Jones, temporarily. . . .

. . . Then, waking, it was about to be dawn. He no
longer felt the earth and the tree save when he moved. It
seemed to him that his thighs must be flattened like a table-
top and that his back had assumed depressions into which the
projections of the tree trunk fitted like the locked rims of
wheels.

There was a rumor of light eastward, somewhere beyond her
house and the room where she lay in the soft familiar intimacy
of sleep, like a faintly blown trumpet; soon perspective returned to a mysterious world, and instead of being a huge
portentous shadow among lesser shadows, Jones was only a
fat young man in baggy tweed, white and pathetic and snor-
ing on his back.

George Farr, waking, saw him so, saw earth stains on
him and a faint incandescence of dew. George Farr bore
earth stains himself and his tie was a hangman's knot beneath

his ear. The wheel of the world, slowing through the hours of darkness, passed the dead center point and gained momentum. After a while Jones opened his eyes, groaning. He rose stiffly, stretching and spitting, yawning.

"Good time to go in, I think," he said. George Farr, tasting his own sour mouth, moved and felt little pains, like tiny red ants, running over him. He, too, rose and they stood side by side. They yawned again.

Jones turned fatly, limping a little.

"Good-night," he said.

"Good-night."

The east grew yellow, then red, and day had really come into the world, breaking the slumber of sparrows.

4

But Cecily Saunders was not asleep. Lying on her back in her bed, in her dark room she, too, heard the hushed sounds of night, smelled the sweet scents of spring and dark and growing things: the earth, watching the wheel of the world, the terrible calm, inevitability of life, turning through the hours of darkness, passing its dead center point and turning faster, drawing the waters of dawn up from the hushed cistern of the east, breaking the slumber of sparrows.

5

"May I see him," she pleaded hysterically, "may I? Oh, may I, please?"

Mrs. Powers, seeing her face, said: Why, child! What is it? What is it, darling?"

"Alone, alone. Please. May I? May I?"

"Of course. What——"

"Thank you, thank you." She sped down the hall and crossed the study like a bird.

"Donald, Donald! It's Cecily, sweetheart. Cecily. Don't you know Cecily?"

"Cecily," he repeated mildly. Then she stopped his mouth with hers, clinging to him.

"I will marry you, I will, I will. Donald, look at me. But you cannot, you cannot see me, can you? But I will marry you, to-day, any time: Cecily will marry you, Donald. You cannot see me, can you, Donald? Cecily? Cecily?"

"Cecily?" he repeated.

"Oh, your poor, poor face, your blind, scarred face! But I will marry you. They said I wouldn't, that I mustn't, but yes, yes, Donald my dear love!"

Mrs. Powers, following her, raised her to her feet, removing her arms. "You might hurt him, you know," she said.

CHAPTER VII

1

"Joe."

"Whatcher say, Loot?"

"I'm going to get married, Joe."

"Sure you are, Loot. Some day—" tapping himself on the chest.

"What's that, Joe?"

"I say, good luck. You got a fine girl."

"Cecily . . . Joe?"

"Hello."

"She'll get used to my face."

"Your damn right. Your face is all right. But easy there, don't knock 'em off. Attaboy," as the other lowered his fumbling hand.

"What do I have to wear 'em for, Joe? Get married as well without 'em, can't I?"

"I'll be damned if I know why they make you wear 'em. I'll ask Margaret. Here, lemme have 'em," he said suddenly removing the glasses. "Damn shame, making you keep 'em on. How's that? Better?"

"Carry on, Joe."

2

San Francisco, Cal.,
April 24, 1919.

Margaret dearest—

I miss you so much. If I could only see each other and talk to each other. I sit in my room and I think you are the only woman for me. Girls are not like you they are so young and dumb you cant trust them. I hope you are

246

lonely for me like I am just to know you are sweetheart.
When I kissed you that day I know you are the only woman
for me Margaret. You cannot trust them. I told her hes
just kidding her he wont get her a job in the movies. So
I sit in my room and outside life goes on just the same
though we are thousand miles apart wanting to see you like
hell I think of how happy we will be. I havent told my
mother yet because we have been waiting we ought to tell
her I think if you think so. And she will invite you out here
and we can be together all day riding and swimming and
dancing and talking to each other. If I can arrange busness
affairs I will come for you soon as I can. It is hell without
you I miss you and I love you like hell.

J.

3

It had rained the night before but this morning was soft
as a breeze. Birds across the lawn parabolic from tree to
tree mocked him as he passed lounging and slovenly in his
careless unpressed tweeds, and a tree near the corner of the
veranda, turning upward its ceaseless white-bellied leaves, was
a swirling silver veil stood on end, a fountain arrested forever: carven water.

He saw that black woman in the garden among roses,
blowing smoke upon them from her pursed mouth, bending
and sniffing above them, and he joined her with slow anticipated malice mentally stripping her straight dark unemphatic
dress downward from her straight back over her firm quiet
thighs. Hearing his feet on the gravel, she looked over her
shoulder without surprise. Her poised cigarette balanced on
its tip a wavering plume of vapor and Jones said:

"I have come to weep with you."

She met his stare, saying nothing. Her other hand blanched

upon a solid mosaic of red and green, her repose absorbed
all motion from her immediate atmosphere so that the plume
of her cigarette became rigid as a pencil, flowering its tip
into nothingness.

"I mean your hard luck, losing your intended," he explained.

She raised her cigarette and expelled smoke. He lounged
nearer. his expensive jacket, which had evidently had no
attention since he bought it, sagging to the thrust of his heavy
hands, shaping his fat thighs. His eyes were bold and lazy,
clear as a goat's. She got of him an impression of aped intelligence imposed on an innate viciousness; the cat that
walks by himself.

"Who are your people, Mr. Jones?" she asked after a while.

"I am the world's little brother. I probably have a bar
sinister in my 'scutcheon. In spite of me, my libido seems
to be a complex regarding decency."

What does that mean? she wondered. "What is your
escutcheon, then?"

"One newspaper-wrapped bundle *couchant* and *rampant,*
one doorstep stone, on a field *noir* and damned *froid.* De-
vice: *Quand mangerai-je?*"

"Oh. A foundling." She smoked again.

"I believe that is the term. It is too bad we are con-
temporary: you might have found the thing yourself. I
would not have thrown you down."

"Thrown me down?"

"You can never tell just exactly how dead these soldiers
are, can you? You think you have him and then the devil
reveals as much idiocy as a normal sane person, doesn't he?"

She skillfully pinched the coal from her cigarette end and
flipped the stub in a white twinkling arc, grinding the coal
under her toe. "If that was an implied compliment——"

"Only fools imply compliments. The wise man comes

right out with it, point-blank. Imply criticism—unless the criticized is not within ear-shot."

"It seems to me that is a rather precarious doctrine for one who is—if you will pardon me—not exactly a combative sort."

"Combative?"

"Well, a fighting man, then. I can't imagine you lasting very long in an encounter with—say, Mr. Gilligan."

"Does that imply that you have taken Mr. Gilligan as a—protector?"

"No more than it implies that I expect compliments from you. For all your intelligence, you seem to have acquired next to no skill with women."

Jones, remote and yellowly unfathomable, stared at her mouth. "For instance?"

"For instance, Miss Saunders," she said, wickedly. "You seem to have let her get away from you, don't you?"

"Miss Saunders," repeated Jones, counterfeiting surprise, admiring the way she had turned the tables on him without reverting to sex, "my dear lady, can you imagine anyone making love to her? Epicene. Of course it is different with a man practically dead," he added, "he probably doesn't care much whom he marries, nor whether or not he marries at all."

"No? I understood from your conduct the day I arrived that you had your eye on her. But perhaps I was mistaken after all."

"Granted I had: you and I seem to be in the same fix now, don't we?"

She pinched through the stem of a rose, feeling him quite near her. Without looking at him she said:

"You have already forgotten what I told you, haven't you?" He did not reply. She released her rose and moved slightly away from him. "That you have no skill in seduction. Don't you know I can see what you are leading up to—that you

and I should console one another? That's too childish, even
for you. I have had to play at too many of these sexual
acrostics with poor boys whom I respected even if I didn't
like them." The rose splashed redly against the front of her
dark dress. She secured it with a pin. "Let me give you
some advice," she continued sharply, "the next time you try
to seduce anyone, don't do it with talk, with words. Women
know more about words than men ever will. And they know
how little they can ever possibly mean."

Jones removed his yellow stare. His next move was quite
feminine: he turned and lounged away without a word. For
he had seen Emmy beyond the garden hanging washed clothes
upon a line. Mrs. Powers, looking after his slouching figure,
said Oh. She had just remarked Emmy raising garments to a
line with formal gestures, like a Greek masque.

She watched Jones approach Emmy, saw Emmy, when she
heard his step, poise a half-raised cloth in a formal arrested
gesture, turning her head across her reverted body. Damn the
beast, Mrs. Powers thought, wondering whether or not to follow
and interfere. But what good would it do? He'll only come
back later. And playing Cerberus to Emmy. . . . She removed
her gaze and saw Gilligan approaching. He blurted:

"Damn that girl. Do you know what I think? I think
she——"

"What girl?"

"What's her name, Saunders. I think she's scared of something. She acts like she might have got herself into a jam
of some kind and is trying to get out of it by taking the loot
right quick. Scared. Flopping around like a fish."

"Why don't you like her, Joe? You don't want her to
marry him."

"No, it ain't that. It just frets me to see her change her
mind every twenty minutes." He offered her a cigarette

which she refused and lit one himself. "I'm jealous, I guess," he said, after a time, "seeing the loot getting married when neither of 'em want to 'specially, while I can't get my girl at all. . . ."

"What, Joe? You married?"

He looked at her steadily. "Don't talk like that. You know what I mean."

"Oh, Lord. Twice in one hour." His gaze was so steady, so serious, that she looked quickly away.

"What's that?" he asked. She took the rose from her dress and slipped it into his lapel.

"Joe, what is that beast hanging around here for?"

"Who? What beast?" He followed her eyes. "Oh. That damn feller. I'm going to beat hell out of him on principle, some day. I don't like him."

"Neither do I. Hope I'm there to see you do it."

"Has he been bothering you?" he asked quickly. She gave him her steady gaze.

"Do you think he could?"

"That's right," he admitted. He looked at Jones and Emmy again. "That's another thing. That Saunders girl lets him fool around her. I don't like anybody that will stand for him."

"Don't be silly, Joe. She's just young and more or less of a fool about men."

"If that's your polite way of putting it, I agree with you." His eyes touched her smooth cheek blackly winged by her hair. "If you had let a man think you was going to marry him you wouldn't blow hot and cold like that."

She stared away across the garden and he repeated: "Would you, Margaret?"

"You are a fool yourself, Joe. Only you are a nice fool." She met his intent gaze and he said Margaret? She put her swift strong hand on his arm. "Don't Joe. Please."

He rammed his hands in his pockets, turning away. They walked on in silence.

4

Spring, like a soft breeze, was in the rector's fringe of hair as with upflung head he tramped the porch like an old war-horse who hears again a trumpet after he had long thought all wars were done. Birds in a wind across the lawn, parabolic from tree to tree, and a tree at the corner of the house turning upward its white-bellied leaves in a passionate arrested rush: it and the rector faced each other in ecstasy. A friend came morosely along the path from the kitchen door.

"Good morning, Mr. Jones," the rector boomed, scattering sparrows from the screening vine. The tree to his voice took a more unbearable ecstasy, its twinkling leaves swirled in a never escaping silver skyward rush.

Jones, nursing his hand, replied Good morning in a slow obese anger. He mounted the steps and the rector bathed him in a hearty exuberance.

"Come 'round to congratulate us on the good news, eh? Fine, my boy, fine, fine. Yes, everything is arranged at last. Come in, come in."

Emmy flopped onto the veranda belligerently. "Uncle Joe," she said, shooting at Jones a hot exulting glance. Jones, nursing his hand, glowered at her. (God damn you, you'll suffer for this.)

"Eh? What is it, Emmy?"

"Mr. Saunders is on the 'phone: he wants to know if you'll see him this morning." (I showed you! Teach you to fool with me.)

"Ah, yes. Mr. Saunders coming to discuss plans for the marriage, Mr. Jones."

"Yes, sir." (I'll fix you.)

"What'll I tell him?" (Do it, if you think you can. You never have come off very well yet. You fat worm.)

"Tell him, by all means, that I had intended calling upon him myself. Yes, indeed. Ah, Mr. Jones, we are all to be congratulated this morning."

"Yes, sir." (You little slut.)

"Tell him, by all means, Emmy."

"All right." (I told you I'd do it! I told you you can't fool with me. Didn't I, now?)

"And, Emmy, Mr. Jones will be with us for lunch. A celebration is in order, eh, Mr. Jones?"

"Without doubt. We all have something to celebrate." (That's what makes me so damn mad: you said you would and I let you do it. Slam a door on my hand! Damn you to hell.)

"All right. He can stay if he wants to." (Damn YOU to hell.) Emmy arrowed him another hot exulting glance and slammed the door as a parting shot.

The rector tramped heavily, happily, like a boy. "Ah, Mr. Jones, to be young as he is, to have your life circumscribed, moved hither and yonder at the vacillations of such delightful pests. Women, women! How charming never to know exactly what you want! While we men are always so sure we do. Dullness, dullness, Mr. Jones. Perhaps that's why we like them, yet cannot stand very much of them. What do you think?"

Jones, glumly silent, nursing his hand, said after a while: "I don't know. But it seemed to me your son has had extraordinarily good luck with his women."

"Yes?" the rector said, with interest. "How so?"

"Well (I think you told me that he was once involved with Emmy?), well, he no longer remembers Emmy (damn her soul: slam a door on me) and now he is about to become involved with another whom he will not even have to look at. What more could one ask than that?"

The rector looked at him keenly and kindly a moment. "You have retained several of your youthful characteristics, Mr. Jones."

"What do you mean?" asked Jones, with defensive belligerence. A car drew up to the gate, and after Mr. Saunders had descended, drove away.

"One in particular: that of being unnecessarily and pettily brutal about rather insignificant things. Ah," he added, looking up, "here is Mr. Saunders. Excuse me, will you? You will probably find Mrs. Powers and Mr. Gilligan in the garden," he said, over his shoulder, greeting his caller.

Jones, in a vindictive rage, saw them shake hands. They ignored him and he lounged viciously past them seeking his pipe. It eluded him and he cursed it slowly, beating at his various pockets.

"I had intended calling upon you to-day." The rector took his caller affectionately by the elbow. "Come in, come in."

Mr. Saunders allowed himself to be propelled across the veranda. Murmuring a conventional response the rector herded him heartily beneath the fanlight, down the dark hall and into the study, without noticing the caller's air of uncomfortable reserve. He moved a chair for the guest and took his own seat at the desk. Through the window he could see a shallow section of the tree that, unseen but suggested, swirled upward in an ecstasy of never-escaping silver-bellied leaves.

The rector's swivel chair protested, tilting. "Ah, yes, you smoke cigars, I recall. Matches at your elbow."

Mr. Saunders rolled his cigar slowly in his fingers. At last he made up his mind and lit it.

"Well, the young people have taken things out of our hands, eh?" the rector spoke around his pipe stem. "I will say now that I have long desired it and, frankly, I have expected it. Though I would not have insisted, knowing Donald's condition. But as Cecily herself desires it——"

"Yes, yes," agreed Mr. Saunders, slowly. The rector did not notice.

"You, I know, have been a stanch advocate of it all along. Mrs. Powers repeated your conversation to me."

"Yes, that's right."

"And do you know, I look for this marriage to be better than a medicine for him. Not my own idea," he added, in swift explanation. "Frankly, I was skeptical but Mrs. Powers and Joe—Mr. Gilligan—advanced it first, and the surgeon from Atlanta convinced us all. He assured us that Cecily could do as much if not more for him than anyone. These were his very words, if I recall correctly. And now, since she desires it so much, since you and her mother support her. . . . Do you know," he slapped his caller upon the shoulder, "do you know, were I a betting man I would wager that we will not know the boy in a year's time!"

Mr. Saunders had trouble getting his cigar to burn properly. He bit the end from it savagely, then wreathing his head in smoke he blurted: "Mrs. Saunders seems to have a few doubts yet." He fanned the smoke away and saw the rector's huge face gone gray and quiet. "Not objections, exactly, you understand," he added, hurriedly, apologetically. Damn the woman, why couldn't she have come herself instead of sending him?

The divine made a clicking sound. "This is bad. I had not expected this."

"Oh, I am sure we can convince her, you and I. Especially with Sis on our side." He had forgotten his own scruples, forgotten that he did not want his daughter to marry anyone.

"This is bad," the rector repeated, hopelessly.

"She will not refuse her consent," Mr. Saunders lied hastily. "It is only that she is not convinced as to its soundness, considering Do—Cecily's—Cecily's youth, you see," he finished with inspiration. "On the contrary, in fact. I only brought it up so that we could have a clear understanding. Don't you think it is best to know all the facts?"

"Yes, yes." The rector was having trouble with his own tobacco. He put his pipe aside, pushing it away. He rose and tramped heavily along the worn path in the rug.

"I am sorry," said Mr. Saunders.

(This was Donald, my son. He is dead.)

"But come, come. We are making a mountain out of a mole hill," the rector exclaimed at last, without conviction. "As you say, if the girl wants to marry Donald I am sure her mother will not refuse her consent. What do you think? Shall we call on her? Perhaps she does not understand the situation, that—that they care for each other so much. She has not seen Donald since he returned, and you know how rumors get about. . . ." (This was Donald, my son. He is dead.)

He paused mountainous and shapeless in his casual black, yearning upon the other. Mr. Saunders rose from his chair and the rector took his arm, lest he escape.

"Yes, that is best. We will see her together and talk it over thoroughly before we make a definite decision. Yes, yes," the rector repeated, flogging his own failing conviction, spurring it. "This afternoon, then?"

"This afternoon," Mr. Saunders agreed.

"Yes, that is our proper course. I'm sure she does not understand. You don't think she fully understands?" (This was Donald, my son. He is dead.)

"Yes, yes," Mr. Saunders agreed in his turn.

Jones found his pipe at last and nursing his bruised hand he filled and lit it.

5

She had just met Mrs. Worthington in a store and they had discussed putting up plums. Then Mrs. Worthington, saying good-bye, waddled away slowly to her car. The negro driver helped her in with efficient detachment and shut the door.

I'm spryer than her, thought Mrs. Burney exultantly, watching the other's gouty painful movement. Spite of she's rich and got a car, she added, feeling better through malice, suppressing her own bone-aches, walking spryer than the rich one. Spite of she's got money. And here approaching was that strange woman staying at Parson Mahon's, the one that come here with him and that other man, getting herself talked about, and right. The one everybody expected to marry him and that he had throwed down for that boy-chasing Saunders girl.

"Well," she remarked with comfortable curiosity, peering up into the white calm face of the tall dark woman in her dark dress with its immaculate cuffs and collar, "I hear you are going to have a marriage up at your house. That's so nice for Donald. He's quite sweet on her, ain't he?"

"Yes. They were engaged for a long time, you know."

"Yes, they was. But folks never thought she'd wait for him, let alone take him sick and scratched up like he is. She's had lots of chances since."

"Folks think lots of things that aren't true," Mrs. Powers reminded her. But Mrs. Burney was intent on her own words.

"Yes, she's had lots of chances. But then Donald has too, ain't he?" she asked cunningly.

"I don't know. You see, I haven't known him very long."

"Oh, you ain't? Folks all thought you and him was old friends, like."

Mrs. Powers looked down at her neat cramped figure in its air-proof black without replying.

Mrs. Burney sighed. "Well, marriages is nice. My boy never married. Like's not he would by now: girls was all crazy about him, only he went to war so young." Her peering, salacious curiosity suddenly left her. "You heard about my boy?" she asked with yearning.

"Yes, they told me, Dr. Mahon did. He was a good soldier, wasn't he?"

"Yes. And them folks got him killed with just a lot of men around: nobody to do nothing for him. Seems like they might of took him into a house where women-folks could have eased him. Them others come back spry and bragging much as you please. Trust them officers and things not to get hurt!" Her washed blue eyes brooded across the quiet square. After a time she said: "You never lost no one you loved in the war, did you?"

"No," Mrs. Powers answered, gently.

"I never thought so," the other stated fretfully. "You don't look like it, so tall and pretty. But then, most didn't. He was so young," she explained, "so brave. . . ." She fumbled with her umbrella. Then she said briskly:

"Mahon's boy come back, anyway. That's something. 'Specially as he's taking a bride." She became curious again, obscene: "He's all right, ain't he?"

"All right?"

"I mean for marriage. He ain't—it's just—I mean a man ain't no right to palm himself off on a woman if he ain't——"

"Good morning," said Mrs. Powers curtly, leaving her cramped and neat in her meticulous air-proof black, holding her cotton umbrella like a flag, stubborn, refusing to surrender.

6

"You fool, you idiot, marrying a blind man, a man with nothing, practically dead."

"He is not! He is not!"

"What do you call him then? Aunt Callie Nelson was here the other day saying that the white folks had killed him."

"You know nigger talk doesn't mean anything. They probably wouldn't let her worry him, so she says he——"

"Nonsense. Aunt Callie has raised more children than I can count. If she says he is sick, he is sick."

"I don't care. I am going to marry him."

Mrs. Saunders sighed creakingly. Cecily stood before her, flushed and obstinate. "Listen, honey. If you marry him you are throwing yourself away, all your chances, all your youth and prettiness, all the men that like you: men who are good matches."

"I don't care," she repeated, stubbornly.

"Think. There are so many you can have for the taking, so much you can have: a big wedding in Atlanta with all your friends for bridesmaids, clothes, a wedding trip. . . . And then to throw yourself away. After your father and I have done so much for you."

"I don't care. I am going to marry him."

"But, why? Do you love him?"

"Yes, yes!"

"That scar, too?"

Cecily's face blanched as she stared at her mother. Her eyes became dark and she raised her hand delicately. Mrs. Saunders took her hand and drew her resisting onto her lap.

Cecily protested tautly but her mother held her, drawing her head down to her shoulder, smoothing her hair. "I'm sorry, baby. I didn't mean to say that. But tell me what it is."

Her mother would not fight fair. She knew this with anger, but the older woman's tactics scattered her defenses of anger: she knew she was about to cry. Then it would be all up. "Let me go," she said, struggling, hating her mother's unfairness.

"Hush, hush. There now, lie here and tell me what it is. You must have some reason."

She ceased to struggle and became completely lax. "I haven't. I just want to marry him. Let me go. Please, mamma."

"Cecily, did your father put this idea in your head?"

She shook her head and her mother turned her face up. "Look at me." They stared at each other and Mrs. Saunders repeated: "Tell me what your reason is."

"I can't."

"You mean you won't?"

"I can't tell you." She slipped suddenly from her mother's lap but Mrs. Saunders held her kneeling against her knee. "I won't," she cried, struggling. The other held her tightly. "You are hurting me!"

"Tell me."

Cecily wrenched herself free and stood. "I can't tell you. I have just got to marry him."

"Got to marry him? What do you mean?" She stared at her daughter, gradually remembering old rumors about Mahon, gossip she had forgot. "Got to marry him? Do you mean that you—that a daughter of mine—with a blind man, a man who has nothing, a pauper——?"

Cecily stared at her mother and her face flamed. "You think—you said that to— Oh, you're not my mother: you are somebody else." Suddenly she cried like a child, wide-mouthed, not even hiding her face. She whirled running. "Don't ever speak to me again," she gasped and fled wailing up the stairs. And a door slammed.

Mrs. Saunders sat thinking, tapping her teeth monotonously with a finger nail. After a while she rose, and going to the telephone, she called her husband downtown.

7

Voices

The Town:

I wonder what that woman that came home with him thinks about it, now he's taken another one. If I were that Saunders girl I wouldn't take a man that brought another woman right up to my door, you might say. And that new one, what'll she do now? Go away and get another man, I guess. Hope she'll learn enough to get a well one this time. . . . Funny goings-on in that house. And a preacher of the gospel, too. Even if he is Episcopal. If he wasn't such a nice man. . . .

George Farr:

It isn't true, Cecily, darling, sweetheart. You can't, you can't. After your body prone and narrow as a pool dividing. . . .

The Town:

I hear that boy of Mahon's, that hurt fellow, and that girl of Saunders', are going to get married. My wife said they never would, but I said all the time. . . .

Mrs. Burney:

Men don't know. They should of looked out for him better. Saying he never wanted for nothing. . . .

George Farr:

Cecily, Cecily. . . . Is this death?

The Town:

There's that soldier that came with Mahon. I guess that woman will take him now. But maybe she don't have to. He might have been saving time himself.

Well, wouldn't you, if you was him?

Sergeant Madden:

Powers. Powers. . . . A man's face spitted like a moth on a lance of flame. Powers. . . . Rotten luck for her.

Mrs. Burney:

Dewey, my boy. . . .

Sergeant Madden:

No, ma'am. He was all right. We did all we could. . . .

Cecily Saunders:

Yes, yes, Donald. I will, I will! I will get used to your poor face, Donald! George, my dear love, take me away, George!

Sergeant Madden:

Yes, yes, he was all right. . . . A man on a fire-step, screaming with fear.

George Farr:

Cecily, how could you? How could you?

The Town:

That girl . . . time she was took in hand by somebody. Running around town nearly nekkid. Good thing he's blind, ain't it?

Guess she hopes he'll stay blind, too. . . .

Margaret Powers:

No, no, good-bye, dear dead Dick, ugly dead Dick. . . .

Joe Gilligan:

He is dying, he gets the woman he doesn't want even, while
I am not dying. . . . Margaret, what shall I do? What
can I say?

Emmy:

Come here, Emmy? Ah, come to me, Donald. But he
is dead.

Cecily Saunders:

George, my lover, my poor dear. . . . What have we done?

Mrs. Burney:

Dewey, Dewey, so brave, so young. . . .

(This was Donald, my son. He is dead.)

8

Mrs. Powers mounted the stairs under Mrs. Saunders' curious eyes. The older woman had been cold, almost rude, but
Mrs. Powers had won her point, and choosing Cecily's door
from her mother's directions she knocked.

After a while she knocked again and called: "Miss
Saunders."

Silence was again a hushed tense interval, then Cecily's
muffled voice came through the door:

"Go away."

"Please," she insisted. "I want to see you a moment."

"No, no. Go away."

"But I must see you." There was no reply and she added:
"I have just talked to your mother, and to Dr. Mahon. Let
me come in, won't you?"

She heard movement, a bed, then another interval. Fool,
taking time to powder her face. But you would, too, she
told herself. The door opened under her hand.

Powder only made the traces of tears more visible and

Cecily turned her back as Mrs. Powers entered the room. She could see the indentation of a body on the bed, and a crumpled pillow. Mrs. Powers, not being offered a chair, sat on the foot of the bed, and Cecily, across the room, leaning in a window and staring out, said ungraciously: "What do you want?"

How like her this room is! thought the caller, observing pale maple and a triple mirrored dressing-table bearing a collection of fragile crystal, and delicate clothing carelessly about on chairs, on the floor. On a chest of drawers was a small camera picture, framed.

"May I look?" she asked, knowing instinctively who it was. Cecily, stubbornly presenting her back in a thin, formless garment through which light from the window passed revealing her narrow torso, made no reply. Mrs. Powers approached and saw Donald Mahon bareheaded in a shabby unbuttoned tunic standing before a corrugated iron wall, carrying a small resigned dog casually by the scruff of the neck, like a handbag.

"That's so typical of him, isn't it?" she commented. Cecily said rudely:

"What do you want with me?"

"That's exactly what your mother asked me, you know. She seemed to think I was interfering also."

"Well, aren't you? Nobody asked you to come here." Cecily turned, leaning her hip against the window ledge.

"I don't think it's interference when it's warranted though. Do you?"

"Warranted? Who asked you to interfere? Did Donald do it, or are you trying to scare me off? You needn't tell me Donald asked you to get him out of it: it will be a lie."

"But I'm not: I don't intend to. I'm trying to help you both."

"Oh, you are against me. Everybody's against me, except Donald. And you keep him shut up like a—a prisoner." She turned quickly and leaned her head against the window.

Mrs. Powers sat quietly examining her, her frail revealed body under the silly garment she wore—a webby cloying thing worse than nothing and a fit complement to the single belaced garment it revealed above the long hushed gleams of her stockings. . . . If Cellini had been a hermit-priest he might have imagined her, Mrs. Powers thought, wishing mildly she could see the other naked. At last she rose from the bed and crossed to the window. Cecily kept her head stubbornly averted, and expecting tears, she touched the girl's shoulder. "Cecily," she said, quietly.

Cecily's green eyes were dry, stony, and she moved swiftly across the room with her delicate narrow stride. She stood holding the door open. Mrs. Powers, at the window, did not accept. Did she ever, ever forget herself? she wondered, observing the studied grace of the girl's body turned on the laxed ball of a thigh. Cecily met her gaze with one of haughty commanding scorn.

"Won't you even leave the room when you are asked?" she said, making her swift, coarse voice sound measured and cold.

Mrs. Powers thinking O hell, what's the use? moved so as to lean her thigh against the bed. Cecily, without changing her position, moved the door for emphasis. Standing quietly, watching her studied fragility (her legs are rather sweet, she admitted, but why all this posing for me? I'm not a man) Mrs. Powers ran her palm slowly along the smooth wood of the bed. Suddenly the other slammed the door and returned to the window. Mrs. Powers followed.

"Cecily, why can't we talk about it sensibly?" The girl made no reply, ignoring her, crumpling the curtain in her fingers. "Miss Saunders?"

"Why can't you let me alone?" Cecily flared suddenly, flaming out at her. "I don't want to talk to you about it. Why do you come to me?" Her eyes darkened: they were no longer hard. "If you want him, take him, then. You have every chance you could want, keeping him shut up there so that even I can't see him!"

"But I don't want him. I am trying to straighten things out for him. Don't you know that if I had wanted him I would have married him before I brought him home?"

"You tried it, and couldn't. That's why you didn't. Oh, don't say it wasn't," she rushed on as the other would have spoken. "I saw it that first day. That you were after him. And if you aren't, why do you keep on staying here?"

"You know that's a lie," Mrs. Powers replied, calmly.

"Then what makes you so interested in him, if you aren't in love with him?"

(This is hopeless.) She put her hand on the other's arm. Cecily shrank quickly away and she returned to lean again against the bed. She said:

"Your mother is against this, and Donald's father expects it. But what chance will you have against your mother?" (Against yourself?)

"I certainly don't need any advice from you," Cecily turned her head, her haughtiness, her anger, were gone and in their place was a thin hopeless despair. Even her voice, her whole attitude, had changed. "Don't you see how miserable I am?" she said, pitifully. "I didn't mean to be rude to you, but I don't know what to do, I don't know. . . . I am in such trouble: something terrible has happened to me. Please!"

Mrs. Powers, seeing her face, went to her quickly, putting her arm about the girl's narrow shoulders. Cecily avoided her. "Please, please go."

"Tell me what it is."

"No, no, I can't. Please——"

They paused, listening. Footsteps approaching, stopped beyond the door: a knock, and her father's voice called her name.

"Yes?"

"Dr. Mahon is downstairs. Can you come down?"

The two women stared at each other.

"Come," Mrs. Powers said.

Cecily's eyes went dark again and she whispered, "No, no, no!" trembling.

"Sis," her father repeated.

"Say yes," Mrs. Powers whispered.

"Yes, daddy. I'm coming."

"All right." The footsteps retreated and Mrs. Powers drew Cecily toward the door. The girl resisted.

"I can't go like this," she said, hysterically.

"Yes, you can. It's all right. Come."

Mrs. Saunders, sitting militant, formal and erect upon her chair, was saying as they entered:

"May I ask what this—this woman has to do with it?"

Her husband chewed a cigar. Light falling upon the rector's face held it like a gray bitten mask. Cecily ran to him. "Uncle Joe!" she cried.

"Cecily!" her mother said, sharply. "What do you mean, coming down like that?"

The rector rose, huge and black, embracing her. "Uncle Joe!" she repeated, clinging to him.

"Now, Robert," Mrs. Saunders began. But the rector interrupted her.

"Cecily," he said, raising her face. She twisted her chin and hid her face against his coat.

"Robert," said Mrs. Saunders.

The rector spoke grayly. "Cecily, we have talked it over together, and we think—your mother and father——"

She moved in her silly, revealing garment. "Daddy?" she exclaimed, staring at her father. He would not meet her gaze but sat slowly twisting his cigar. The rector continued:

"We think that you will only—that you— They say that Donald is going to die, Cecily," he finished.

Lithe as a sapling she thrust herself backward against his arm, bending, to see his face, staring at him. "Oh, Uncle Joe! Have you gone back on me, too?" she cried, passionately.

9

George Farr had been quite drunk for a week. His friend, the drug-clerk, thought that he was going crazy. He had become a local landmark, a tradition: even the town soaks began to look upon him with respect, calling him by his given name, swearing undying devotion to him.

In the intervals of belligerent or rollicking or maudlin inebriation he knew periods of devastating despair like a monstrous bliss, like that of a caged animal, of a man being slowly tortured to death: a minor monotony of pain. As a rule, though, he managed to stay fairly drunk. Her narrow body sweetly dividing naked . . . have another drink. . . . I'll kill you if you keep on fooling around her . . . my girl, my girl . . . her narrow . . . 'nother drink . . oh, God, oh, God . . . sweetly dividing for another . . . have drink, what hell I care, oh, God, oh, God, oh, God, oh, God. . . .

Though "nice" people no longer spoke to him on the streets he was, after a fashion, cared for and protected by casual acquaintances and friends both black and white, as in the way of small towns particularly and of the "inferior" classes anywhere.

He sat glassy-eyed among fried smells, among noises, at an oilcloth-covered table.

"Clu—hoverrrrrr blarrrr—sums, clo—ver blarrrr—sum-mmzzzz," sang a nasal voice terribly, the melody ticked off at spaced intervals by a small monotonous sound, like a clock-bomb going off. Like this:

Clo (tick) ver (tick) rrr (tick) (tick) bl (tick) rrs (tick) sss (tick) umm (tick) zzz.

Beside him sat two of his new companions, quarreling, spitting, holding hands and weeping over the cracked interminability of the phonograph record. "Clo verrrr blar—sums," it repeated with saccharine passion; when it ran down they repaired to a filthy alley behind the filthier kitchen to drink of George Farr's whisky. Then they returned and played the record through again, clutching hands while frank tears slid down their otherwise unwashed cheeks. "Clooooooooover blaaaaaarsummmmsss. . . ."

Truely vice is a dull and decorous thing: no life in the world is as hard, requiring so much sheer physical and moral strength as the so-called "primrose path." Being "good" is much less trouble.

"Clo—ver blar—sums. . . ."

. . . After a while his attention was called to the fact that someone had been annoying him for some time. Focusing his eyes he at last recognized the proprietor in an apron on which he must have dried his dishes for weeks. "What'n 'ell y' want?" he asked, with feeble liquid belligerence, and the man finally explained to him that he was wanted on the telephone in a neighboring drug-store. He rose, pulling himself together.

"Clu—hooooooooover blar—sums. . . ."

After a few years he languished from a telephone mouthpiece holding himself erect, watching without interest a light globe over the prescription desk describing slow concentric circles.

"George?" There was something in the unknown voice speaking his name, such anguish, as to almost shock him sober. "George."

"This George . . . hello. . . .

"George, it's Cecily. Cecily. . . ."

Drunkenness left him like a retreating wave. He could feel his heart stop, then surge, deafening him, blinding him with his own blood.

"George. . . . Do you hear me?" (Ah, George, to have been drunk now!) (Cecily, oh, Cecily!) "Yes! Yes!" gripping the instrument as though this would keep her against escape. "Yes, Cecily? Cecily! It's George. . . ."

"Come to me, now. At once."

"Yes, yes. Now?"

"Come, George, darling. Hurry, hurry. . . ."

"Yes!" he cried again. "Hello, hello!" The line made no response. He waited but it was dead. His heart pounded and pounded, hotly; he could taste his own hot bitter blood in his throat. (Cecily, oh, Cecily!)

He plunged down the length of the store and while a middle-aged clerk filling a prescription poised his bottle to watch in dull amazement, George Farr tore his shirt open at the throat and thrust his whole head beneath a gushing water tap in a frenzy of activity.

(Cecily, oh, Cecily!)

10

He seemed so old, so tired as he sat at the head of the table toying with his food, as if the very fiber of him had lost all resilience. Gilligan ate with his usual informal appetite and Donald and Emmy sat side by side so that Emmy could help him. Emmy enjoyed mothering him, now that she could never

have him again for a lover; she objected with passionate ardor
when Mrs. Powers offered to relieve her. The Donald she
had known was dead; this one was but a sorry substitute,
but Emmy was going to make the best of it, as women will.
She had even got accustomed to taking her food after it had
cooled.

Mrs. Powers sat watching them. Emmy's shock of no
particular color hair was near his worn head in intent devotion, her labor-worried hand seemed to have an eye of its
own, so quick, so tender it was to anticipate him and guide
his hand with the food she had prepared for him. Mrs.
Powers wondered which Donald Emmy loved the more, wondering if she had not perhaps forgotten the former one completely save as a symbol of sorrow. Then the amazing logical
thought occurred to her that here was the woman for Donald
to marry.

Of course it was. Why had no one thought of that before? Then she told herself that no one had done very much
thinking during the whole affair, that it had got on without
any particular drain on any intelligence. Why did we take
it for granted that he must marry Cecily and no other? Yet
we all accepted it as an arbitrary fact and off we went with
our eyes closed and our mouths open, like hounds in full cry.

But would Emmy take him? Wouldn't she be so frightened at the prospect that she'd be too self-conscious with him
afterward to care for him as skillfully as she does now;
wouldn't it cause her to confuse in her mind to his detriment
two separate Donalds—a lover and an invalid? I wonder
what Joe will think about it.

She looked at Emmy impersonal as Omnipotence, helping
Donald with effacing skill, seeming to envelop him, yet never
touching him. Anyway, I'll ask her, she thought, sipping her
tea.

Night was come. Tree-frogs, remembering last night's rain, resumed their monotonous molding of liquid beads of sound; grass blades and leaves losing shapes of solidity gained shapes of sound: the still suspire of earth, of the ground preparing for slumber; flowers by day, spikes of bloom, became with night spikes of scent; the silver tree at the corner of the house hushed its never-still never-escaping ecstasy. Already toads hopped along concrete pavements drinking prisoned heat through their dragging bellies.

Suddenly the rector started from his dream. "Tut, tut. We are making mountains from mole hills, as usual. If she wants to marry Donald I am sure her people will not withhold their consent always. Why should they object to their daughter marrying him? Do you know——"

"Hush!" she said. He looked up at her startled, then seeing her warning glance touch Mahon's oblivious head, he understood. She saw Emmy's wide shocked eyes on her and she rose at her place. "You are through, aren't you?" she said to the rector. "Suppose we go to the study."

Mahon sat quiet, chewing. She could not tell whether or not he heard. She passed behind Emmy and leaning to her whispered: "I want to speak to you. Don't say anything to Donald."

The rector, preceding her, fumbled the light on in the study. "You must be careful," she told him, "how you talk before him, how you tell him."

"Yes," he agreed apologetically. "I was so deep in thought."

"I know you were. I don't think it is necessary to tell him at all, until he asks."

"And that will never be. She loves Donald: she will not let her people prevent her marrying him. I am not customarily in favor of such a procedure as instigating a young woman to marry against her parents' wishes, but in this case. . . . You do not think that I am inconsistent, that I am partial because my son is involved?"

"No, no. Of course not."

"Don't you agree with me, that Cecily will insist on the wedding?"

"Yes, indeed." What else could she say?

Gilligan and Mahon had gone and Emmy was clearing the table when she returned. Emmy whirled upon her.

"She ain't going to take him? What was Uncle Joe saying?"

"Her people don't like the idea. That's all. She hasn't refused. But I think we had better stop it now, Emmy. She has changed her mind so often nobody can tell what she'll do."

Emmy turned back to the table, lowering her head, scraping a plate. Mrs. Powers watched her busy elbow, hearing the little clashing noises of china and silver. A bowl of white roses shattered slowly upon the center of the table.

"What do you think, Emmy?"

"I don't know," Emmy replied, sullenly. "She ain't my kind. I don't know nothing about it."

Mrs. Powers approached the table. "Emmy," she said. The other did not raise her head, made no reply. She turned the girl gently by the shoulder. "Would you marry him, Emmy?"

Emmy straightened hotly, clutching a plate and a fork. "Me? Me marry him? Me take another's leavings? (Donald, Donald.) And her leavings, at that, her that's run after every boy in town, dressed up in her silk clothes?"

Mrs. Powers moved back to the door and Emmy scraped dishes fiercely. This plate became blurred, she blinked and saw something splash on it. She shan't see me cry! she

whispered passionately, bending her head lower, waiting for
Mrs. Powers to ask her again. (Donald, Donald. . . .)

When she was young, going to school in the spring, having
to wear coarse dresses and shoes while other girls wore silk
and thin leather; being not pretty at all while other girls
were pretty——

Walking home to where work awaited her while other girls
were riding in cars or having ice cream or talking to boys
and dancing with them, with boys that had no use for her;
sometimes he would step out beside her, so still, so quick, all
of a sudden—and she didn't mind not having silk.

And when they swam and fished and roamed the woods
together she forgot she wasn't pretty, even. Because he was
beautiful, with his body all brown and quick, so still . . .
making her feel beautiful, too.

And when he said Come here, Emmy, she went to him, and
wet grass and dew under her and over her his head with the
whole sky for a crown, and the moon running on them like
water that wasn't wet and that you couldn't feel. . . .

Marry him? Yes! Yes! Let him be sick: she would
cure him; let him be a Donald that had forgotten her—she
had not forgotten: she could remember enough for both of
them. Yes! Yes! she cried, soundlessly, stacking dishes,
waiting for Mrs. Powers to ask her again. Her red hands
were blind, tears splashed fatly on her wrists. Yes! Yes!
trying to think it so loudly that the other must hear. She
sha'n't see me cry! she whispered again. But the other woman
only stood in the door watching her busy back. So she
gathered up the dishes slowly, there being no reason to linger
any longer. Keeping her head averted she carried the dishes
to the pantry door, slowly, waiting for the other to speak
again. But the other woman said nothing and Emmy left the
room, her pride forbidding her to let the other see her tears.

II

The study was dark when she passed, but she could see the rector's head in dim silhouette against the more spacious darkness outside the window. She passed slowly onto the veranda. Leaning her quiet tall body against a column in the darkness beyond the fan of light from the door she listened to the hushed myriad life of night things, to the slow voices of people passing unseen along an unseen street, watching the hurried staring twin eyes of motor cars like restless insects. A car slowing, drew up to the corner, and after a while a dark figure came along the pale gravel of the path, hurried yet diffident. It paused and screamed delicately in midpath, then it sped on toward the steps, where it stopped again and Mrs. Powers stepped forward from beside her post.

"Oh," gasped Miss Cecily Saunders, starting, lifting her hand slimly against her dark dress. "Mrs. Powers?"

"Yes. Come in, won't you?"

Cecily ran with nervous grace up the steps. "It was a f-frog," she explained between her quick respirations. "I nearly stepped—ugh!" She shuddered, a slim muted flame hushed darkly in dark clothing. "Is Uncle Joe here? May I—" her voice died away diffidently.

"He is in the study," Mrs. Powers answered. What has happened to her? she thought. Cecily stood so that the light from the hall fell full on her. There was in her face a thin nervous despair, a hopeless recklessness, and she stared at the other woman's shadowed face for a long moment. Then she said Thank you, thank you, suddenly, hysterically, and ran quickly into the house. Mrs. Powers looked after her, then following, saw her dark dress. She is going away, Mrs. Powers thought, with conviction.

Cecily flew on ahead like a slim dark bird, into the unlighted

study. "Uncle Joe?" she said, poised, touching either side
of the door-frame. The rector's chair creaked suddenly.

"Eh?" he said, and the girl sailed across the room like a
bat, dark in the darkness, sinking at his feet, clutching his
knees. He tried to raise her but she clung to his legs the
tighter, burrowing her head into his lap.

"Uncle Joe, forgive me, forgive me!"

"Yes, yes. I knew you would come to us. I told them——"

"No, no. I—I— You have always been so good, so sweet
to me, that I couldn't. . . ." She clutched him again fiercely.

"Cecily, what is it? Now, now, you mustn't cry about it.
Come now, what is it?" Knowing a sharp premonition he
raised her face, trying to see it. But it was only a formless
soft blur warmly in his hands.

"Say you forgive me first, dear Uncle Joe. Won't you?
Say it, say it. If you won't forgive me, I don't know what'll
become of me." His hands slipping downward felt her delicate tense shoulders and he said:

"Of course, I forgive you."

"Thank you. Oh, thank you. You are so kind—" she
caught his hand, holding it against her mouth.

"What is it, Cecily?" he asked, quietly, trying to soothe
her.

She raised her head. "I am going away."

"Then you aren't going to marry Donald?"

She lowered her head to his knees again, clutching his hand
in her long nervous fingers, holding it against her face. "I
cannot, I cannot. I am a—I am not a good woman any more,
dear Uncle Joe. Forgive me, forgive me. . . ."

He withdrew his hand and she let herself be raised to her
feet, feeling his arms, his huge kind body. "There, there,"
patting her back with his gentle heavy hand. "Don't cry."

"I must go," she said at last, moving slimly and darkly

against his bulk. He released her. She clutched his hand again sharply, letting it go. "Good-bye," she whispered, and fled swift and dark as a bird, gracefully to a delicate tapping of heels, as she had come.

She passed Mrs. Powers on the porch without seeing her and sped down the steps. The other woman watched her slim dark figure until it disappeared . . . after an interval the car that had stopped at the corner of the garden flashed on its lights and drove away. . . .

Mrs. Powers, pressing the light switch, entered the study. The rector stared at her as she approached the desk, quiet and hopeless.

"Cecily has broken the engagement, Margaret. So the wedding is off."

"Nonsense," she told him sharply, touching him with her firm hand. "I'm going to marry him myself. I intended to all the time. Didn't you suspect?"

12

San Francisco, Cal.,
April 25, 1919.

Darling Margaret—

I told mother last night and of coarse she thinks we are too young. But I explained to her how times have changed since the war how the war makes you older than they used to. I see fellows my age that did not serve specially flying which is an education in itself and they seem like kids to me because at last I have found the woman I want and my kid days are over. After knowing so many women to found you so far away when I did not expect it. Mother says for me to go in business and make money if I expect a woman to marry me so I am going to start in to-morrow I have got

the place already. So it will not be long till I see you and
take you in my arms at last and always. How can I tell you
how much I love you you are so different from them. Lov-
ing you has already made me a serious man realizing responsa-
bilities. They are all so silly compared with you talking of
jazz and going some place where all the time I have been
invited on parties but I refuse because I rather sit in my
room thinking of you putting my thoughts down on paper let
them have their silly fun. I think of you all ways and if it
did not make you so unhappy I want you to think of me
always. But don't I would not make you unhappy at all my
own dearest. So think of me and remember I love you only
and will love you only will love you all ways.

Forever yours

JULIAN.

13

The Baptist minister, a young dervish in a white lawn tie,
being most available, came and did his duty and went away.
He was young and fearfully conscientious and kind-hearted;
upright and passionately desirous of doing good: so much so
that he was a bore. But he had soldiered after a fashion and
he liked and respected Dr. Mahon, refusing to believe that
simply because Dr. Mahon was Episcopal he was going to hell
as soon as he died.

He wished them luck and fled busily away, answering his
own obscure compulsions. They watched his busy energetic
backside until he was out of sight, then Gilligan silently
helped Mahon down the steps and across the lawn to his
favorite seat beneath the tree. The new Mrs. Mahon walked
silently beside them. Silence was her wont, but not Gilligan's.
Yet he had spoken no word to her. Walking near him she
put out her hand and touched his arm: he turned to her a face

so bleak, so reft that she knew a sharp revulsion, a sickness with everything. (Dick, Dick. How well you got out of this mess!) She looked quickly away, across the garden, beyond the spire where pigeons crooned the afternoon away, unemphatic as sleep, biting her lips. Married, and she had never felt so alone.

Gilligan settled Mahon in his chair with his impersonal half-reckless care. Mahon said:

"Well, Joe, I'm married at last."

"Yes," answered Gilligan. His careless spontaneity was gone. Even Mahon noticed it in his dim oblivious way. "I say, Joe."

"What is it, Loot?"

Mahon was silent and his wife took her customary chair, leaning back and staring up into the tree. He said at last: "Carry on, Joe."

"Not now, Loot. I don't feel so many. Think I'll take a walk," he answered, feeling Mrs. Mahon's eyes on him. He met her gaze harshly, combatively.

"Joe," she said quietly, bitterly.

Gilligan saw her pallid face, her dark unhappy eyes, her mouth like a tired scar and he knew shame. His own bleak face softened.

"All right, Loot," he said, quietly matching her tone, with a trace of his old ambiguous unseriousness. "What'll it be? Bust up a few more minor empires, huh?"

Just a trace, but it was there. Mrs. Mahon looked at him again with gratitude and that old grave happiness which he knew so well, unsmiling but content, which had been missing for so long, so long; and it was as though she had laid her firm strong hand on him. He looked quickly away from her face, sad and happy, not bitter any more.

"Carry on, Joe."

CHAPTER VIII

San Francisco, Cal,
April 27, 1919.

My dearest sweetheart—

Just a line to let you know that I have gone into business into the banking business making money for you. To give ourselves the position in the world you deserve and a home of our own. The work is congenal talking to other people in the business that don't know anything about aviation. All they think about is going out to dance with men. Everyday means one day less for us to be with you forever. All my love.

Yours forever

JULIAN.

2

Nine day or ninety day or nine hundred day sensations have a happy faculty for passing away into the oblivion whence pass sooner or later all of man's inventions. Keeps from getting the world all cluttered up. You say right off that this is God's work. But it must be a woman: no man could be so utilitarian. But then, women preserve only those things which can or might be used again. So this theory is also exploded.

After a while there were no more of the local curious to call; after a while those who had said I told you so when Miss Cecily Saunders let it be known that she would marry the parson's son and who said I told you so when she did not marry the parson's son forgot about it. There were other

things to think and talk of: this was the lying-in period of
the K. K. K. and the lying-out period of Mr. Wilson, a
democratish gentleman living in Washington, D. C.

Besides, it was all legal now. Miss Cecily Saunders was
safely married—though nobody knows where they was from
the time they drove out of town in George Farr's car until
they was properly married by a priest in Atlanta the next
day (but then I always told you about that girl). They
all hoped for the worst. And that Mrs. What's-her-name, that
tall black-headed woman at Mahon's, had at last married
someone, putting an end to that equivocal situation.

And so April became May. There were fair days when
the sun, becoming warmer and warmer, rising, drank off the
dew, and flowers bloomed like girls ready for a ball, then
drooped in the langourous fulsome heat like girls after the
ball; when earth, like a fat woman, recklessly trying giddy hat
after hat, trying a trimming of apple and pear and peach,
threw it away; tried narcissi and jonquil and flag: threw it
away—so early flowers bloomed and passed and later flowers
bloomed to fade and fall, giving place to yet later ones. Fruit
blossoms were gone, pear was forgotten: what were once tall
candlesticks, silvery with white bloom, were now tall jade
candlesticks of leaves beneath the blue cathedral of sky
across which, in hushed processional, went clouds like choir-
boys slow and surpliced.

Leaves grew larger and greener until all rumor of azure and
silver and pink had gone from them; birds sang and made
love and married and built houses in them and in the tree
at the corner of the house that yet swirled its white-bellied
leaves in never-escaping skyward ecstasies; bees broke clover
upon the lawn interrupted at intervals by the lawn mower and
its informal languid conductor.

Their mode of life had not changed. The rector was neither

happy nor unhappy, neither resigned nor protesting. Occasionally he entered some dream within himself. He conducted
services in the dim oaken tunnel of the church while his flock
hissed softly among themselves or slept between the responses,
while pigeons held their own crooning rituals of audible slumber in the spire that, arcing across motionless young clouds,
seemed slow and imminent with ruin. He married two people
and buried one: Gilligan found this ominous and said so aloud;
Mrs. Mahon found this silly and said so aloud.

Mrs. Worthington sent her car for them at times and they
drove into the country regretting the dogwood, the three of
them (two of them did, that is, Mahon had forgotten what
dogwood was); the three of them sat beneath the tree while
one of them wallowed manfully among polysyllabics and another of them sat motionless, neither asleep nor awake. They
could never tell whether or not he heard. Nor could they
ever tell whether or not he knew whom he had married. Perhaps he didn't care. Emmy, efficient and gentle, mothering
him, was a trifle subdued. Gilligan still slept on his cot at
the foot of Mahon's bed, lest he be needed.

"You two are the ones who should have married him," his
wife remarked with quiet wit.

3

Mrs. Mahon and Gilligan had resumed their old status of
companionship and quiet pleasure in each other's company.
Now that he no longer hoped to marry her she could be freer
with him.

"Perhaps this is what we needed, Joe. Anyway, I never
knew anyone I liked half this much."

They walked slowly in the garden along the avenue of roses
which passed beneath the two oaks, beyond which, against

a wall, poplars in a restless formal row were like columns of a temple.

"You're easy pleased then," Gilligan answered with sour assumed moroseness. He didn't have to tell her how much he liked her.

"Poor Joe," she said. "Cigarette, please."

"Poor you," he retorted, giving her one. "I'm all right. I ain't married."

"You can't escape forever, though. You are too nice:—safe for the family: will stand hitched."

"Is that a bargain?" he asked.

"Sufficient unto the day, Joe. . . ."

After a while he stayed her with his hand. "Listen." They halted and she stared at him intently.

"What?"

"There's that damn mocking bird again. Hear him? What's he got to sing about, you reckon?"

"He's got plenty to sing about. April's got to be May, and still spring isn't half over. Listen. . . ."

4

Emmy had become an obsession with Januarius Jones, such an obsession that it had got completely out of the realm of sex into that of mathematics, like a paranoia. He manufactured chances to see her, only to be repulsed; he lay in wait for her like a highwayman, he begged, he threatened, he tried physical strength, and he was repulsed. It had got to where, had she acceded suddenly, he would have been completely reft of one of his motivating impulses, of his elemental impulse to live: he might have died. Yet he knew that if he didn't get her soon he would become crazy, an imbecile.

After a time it assumed the magic of numbers. He had failed twice: this time success must be his or the whole cosmic scheme would crumble, hurling him, screaming, into blackness, where no blackness was, death where death was not. Januarius Jones, by nature and inclination a Turk, was also becoming an oriental. He felt that his number must come: the fact that it would not was making an idiot of him.

He dreamed of her at night, he mistook other women for her, other voices for hers; he hung skulking about the rectory at all hours, too wrought up to come in where he might have to converse sanely with sane people. Sometimes the rector, tramping huge and oblivious in his dream, flushed him in out-of-the-way corners of concealment, flushed him without surprise.

"Ah, Mr. Jones," he would say, starting like a goaded elephant, "good morning."

"Good morning, sir," Jones would reply, his eyes glued on the house.

"You are out for a walk?"

"Yes, sir. Yes, sir." And Jones would walk hurriedly away in an opposite direction as the rector, entering his dream again, resumed his own.

Emmy told Mrs. Mahon of this with scornful contempt.

"Why don't you tell Joe, or let me tell him?" Mrs. Mahon asked.

Emmy sniffed with capable independence. "About that worm? I can take care of him, all right. I do my own fighting."

"And I bet you are good at it, too."

And Emmy said: "I guess I am."

5

April had become May.

Fair days, and wet days in which rain ran with silver lances over the lawn, in which rain dripped leaf to leaf while birds still sang in the hushed damp greenness under the trees, and made love and married and built houses and still sang; in which rain grew soft as the grief of a young girl grieving for the sake of grief.

Mahon hardly ever rose now. They had got him a movable bed and upon this he lay, sometimes in the house, sometimes on the veranda where the wistaria inverted its cool lilac flame, while Gilligan read to him. They had done with Rome and they now swam through the tedious charm of Rousseau's "Confessions" to Gilligan's hushed childish delight.

Kind neighbors came to inquire; the specialist from Atlanta came once by request and once on his own initiative, making a friendly call and addressing Gilligan meticulously as "Doctor," spent the afternoon chatting with them, and went away. Mrs. Mahon and he liked each other immensely. Dr. Gary called once or twice and insulted them all and went away nattily smoking his slender rolled cigarettes. Mrs. Mahon and he did not like each other at all. The rector grew grayer and quieter, neither happy nor unhappy, neither protesting nor resigned.

"Wait until next month. He will be stronger then. This is a trying month for invalids. Don't you think so?" he asked his daughter-in-law.

"Yes," she would tell him, looking out at the green world, the sweet, sweet spring, "yes, yes."

6

It was a postcard. You buy them for a penny, stamp and all. The post office furnishes writing material free.

"Got your letter. Will write later. Remember me to Gilligan and Lieut. Mahon.   "JULIAN L."

7

Mahon was asleep on the veranda and the other three sat beneath the tree on the lawn, watching the sun go down. At last the reddened edge of the disc was sliced like a cheese by the wistaria-covered lattice wall and the neutral buds were a pale agitation against the dead afternoon. Soon the evening star would be there above the poplar tip, perplexing it, immaculate and ineffable, and the poplar was vain as a girl darkly in an arrested passionate ecstasy. Half of the moon was a coin broken palely near the zenith and at the end of the lawn the first fireflies were like lazily blown sparks from cool fires. A negro woman passing crooned a religious song, mellow and passionless and sad.

They sat talking quietly. The grass was becoming gray with dew and she felt dew on her thin shoes. Suddenly Emmy came around the corner of the house running and darted up the steps and through the entrance, swift in the dusk.

"What in the world—" began Mrs. Mahon, then they saw Jones, like a fat satyr, leaping after her, hopelessly distanced. When he saw them he slowed immediately and lounged up to them slovenly as ever. His yellow eyes were calmly opaque but she could see the heave of his breathing. Convulsed with laughter she at last found her voice.

"Good evening, Mr. Jones."

"Say," said Gilligan with interest, "what was you——"

"Hush, Joe," Mrs. Mahon told him. Jones' eyes, clear and yellow, obscene and old in sin as a goat's, roved between them.

"Good evening, Mr. Jones." The rector became abruptly aware of his presence. "Walking again, eh?"

"Running," Gilligan corrected, and the rector repeated Eh? looking from Jones to Gilligan.

Mrs. Mahon indicated a chair. "Sit down, Mr. Jones. You must be rather fatigued, I imagine."

Jones stared toward the house, tore his eyes away and sat down. The canvas sagged under him and he rose and spun his chair so as to face the dreaming façade of the rectory. He sat again.

"Say," Gilligan asked him, "what was you doing, anyway?"

Jones eyed him briefly, heavily. "Running," he snapped, turning his eyes again to the dark house.

"Running?" the divine repeated.

"I know: I seen that much from here. What was you running for, I asked."

"Reducing, perhaps," Mrs. Mahon remarked, with quiet malice.

Jones turned his yellow stare upon her. Twilight was gathering swiftly. He was a fat and shapeless mass palely tweeded. "Reducing, yes. But not to marriage."

"I wouldn't be so sure of that if I were you," she told him. "A courtship like that will soon reduce you to anything, almost."

"Yeh," Gilligan amended, "if that's the only way you got to get a wife you'd better pick out another one besides Emmy. You'll be a shadow time you catch her. That is," he added, "if you aim to do your courting on foot."

"What's this?" the rector asked.

"Perhaps Mr. Jones was merely preparing to write a poem. Living it first, you know," Mrs. Mahon offered. Jones looked at her sharply. "Atalanta," she suggested in the dusk.

"Atlanta?" repeated Gilligan, "what——"

"Try an apple next time, Mr. Jones," she advised.

"Or a handful of salt, Mr. Jones," added Gilligan in a thin

falsetto. Then in his natural voice. "But what's Atlanta got to——"

"Or a cherry, Mr. Gilligan," said Jones viciously. "But then, I am not God, you know."

"Shut your mouth, fellow," Gilligan told him roughly.

"What's this?" the rector repeated. Jones turned to him heavily explanatory:

"It means, sir, that Mr. Gilligan is under the impression that his wit is of as much importance to me as my actions are to him."

"Not me," denied Gilligan with warmth. "You and me don't have the same thoughts about anything, fellow."

"Why shouldn't they be?" the rector asked. "It is but natural to believe that one's actions and thoughts are as important to others as they are to oneself, is it not?"

Gilligan gave this his entire attention. It was getting above his head, beyond his depth. But Jones was something tangible, and he had already chosen Jones for his own.

"Naturally," agreed Jones with patronage. "There is a kinship between the human instruments of all action and thought and emotion. Napoleon thought that his actions were important, Swift thought his emotions were important, Savonarola thought his beliefs were important. And they were. But we are discussing Mr. Gilligan."

"Say—" began Gilligan.

"Very apt, Mr. Jones," murmured Mrs. Mahon above the suggested triangle of her cuffs and collar. "A soldier, a priest and a dyspeptic."

"Say," Gilligan repeated, "who's swift, anyway? I kind of got bogged up back there."

"Mr. Jones is, according to his own statement. You are Napoleon, Joe."

"Him? Not quite swift enough to get himself a girl,

though. The way he was gaining on Emmy— You ought
to have a bicycle," he suggested.

"There's your answer, Mr. Jones," the rector told him.
Jones looked toward Gilligan's fading figure in disgust, like
that of a swordsman who has been disarmed by a peasant with
a pitchfork.

"That's what association with the clergy does for you," he
said crassly.

"What is it?" Gilligan asked. "What did I say wrong?"

Mrs. Mahon leaned over and squeezed his arm. "You didn't
say anything wrong, Joe. You were grand."

Jones glowered sullenly in the dusk. "By the way," he
said, suddenly, "how is your husband to-day?"

"Just the same, thank you."

"Stands wedded life as well as can be expected, does he?"
She ignored this. Gilligan watched him in leashed anticipation. He continued: "That's too bad. You had expected
great things from marriage, hadn't you? Sort of a miraculous
rejuvenation?"

"Shut up, fellow" Gilligan told him. "Whatcher mean,
anyway?"

"Nothing, Mr. Galahad, nothing at all. I merely made a
civil inquiry. . . . Shows that when a man marries, his troubles
continue, doesn't it?"

"Then you oughtn't to have no worries about your troubles,"
Gilligan told him savagely.

"What?"

"I mean, if you don't have no better luck than you have
twice that I know of——"

"He has a good excuse for one failure, Joe," Mrs. Mahon
said.

They both looked toward her voice. The sky was bowled
with a still disseminated light that cast no shadow and branches

of trees were rigid as coral in a mellow tideless sea. "Mr. Jones says that to make love to Miss Saunders would be epicene."

"Epicene? What's that?"

"Shall I tell him, Mr. Jones? or will you?"

"Certainly. You intend to, anyway, don't you?"

"Epicene is something you want and can't get, Joe."

Jones rose viciously. "If you will allow me, I'll retire, I think," he said savagely. "Good evening."

"Sure," agreed Gilligan with alacrity, rising also. "I'll see Mr. Jones to the gate. He might get mixed up and head for the kitchen by mistake. Emmy might be one of them epicenes, too."

Without seeming to hurry Jones faded briskly away. Gilligan sprang after him. Jones, sensing him, whirled in the dusk and Gilligan leaped upon him.

"For the good of your soul," Gilligan told him joyously. "You might say that's what running with preachers does for you, mightn't you?" he panted as they went down.

They rolled in dew and an elbow struck him smartly under the chin. Jones was up immediately and Gilligan, tasting his bitten tongue, sprang in pursuit. But Jones retained his lead. "He has sure learned to run from somebody," Gilligan grunted. "Practicing on Emmy so much, I guess. Wisht I was Emmy, now—until I catch him."

Jones doubled the house and plunged into the dreaming garden. Gilligan, turning the corner of the house, saw the hushed expanse where his enemy was, but his enemy, himself, was out of sight. Roses bloomed quietly under the imminence of night, hyacinths swung pale bells, waiting for another day. Dusk was a dream of arrested time, the mocking bird rippled it tentatively, and everywhere blooms slept passionately, waiting for to-morrow. But Jones was gone.

He stopped to listen upon the paling gravel, between the slow unpickable passion of roses, seeing the pale broken coin of the moon attain a richer luster against the unemphatic sky. Gilligan stilled his heaving lungs to listen, but he heard nothing. Then he began systematically to beat the firefly-starred scented dusk of the garden, beating all available cover, leaving not a blade of grass unturned. But Jones had got clean away; the slow hands of dusk had removed him as cleanly as the prestidigitator rieves a rabbit from an immaculate hat.

He stood in the center of the garden and cursed Jones thoroughly on the off-chance that he might be within hearing, then Gilligan slowly retraced his steps, retracing the course of the race through the palpable violet dusk. He passed the unlighted house where Emmy went somewhere about her duties, where at the corner of the veranda near the silver tree's twilight-musicked ecstasy Mahon slept on his movable bed and on across the lawn, while evening, like a ship with twilight-colored sails, dreamed on down the world.

The chairs were formless blurs beneath the tree and Mrs. Mahon's presence was indicated principally by her white collar and cuffs. As he approached, he could see dimly the rector reclined in slumber, and the woman's dark dress shaped her against the dull white of her canvas chair. Her face was pallid, winged either side by her hair. She raised her hand as he drew near.

"He's asleep," she whispered, as he sat beside her.

"He got away, damn him," he told her, in exasperation.

"Too bad. Better luck next time."

"You bet. And there'll be a next time soon as I see him again."

Night was almost come. Light, all light, passed from the world, from the earth, and leaves were still. Night was almost come, but not quite; day was almost gone, but not quite. Her shoes were quite soaked in dew.

"How long he has slept." She broke the silence diffidently. "We'll have to wake him soon for supper."

Gilligan stirred in his chair and almost as she spoke the rector sat hugely and suddenly up.

"Wait, Donald," he said, lumbering to his feet. With elephantine swiftness he hurried across the lawn toward the darkly dreaming house.

"Did he call?" they spoke together, in a dark foreboding. They half rose and stared toward the house, then at each other's indistinct, white face. "Did you—?" the question hung poised in the dusk between them and here was the evening star bloomed miraculously at the poplar's tip and the slender tree was a leafed and passionate Atalanta, poising her golden apple.

"No, did you?" he replied.

But they heard nothing.

"He dreamed," she said.

"Yes," Gilligan agreed. "He dreamed."

8

Donald Mahon lay quietly conscious of unseen forgotten spring, of greenness neither recalled nor forgot. After a time the nothingness in which he lived took him wholly again, but restlessly. It was like a sea into which he could neither completely pass nor completely go away from. Day became afternoon, became dusk and imminent evening: evening like a ship, with twilight-colored sails, dreamed down the world darkly toward darkness. And suddenly he found that he was passing from the dark world in which he had lived for a time he could not remember, again into a day that had

long passed, that had already been spent by those who lived
and wept and died, and so remembering it, this day was his
alone: the one trophy he had reft from Time and Space. *Per
ardua ad astra.*

I never knew I could carry this much petrol, he thought in
unsurprised ubiquity, leaving a darkness he did not remember
for a day he had long forgot, finding that the day, his own
familiar day, was approaching noon. It must be about ten
o'clock, for the sun was getting overhead and a few degrees
behind him, because he could see the shadow of his head
bisecting in an old familiarity the hand which held the control
column and the shadow of the cockpit rim across his flanks,
filling his lap, while the sun fell almost directly downward
upon his other hand lying idly on the edge of the fuselage.
Even the staggered lower wing was partly shadowed by the
upper one.

Yes, it is about ten, he thought, with a sense of familiarity.
Soon he would look at the time and make sure, but now. . . .
With the quick skill of practice and habit he swept the
horizon with a brief observing glance, casting a look above,
banking slightly to see behind. All clear. The only craft in
sight were far away to the left: a cumbersome observation
'plane doing artillery work; a brief glance divulged a pair of
scouts high above it, and above these he knew were probably two more.

Might have a look, he thought, knowing instinctively that
they were Huns, calculating whether or not he could reach
the spotter before the protecting scouts saw him. No, I guess
not, he decided. Better get on home. Fuel's low. He
settled his swinging compass needle.

Ahead of him and to the right, far away, what was once
Ypres, was like the cracked scab on an ancient festering
sore; beneath him were other shining sores lividly on a corpse

that would not be let to die. . . . He passed on lonely and
remote as a gull.

Then, suddenly, it was as if a cold wind had blown upon
him. What is it? he thought. It was that the sun had
been suddenly blotted from him. The empty world, the sky,
were yet filled with lazy spring sunlight, but the sun that had
been full upon him, had been brushed away as by a hand.
In the moment of realizing this, cursing his stupidity, he dived
steeply, slipping to the left. Five threads of vapor passed
between the upper and lower planes, each one nearer his
body, then he felt two distinct shocks at the base of his
skull and vision was reft from him as if a button somewhere
had been pressed. His trained hand nosed the machine up
smartly, and finding the Vickers release in the darkness, he
fired into the bland morning marbled and imminent with
March.

Sight flickered on again, like a poorly made electrical contact, he watched holes pitting into the fabric near him like
a miraculous small-pox and as he hung poised firing into the
sky a dial on his instrument board exploded with a small
sound. Then he felt his hand, saw his glove burst, saw his
bared bones. Then sight flashed off again and he felt himself lurch, falling until his belt caught him sharply across
the abdomen, and he heard something gnawing through his
frontal bone, like mice. You'll break your damn teeth, there,
he told them, opening his eyes.

His father's heavy face hung over him in the dusk like a
murdered Cæsar's.

He knew sight again and an imminent nothingness more
profound than any yet, while·evening, like a ship with twilight-
colored sails, drew down the world, putting calmly out to an
immeasurable sea. "That's how it happened," he said, staring
at him.

CHAPTER IX

I

Sex and death: the front door and the back door of the world. How indissolubly are they associated in us! In youth they lift us out of the flesh, in old age they reduce us again to the flesh; one to fatten us, the other to flay us, for the worm. When are sexual compulsions more readily answered than in war or famine or flood or fire?

Jones, lurking across the street, saw the coast clear at last.

(First, marched a uniformed self-constituted guard, led by a subaltern with three silver V's on his sleeve and a Boy Scout bugler furnished by the young Baptist minister, a fiery-eyed dervish, who had served in the Y. M. C. A.)

And then, fatly arrogant as a cat, Jones let himself through the iron gate.

(The last motor car trailed slowly up the street and the casuals gathered through curiosity—the town should raise a monument to Donald Mahon, with effigies of Margaret Mahon-Powers and Joe Gilligan for caryatides—and the little blackguard boys, both black and white, and including young Robert Saunders, come to envy the boy bugler, drifted away.)

And still cat-like, Jones mounted the steps and entered the deserted house. His yellow goat's eyes became empty as he paused, listening. Then he moved quietly toward the kitchen.

(The procession moved slowly across the square. Country people, in town to trade, turned to stare vacuously, merchant and doctor and lawyer came to door and window to look; the city fathers, drowsing in the courthouse yard, having successfully circumvented sex, having reached the point where death would look after them instead of they after death, waked and looked and slept again. Into a street, among and between horses and mules tethered to wagons, it passed, into a street bordered by shabby negro stores and shops, and here was Loosh standing stiffly at salute as it passed. "Who dat, Loosh?" "Mist' Donald Mahon." "Well, Jesus! we all gwine dat way, some day. All roads leads to de graveyard.")

Emmy sat at the kitchen table, her head between her hard elbows, her hands clasping behind her in her hair. How long she had sat there she did not know but she had heard them clumsily carrying him from the house and she put her hands over her ears, not to hear. But it seemed as if she could hear in spite of her closed ears those horrible, blundering, utterly unnecessary sounds: the hushed scraping of timid footsteps, the muted thumping of wood against wood, that passing, left behind an unbearable unchastity of stale flowers— as though flowers themselves getting a rumor of death became corrupt—all the excruciating ceremony for disposing of human carrion. So she had not heard Mrs. Mahon until the other touched her shoulder. (I would have cured him! If they had just let me marry him instead of her!) At the touch Emmy raised her swollen, blurred face, swollen because she couldn't seem to cry. (If I could just cry. You are prettier than me, with your black hair and your painted mouth. That's the reason.)

"Come, Emmy," Mrs. Mahon said.

"Let me alone! Go away!" she said, fiercely. "You got him killed: now bury him yourself."

"He would have wanted you to come, Emmy," the other woman said, gently.

"Go away, let me alone, I tell you!" She dropped her head to the table again, bumping her forehead. . . .

There was no sound in the kitchen save a clock. Life. Death. Life. Death. Life. Death. Forever and ever. (If I could only cry!) She could hear the dusty sound of spar-

rows and she imagined she could see the shadows growing
longer across the grass. Soon it will be night, she thought,
remembering that night long, long ago, the last time she had
seen Donald, her Donald—not that one! and he had said,
"Come here, Emmy," and she had gone to him. Her Donald
was dead long, long ago. . . . The clock went Life. Death.
Life. Death. There was something frozen in her chest, like
a dish-cloth in winter.

(The procession moved beneath arching iron letters. Rest
in Peace in cast repetition: Our motto is one for every cemetery, a cemetery for everyone throughout the land. Away,
following where fingers of sunlight pointed among cedars,
doves were cool, throatily unemphatic among the dead.)

"Go away," Emmy repeated to another touch on her
shoulder, thinking she had dreamed. It was a dream! she
thought and the frozen dish-rag in her chest melted with unbearable relief, becoming tears. It was Jones who had touched
her, but anyone would have been the same and she turned in
a passion of weeping, clinging to him.

(I am the Resurrection and the Life, saith the Lord. . . .)

Jones' yellow stare enveloped her like amber, remarking
her sun-burned hair and her foreshortened thigh, wrung by
her turning body into high relief.

(Whosoever believeth in Me, though he were dead. . . .)

My God, when will she get done weeping? First she
wets my pants, then my coat. But this time she'll dry it
for me, or I'll know the reason why.

(. . . yet shall he live. And whosoever liveth and believeth
in Me shall never die. . . .)

Emmy's sobbing died away: she knew no sensation save
that of warmth and languorous contentment, emptiness, even
when Jones raised her face and kissed her. "Come, Emmy,"
he said, raising her by the armpits. She rose obediently,

leaning against him warm and empty, and he led her through the house and up the stairs to her room. Outside the window, afternoon became abruptly rain, without warning, with no flapping of pennons nor sound of trumpet to herald it.

(The sun had gone, had been recalled as quickly as a usurer's note and the doves fell silent or went away. The Baptist dervish's Boy Scout lipped his bugle, sounding taps.)

2

"Hi, Bob," called a familiar voice, that of a compatriot. "Le's gwup to Miller's. They're playing ball up there."

He looked at his friend, making no reply to the greeting, and his expression was so strange that the other said: "Whatcher looking so funny about? You ain't sick, are you?"

"I don't haf to play ball if I don't want to, do I?" he replied, with sudden heat. He walked on while the other boy stood watching him with open mouth. After a while, he, too, turned and went on, stopping once or twice to look again at his friend become suddenly strange and queer. Then he passed, whooping from sight, forgetting him.

How strange everything looked! This street, these familiar trees—was this his home here, where his mother and father were, where Sis lived, where he ate and slept, lapped closely around with safety and solidity, where darkness was kind and sweet for sleeping? He mounted the steps and entered, wanting his mother. But, of course, she hadn't got back from— He found himself running suddenly through the hall toward a voice raised in comforting, crooning song. Here was a friend mountainous in blue calico, her elephantine thighs undulating, gracious as the wake of a ferry boat as she moved between table and stove.

She broke off her mellow, passionless song, exclaiming: "Bless yo' heart, honey, what is it?"

But he did not know. He only clung to her comforting, voluminous skirt in a gust of uncontrollable sorrow, while she wiped biscuit dough from her hands on a towel. Then she picked him up and sat upon a stiff-backed chair, rocking back and forth and holding him against her balloon-like breast until his fit of weeping shuddered away.

Outside the window the afternoon became abruptly rain, without warning, with no flapping of pennons nor sound of trumpet to herald it.

3

There was nothing harsh about this rain. It was gray and quiet as a benediction. The birds did not even cease to sing, and the west was already thinning to a moist and imminent gold.

The rector, bareheaded, walked slowly, unconscious of the rain and the dripping trees, beside his daughter-in-law across the lawn, houseward, and they mounted the steps together, passing beneath the dim and unwashed fanlight. Within the hall he stood while water ran down his face and dripped from his clothing in a series of small sounds. She took his arm and led him into the study and to his chair. He sat obediently and she took his handkerchief from the breast of his coat and wiped the rain from his temples and face. He submitted, fumbling for his pipe.

She watched him as he sprinkled tobacco liberally over the desk-top, trying to fill the bowl, then she quietly took it from his hand. "Try this. It is much simpler," she told him, taking a cigarette from her jacket pocket and putting it in his mouth. "You have never smoked one, have you?"

"Eh? Oh, thank you. Never too old to learn, eh?"

She lit it for him and then she quickly fetched a glass from the pantry. Kneeling beside the desk she drew out drawer after drawer until she found the bottle of whisky. He seemed to have forgotten her until she put the glass in his hand.

Then he looked up at her from a bottomless, grateful anguish and she sat suddenly on the arm of his chair, drawing his head against her breast. His untasted drink in one hand and his slowly burning cigarette lifting an unshaken plume of vapor from the other; and after a while the rain passed away and the dripping eaves but added to the freshened silence, measuring it, spacing it off; and the sun breaking through the west took a last look at the earth before going down.

"So you will not stay," he said at last, repeating her unspoken decision.

"No," she said, holding him.

4

Before her descending, the hill crossed with fireflies. At its foot among dark trees was unseen water and Emmy walked slowly on, feeling the tall wet grass sopping her to the knees, draggling her skirt.

She walked on and soon was among trees that as she moved, moved overhead like dark ships parting the star-filled river of the sky, letting the parted waters join again behind them with never a ripple. The pool lay darkly in the dark: sky and trees above it, trees and sky beneath it. She sat down on the wet earth, seeing through the trees the moon becoming steadily brighter in the darkening sky. A dog saw it also and bayed: a mellow, long sound that slid immaculately down a hill of silence, yet at the same time seemed to linger about her like a rumor of a far despair.

Tree trunks taking light from the moon, streaks of moonlight in the water—she could almost imagine she saw him standing there across the pool with her beside him; leaning above the water she could almost see them darting keen and swift and naked, flashing in the moon.

She could feel earth strike through her clothes against legs and belly and elbows . . . the dog bayed again, hopeless and sorrowful, dying, dying away. . . . After a while she rose slowly, feeling her damp clothes, thinking of the long walk home. To-morrow was washday.

5

"Damn!" said Mrs. Mahon, staring at the bulletin board. Gilligan, setting down her smart leather bags against the station wall, remarked briefly:

"Late?"

"Thirty minutes. What beastly luck!"

"Well, can't be helped. Wanta go back to the house and wait?"

"No, I don't. I don't like these abortive departures. Get my ticket, please." She gave him her purse and standing on tiptoe to see her reflection in a raised window she did a few deft things to her hat. Then she sauntered along the platform to the admiration of those casuals always to be found around small railway stations anywhere in these United States. And yet Continentals labor under the delusion that we spend all our time working!

Freedom comes with the decision: it does not wait for the act. She felt freer, more at peace with herself than she had felt for months. But I won't think about that, she decided deliberately. It is best just to be free, not to let it into the conscious mind. To be consciously anything argues a comparison, a bond with antithesis. Live in your dream, do not attain it—else comes satiety. Or sorrow, which is worse, I wonder? Dr. Mahon and his dream: reft, restored, reft again. Funny for someone, I guess. And Donald, with his scar and his stiffened hand quiet in the warm earth, in the warmth and the dark, where the one cannot hurt him and the other he will not need. No dream for him! The ones with whom he now sleeps don't care what his face looks like. *Per ardua ad astra*. . . . And Jones, what dream is his? "Nightmare, I hope," she said aloud, viciously, and one collarless and spitting tobacco said Ma'am? with interest.

Gilligan reappeared with her ticket.

"You're a nice boy, Joe," she told him, receiving her purse. He ignored her thanks. "Come on, let's walk a ways."

"Will my bags be all right there, do you think?"

"Sure." He looked about, then beckoned to a negro youth reclining miraculously on a steel cable that angled up to a telephone pole. "Here, son."

The negro said Suh? without moving. "Git up dar, boy. Dat white man talkin' to you," said a companion, squatting on his heels against the wall. The lad rose and a coin spun arcing from Gilligan's hand.

"Keep your eye on them bags till I come back, will you?"

"Awright, cap'm." The boy slouched over to the bags and became restfully and easily static beside them, going to sleep immediately, like a horse.

"Damn 'em, they do what you say, but they make vou feel so—so——"

"Immature, don't they?" she suggested.

"That's it. Like you was a kid or something and that they'd look after you even if you don't know exactly what you want."

"You are a funny sort, Joe. And nice. Too nice to waste." Her profile was sharp, pallid against a doorway darkly opened. "I'm giving you a chance not to waste me."

"Come on, let's walk a bit." She took his arm and moved slowly along the track, conscious that her ankles were being examined. The two threads of steel ran narrowing and curving away beyond trees. If you could see them as far as you can see, further than you can see. . . .

"Huh?" asked Gilligan, walking moodily beside her.

"Look at the spring, Joe. See, in the trees: summer is almost here, Joe."

"Yes, summer is almost here. Funny, ain't it? I'm always kind of surprised to find that things get on about the same, spite of us. I guess old nature does too much of a wholesale business to ever be surprised at us, let alone worrying if we ain't quite the fellows we think we ought to of been."

Holding his arm, walking a rail: "What kind of fellows do we think we ought to have been, Joe?"

"I don't know what kind of a fel—I mean girl you think you are and I don't know what kind of a fellow I think I am, but I know you and I tried to help nature make a good job out of a poor one without having no luck at it."

Flat leaves cupped each a drop of sunlight and the trees seemed coolly on fire with evening. Here was a wooden footbridge crossing a stream and a footpath mounting a hill. "Let's sit on the rail of the bridge," she suggested, guiding him toward it. Before he could help her she had turned her back to the rail and her straightening arms raised her easily. She hooked her heels over a lower rail and he mounted beside her. "Let's have a cigarette."

She produced a pack from her handbag and he accepted one, scraping a match. "Who has had any luck in this business?" she asked.

"The loot has."

"No, he hasn't. When you are married you are either lucky or unlucky, but when you are dead you aren't either: you aren't anything."

"That's right. He don't have to bother about his luck any more. . . . The padre's lucky, though."

"How?"

"Well, if you have hard luck and your hard luck passes away, ain't you lucky?"

"I don't know. You are too much for me now, Joe."

"And how about that girl? Fellow's got money, I hear, and no particular brains. She's lucky."

"Do you think she's satisfied?" Gilligan gazed at her attentively, not replying. "Think how much fun she could have got out of being so romantically widowed, and so young. I'll bet she's cursing her luck this minute."

He regarded her with admiration. "I always thought I'd like to be a buzzard," he remarked, "but now I think I'd like to be a woman."

"Good gracious, Joe. Why in the world?"

"Now, long as you're being one of them sybils, tell me about this bird Jones. He's lucky."

"How lucky?"

"Well, he gets what he wants, don't he?"

"Not the women he wants."

"Not exactly. Certainly he don't get all the women he wants. He has failed twice to my knowledge. But failure don't seem to worry him. That's what I mean by lucky. Their cigarettes arced together into the stream, hissing. "I guess brass gets along about as well as anything else with women."

"You mean stupidity."

"No, I don't. Stupidity. That's the reason I can't get the one I want."

She put her hand on his arm. "You aren't stupid, Joe. And you aren't bold, either."

"Yes, I am. Can you imagine me considering anybody else's feelings when they's something I want?"

"I can't imagine you doing anything without considering someone else's feelings."

Offended, he became impersonal. " 'Course you are entitled to your own opinion. I know I ain't bold like the man

in that story. You remember? accosted a woman on the
street and her husband was with her and knocked him down.
When he got up, brushing himself off, a man says: 'For heaven's
sake, friend, do you do that often?' and the bird says: 'Sure.
of course I get knocked down occasionally, but you'd be surprised.' I guess he just charged the beating to overhead,"
he finished with his old sardonic humor.

She laughed out. Then she said: "Why don't you try
that, Joe?"

He looked at her quietly for a time. She met his gaze
unwavering and he slipped to his feet facing her, putting his
arm around her. "What does that mean, Margaret?"

She made no reply and he lifted her down. She put her
arms over his shoulders. "You don't mean anything by it,"
he told her quietly, touching her mouth with his. His clasp
became lax.

"Not like that, Joe."

"Not like what?" he asked stupidly. For answer she drew
his face down to hers and kissed him with slow fire. Then
they knew that after all they were strangers to each other.
He hastened to fill an uncomfortable interval. "Does that
mean you will?"

"I can't, Joe," she answered, standing easily in his arms.

"But why not, Margaret? You never give me any reason."

She was silent in profile against sunshot green. "If I didn't
like you so much, I wouldn't tell you. But it's your name,
Joe. Gilligan. I couldn't marry a man named Gilligan."

He was really hurt. "I'm sorry," he said dully. She laid
her cheek against his. On the crest of the hill tree trunks
were a barred grate beyond which the fires of evening were
dying away. "I could change it," he suggested.

Across the evening came a long sound. "There's your
train," he said.

She thrust herself slightly from him, to see his face. "Joe, forgive me. I didn't mean that——"

"That's all right," he interrupted, patting her back with awkward gentleness. "Come on, let's get back."

The locomotive appeared blackly at the curve, plumed with steam like a sinister squat knight and grew larger without seeming to progress. But it was moving and it roared past the station in its own good time, bearing the puny controller of its destiny like a goggled greasy excrescence in its cab. The train jarred to a stop and an eruption of white-jacketed porters.

She put her arms about him again to the edification of the by-standers. "Joe, I didn't mean that. But don't you see, I have been married twice already, with damn little luck either time, and I just haven't the courage to risk it again. But if I could marry anyone, don't you know it would be you? Kiss me, Joe." He complied. "Bless your heart, darling. If I married you you'd be dead in a year, Joe. All the men that marry me die, you know."

"I'll take the risk," he told her.

"But I won't. I'm too young to bury three husbands." People got off, passed them, other people got on. And above all like an obligato the vocal competition of cab-men. "Joe, does it really hurt you for me to go?" He looked at her dumbly. "Joe!" she exclaimed, and a party passed them. It was Mr. and Mrs. George Farr: they saw Cecily's stricken face as she melted graceful and fragile and weeping into her father's arms. And here was Mr. George Farr morose and thunderous behind her. Ignored.

"What did I tell you?" Mrs. Mahon said, clutching Gilligan's arm.

"You're right," he answered, from his own despair. "It's a sweet honeymoon he's had, poor devil."

The party passed on around the station and she looked at Gilligan again. "Joe, come with me."

"To a minister?" he asked with resurgent hope.

"No, just as we are. Then when we get fed up all we need do is wish each other luck and go our ways." He stared at her, shocked. "Damn your Presbyterian soul, Joe. Now you think I'm a bad woman."

"No I don't, ma'am. But I can't do that. . . ."

"Why not?"

"I dunno: I just can't."

"But what difference does it make?"

"Why, none, if it was just your body I wanted. But I want—I want——"

"What do you want, Joe?"

"Hell. Come on, let's get aboard."

"You are coming, then?"

"You know I ain't. You knew you were safe when you said that."

He picked up her bags. A porter ravished them skillfully from him and he helped her into the car. She sat upon green plush and he removed his hat awkwardly, extending his hand. "Well, good-bye."

Her face pallid and calm beneath her small white and black hat, above her immaculate collar. She ignored his hand.

"Look at me, Joe. Have I ever told you a lie?"

"No," he admitted.

"Then don't you know I am not lying now? I meant what I said. Sit down."

"No, no. I can't do it that way. You know I can't."

"Yes. I can't even seduce you, Joe. I'm sorry. I'd like to make you happy for a short time, if I could. But I guess it isn't in the cards, is it?" She raised her face and he kissed her.

"Good-bye."

"Good-bye, Joe."

But why not? he thought with cinders under his feet, why not take her this way? I could persuade her in time, perhaps before we reached Atlanta. He turned and sprang back on board the train. He hadn't much time and when he saw that her seat was empty he rushed through the car in a mounting excitement. She was not in the next car either.

Have I forgotten which car she is in? he thought. But no, that was where he had left her, for there was the negro youth, still motionless opposite the window. He hurried back to take another look at her place. Yes, there were her bags. He ran, blundering into other passengers, the whole length of the train. She was not there.

She has changed her mind and got off, looking for me, he thought, in an agony of futile endeavor. He slammed open a vestibule and leaped to the ground as the train began to move. Careless of how he must look to the station loungers he leaped toward the waiting room. It was empty, a hurried glance up and down the platform did not discover her and he turned despairing to the moving train.

She must be on it! he thought furiously, cursing himself because he had not stayed on it until she reappeared. For now the train was moving too swiftly and all the vestibules were closed. Then the last car slid smoothly past and he saw her standing on the rear platform where she had gone in order to see him again and where he had not thought of looking for her.

"Margaret!" he cried after the arrogant steel thing, running vainly down the track after it, seeing it smoothly distancing him. "Margaret!" he cried again, stretching his arms to her, to the vocal support of the loungers.

"Whup up a little, mister," a voice advised. "Ten to one

on the train," a sporting one offered. There were no takers.

He stopped at last, actually weeping with anger and despair, watching her figure, in its dark straight dress and white collar and cuffs, become smaller and smaller with the diminishing train that left behind a derisive whistle blast and a trailing fading vapor like an insult, moving along twin threads of steel out of his sight and his life.

. . . At last he left the track at right angles and climbed a wire fence into woods where spring becoming languorous with summer turned sweetly nightward, though summer had not quite come.

6

Deep in a thicket from which the evening was slowly dissolving a thrush sang four liquid notes. Like the shape of her mouth, he thought, feeling the heat of his pain become cool with the cooling of sunset. The small stream murmured busily like a faint incantation and repeated alder shoots leaned over it Narcissus-like. The thrush, disturbed, flashed a modest streak of brown deeper into the woods, and sang again. Mosquitoes spun about him, unresisted: he seemed to get ease from their sharp irritation. Something else to think about.

I could have made up to her. I would make up to her for everything that ever hurt her, so that when she remembered things that once hurt her she'd say: Was this I? If I could just have told her! Only I couldn't seem to think of what to say. Me, that talks all the time, being stuck for words. . . . Aimlessly he followed the stream. Soon it ran among violet shadows, among willows and he heard a louder water. Parting the willows he came upon an old mill-race and a small lake calmly repeating the calm sky and the opposite dark trees. He saw fish gleaming dully upon the earth, and the buttocks of a man.

"Lost something?" he asked, watching ripples spread from the man's submerged arm. The other heaved himself to his hands and knees, looking up over his shoulder.

"Dropped my terbaccer," he replied, in an unemphatic drawl. "Don't happen to have none on you, do you?"

"Got a cigarette, if that'll do you any good." Gilligan offered his pack and the other, squatting back on his heels, took one.

"Much obliged. Feller likes a little smoke once in a while, don't he?"

"Fellow likes a lot of little things in this world, once in a while."

The other guffawed, not comprehending, but suspecting a reference to sex. "Well, I ain't got any o' that, but I got the next thing to it." He rose, lean as a hound, and from beneath a willow clump he extracted a gallon jug. With awkward formality he tendered it. "Allers take a mite with me when I go fishin'," he explained. "Seems to make the fish bite more 'n the muskeeters less."

Gilligan took the jug awkwardly. What in hell did you do with it? "Here, lemme show you," his host said, relieving him of it. Crooking his first finger through the handle the man raised the jug with a round back-handed sweep to his horizontal upper arm, craning his neck until his mouth met the mouth of the vessel. Gilligan could see his pumping adam's apple against the pale sky. He lowered the jug and drew the back of his hand across his mouth. "That's how she's done," he said, handing the thing to Gilligan.

Gilligan tried it with inferior success, feeling the stuff chill upon his chin, sopping the front of his waistcoat. But in his throat it was like fire: it seemed to explode pleasantly as soon as it touched his stomach. He lowered the vessel, coughing.

"Good God, what it it?"

The other laughed hoarsely, slapping his thighs. "Never

drunk no corn before, hain't you? But how does she feel inside? Better'n out, don't she?"

Gilligan admitted that she did. He could feel all his nerves like electric filaments in a bulb: he was conscious of nothing else. Then it became a warmth and an exhilaration. He raised the jug again and did better.

I'll go to Atlanta to-morrow and find her, catch her before she takes a train out of there, he promised himself. I will find her: she cannot escape me forever. The other drank again and Gilligan lit a cigarette. He too knew a sense of freedom, of being master of his destiny. I'll go to Atlanta to-morrow, find her, make her marry me, he repeated. Why did I let her go?

But why not to-night? Sure, why not to-night? I can find her! I know I can. Even in New York. Funny I never thought of that before. His legs and arms had no sensation, his cigarette slipped from his nerveless fingers, and reaching for the tiny coal he wavered, finding that he could no longer control his body. Hell, I ain't that drunk, he thought. But he was forced to admit that he was. "Say, what was that stuff, anyway? I can't hardly stand up."

The other guffawed again, flattered. "Ain't she, though? Make her myself, and she's good. You'll git used to it, though. Take another." He drank it like water, with unction.

"Dam'f I do. I got to get to town."

"Take a little sup. I'll put you on the road all right."

If two drinks make me feel this good I'll scream if I take another, he thought. But his friend insisted and he drank again. "Let's go," he said, returning the jug.

The man carrying "her" circled the lake. Gilligan blundered behind him, among cypress knees, in occasional mud. After a time he regained some control over his body and they

came to a break in the willows and a road slashed into the
red sandy soil.

"Here you be, friend. Jest keep right to the road. 'Tain't
over a mile."

"All right. Much obliged to you. You've sure got a son-
of-a-gun of a drink there."

"She's all right, ain't she?" the other agreed.

"Well, good night." Gilligan extended his hand and the
other grasped it formally and limply and pumped it once
from a rigid elbow.

"Take keer of yourself."

"I'll try to," Gilligan promised. The other's gangling
malaria-ridden figure faded again among the willows. The
road gashed across the land, stretched silent and empty before him, and below the east was a rumorous promise of moonlight. He trod in dust between dark trees like spilled ink
upon the pale clear page of the sky, and soon the moon was
more than a promise. He saw the rim of it sharpening the
tips of trees, saw soon the whole disc, bland as a saucer.
Whippoorwills were like lost coins among the trees and one
blundered awkwardly from the dust almost under his feet.
The whisky died away in the loneliness, soon his temporarily
mislaid despair took its place again.

After a while passing beneath crossed skeletoned arms
on a pole he crossed the railroad and followed a lane between
negro cabins, smelling the intimate odor of negroes. The
cabins were dark but from them came soft meaningless
laughter and slow unemphatic voices cheerful yet somehow
filled with all the old despairs of time and breath.

Under the moon, quavering with the passion of spring
and flesh, among whitewashed walls papered inwardly with
old newspapers, something pagan using the white man's conventions as it used his clothing, hushed and powerful, not
knowing its own power:

"Sweet chariot . . . comin' fer to ca'y me home. . . ."

Three young men passed him, shuffling in the dust, aping their own mute shadows in the dusty road, sharp with the passed sweat of labor: "You may be fas', but you can't las'; cause yo' mommer go' slow you down."

He trod on with the moon in his face, seeing the cupolaed clock squatting like a benignant god on the courthouse against the sky, staring across the town with four faces. He passed yet more cabins where sweet mellow voices called from door to door. A dog bayed the moon, clear and sorrowful, and a voice cursed it in soft syllables.

". . . .sweet chariot, comin' fer to ca'y me home . . . yes, Jesus, comin' fer to ca'y me hoooooome. . . . ."

The church loomed a black shadow with a silver roof and he crossed the lawn, passing beneath slumbrous ivied walls. In the garden the mocking bird that lived in the magnolia rippled the silence, and along the moony wall of the rectory, from ledge to ledge, something crawled shapelessly. What in hell, thought Gilligan, seeing it pause at Emmy's window.

He leaped flower beds swiftly and noiselessly. Here was a convenient gutter and Jones did not hear him until he had almost reached the window to which the other clung. They regarded each other precariously, the one clinging to the window, the other to the gutter.

"What are you trying to do?" Gilligan asked.

"Climb up here a little further and I'll show you," Jones told him snarling his yellow teeth.

"Come away from there, fellow."

"Damn my soul, if here ain't the squire of dames again. We all hoped you had gone off with that black woman."

"Are you coming down, or am I coming up there and throw you down?"

"I don't know: am I? Or are you?"

For reply Gilligan heaved himself up, grasping the window ledge. Jones, clinging, tried to kick him in the face but Gilligan caught his foot, releasing his grasp on the gutter. For a moment they swung like a great pendulum against the side of the house, then Jones' hold on the window was torn loose and they plunged together into a bed of tulips. Jones was first on his feet and kicking Gilligan in the side he fled. Gilligan sprang after him and overtook him smartly.

This time it was hyacinths. Jones fought like a woman, kicking, clawing, biting, but Gilligan hauled him to his feet and knocked him down. Jones rose again and was felled once more. This time he crawled and grasping Gilligan's knees pulled him down. Jones kicked himself free and rising fled anew. Gilligan sat up contemplating pursuit, but gave it up as he watched Jones' unwieldy body leaping away through the moonlight.

Jones doubled the church at a good speed and let himself out at the gate. He saw no pursuit so his pace slackened to a walk. Beneath quiet elms his breath became easier. Branches motionlessly leafed were still against stars, and mopping his face and neck with his handkerchief he walked along a deserted street. At a corner he stopped to dip his handkerchief in a trough for watering horses, bathing his face and hands. The water reduced the pain of the blows he had received and as he paced fatly on from shadow to moonlight and then to shadow again, dogged by his own skulking and shapeless shadow, the calm still night washed his recent tribulation completely from his mind.

From shadowed porches beyond oaks and maples, elms and magnolias, from beyond screening vines starred with motionless pallid blossoms came snatches of hushed talk and sweet broken laughter. . . . Male and female created He them, young. Jones was young, too. 'Yet ah, that Spring should vanish with the Rose! That Youth's sweet-scented Manuscript should close! The Nightingale that in the Branches sang, Ah, whence, and whither flown again, who knows! . . .' Wish I had a girl to-night, he sighed.

The moon was serene: 'Ah, Moon of my Delight, that knows't no wane, The Moon of Heav'n is rising once again: How oft hereafter rising shall she look Through this same Garden after me—in vain!' But how spring itself is imminent with autumn, with death: 'As autumn and the moon of death draw nigh The sad long days of summer herein lie And she too warm in sorrow 'neath the trees Turns to night and weeps, and longs to die.' And in the magic of spring and youth and moonlight Jones raised his clear sentimental tenor.

"Sweetheart, sweetheart, sweetheart."

His slow shadow blotted out the pen strokes of iron pickets but when he had passed, the pen strokes were still there upon the dark soft grass. Clumps of petunia and cannas broke the smooth stretch of lawn and above the bronze foliage of magnolias the serene columns of a white house rose more beautiful in simplicity than death.

Jones leaned his elbows on a gate, staring at his lumpy shadow at his feet, smelling cape jasmine, hearing a mocking-bird somewhere, somewhere. . . . Jones sighed. It was a sigh of pure ennui.

7

On the rector's desk was a letter addressed to Mr. Julian Lowe, ——— St., San Francisco, Cal., telling him of her marriage and of her husband's death. It had been returned by the postoffice department stamped, "Removed. Present address unknown."

8

Gilligan, sitting in the hyacinth bed, watched Jones' flight. "He ain't so bad for a fat one," he admitted, rising. "Emmy'll sure have to sleep single to-night." The mocking bird in the magnolia, as though it had waited for hostilities to cease, sang again.

"What in hell have you got to sing about?" Gilligan shook his fist at the tree. The bird ignored him and he brushed dark earth from his clothes. Anyway, he soliloquized, I feel better. Wish I could have held the bastard, though. He passed from the garden with a last look at the ruined hyacinth bed. The rector, looming, met him at the corner of the house, beneath the hushed slumbrous passion of the silver tree.

"That you, Joe? I thought I heard noises in the garden."

"You did. I was trying to beat hell out of that fat one, but I couldn't hold the so—I couldn't hold him. He lit out."

"Fighting? My dear boy!"

"It wasn't no fight; he was too busy getting away. It takes two folks to fight, padre."

"Fighting doesn't settle anything, Joe. I'm sorry you resorted to it. Was anyone hurt?"

"No, worse luck," Gilligan replied ruefully, thinking of his soiled clothes and his abortive vengeance.

"I am glad of that. But boys will fight, eh, Joe? Donald fought in his day."

"You damn right he did, reverend. I bet he was a son-of-a-gun in his day."

The rector's heavy lined face took a flared match, between his cupped hands he sucked at his pipe. He walked slowly in the moonlight across the lawn, toward the gate. Gilligan followed. "I feel restless to-night," he explained. "Shall we walk a while?"

They paced slowly beneath arched and moon-bitten trees, scuffing their feet in shadows of leaves. Under the moon lights in houses were yellow futilities.

"Well, Joe, things are back to normal again. People come

and go, but Emmy and I seem to be like the biblical rocks. What are your plans?"

Gilligan lit a cigarette with ostentatiousness, hiding his embarrassment. "Well, padre, to tell the truth, I ain't got any. If it's all the same to you I think I'll stay on with you a while longer."

"And welcome, dear boy," the rector answered heartily. Then he stopped and faced the other, keenly. "God bless you, Joe. Was it on my account you decided to stay?"

Gilligan averted his face guiltily. "Well, padre——"

"Not at all. I won't have it. You have already done all you can. This is no place for a young man, Joe."

The rector's bald forehead and his blobby nose were intersecting planes in the moonlight. His eyes were cavernous. Gilligan knew suddenly all the old sorrows of the race, black or yellow or white, and he found himself telling the rector all about her.

"Tut, tut," the divine said, "this is bad, Joe." He lowered himself hugely to the edge of the sidewalk and Gilligan sat beside him. "Circumstance moves in marvellous ways, Joe."

"I thought you'd a said God, reverend."

"God is circumstance, Joe. God is in this life. We know nothing about the next. That will take care of itself in good time. 'The Kingdom of God is in man's own heart,' the Book says."

"Ain't that a kind of funny doctrine for a parson to get off?"

"Remember, I am an old man, Joe. Too old for bickering or bitterness. We make our own heaven or hell in this world. Who knows; perhaps when we die we may not be required to go anywhere nor do anything at all. That would be heaven."

"Or other people make our heaven and hell for us."

The divine put his heavy arm across Gilligan's shoulder. "You are suffering from disappointment. But this will pass away. The saddest thing about love, Joe, is that not only the love cannot last forever, but even the heartbreak is soon forgotten. How does it go? 'Men have died and worms have eaten them, but not for love.' No, no," as Gilligan would have interrupted, "I know that is an unbearable belief, but all truth is unbearable. Do we not both suffer at this moment from the facts of division and death?"

Gilligan knew shame. Bothering him now, me with a fancied disappointment! The rector spoke again. "I think it would be a good idea for you to stay, after all, until you make your future plans. So let's consider it closed, eh? Suppose we walk further—unless you are tired?"

Gilligan rose in effusive negation. After a while the quiet tree-tunnelled street became a winding road, and leaving the town behind them they descended and then mounted a hill. Cresting the hill beneath the moon, seeing the world breaking away from them into dark, moon-silvered ridges above valleys where mist hung slumbrous, they passed a small house, sleeping among climbing roses. Beyond it an orchard slept the night away in symmetrical rows, squatting and pregnant. "Willard has good fruit," the divine murmured.

The road dropped on again descending between reddish gashes, and across a level moon-lit space, broken by a clump of saplings, came a pure quivering chord of music wordless and far away.

"They are holding services. Negroes," the rector explained. They walked on in the dust, passing neat tidy houses, dark with slumber. An occasional group of negroes passed them, bearing lighted lanterns that jetted vain little flames futilely into the moonlight. "No one knows why they do that," the divine replied to Gilligan's question. "Perhaps it is to light their churches with."

The singing drew nearer and nearer; at last, crouching among a clump of trees beside the road, they saw the shabby church with its canting travesty of a spire. Within it was a soft glow of kerosene serving only to make the darkness and the heat thicker, making thicker the imminence of sex after harsh labor along the mooned land; and from it welled the crooning submerged passion of the dark race. It was nothing, it was everything; then it swelled to an ecstasy, taking the white man's words as readily as it took his remote God and made a personal Father of Him.

Feed Thy Sheep, O Jesus. All the longing of mankind for a Oneness with Something, somewhere. Feed Thy Sheep, O Jesus. . . . The rector and Gilligan stood side by side in the dusty road. The road went on under the moon, vaguely dissolving without perspective. Worn-out red-gutted fields were now alternate splashes of soft black and silver; trees had each a silver nimbus, save those moonward from them, which were sharp as bronze.

Feed Thy Sheep, O Jesus. The voices rose full and soft. There was no organ; no organ was needed as above the harmonic passion of bass and baritone soared a clear soprano of women's voices like a flight of gold and heavenly birds. They stood together in the dust, the rector in his shapeless black, and Gilligan in his new hard serge, listening, seeing the shabby church become beautiful with mellow longing, passionate and sad. Then the singing died, fading away along the mooned land inevitable with to-morrow and sweat, with sex and death and damnation; and they turned townward under the moon, feeling dust in their shoes.

THE END